WARNING SHOT!

Sandra started to raise her head. "I guess I did overreact. Sorry to be so chicken . . ."

I pushed her down again, as the room she'd just left exploded with a flat, hard bang that blew the connecting door open again and shook a picture off the common wall. A little whitish smoke drifted in through the open doorway. I held Sandra long enough to make sure she wasn't going to break down; but Matthew had picked a good unhysterical type.

"We'd better find you a shirt," I said. "It looks as if we might have company. . . ."

Fawcett Gold Medal Books
by Donald Hamilton:

THE MONA INTERCEPT

Matt Helm Series:

THE
DEMOLISHERS

Donald Hamilton

FAWCETT GOLD MEDAL • NEW YORK

A Fawcett Gold Medal Book
Published by Ballantine Books
Copyright © 1987 by Donald Hamilton

Library of Congress Catalog Card Number: 87-90865

ISBN 0-449-13233-1

Manufactured in the United States of America

First Edition: November 1987

CHAPTER 1

MAC was sitting at his desk as usual, with the bright window behind him. This made his expression difficult to read, which was the idea; but I gathered he didn't feel that the instructions he'd just given me were open to question, although, of course, we were both aware that most instructions given in that office are pretty questionable by ordinary standards.

I said, "No, sir."

He frowned quickly. "What?"

I said, "No, sir, I won't go after Herman Heinrich Bultman. If he must be handled, let the CIA handle him; he's their boy. Or was once; and they still wake up nights sweating, wondering if he's told anybody who hired him for that Cuba mission that cost him his left foot." I grimaced. "Bultman was a fool to get sucked into that one; but they do get proud. He's not the first character in that line of work who's let himself be conned into trying for The Beard in order to show that he was the best; that he could succeed where everyone else had failed. Of course the money was a consideration, too. But he should have known that, whether he made it or not, and particularly if, as it turned out, he didn't, those publicity-shy folks down at Langley would figure on silencing him afterwards. Only it turned out they weren't quite up to the job, so they wished it off on us."

Mac made an impatient gesture. "That is ancient his-

1

tory, Eric." In that office, and while engaged in the exercise of my profession, I'm Eric, although I use other names as well. In my normal civilian life, what little there is of it, I'm known as Matthew Helm. Mac went on: "The misguided attempt on Castro's life is past and forgotten; it has no bearing on our present . . ."

I shook my head quickly. "The boys and girls down in Virginia don't forget much, sir. Bultman's still on their shit list and they want him off, permanently. Well, I went after him once for them down in Costa Verde, and got lucky. I outshuffled him and outnumbered him and got the drop on him. I made him swear that he'd never, ever open his mouth on the subject of Cuba. They'd told me to silence him, hadn't they?" I grinned. "That wasn't exactly what they'd had in mind, I guess, but I needed Bultman's cooperation on another project, as you'll recall. As a matter of fact, whatever else he may be, the Kraut seems to be a man of his word; his promise has turned out to be as good as a bullet in the brain. Now they've come up with another important reason for us to eliminate Herr Bultman. Personally, I think they'll keep finding new reasons to wipe him out until they get the job done. Correction: until they get somebody else to get it done for them. Like us. But not me, sir. The reason they've come up with this time isn't good enough. I want no part of it, thanks."

Theoretically, our wants and don't-wants are quite irrelevant in that office, but I've worked for him a long time and have earned a certain amount of latitude.

Mac said, "You are showing great consideration for a man who's an assassin for sale, a hired gun."

I said, "I've killed upon occasion. You should know; you sent me out to do it. Hell, you're trying to send me out to do it now. And for doing it, when I do it, I'm paid a pretty good salary by the U.S. government. Not what I'm worth, of course, but pretty good. What does that make me? Let's not have any loose talk in here about hired guns, sir. Anyway, Bultman has retired from the hitman wars.''

''Had retired.''

''Well, this isn't really his old line of work. And who turned him active again, if you want to call it that? And how did they do it? If people are going to be that stupidly, arrogantly vicious, they deserve what they get, even if what they get is a professional killer on the prowl.''

Mac spoke without expression: ''You are the only one of our people who's had an opportunity to study the subject in action and at close range. Another agent's chances of success, even of survival, would be considerably smaller than yours.''

I said, ''You don't have to send anybody, sir. Tell them to take their lousy job and shove it back across the Potomac where it belongs.''

''We are not here to tell people to take their lousy jobs and shove them, Eric. The lousy jobs are exactly what this organization was created to handle. The ones too lousy for anybody else.''

Our business is classified as counterassassination by the people who know what we do, but there aren't many of those. In other words, when the knifers, snipers, and bombers get too rough for other agencies to handle, they call on us.

I said, ''What you said works both ways. I've had a chance to study Herman, but he's also had a chance to study me. It cancels out. The man only has one flesh-and-blood foot, but he was getting along all right with the tin one when I saw him last. I have a hunch he suffered some other injuries on that ill-fated expedition that we don't know about, or he wouldn't have gone out of business later the way he did. But regardless, crippled or whole, sick or well, he's the old lobo from the top of the mountain, as the CIA found out the hard way. And I'm

3

not going to tackle him again for them and a bunch of Caribbean islanders who haven't got any more sense than to make a deadly enemy of a basically nonpolitical character like Bultman by doing the one thing that would make him blow his stack, stolid Kraut though he is. Those uniformed Latin characters with their casual submachine guns are always a bit trigger-happy, but this time they outdid themselves and really played hell.''

"There were sound medical reasons for the regulations that were enforced in Bultman's case; although the enforcement may have been a bit arbitrary." Mac frowned at me across the desk. "So it's the dog."

I said, "You're damned right it's the dog, sir."

Mac spoke carefully: "The island of Gobernador—these days the sovereign nation of Gobernador—is an important link in our Caribbean defense system. Whatever your opinion may be, the government of the United States of America considers it more important than one elderly German shepherd dog." When I didn't say anything, Mac went on without expression. "Are you aware that the German shepherd is not German and has never been known to herd a sheep? Originally, it came to this country as the Alsatian wolf dog. It found few buyers under that label, so the name was changed quite arbitrarily and inaccurately to make the product sound more attractive. It still, in many specimens, retains its savage propensities.''

I said, "Sure. There's always a fashionable devil dog. For a while it was the Doberman pinscher. Then the pit bull became the Monster Canine of the Year. Currently, I believe, the Rottweiler is the beast at the head of the eat-you-up list. I'm just waiting for the day they discover the Homicidal Pekingese. Anyway, the temperament of Bultman's mutt is irrevelant here. It didn't bite anybody, it was just there, an elderly German shepherd bitch named Marlene for Marlene Dietrich. It throws an interesting light on Tough-Guy Bultman, his naming his pet for a long-ago movie star. And whatever the U.S. government may think, Herman Bultman considers the lousy island strictly expendable and I don't blame him. Under similar circumstances, I'd be looking for help to sink it into the sea, myself. Apparently, he's found his help in the anti-government movement; and more power to him.''

"You're being dangerously sentimental, Eric." Mac cleared his throat and controlled his irritation. He went on with his briefing remorselessly, as if there had been no objection from me. "Gobernador consists of two islands. Isla del Norte is a fairly barren rock, sparsely settled. It contains important U.S. installations of a fairly secret nature—secret enough that we don't need to know what they are, or so we're told, as usual. The government of the newly independent nation has given us long-term leases; but if it should be overthrown, those leases could be, and probably would be, abrogated by those who would come to power next, who'd be at least anti-American if not actively pro-communist." He paused. When I made no comment, he continued: "Isla del Sur is fertile and quite densely populated. It contains the capital city up in the mountains, Santa Isabella; and down on the coast, the principal harbor, Puerto del Sol, where your friend had his trouble."

"Hell, he's no friend of mine," I said. "Just because I sympathize with his current motives doesn't mean I like him. That's one cold, ruthless sonofabitch, and anybody idiot enough to hit him in his one soft spot . . ."

"I am certain that, if they had known with whom they were dealing, the port officials would have treated him more tenderly, Eric." Mac's voice was tart. "Unfortunately the name Bultman is not a household word in the Caribbean."

"If the rumors I've heard are correct, it soon will be," I said.

Mac winced. "Yes, that is the problem with which we are trying to deal."

I went on: "Certain people never learn that if they push enough folks around long enough, sooner or later they'll start shoving somebody who won't take it. He'll blow right up in their faces and demolish them and the surrounding landscape; and they—those who are left—will scream about how misunderstood and abused they are, and why didn't somebody *tell* them the guy was dangerous so they could be nice to him? It never seems to occur to them that there's a very simple answer: just be nice to everybody." I grimaced. "In Bultman they hit a prime specimen of demolisher; and now that they've triggered him they want us to abort the explosion? How optimistic can you get?"

Mac ignored this foray into philosophy, if you want to call it that. He went on stiffly: "What I am trying to point out is that we have a vested interest in the current government of Islas Gobernador. We do not want it replaced by a less friendly regime, or a steaming hole in the ocean. Apparently Bultman is now busily whipping into shape a motley collection of terrorists and revolutionaries that could never have accomplished anything on their own except the usual kind of protest assassinations and abductions and random bombings. But the man has considerable military experience, as you know, and he's being allowed to carry out his recruiting and training on a neighboring island that has an interest in fomenting disturbances on Gobernador. Under this protection, Bultman is forming a disciplined strike force that may become a real threat to the stability of the region."

"He's just the boy to do it," I said. "He's not a lone-wolf type like me; that time I outmaneuvered him with paramilitary help was strictly an exception. But Bultman always did run his operations like clockwork commando raids, using plenty of manpower, even when his target was a single individual." I drew a long breath. "Look, sir, it's no use pulling that anti-commie stuff on me. I've had too many missions sold me as the last faint hope of democracy. I think I've proved a number of times that I'm as patriotic as the next guy, but you can't tell me that a few antennas or whatever, on a Caribbean rock, are going to make the difference between our national existence and nonexistence."

Mac studied me coldly. "I won't insult you by suggesting that you are afraid of taking on this mission; but I find your reason for refusing quite unconvincing."

I said, "That's because you're not a dog man, sir."

"I should hope not," he said. "Nor am I cat man or a ferret man or a monkey man or a parakeet man, or a little-white-mouse man. And I would have thought at your age you'd be cured of that childish pet nonsense."

"Age has nothing to do with it," I said. "A dog can mean just as much to an older person as it does to a kid, maybe more. And calling my attitude names doesn't change anything. I grew up with hunting dogs and you know it; you may even recall a couple of assignments where my familiarity with dogs came in quite handy. As a matter of fact, I picked up a pup on my recent jaunt to Scandinavia. He's in a training kennel in Texas right now and I hope to take him duck hunting shortly—the season opens in a couple of weeks—and see just what kind of a retriever my Svenska relatives wished off on me. And even though I haven't had much time to get acquainted with him, I strongly recommend that nobody lift a finger against him, because my reaction would be exactly the same as Bultman's." I stared right back across the desk. "You'll never understand that, sir. You told me once that you were brought up to be afraid of them; and that it gave you a lot of trouble when you had to revise our methods of dealing with attack and guard dogs."

Mac said dryly, "To be frank, my attitude is that of

7

the late W. C. Fields: Any man who hates dogs can't be all bad. A slight exaggeration, but close enough."

"As I recall, Fields included children also."

Mac disregarded that, frowning at me across the desk. "You can't be serious about refusing this mission simply because the target is a fellow dog lover." When I didn't respond to that, he went on sharply: "Nobody is asking you to *hurt* any dogs, Eric! All you have been instructed to do is deal with a dangerous man . . . ."

"A dangerous man who, crippled and perhaps not altogether well, had retired from being dangerous," I said. "Okay, let's pull it all out and look at it, including the parts you neglected to mention. Bultman was living on board his boat, a thirty-two-foot sloop, and doing no harm to anybody—you never know who you'll find taking off in a boat these days. He was sailing through the Caribbean by easy stages, alone except for his ancient Alsatian bitch. He got caught by the fringe of a hurricane, his boat sustained some damage, and he limped into the nearest port, which happened to belong to a new island nation that's free of rabies and hopes to stay that way by keeping all strange canines out. Their privilege; but there's also an ancient tradition about affording refuge to distressed mariners."

Mac said, "Just because an arrogant official exceeded his instructions . . ."

I said, "We don't know what his instructions were, sir. *Now* it's being claimed that he exceeded them, now that the shit has hit the fan; but that's the way of governments everywhere. Anyway, under similar circumstances more reasonable countries with the same kind of antirabies regulations just quarantine the dog. Not Islas Gobernador. Those clowns didn't even give Bultman the choice of putting back to sea with his damaged boat and his four-legged companion. They simply hauled the old lady shepherd onto the dock and shot her to death right under her master's eyes." I drew a long breath. "And Herman Heinrich Bultman kept his temper and said *sí, señor*, and *por favor, señor*. He got out of there without killing anybody, and I know exactly why. He didn't just want the few he could get by grabbing one of the machine pistols that are always waving in the breeze in a place like that, and cleaning off the dock with a few well-aimed bursts. Suddenly they'd given him a new purpose in life, something interesting to do in his retirement. Now he's going to use everything he learned in all his years as a soldier of fortune and professional assassin to carry off one final, efficient, Bultman operation: wiping out, not only the trigger-happy officials who did the job, but the lousy government that put them there to do it."

After a moment, Mac said, "I don't condone what was done, of course. But to suggest that the death of one animal justifies in any way the kind of bloody revolt this man is planning . . ."

I sighed. "I knew we'd get to that after-all-it's-just-an-animal routine eventually, sir. But Bultman isn't doing what he's doing for an elderly bitch that would soon have died of natural causes anyway. He's doing it for his *right* to keep an elderly bitch and, when her time was up, let her die in peace with her old gray head in his lap."

"Very touching, Eric, but . . ."

I said, "I won't go after him, sir. I won't say he's justified in what he's doing. As you point out, it was only an animal, and a lot of human beings are going to die for it. But I can't go after him because, as I said before, if it had been my dog, I'd have reacted in exactly the same way; so how can I hunt down the man for that? As a kid out west I learned that if you mess with a man's horse or his dog you've only yourself to blame for what happens next. It's time these people learned it, too, and I'm not about to stop Bultman from advancing their education. If you want my resignation, it will be

on your desk as soon as one of the girls downstairs can
type it up . . . ."

CHAPTER 2

WHEN I was a boy, a Labrador retriever was always black. I was aware that the yellows and chocolates
were permissible variations, but I can't recall ever seeing
one of those offbeat canines. Nowadays, however, every
dog breeder is striving for something new and different.
The yellow Lab has been rescued from obscurity and is
starting to take over from the black.

The pup that had been given me by the Swedish relatives on whose farm I'd stayed the previous spring ranged
in color from pale red gold on the back to straw white
on the chest. He was the biggest juvenile Labrador I'd
seen. At eighteen months he weighed over a hundred
pounds, with enormous feet and a head like a bear. His
greeting was overwhelming, like being mauled by a
grizzly; but I didn't mind. I mean, it showed that he
remembered me and, dammit, love is where you find it.
There aren't that many humans around eager to hug and
kiss me.

"Grown a bit, ain't he?" Bert Hapgood said, grinning. He was a lean dark man in jeans and a denim jacket.
"Down, pup, down! I ought to charge you extra, Matt,
the grub he puts away. In the morning you can shoot him
a duck or two and see what he's learned about handling
them. . . ."

Bert and his handsome, brown-haired wife, Doreen, ran what might be called a combination operation. They had their kennels, and they boarded and trained dogs throughout the year; but they also had boats in which they took people fishing in the appropriate seasons, and they had a considerable amount of local marshland under lease, on which they ran guided hunts in the fall and early winter from their rustic hunting lodge on the shore of the Gulf of Mexico. It was a weathered building raised on stilts like the beach houses I'd passed on my way there, so high storm tides could wash underneath without damage. From my room, spartan but comfortable enough, I could hear the surf until I fell asleep thinking about tomorrow's hunt.

It was an improvement over some night thoughts I'd been having. I kept telling myself that I'd survived longer in the business than most, and that it had been only sensible to quit before the statistics of my profession caught up with me; but I'd have liked to have it happen in a more friendly fashion. I assured myself that it was ridiculous to entertain any sentimental or regretful thoughts about Mac; might as well start getting mushy about the public executioner. Still, we'd worked together a hell of a lot of years . . . But that night in Texas I thought only about ducks and dogs and shotguns, and fell asleep in record time.

In the morning, after a hearty breakfast, we loaded the yellow pup into a crate in the back of Bert's four-wheel-drive pickup and headed east along the highway, with another carload of hunters following along behind. It was a clear morning, with a good breeze and the sky already lightening in the east. The road followed the Gulf. Sizable waves were still breaking on the beach to the right. To the left was an endless expanse of marsh, into which Bert turned after a while, following an old, overgrown levee of some kind. At the end of it was a swampy pond.

11

On the far side of the pond I could make out, in the growing light, a duck blind with a couple of dozen decoys floating in front of it.

"It's deeper than it looks; you'll need the pup to fetch whatever you drop out there," Bert said, leading me to the edge. "That's why I gave you this spot, so you can see some water work. Don't expect him to be steady when the gun fires; we haven't insisted on that yet. I wanted to get him good and eager first. I'll be back for you around nine; they generally stop flying about then. Good luck."

The pup, released when we got out of the pickup, was already swimming happily in the pond, something I was pleased to see. They're supposed to be water dogs, but they don't all know it. I called him in, as Bert drove off to take care of his other clients. After the usual ritual of shaking himself all over me, the dripping youngster accompanied me around the pond to the blind, which consisted of several barrels sunk in the mud, concealed by reeds and brush. I climbed into the left-hand barrel, which seemed to be most strategically located. It was reasonably dry and had a comfortable seat. I loaded my shotgun, an old Remington automatic I'd had for years. I whistled in the pup and parked him on a water-level wooden platform beside me that had been built for the purpose.

Oddly enough considering where he'd been born, his name was Happy. The Swedes seemed to like picking their dog names from the English language, judging by the three-generation pedigree I'd been given that was nicely sprinkled with champions of one kind or another— I didn't know what the European titles signified, but they looked impressive. We sat and watched the marsh come to life as the sun rose; the reedy vista gradually turning from dawn gray to daylight gold. Some shots were fired in the distance; then the pup stiffened, staring off to the

12

left at an incoming single that was obviously seeking the company of the friendly-looking group of decoys.

It was a teal, a small duck, but I wasn't being particular this morning; I just wanted to see my dog work. I waited for a close and easy shot. When I rose at last the teal, just lowering its flaps for the landing, flared away to the left, low over the decoys. I let it get clear so I wouldn't blast Bert's imitation ducks, and fired. Rifle shooting is a deliberate science; shotgun shooting is the instinctive art of sweeping a fast-flying target out of the sky with swinging gunbarrel. This shot felt good, and was good.

At the report, and the resulting splash beyond the decoys, Happy launched himself like a rocket, sending spray flying in all directions. He surged out there, swimming powerfully—no heads-up puppy-paddling here—and came back with the colorful little teal drake cradled in his mouth. He made the delivery in proper fashion. There's always something special about the first bird brought you by a new young dog; and we admired it together and I scratched his ears and told him what a great retriever he was.

It had been a long time since I'd owned a dog and I hadn't realized how much I'd missed having one. But as I praised the pup, the instinct developed by years of survival in a nonsurviving business was whispering in my ear that it was too soon for me to relax and consider myself a normal, dog-loving, private citizen. I wasn't through with them yet, the deadly ones, the killers I'd hunted all my life, not because I hated them so much, but because somebody had to hunt them and it took another hunter to do the job. They were still out there, somewhere; and I'd better keep a sharp eye on everything I valued, even a dog, because they could strike anywhere . . . .

I brought my mind back to ducks, but too late: a pair

13

of pintails had dipped low over the blocks and disappeared before I could get to my feet and get the gun to my shoulder. I'd barely sat down again when a larger bunch of assorted ducks pitched in to the decoys. They flared in all directions as I rose; the sky seemed to be full of them. I picked the one that made the best target, and hit it, and saw it fall. Happy was after it instantly, a yellow streak exploding from the blind. I swung on another and missed, but corrected my lead and dropped it into the marsh behind us.

Suddenly the sky was empty again. I reloaded and waited for the pup to bring me the duck that had landed in the water, a shoveler drake with an outsize bill, very gaudy and handsome; but they usually taste a little fishy. However, Happy was proud of it, and that was what counted today. He hadn't seen the second fall, but he followed me back there and went to work willingly, searching where I indicated. Soon he hit the scent and dug the bird out of the tall reeds, a nice pintail, the best duck of the day so far. Then back into the blind in time to repel the next airborne assault . . .

By the time Bert's truck appeared, I was sitting on the levee on the outer side of the pond, where it was more or less dry. I was field-dressing my ducks while Happy kept telling me that there were still birds flying, so why weren't we shooting them? He didn't understand about game laws and bag limits.

"Looks like you did all right," Bert said, coming up. "Any problems?"

"Yeah, this dumb dog doesn't know when to quit," I said. I grinned, scratching the pup's ears and trying to keep him from climbing into my lap. "No, no problems. He did just fine."

"I was a bit worried when you first brought him here," Bert said. "We've had some yellow Labs that didn't have a lot of hunt in them, if you know what I mean; not

14

compared to the usual run of blacks. But this one's turning out pretty good. Give us a little more time to teach him manners and you'll have yourself a retriever."

When we drove up to the lodge in the bright morning sunshine, a big car was parked by the stairs that led up to the veranda that ran around three sides of the raised building. Bert glanced at it curiously.

"Rental car from the airport," he said. "But we're not expecting any . . . Doreen?"

His wife was coming down the wooden stairs, looking slender and competent in jeans and a checked shirt. She didn't respond to her husband's implied question, but came straight to me.

"You've got some visitors, Matt," she said. "They're waiting for you in the living room."

"Visitors?"

Instinctively, I unzipped the shotgun case I was holding and reached into my hunting coat pocket for shells. If people had gone to the trouble of tracking me here, I preferred not to meet them unarmed. A duck load will do as well as buckshot at short ranges.

Doreen laughed in an odd, strained way. "Oh, no, you won't need a gun, Matt. It's nothing like that. But . . . but I'm afraid you'd better brace yourself for bad news. I'm sorry."

I looked at her for a moment, but she obviously wasn't going to tell me, so I went past her and up the stairs and around the veranda to the front door. The sea view was great from up here, except for a few oil rigs, but I wasn't into scenery at the moment. I slid the door back and stepped inside, closing it behind me, a little hampered because I still held the cased shotgun.

Of the two women who sat on the sofa side by side, the smaller was the one who'd have drawn a normal man's attention first. Basically a pretty girl, and quite young, she was spectacularly beat-up-looking at the moment. In

15

the glance I gave her, I noted a sling, a head bandage, and some ugly facial bruises; but I'd already recognized the woman beside her and couldn't be bothered with taking the inventory any further. To hell with the battered kid. I wasn't a normal man. I was an ex-husband facing his former wife. She rose as I crossed the room towards her.

"Hello, Beth," I said.

"Matt." She swallowed hard. "I . . . I can't say it, Matt. It's easier if you read it. Here."

She held out a page torn from a newspaper, folded to put a certain story on top. Tucking the shotgun under my arm, I took it and studied it warily. At first glance it was just another terrorist incident. A bomb had been flung into a small restaurant called La Mariposa, in West Palm Beach, Florida. I read on and came to the kicker: *Killed by the blast were . . . Ernesto Bustamente, West Palm Beach, Fla.; Simon Greenberg and Rosa Greenberg, New York, N.Y.; Matthew Helm, Jr., Old Saybrook, Conn. . . .*

Mac would have been proud of me. My first thought was that my older boy was dead, murdered by a bunch of terrorist thugs, while my instinct was telling me to keep a careful eye on a damn dog.

CHAPTER 3

I LOOKED from the newspaper page to the woman I'd once married. She hadn't changed very much. She still had that fresh, healthy, almost boyish, New-England-nice-girl look. Just slightly taller than average, she had light brown hair that still showed no hint of gray. Her figure, in blue tweed, was still slim and youthful; and her legs were still fine in sheer nylon. Her blue shoes had moderate heels. The color of her expensive suit, and matching cashmere sweater, emphasized the blueness of her eyes. There was something intent and hypnotic about the way they watched me. I didn't gather that she was in a very stable mental state at the moment; but, then, who was?

She was no longer my wife, of course. Her name was Logan now and had been for more years than I cared to remember, Mrs. Lawrence Logan, but we still shared something unique that belonged only to us: the memory of a small child in a crib, our first. There had been two after that, and we'd eventually become hardened to parenthood, but the first is the scary one, particularly when you're as young as we were. You don't know anything about it, either of you, in spite of the baby books you've been reading. You're afraid of holding it too hard and breaking it, or not hard enough and dropping it. You can't believe it's really alive. You expect it to stop breathing any minute. . . .

"Kill them," Beth said very softly, regarding me with that intent blue-eyed look. "That's what you do, isn't it, Matt? That's why I left you, when I finally learned that about you, all those years ago. I was . . . a rather gentle person back then. But now I've come back asking you to find them and kill them for me. For us. For . . . for Matthew. Kill all of them!"

Then she buried her face in her hands and began to cry. She swayed dangerously and I thought she was about to collapse. I started forward, but the kid got to her first, and led her back to the sofa, and looked up at me.

"Would you mind putting away that firearm, Mr. Helm?" she asked calmly. "Guns make me very nervous."

"Yes, ma'am," I said, and zipped up the case and set the shotgun in the corner. Then I went to the little bar across the room and found three glasses and my private bottle. The Hapgoods didn't have a license. You provided your own booze; they just supplied what you drank it with and out of. I took two glasses to the sofa, set one on the end table for Beth, and gave the other to the girl, although I wasn't quite sure about the ethics of that. She was really pretty young. "Scotch is what there is," I said.

"Thank you," said the beat-up kid, still with an arm around Beth. "Incidentally, Mr. Helm, I'm your daughter-in-law. We sent you announcements and invitations at the time, if you'll remember, two years ago."

"I remember," I said. "You were both still in college."

"Is that why you didn't come, because you disapproved?"

I shook my head. "A man in my line of work does better to stay away from public occasions involving his kids. There were other reasons why I figured the cere-

18

mony would proceed better without me. I didn't think one absentee daddy would be missed."

"You were wrong," she said stiffly. "But I believe we thanked you properly for the present and the check."

"You did," I said. I looked at her for a moment. "So you're Cassandra. Cassandra Varek as was, if I remember correctly. Cassie or Sandra?"

"Sandra. I might answer to Sandy if you yelled loudly enough." We'd both been intent upon the business of getting acquainted; now the kid glanced at Beth, who'd stopped sobbing and was groping in her purse for a handkerchief. Sandra asked me, "Where's a bathroom?"

"Through those doors and down the hall to the right." But when she'd helped Beth up and started to lead her that way, I said, "Wait a minute. Why don't you take her to my room? There's a small john there, and she can rest on the bed if she wants to. Out the front door and around the veranda to the left. Here's the key; the number's on it."

When the girl returned alone, I was leaning against the bar, sipping the drink I'd made for myself, although I didn't want it very badly. I'm not a morning drinker. But it seemed like something that should be done, a gesture that should be made. You get a big tragic shock, you take a stiff drink, right? Sandra made a detour to pick up her glass and came over to face me.

"Elizabeth will be all right. She's just been holding it in, and it was a long plane ride."

"Sure."

"She doesn't mean it, of course. What she said to you. She's not really a vengeful person."

I studied her carefully, trying to estimate what she'd look like when she wasn't a walking disaster area, this girl my son had married. She was shorter than Beth, sturdy and dark, with black hair cut very short. Perhaps, after having a significant part of it shaved away to permit

19

treatment of the head injury, she'd decided to chop it off totally and let it all grow back at once. The area of tape above her right ear was quite extensive.

She had a rather wide dark face, snub-nosed and full-lipped, with thick eyebrows that had never heard of tweezers. It was a good strong face, very attractive in a young and sultry way. I wouldn't have judged it to be the face of a girl who'd fear guns and forgive her enemies; but on the subject of girls I've been wrong before. Her eyes were brown, and there was an ugly discoloration around the right one; she also had a bruise on the side of her chin. The sling I'd noted earlier supported her right arm. There were small dressings on both hands. She was wearing a tailored gray pantsuit with a black blouse, open at the throat. I could see through her trousers a suggestion of a bandage on her right thigh; I'd already noticed that she favored that leg slightly.

She was aware of my scrutiny, of course, and she spoke without expression: "Twenty-seven stitches in the leg. A lot more in the scalp; but I think they take smaller stitches up there for cosmetic reasons. Greenstick fracture of the radius bone; that's the smaller one in the forearm. My hands got pretty well sliced up as you can see; my knees look like hamburger. Of course I'm black and blue practically all over, turning a beautiful green in spots. My ears only stopped ringing from the blast a couple of days ago. Does that satisfy your curiosity?"

"It's a wonder they let you out of the hospital," I said. "The flight from Washington can't have been much fun for you."

She shrugged. "I'm tough. I don't like hospitals. How did you know we came from Washington?"

"It's the only place you could have learned where to find me. Although I don't check in there any longer, my former chief has ways of keeping track. But he wouldn't have given you this address over the phone. I wouldn't have thought he'd give it to you at all."

"Elizabeth said she'd met him once before, your boss, many years ago when you were being divorced. He looked her up then and tried to persuade her to change her mind about leaving you."

I said, "My ex-boss, please. My former chief, I said. I quit two weeks ago."

"So he told us; but he let Elizabeth come to see him anyway, for old times' sake, I guess." Sandra shrugged. "I went with her, because she's still a bit shaky—and of course I had a personal interest, too. That's a polite and soft-spoken man, but I wouldn't want to get him mad at me. I don't think he's a very kindly person, really."

I laughed. "We're not a kindly outfit. My own humanitarian impulses can hardly be called dominant. What did he say?"

"He wanted to know why Elizabeth was looking for you. When she told him, he was very sympathetic and gave her this address. He said he thought you were probably here, since the waterfowl season was opening today and you had a new hunting dog you wanted to try out." The kid laughed shortly, watching me. "What is it, some kind of a compulsion, Mr. Helm, that you just can't stop shooting things?"

It's never any use arguing with them, young or old, when they get on that kick. "Man gets in a rut, I guess," I said. "But you'd better call me Matt. All this formality doesn't go with such high-minded disapproval."

She said, "Maybe my disapproval isn't so very high-minded . . . Matt. Maybe I don't really care what you shoot. Maybe I'm just trying to give you a hard time for other reasons."

"Reasons such as?"

She licked her lips. "Maybe I'm remembering a very nice guy, a guy you might even have liked if you'd made

21

an effort to know him. A guy who'd have enjoyed having a father, even an offbeat daddy like you. But you were never there. Oh, there were occasional letters, and presents when presents were indicated, and a check now and then, but never a warm body, not even at his wedding, not even at his graduation."

I said, "I gave you my reasons. And Larry Logan makes a pretty good substitute papa. I checked him out."

Sandra shook her head. "Elizabeth's husband is very much okay, and he did what he could to fill the daddy spot, but a stepfather isn't the same thing even when he's adopted his new wife's kiddies legally and given them his name. If you'd died and Elizabeth had remarried, that would have been bearable. But knowing that you were still around, somewhere, and just couldn't be bothered with your own son, with any of your children . . ." She drew a long breath. "Of course, that was what drew us together in college, Matthew and me. We had it in common. My daddy was a lot like you in many ways. My mother died when I was very young, and he couldn't be bothered with being a papa, either. So he wished me off on nurses and governesses and boarding schools, and never once . . . Well, to hell with that. Sorry. I didn't mean to inflict my bleak childhood on you."

I said, "Did Beth know how Matthew felt?"

Sandra grimaced. "What you want to know is, did she make him feel that way, did she turn her children against their father deliberately, like many divorced wives? No, of course she didn't, she's too nice a lady. In fact, Elizabeth has been defending you stoutly all these years, telling your kids how busy you were saving the world for democracy, or something; and how you couldn't visit them anyway, even when you had time, because you were afraid somebody who didn't like you, somebody you'd injured in the line of duty, say, might strike at your family if they knew it existed. That routine you just used on me. I don't think it's a very plausible excuse for neglecting your kids, Mr. Helm . . . Matt, and they didn't think so either. It might have been better if you'd been honest and simply let them know you weren't interested, the way my daddy did. At least I could console myself, a little, with the fact that I hadn't been sired by a hypocrite."

I asked, "Is that why Matthew changed his name back to Helm?"

She said, "Yes, he wanted to show that he was still your son, even though you'd practically disowned him, getting Larry to adopt him and make him a little Logan. I don't blame him. He wanted you to know, I suppose, that there *was* another Matthew Helm around whether you liked it or not, and that he'd seen through your ridiculous pretense of trying to protect him by giving him another name and staying away from him, when what you were really doing was washing your hands of him and the rest of your offspring!"

I regarded her for a moment. "Do you believe that, Sandra? Now?"

"Of course I do! What do you mean, now? What's changed?"

"Look in the mirror," I said. "I'd say there were some changes, wouldn't you?"

"I don't understand what you—"

I said harshly, "Use your brains, little girl! If any. There you are, all stitched up like the bride of Frankenstein, and there is Matthew, dead, and you still call my precautions ridiculous?" She started to speak, but I went on anyway: "You're blaming me for not seeing my kids often enough. I'm blaming myself for maybe seeing them too often. I did drop in on them once in a great while, you know. Maybe I shouldn't have allowed myself even those few visits."

She said, shocked, "You can't think . . . But that's crazy!"

23

"Well, maybe it wouldn't have made any difference, under the circumstances," I said. "That's something I have to find out."

"Now you're talking riddles," she said angrily. "And you can't truly believe that . . . that somebody blew up a whole restaurant and killed five people in addition to your son, and put a dozen more into the hospital including me, just because they were mad at you! That's . . . that's *paranoid*!"

I said, "I've spent most of my life in a paranoid profession; you can't expect me to change overnight."

"But we *know* who's responsible for that bomb!" she protested. "It's right there in the clipping you just read. A terrorist gang calling itself the Caribbean Legion of Liberty. The CLL. Why do they all go in for those idiot acronyms? They're against what they call American imperialist domination of all those little island countries down there. Fuck the Monroe Doctrine, or words to that effect. At the moment they're particularly concerned with a place called Gobernador that just gained its independence recently—but they claim it's not really independent. They say we only helped it gain its freedom from its previous imperialist oppressor so we could take it over for our missile bases or tracking stations or whatever we have down there. They want to replace the present regime, which they claim is a puppet government controlled from Washington, with a true People's Republic of Islas Gobernador . . . . Anyway, the West Palm Beach bombing was clearly a political protest against American foreign policy by a recognized gang of international terrorists; they've done the same thing elsewhere. It can't possibly have been a personal attack on you."

"Can't it?" I asked. "Even if the bombing was the work of a genuine gang of terrorists, who aimed them at that particular little restaurant? Who ever heard of a hash joint called La Mariposa, the Butterfly? The Palm

24

Beaches are full of targets that make more sense politically; and why West Palm Beach anyway? Why not stage the blast in Miami, a major city, and really shake up the lousy *Americanos*? The casualty list shows no important people to explain why that particular food dispensary was chosen for their explosive attentions; no ambassadors or presidential advisers or senators or congressmen, not even any generals or admirals. Just a bunch of ordinary citizens; some locals, some tourists. And Matthew Helm, Jr. What the hell were the two of you doing in Florida, anyway?''

She made a wry face. ''We were watching my daddy get married to still another tramp, under the waving palms of the ten-acre backyard of his cozy little twenty-room Palm Beach cottage. It always draws me back, the humble home of my childhood, with its tender memories of surly bodyguards and snarling guard dogs and alarms that I was always setting off in my snoopy childish way. It's a wonder I didn't get myself shot.''

''I see. So you've got yourself a stepmother.''

She made a wry face. ''There's been a long parade of them. The blushing brides last him two or three years, maybe five, and then he pays them off according to his standard matrimonial contract—he got the lawyers to write up an ironclad one after a bright dame stung him badly back when I was a little girl—and uses temporaries for a while. But I guess he prefers live-in sex; he always finds another one to marry sooner or later. I'm gaining on them. They look younger all the time; or maybe they stay the same age and I just keep getting older. Well, I guess this one's crowding thirty, although she won't admit it. She's very sweet to me. They all are at the start.'' The kid shrugged. ''Anyway, Matthew and I just had to get away from that madhouse on the ocean, so we decided to sneak away from all the nuptial gaiety and have dinner together in a quiet little place. . . . Quiet!'' She

25

moved her shoulders awkwardly. "So much for that brilliant idea."

"Yes," I said. "And I'm still wondering just how it happened that these political crazies just happened to select for their political demonstration an obscure eatery where my son just happened to be dining with his wife."

She said, "And I still think you've got paranoia problems. I suggest a visit to the shrink."

She was an irritating girl, and she looked like hell at the moment, but I was beginning to have considerable respect for her. She had the guts not to sit around feeling sorry for her poor little damaged and widowed self, and I liked the way she spoke her mind in spite of my considerable seniority and the relationship between us, whatever it might be now that Matthew was dead.

"Well, maybe," I said. "But in any case, do I gather that you're all for these noble Caribbean patriots, since you seem to be trying to keep me from going after them, telling me how Beth doesn't *really* want them all killed no matter what she came a few thousand miles to ask me?" I watched her closely. "Am I to understand that you don't want anybody to hurt a hair of their cute little heads?"

"I didn't say that!" She shook her head vigorously and winced as the gesture reminded her of her injuries. She went on fiercely, "I hate them; of course I hate them! I never did a thing to harm their lousy little island, wherever the hell it is, and neither did Matthew; and now he's dead and I have the rest of my life to remember that awful moment, those dark hating faces outside the restaurant window, and the glass shattering like that, and his weight on top of me as he knocked me out of my chair and covered me with his body. And then that awful noise like the end of the world and everything crashing down on us. And . . . and afterwards crawling through the broken glass and rubble and spilled food and broken dishes with

26

my clothes in rags and my scalp hanging into my eyes and my arm not working right and blood all over me, my own blood, Matthew's blood. That's when I cut my hands and knees like that, but I didn't even know I was doing it. I was trying to find somebody to help him. . . . Yes, I hate them! Yes, I want to see them caught and punished! But legally by the proper authorities, not by you!''

"Caught is caught. Punished is punished," I said.

"No, it isn't, and you know it! The law is one thing and private vengeance, private violence, is something totally different, something the world has too much of already and has to get rid of if we're ever going to live together in peace.''

When they start talking about living in peace, under present world conditions, they lose me completely. I'm not that good at daydreaming.

"Do you think Matthew would have wanted his murderers to get away with it?" I asked. When she glanced at me sharply, I said, "It's not a rhetorical question. As you've pointed out so diplomatically, I didn't know my son very well. Was he a turn-the-other-cheek kid?''

She hesitated. "I'm sorry if . . . I didn't really mean to hurt you.''

I grinned briefly. "The hell you didn't.''

"All right, I suppose I did. Yes, Matthew was a non-violent person; that was another thing we had in common. I guess we were both rebelling against our macho male parents. You with your ugly government work, my daddy with his . . . Well, never mind that; but even in his private life he was always shooting things, just like you. Pistols and rifles and shotguns everywhere. Even Larry Logan hasn't always been the peaceful ranching gentleman he seems, as you probably know; and his house isn't exactly weaponless, although he keeps them pretty much out of sight for Elizabeth's sake.'' Sandra frowned. "I don't know why she didn't just go to her current husband when she got this revenge obsession. Larry was very fond of Matthew, and I have a feeling he can still be a pretty tough character when he puts his mind to it. It would have saved her all this trouble tracking you down.''

I said, ''You're not thinking. If she loves the guy, would she want to involve him and get blood on his hands? Although he took his stepfather duties seriously, it's not really his son who was killed.''

''I guess that makes sense, if anything does in this crazy mess.'' Sandra shook her head ruefully. ''Anyway, to answer your original question, yes, Matthew would certainly have wanted his murderers to get away with it rather than have his mother spend the rest of her life with a bloody vendetta on her conscience, that she'd set into motion when she wasn't her normal, gentle self.''

I said, ''Never mind Beth's conscience. Whatever happens, it won't be her responsibility.''

''What do you mean?''

''I'm not quite the wild man my son seems to have thought me, judging by what he's apparently told you about me.'' I regarded the girl grimly. ''I don't go around killing people just because I'm mad at them, even if I have a very good reason, like my boy's murder. Nor do I grab a gun and start blasting away merely because I'm asked to by a lady I was once rather fond of. There's only one person from whom I'll take that kind of instructions, and I'm not working for him any longer. At least I don't think I am.''

Sandra drew a long breath. ''Then you're not going to do it?''

''I didn't say that. The message I'm trying to convey is that, except where ducks and other gamebirds are concerned, I don't take up weapons for personal reasons.''

''I don't understand. What other reasons could there be. . . ?''

Mac's timing was good; it always is. The hall door

opened and Doreen Hapgood beckoned to me. "You have a call from Washington. You can take it in my office."

"Excuse me a moment, Sandra." I took my time walking in there. Let him wait a little. I picked up the phone and said, "Eric here."

The voice that answered was the right one. I'd never doubted that it would be. "You will have spoken with the ladies I sent you by this time," Mac said.

"Yes, sir."

"Please accept my condolences."

"Yes, sir."

"Mrs. Logan informed me where your other two children are living. I have taken the liberty of having them covered, discreetly, just as a precaution."

I'd had it on my mind. I was glad there was somebody around who thought along the same ugly, paranoid lines as I did. It was nice of him to arrange for the kids' protection without even being asked. He always scares me most when he's being nice.

"Thank you, sir," I said.

"You have certain questions, I suppose."

"Yes, sir."

"I thought you might. And I have no answers. They must be found elsewhere. But you will want to make certain of that. If you drive to Houston right away, you can catch a two o'clock flight that will get you into Washington this evening. Reservations have been made for you. A car will be waiting to bring you here; the driver will identify himself in the usual way."

"Yes, sir," I said; and the line went dead.

CHAPTER 4

THE agency car dropped me four blocks from the office, as usual. Unless you're crippled temporarily, which happens in this business, you don't pull up in front when you answer the summons; too much vehicular traffic is deemed undesirable. Furthermore, a short hike lets you make a few routine checks, so you can brush off at least the most obvious insects that might have attached themselves to you, or send out the exterminators with the DDT if it seems desirable.

The driver was taking care of my suitcase, so I had nothing to carry. It was a nice fall night, good for walking. I didn't mind stretching my legs after the plane ride. However, it was a poorly lighted part of town and, as a private citizen, I'd avoided the problems of bringing a gun by air. I therefore took out the little Gerber knife I'd acquired recently and flicked it open, carrying it so the pretty pear-shaped blade would not reflect what light there was. I mean, I don't run wild rapids without a life preserver; and I don't walk wild Washington streets unarmed. I'm full of admiration for the brave citizens who do; but I'm still here and some of them aren't.

There's an inconspicuous entrance a couple of buildings away that'll get you inside unseen by way of some tricky cellar passages; but Mac hadn't indicated we were operating under that kind of security tonight. I used the customary side door. There aren't any obvious checks or controls on any of the entrances; but an unidentified stranger wouldn't get very far inside. The place is always better at night, nice and peaceful. There's only a skeleton crew downstairs; and the upstairs offices are empty except for the one in which he's waiting for you, no bigger than the others and no more elaborately furnished. But at night you see him against a background of drawn blinds instead of that damn bright window. The building is almost quiet, and even kind of cozy—well, the way I suppose a lion's den is cozy if you're a lion—and sometimes he relaxes and has a drink with you if you look as if you need it. Or if he has a reason for wanting to put you at your ease.

As I settled into my chair, glass in hand, a handsome dark girl in tailored gray slacks came in and walked around the desk to lay a paper before him. Her black hair was pulled severely back from her face, and she was wearing a mannish shirt complete with necktie. She gave me a brief, cool glance as she waited for him to read what she'd given him, letting me know that she wasn't a bit impressed by field personnel, even senior field personnel. Any meathead could go out and shoot people; what took intelligence was working the computers and keeping the backup organization running smoothly so that when we got ourselves into a mess out there, as we usually did, somebody knew what buttons to push to get us out. The girl looked down again, as Mac scribbled something on the paper and gave it back to her.

"Keep working on it, please," he said. "See if you can't get a hint as to where at least one of them likes to hide out when the pressure gets heavy. . . . Oh. Miss Dana Delgado, Mr. Matthew Helm."

"I know." Her voice was as cool as her look.

Mac spoke to me: "Miss Delgado is our computer expert specializing in Caribbean terrorist organizations. She has produced some interesting information about the administrative structure of the Caribbean Legion of Liberty, and a few names. She is trying to locate the owners of those names by means of their habits as recorded in the computer. . . . Thank you, Miss Delgado.''

We don't use the code names when dealing with the office people. The girl nodded and went out without telling me what a great pleasure it had been to meet me. I seemed to be encountering nothing but hostile brunettes lately; although my parting from my daughter-in-law had actually been pleasant enough and she'd said she hoped we'd meet again and if I should happen to be in Palm Beach I should stop by her daddy's umpty-million-buck beach cottage and see her; she'd be there for a while, until she'd got rid of her stitches and grown some hair. Address. Telephone number. Please do come.

Then I'd said a hasty good-bye to Beth, but the grief we shared hadn't been enough to overcome the years we'd been apart and the fact that she was the wife of another man, to whose Nevada ranch she was returning. The pup's good-byes had been less restrained; in fact he'd almost overwhelmed me with his affection.

So now I was watching an unfriendly young woman go out of Mac's office and deciding that her retreating rump, while intriguing, was not designed for trousers. Not that she had an overly large butt; it was really rather a neat behind, but it was too feminine, both in contour and in operation, for what is still, at least in my old-fashioned opinion, basically a masculine garment. Or maybe I was just thinking snide thoughts about the lady because she so obviously didn't approve of me.

''Eric.''

''Yes, sir.''

Mac was studying me thoughtfully. ''We had better clear the decks first, don't you think?'' he said. ''I believe you have something you wish to ask me.''

''No, sir.'' I shook my head. ''We've worked together

a long time. You know what I'm thinking; what I have to be thinking. You know what I'll do if I ever find proof pointing that way. There's nothing that needs to be discussed between us."

He said, "I disagree. It will be better to have it in the open. That way there can be no misunderstandings." He regarded me for a moment longer; when I shrugged, he went on: "What we have here is a troubling coincidence, am I correct?"

"Troubling is a nice word."

"The facts are that you turned down a mission directed against certain people. Within a very short time, those people were apparently responsible for the death of a member of your family. As a result, you may now be willing to reverse your previous decision and accept the job you refused, hoping to retaliate. But you cannot help but ask yourself if someone planned it that way." He smiled thinly. "Someone, for instance, like me."

I gave him a small grin. "Well, you're the obvious candidate, sir. You know me, you know about my family even though I've been careful not to leave many tracks leading that way, and you have contacts in strange places; setting up a blast wouldn't be hard for you. And you were pretty unhappy with me when I left here two weeks ago."

"Well, you must admit you were behaving very unreasonably."

I grinned. "I don't admit it, but let's not start that argument again. Regardless of who was reasonable and who wasn't, the fact was that I'd refused a mission for reasons you considered quite inadequate, even going so far as to hand in my resignation. For a lousy German shepherd bitch! You could have figured it was time I was brought to my senses and shown the difference between people and dogs. Besides, knowing Bultman, I was the only man around with a reasonable chance of carrying

33

out the operation successfully, at least in your opinion. You may have convinced yourself that the welfare of our country demanded that drastic measures be taken to regain my services. You've pulled some pretty raw stuff in the past to get people to do what you wanted."

He nodded calmly. "Yes. It is what I expected you to think. And I will not claim that I am incapable of sacrificing an agent's family for the good of a mission. In fact, in certain situations, I would expect him to make the sacrifice himself."

I spoke carefully: "Of course it's only one possibility; but you wouldn't believe me if I said it had never occurred to me."

"Let us say I would be disappointed in you. It would indicate that you were a fool or that you thought I was."

I said, "Of course, there's a flaw in my reasoning. The mission we discussed here a couple of weeks ago involved only one man, Bultman. There's no indication, as far as I know, that he was responsible for the West Palm Beach incident in which my son died, so why should it change my mind about going after him?"

Mac gave me his meager smile again. "Perhaps I should not answer that question, but I will. Bultman may not be the man who gave the orders; but he will almost certainly defend those who did, and those who carried them out. The Caribbean Legion has contributed substantial manpower to the force he is assembling on Hawkins Island, which is currently part of the sovereign nation of Montego—the part closest to Gobernador."

"What's a Montego?" I asked.

"When a certain colonial presence in this oceanic area was withdrawn, the islands involved split themselves up into a number of nationalistic groupings, Gobernador and Montego being the two in which we're interested. Not that we'd be concerned about the latter in the normal course of events; but the president of Montego, Alfredo

Gorman, disapproves of the boundaries that were drawn by the Convention of 1979. He feels that the Islas Gobernador should have been awarded to Montego instead of being given their independence. He is encouraging Bultman in the hope that a revolutionary struggle over there will open the door for Montegan intervention; and of course Bultman cares little who overthrows the present government in Santa Isabella, as long as somebody does. He'll welcome help from President Gorman, although some of his followers would rather make a pact with the devil. They are under the impression they are struggling to free their country from one oppressive regime; they have no desire to trade it for another. Of course they are not aware that, in reality, they are merely fighting to avenge a dead dog.''

''Yes, sir,'' I said. ''Personally, I think this self-determination thing has been overdone; they're making new little countries faster than I can find them on the map.''

We were talking around the awkward subject. Mac brought us back to it. ''If any part of Bultman's strike force, including the Legion, is threatened, Bultman will be obliged to deal with the threat, or his leadership of this violent coalition will be undermined. So whoever is instructed to take action against these terrorists will eventually have to deal with Bultman; he'll have no choice.''

I asked, ''Has such action been ordered?''

''Miss Delgado informs me that the Caribbean Legion of Liberty is a fairly diffuse organization of volunteer hotheads, but that it is directed by a nucleus that calls itself the Council of Thirteen, because that was the original number of members when the gang was formed. Although they now claim a membership in the thousands, and actually do have a couple of hundred active followers, they've retained the original number for the govern-

35

ing council. It is presided over by one *El Martillo*, The Hammer, real name unknown."

"*El Martillo*," I said sourly. "They sure love to give themselves those menace-names. Remember our little jungle problem down in Central America, years ago, with the guy who called himself *El Fuerte*, The Strong One?"

"Yes, I remember," Mac said. He paused briefly, and went on: "We have been instructed to terminate the Council of Thirteen."

I looked at him for a moment across the desk. Then I got up and went to the corner bookcase that opened to form a rudimentary bar. I poured myself another drink.

"It would be nice if they'd make up their cotton-picking little minds," I said without turning my head. "One moment we're supposed to negotiate peacefully with these wild-eyed characters and make them see the error of their ways; and the next we're ordered to stage a bloody massacre and wipe them all off the face of the earth. I just hope the folks handing down these violent instructions hold on to their tough attitude long enough to back up the poor guy who winds up with thirteen stiffs to his credit, if you want to call it credit. More likely they'll wash their hands of him once the gore has been spilled. It wouldn't be the first time they've gone chicken after giving the hard-nosed orders."

Mac said, "Seventeen."

"What?"

"There are seventeen numbered spaces on the list, although we have few names as yet to go with the numbers. Miss Delgado is doing her best to fill in the blanks. We are instructed to destroy the nucleus of this terrorist organization in order to demonstrate that this country will no longer tolerate such murderous activities, and any group that indulges in them can expect to be demolished."

"That's the directive of today," I said sourly. "What do you suppose will be the directive of tomorrow?"

Mac ignored that and continued: "We are to exterminate all thirteen members of the Council including, of course, *El Martillo*. He rates as Number Two on our list." When I stirred, about to ask the obvious question, Mac said, "Be patient, we'll come to Number One presently. Also we must identify, run down, and eradicate those who actually carried out the bombing of La Mariposa restaurant—witnesses indicate that there were three, two men and a woman. Of course, they may be members of the Council; if so, the number of targets will have to be adjusted accordingly since it is not practical to kill them twice, once for each category in which we have them classified." His voice was dry.

"Does our computer lady have any leads in that direction?"

"Not yet, but she keeps hoping. In addition, we are authorized, indeed we are encouraged, to deal ruthlessly with any other members of the gang who attempt to interfere. The more the merrier. And finally, we are instructed to dispose of Herman Heinrich Bultman, since it is felt that he bears the ultimate responsibility for the atrocity, being the commander of the insurrectionary force with which the Legion is currently associated. In fact, he has the honor of being placed at the top of our list."

I sighed. "Here we go again. They never give up, do they? If one reason for hitting the Kraut isn't good enough, they dig up another. I hate to be forever defending the homicidal sonofabitch; but the fact is that random explosions aren't his style, and he'd never have been stupid enough to authorize an action that would antagonize whatever support his invasion might otherwise have gained here in the U.S. What probably happened was that some wild-eyed CLL characters, maybe not even part

37

of Bultman's paramilitary outfit, decided to go off and make a little noise on their own. If it actually was the Legion." I shook my head. "Hell, I'm as vengeful as the next guy, but I do like to go for the right throat when I go."

Mac said deliberately, "Yes, I am counting on that."

I spoke without expression: "You don't have to worry, sir. I won't come after you until I have proof."

"And of course it will accomplish nothing for me to assure you that I had nothing whatever to do with your boy's death."

"Of course not," I said. "You'd tell me that in any case. We're all terrible liars here. And who was it who trained us never to believe anything anybody told us?"

He regarded me bleakly for a moment, and asked, "While you are making up your mind whether or not to shoot me, will you accept reinstatement and take on this assignment for us?"

There was a little silence. The fact was, of course, that I didn't really believe he'd set up the West Palm incident, not because he wasn't capable of it, but simply because he was smart enough to know I'd never accept it as an act of random terrorism. Still, his ruthlessness was well documented, and his motives were often impenetrable, so the possibility remained a possibility even though we were playing rough word games with it.

I said, "Do I have a choice? How else am I going to keep an eye on you, sir? I'll take the job with a couple of reservations."

"Name them."

"First, I won't go after Bultman; but I won't hesitate to take care of him—assuming that I can, he's pretty good—if he comes after me."

Mac smiled faintly. "Are you saving face by not re-treating from your previous position, Eric? Very well, I accept that condition. There's no chance whatever that

Herr Bultman will let you carry out the rest of this assignment without trying to stop you. What else?"

I said, "It's possible that the CLL is claiming credit for an explosion that wasn't theirs." I watched him across the scarred old desk. "Whoever was striking at me through Matthew had a choice: He could point an existing terrorist organization in the right direction or, if he had no influential contacts among a suitable bunch of crazies, he could make up a little bomb squad of his own and, after the blast, publicize it as the work of the Legion. Those nuts wouldn't deny it; hell, they'd claim credit for the eruption of Mount Saint Helens if they thought anybody'd believe them. And if it turns out that the CLL is actually innocent, the deal is off."

Mac said, "Again, it is a risk I am willing to run. All our evidence indicates that they were responsible; and I know of no one else who has been hiring explosives experts recently." He looked me straight in the eyes. "Myself included."

I said, "Even if I take your word for that, you may not have been checking on the right people."

He frowned. "What are you driving at, Eric?"

"We've got to keep in mind the possibility that our basic premise is all haywire. There's a chance that whoever arranged that bombing wasn't interested in me at all."

Mac said impatiently, "Of course. There has always been a remote chance that it was a straight political act after all, unlikely as it may seem, and that your son's death was a complete coincidence. Such things do happen. But I am very wary of coincidences in this business."

I said, "So am I, but there was someone else present whom you seem to have overlooked." I leaned forward to set my empty glass on the desk, and sat back again. I said, "Two years ago, when I returned from an assign-

39

ment to find Matthew's wedding announcements among the mail that had accumulated in my absence, I took the liberty of using our facilities to conduct an investigation. The results are in my file. Correction, you keep separate dossiers on agents' families, don't you? So the stuff about the girl would probably have wound up in Matthew's file.''

"You mean that young Mrs. Helm . . ."

"My researches indicated that my daughter-in-law-to-be was a fairly interesting young lady. Somehow she'd wound up at the same university as my son, Northwestern, studying journalism, after surviving one of those East Coast lady-factories, you know, the expensive boarding schools where they teach you not to blow your nose on your napkin.''

"Northwestern?" Mac said. "I thought everyone truly interested in journalism went to the University of Missouri.''

"You're behind the times, sir," I said. "Missouri is still at the top, but nowadays Northwestern's school of journalism is supposed to be right up there alongside it. And for a young person Evanston, Illinois, right next to the gaudy metropolis of Chicago, might have some attractions that Columbia, Missouri, doesn't. As a matter of fact, Matthew actually went to Northwestern because they offered him a scholarship. The girl might have been sent there because her papa preferred having her near Chicago where he had connections who could keep an eye on her.''

"What connections? Who is this girl, anyway?"

I said, "Reading the stuff our people dug up on her, I came across nothing unfavorable to her personally. Some young women do remain almost human in spite of having been subjected to those cruel early disciplines, like learning what fork to use and how to hold a teacup; and if my son wanted to marry an embryo lady reporter, that

40

was his business. I did think they were rushing it a bit, getting married in their junior year like that, but even if I'd wanted to make them hold off until graduation, it was a little late for me to throw my weight around as a papa. As it turned out, well, I'd hate to be sitting here knowing that I'd kept my boy from having had two years of happiness with his girl, since that's all he'll ever have, now. At least he had his marriage and a few months at a reasonable job in his chosen field . . . Well, to hell with that.''

Downstairs, somebody started up a printer of some kind. It sent a distant chattering noise through the building. I wondered if the aloof Miss Delgado was punching the buttons.

Mac, having offered his condolences once, seemed to feel that no further sympathy was needed. He asked, ''What about the parents?''

I said, ''Yes, sir. Sandra's mother was apparently more than respectable, the daughter of a certain Homer Putnam Ganson, who'd inherited a lot of railroad money and made it grow. Unfortunately, Sally Ganson seems to have been a rebellious girl who went slumming once too often and fell for a very undesirable young man. I presume Homer put his foot down, thereby making a runaway marriage inevitable. There was a reconciliation of sorts, although I doubt that Homer ever took his son-in-law to his bosom; and when the old man died, everything went to the young couple, including the Palm Beach estate where Sandra grew up between boarding schools, her mother having in the meantime managed to get herself killed in an one-car accident that could have been self-inflicted, if you know what I mean. I gather it was not a happy household.''

Mac said, ''The suspense is considerable, Eric. Just who was this undesirable young man who married the reckless young heiress?''

"My son's father-in-law's name is Varek. Alexander K. Varek. K for Konstantin."

Mac frowned. "*Sonny* Varek?"

"That's who," I said.

He shook his head ruefully. "The material must have come across my desk on a busy day; apparently I didn't give it proper attention. Otherwise I would certainly have commented on the fact that one of my operatives was now related by marriage to a member in good standing of the Mob, or however it is known nowadays. The Syndicate? I believe Varek specialized in drugs, did he not?"

I said, "To some extent. Like most of them, he had a lot of things going for him. I gather he's retired now, to the extent that those guys are permitted to retire. But you can see that his past activities, both in the rackets and the smuggling trade, could easily have given somebody a motive for blowing up his daughter, either using a weirdo organization like the CLL or just laying the blame on them knowing they'd accept it happily."

CHAPTER 5

YOUNG Mrs. Cassandra Helm picked me up at the airport in a black Mercedes three blocks long. There was a chauffeur in uniform who, I noted, carried a two-inch-barreled bellygun holstered on his right hip under his whipcord coat, which he did not button. He was a large, dark gent, shorter than my six-four but heavier than my two hundred, and he gave me a cold inspection and saw nothing because the stuff I'd drawn from the armorer was in my suitcase and the little folding knife, with its space-age plastic grip, was flat enough and light enough not to make itself conspicuous in my pants pocket. Never mind how I get that past the airport scanners. We have our little professional secrets; unfortunately this particular trick doesn't work with heavier stuff like firearms.

Sandra hadn't met me at the gate; she'd just described the car over the phone and told me where to find it. She didn't get out to greet me now; but when I slid in beside her she gave me a good enough smile of welcome.

"I'm glad you could come," she said.

"It's nice of you to put me up on such short notice," I said.

The chauffeur was putting my suitcase into the trunk of the car. He got behind the wheel and took us away without instructions. There was glass between him and us.

"Bodyguard?" I asked.

"Yes. He wouldn't let me meet your plane, said he couldn't protect me in there with all those people. Sorry. He also makes sure I behave myself like a proper widow. He's supposed to report any indiscretions to Daddy. He's got very good ears and a mike to help him . . . . Don't you, Leonard?" When there was no answer, she repeated: "Don't you, Leonard?"

A metallic voice answered, "Yes, Mrs. Helm."

She grinned, and said ruefully, "Even without Leonard to protect my reputation, among other things, I'd have a problem being indiscreet looking like this, wouldn't I? But at least I can get my right eye all the way open again."

Actually, there had been considerable improvement since I'd last seen her. The discoloration around the eye had faded and the swelling had, as she'd said, subsided. Her hands were no longer bandaged, and neither was her head. The cropped hair had grown back a little; but you could see the scar like an erratic furrow wandering through a field of cut wheat, except that the colors were all wrong, of course. I liked the way she seemed to feel no need to hide it under a hat or scarf, telling everybody: *Okay, so they had to stitch my scalp back on, so what business is it of yours, Buster?*

She was overdressed for the place, Florida, and the time of day, early afternoon, in a black silk dress and black nylons. I couldn't help noting that, for a short girl, she had legs that were very shapely, with strong calves and slim, lovely ankles. High-heeled black pumps improved the view. Even though my son was dead, it made me feel guilty, admiring the legs of my daughter-in-law. Incest? She held a black silk envelope purse in her lap. It had something inside that was too big and blocky for a compact. She had discarded her sling.

"Daddy insists on proper mourning in public," she said, with a gesture towards the black dress. "Daddy's a great one for appearances nowadays. Thank God, the doctor said I could leave off the splint and sling now if I was careful. It wasn't a real break, you know, just a kind of a crack. This is West Palm Beach, as you probably know." She raised her voice: "Leonard, drive us past La Mariposa, please."

The tinny voice said, "But, Mrs. Helm . . ."

"They're not likely to be waiting for us with another bomb after all this time, are they? Go on, take us there."

"Yes, ma'am."

It was a bright Florida day but, except for the palm trees, the city through which we drove could have been located in any sunny state with blue skies—I'd seen the same sprawling, ticky-tacky neighborhoods spring up all over New Mexico, which used to be a nice place to live back when I was growing up there. Maybe Florida was, too, at the time.

44

From the rugged feel of the Mercedes suspension—usually they ride like silk—I judged that the car was carrying more weight than it appeared to, presumably armor of some kind. The windows weren't ordinary passenger-car glass and the windshield refracted the light oddly. Leonard spoke into his mike, but on a wavelength we were not receiving. A couple of surreptitious glances aft had already let me know there was a covering car behind; presumably he was communicating with the driver. At first I couldn't spot anybody breaking trail up ahead, but after a dozen blocks I got that one, too, sorted out from the casual traffic.

Sandra glanced at me with a rueful little smile. "I hope you don't mind if I hold your hand when we get there. I know I've got to look at it again or I'll never really get over it, but I haven't had the nerve to do it alone. Like I haven't had the nerve to return to Connecticut and go through . . . go through Matthew's things."

"Old Saybrook, Connecticut. That's on the Connecticut River, right?"

"Yes. He got a job with the *New Haven Post-Courier* right after graduation; and that was the closest place we could find that was really nice. It was a thirty-mile commute, but the turnpike made it not too bad since he worked odd hours and usually missed the big morning and evening rush. There's also a train. We had a small house on the edge of town, not waterfront but handy to the beach and the launch ramp for the little boat we kept parked in the driveway. Graduation present to me from Daddy. Did you know that Matthew had never sailed in his life until I taught him?"

"Well, he was brought up on Larry Logan's ranch in Nevada, the driest state in the Union," I said. I glanced at her. "This restaurant we're going to, have you done any more thinking about what happened there?"

She shook her head quickly. "Not except when I can't help it. Sometimes . . . sometimes at night I have to live it all over again; but I'm getting it under control, I think. I don't wake up whimpering and sweating so often lately."

"Maybe you should see a psychiatrist."

"I said I was getting over it. I don't need a shrink messing with my psyche."

"Well, I hate to pick at the sore spot, but . . . you said you saw some dark hating faces outside the window just before the bomb came through the glass. Would you recognize them again?"

"Oh, God, don't start that routine! I've had it from Daddy and the cops and several bunches of federal creeps, not to mention daily-, weekly-, and monthly-type reporters and writers. Terrorism is the fashionable menace of the year, beating out smoking and cancer and drunken driving. No, dammit, I can't draw you pictures of them; I can't even describe them. I wouldn't know them if I saw them on the street. Like I told all those nosies, one seemed to be a woman; she was wearing a skirt, a full peasant thing of some kind, although you'd think she'd do her bombing in jeans, wouldn't you? But maybe she carried it hidden under that big skirt. Otherwise, aside from the fact that they weren't blond or albino, I can't tell you anything about them."

"What federal creeps?" I asked.

"Oh, God, I don't know! One pair of clowns all dressed up in three-piece suits and ties. And there were some other civilian types, more informal, in sports shirts and slacks, also U.S. government they said; not to mention the local plainclothes cops who'll still look like cops when they put on their angel robes and wings, if St. Pete lets them through the Gates, which isn't likely. Who needs fuzz in Heaven?"

"It sounds as if they really put you through it," I said.

46

"It was Daddy they were really after, to hell with the innocent little terrorists. The way they acted, you'd have thought it was a federal and state crime to have you daughter and son-in-law blown up by a bomb." She glanced at me. "You know about Daddy?"

"Yes. I checked you out before the wedding."

"I didn't know whether you knew or not, when we were talking back there in Texas."

I grinned. "You kept scrambling like hell to talk around it. But we've got a good research department. I probably know stuff about your daddy even the cops don't know. If you report that, Leonard, tell Sonny Varek not to worry. His business isn't our business."

"I'll tell him," the microphone said. "It'll be a great big load off his mind, I'm sure."

Sandra laughed shortly. "All the official comings and goings just confirmed our neighbors' opinions that we were highly undesirable residents for their pure Palm Beach. They're very restricted in that high-class community over on the ocean side of the Intracoastal Waterway, which is wide enough there to be called a lake. Lake Worth. They'd get rid of us if they could. I mean, even with all his money, Daddy couldn't have bought our place there; they'd have blocked him somehow. Gangsters and niggers keep out. But they couldn't keep him from marrying it." She gave me another sharp glance. "Talking about marriage, if you knew all about me two years ago, why didn't you come charging along to save your precious son from that dreadful female he'd dredged up out of the slimy underworld?"

I laughed. "Telling people whom they can't marry isn't a very profitable occupation. I was more concerned about the way you kids were jumping the gun; I'd have liked to see you wait until you were out of school. As it turned out . . ." I cleared my throat. "As it turned out, obviously you did the right thing, and I'm glad I minded

47

my own business. As far as your family was concerned, I figured that if your pop could stand having a Helm in his family, I could stand having a Varek in mine.''

She laughed. "That was very tolerant of you. Daddy's attitude was pretty much the same. Matthew . . . Matthew said he knew how Romeo and Juliet must have felt, squished between the feuding Montagues and Capulets, except that you both turned out to be more reasonable than we expected . . .'' She stopped and gripped my arm hard, leaning forward to look out the car window. "Oh, God, here we are! La Mariposa is right around the corner ahead. . . . Slow down a little, please, Leonard.''

"Yes, ma'am.''

We turned into a narrow side street of old two- and three-story buildings; storefronts at street level and offices above. The restaurant was on the right about halfway down the block; it wasn't hard to spot. Raw plywood, braced by two-by-fours, covered the large front window. The sign hanging over the door, scarred by flying debris from the explosion, showed a colorful butterfly: La Mariposa. The only butterfly I recognize is the Monarch; this seemed to be a gaudy distant cousin. A cardboard placard on the door, black with glowing red letters, read: CLOSED.

As we cruised by, Sandra drew a long, shaky breath, but her voice was quite steady when she spoke. "It's too bad, they used to serve the best enchiladas in town. All right, Leonard, you can take us home now.'' She released my arm and smoothed my coat sleeve. "Sorry. Circulation will probably return in a couple of hours. . . .''

She stopped. An elderly car had come screeching around the corner ahead; now it slued around broadside to block the street. Leonard reacted instantly; I felt the Mercedes leap forward and swing sharply as he tried the maneuver that was still called the bootlegger's turn back when I was a boy, although the rum runners had mostly vanished with repeal. Times change, but happy-stuff still gets transported illegally, so maybe they call it the drug smuggler's turn nowadays. Leonard hit the gas hard to break the rear wheels loose and skid the heavy car around in the narrow street; but he never made it. Something punched through the top edge of the thick windshield and took away most of his head and splashed it over the heavy glass that separated us.

The report of the ambush weapon was loud even inside the closed car. I placed it above street level, ahead and to the right. So unload to the left. The Mercedes was still rolling, unguided now; as it jumped the curb I grabbed Sandra's purse from her lap and threw the same arm around her. I hit the door handle with my free hand and threw myself out, dragging the girl out with me. A moment later, the violent, ringing report came again and a projectile smashed into the rear of the car where we'd been. I caught a glimpse of the muzzle flash at a second-story window, level with the roadblock and on the same side of the street as the restaurant.

I hauled the girl to her feet and shoved at her, trying to head her towards that side of the street, but she resisted me, wanting to get back to the car for some reason. It had come to rest across the sidewalk with its front end buried in the side of a building. She'd cost us too much time, and I swore and slammed her roughly to the ground again, as the heavy weapon fired and something very authoritative blasted through the air above us with a supersonic crack and screamed off the pavement beyond us. I yanked the girl upright once more and slapped her face hard.

"Snap out of it, stupid! That doorway over there. *Run!*"

She obeyed, limping for a couple of steps with one high-heeled shoe already lost; then kicking off the other and hoisting her narrow dress and running like a deer in her stocking feet. Under other circumstances I'd have found the sight intriguing, but the clock was ticking in my head. Clearly it was a single-shot weapon and so far he'd taken about five seconds to reload . . . . We made it in four and he didn't shoot at us again. Presumably we'd been too fast for him; now we'd reached a place he couldn't cover, on the same side of the street and below him. I'd hoped for that. There had been some small stuff flying around, but nothing had hit me.

"You okay?" I asked Sandra, as I crammed myself into the doorway beside her, trying to make myself skinnier than I really am.

She nodded breathlessly. There was another shot from the heavy artillery and some small-arms fire, both single-shot and automatic; we had us a real little war. I saw that the cannon in the window had just taken out a headlight and most of a fender of the car that had been following us, smacking it as it turned the corner after us. But the vehicle was still operative; it was backing hastily out of the danger zone.

It had left two men behind. Widely separated, one on each side of the street, they were crouching as they moved forward to attack, firing machine pistols in professional little three- and four-shot bursts. One was hosing down the ancient car that blocked the street, from which shots had been coming. The other was trying for the high window—but he didn't walk his bullets onto the target fast enough. The heavy weapon fired and the projectile picked him up and threw him backwards to land on his shoulders with his legs kicking high into the air before flopping down limply onto the sidewalk. That's the dramatic way they often die in the movies when shot, but I'd never before seen it happen in real life since real rifle and pistol bullets don't have that much power. But this slug did.

The weapon the dead man had been holding had slid

out into the street, but much too far away for me to try for it. I opened the purse I held and took out the small automatic pistol I'd spotted earlier through the thin silk. I closed the purse and put it into Sandra's hands, noting that they were no longer very clean after our tumbling act in the street.

"Sorry I had to slug you; there wasn't time to argue," I said.

She dismissed the incident with a quick shake of her head. "I didn't mean . . . I was all confused, poor Leonard, everything happening so fast, and Daddy said we were supposed to stay with the car no matter what, it's bulletproof."

"Bulletproof, hell!" I said. "That's a big fifty up there, probably with AP ammo. It can make a sieve of a real armored car, let alone a fancy sedan with some tin stuck on it." Now there was gunfire down the street beyond the roadblock; apparently our lead car was engaging the enemy from behind. A bullet hit the building above us and ricocheted away with a nasty, wavering, dying shriek. I said, "Let's beat it and let the boys fight World War Three without us. Are you ready for another sprint?"

There was dirt on Sandra's face as well as on her hands, but her grin was clean and bright. I couldn't help thinking that my son seemed to have found himself quite a girl; it was too bad he hadn't lived to enjoy his marriage.

She said, "Speedy Sandy is right with you, sir. Or a little ahead."

"Good girl. Stay on this sidewalk close to the wall so the big gun can't reach you. Head for the main street we came from, and don't stop for anything. . . . *Go!*"

As we lunged out of our shelter, such as it was, I found myself hoping that the remaining gunner from the following car wasn't in the habit of shooting everything that moved. He wasn't. Seeing us pop into sight, he stepped away from the wall to give us room to pass and, from the kneeling position, laid down a long burst of covering fire; then we were around the corner. The driver was there holding a big Browning 9mm pistol, ready to take out anything hostile that followed us. I shoved the girl at him.

"She's all yours, keep her safe," I said.

Sandra, badly winded, gasped, "Matt, where are you going?"

But I was already crossing the big street at a run. The building over there was two stories high; and from a couple of the second-floor windows there would be a good view down the side street on which La Mariposa was located. One was labeled neatly, in gold lettering: RAMIRO S. SANCHEZ—ATTORNEY-AT-LAW. The other was shabbier and painted: CROWN NUMISMATICS AND PHILATELY—STAMPS AND COINS. I thought that was kind of backwards, and the coins went with the numismatics, but it was no time for semantic technicalities. I paused briefly to check my borrowed gun, and found it loaded and ready, cartridge chambered, safety on. I headed for the door between the storefronts that presumably served the offices above.

It was open for customers. Inside, a hall ran clear through the building to another door in the rear. Maybe there was a parking lot back there. The lighting was dim and it was like seeing daylight through a long tunnel. A lighted sign on the left, about halfway down the corridor, indicated a stairway going up to the right. I paused to listen and it was my day for lucky guesses; somebody was coming down it in a hurry. I moved forward cautiously, wishing the stairs had run the other way; it's hard for a right-handed man to shoot around a corner to the right without making a target of himself. I can shoot left-handed if I have to, but I wasn't going to compound the uncertainty of an unknown guy by using my weak hand.

52

I gambled that I wasn't dealing with a pro, and pulled the old loudmouth gag, bellowing: "Jim, you go on through and cover the back; I'll see what's up the stairs."

The sound of my voice was shocking in that quiet building. I heard my man, or woman, stop momentarily on the stairs. Then the footsteps started retreating upwards towards the second floor. I stepped out, gun ready. It was a man, as near as I could tell in the dim light of the stairway; long hair and jeans and T-shirts are no longer reliable means of sex determination. He sensed me behind and below him, and spun around with a gun in his hand, which made him no innocent lawyer or rare-stamp dealer. Or client or customer. I hoped. It's always nervous when you need them alive. You can't afford to shoot them where it's permanent. You have to try for a merely disabling hit, and so run a much greater risk of getting shot yourself. I aimed for the calf of his leg and fired. He came down right away, losing his weapon, a considerable relief.

But when I got to him, I stopped being so pleased with my marksmanship. Sandra's pistol had thrown high, and the man's right pants leg was already soaked with blood; it was pumping from a wound in his thigh in a volume indicating that I'd probably got the femoral artery. I pocketed the automatic hastily, and the cheap revolver I'd picked up on the stairs. I got out my knife and flicked it open. I pushed the wounded man flat on the stairs, on his back, and showed him the wicked little blade.

"No," he gasped. "Please, no. *Por favor, señor.* I am wounded, I bleed. Help me!"

He was a man, but just man enough to grow a thin little moustache to prove his masculinity: a pretty, slight, dark, scared boy with shoulder-length black hair that needed washing.

"I want a name," I said harshly. "The lady in the peasant skirt with the bomb. *Mujer con bomba.* What is her name?'' When he didn't respond, I laid the knife blade against his cheek and slid the point close enough to his left eye that he'd be able to see it blocking part of his vision, blurred and shiny and menacing. *''La nombre!* You must give me the name, first; then we'll fix that leg for you. The woman who helped bomb the restaurant. Her name or I'll gouge out your fucking eyeball and make you eat it. *Dígame la nombre de la dama, pronto!* Come on, come on, give!''

He licked his lips. ''Angel,'' he whispered weakly. ''The little angel . . .''

Then he died. Hearing a sound below me, I turned quickly, but it was only the driver of the escort car with his big Browning, and Sandra looking up the stairs at me with wide, shocked eyes.

CHAPTER 6

THE evacuation was run more efficiently than the military engagement had been. As we came out of the building, a sedan pulled up in front of us. Beside the driver sat the surviving gunner who'd covered our retreat from the shot-up Mercedes. He jumped out to open the rear door for Sandra.

''I retrieved your shoes, Mrs. Helm; I thought you might like them back,'' he said, straight-faced. He glanced my way. ''And your suitcase, Mr. Helm . . . Get in, please, both of you. Richard will take you home; we'll clean up here.''

Then Richard was driving us away. Sirens wailed in the distance. After a little, Sandra reached for the dusty black pumps on the seat beside her and started to put them on her feet. She stopped upon discovering that her stockings, never designed for direct contact with the pavement, had pretty well disintegrated down there. Her knees were also emerging through the laddered nylon. She started to reach up under her skirt, unselfconsciously, raising herself off the seat so she could strip off the ruined panty hose; then she stopped with a quick, embarrassed glance my way.

It was an odd little moment. I knew that if I'd been her contemporary, she'd have had no hesitation about discarding the garment that had come to grief; and if it gave me any ideas, to hell with me. But now that the excitement was over, she was remembering that I was twice her age. Older people had funny ideas. We'd been getting along fine; she didn't want to spoil it by offending my notions of maidenly modesty, whatever they might be.

She spoke carefully: "I hope you have no serious objection to bottomless girls, Matt."

I grinned. "I've never had any prejudice against topless, why should I object to bottomless?"

Relieved, she wriggled out of the panty hose, dropping them on the car floor. She stuck her bare feet into her shoes and smoothed down her dress, which was smudged but intact. She checked her injured arm.

"Well, I don't seem to have developed any new bone cracks," she said dryly. "But it seems that I can't get dressed up nowadays that I don't get a load of bricks dumped on me. God, look at my knees, I just got the Band-Aids off and now they're all skinned again! With a father-in-law like I've got, punching me in the face and knocking me down in the street, who needs terrorists?" She glanced at me quickly. "Please don't take me seriously. I'm just prattling away. Reaction, I guess. I know you saved my life, and I didn't make it easy for you. Is it proper to say thank you?''

"Proper, but unnecessary," I said.

"I'm grateful, really. But you're not a very nice man, are you?''

"Nobody ever told you I was, did they? Certainly I didn't.''

"He was just a boy," she said.

"There's an old country saying: If they's big enough they's old enough.''

She said, "I don't think that was meant to apply here.''

I said, "I don't understand your complaint. You're a mere slip of a girl but nobody hesitated to blow you up with a bomb. Matthew was just a boy, himself, by some standards, but they didn't spare him. Why should I worry about a punk's birthday when he's waving a gun at me?'' I cleared my throat. "As far as I'm concerned, anybody who's old enough to shoot is old enough to get shot. Am I supposed to let somebody empty a cheap .22 into me just because his ID says he can't drink legally yet? Anyway, I was aiming for his lower leg. Don't you ever sight in your weapons? That damn peashooter of yours throws over a foot high at fifteen feet.''

"It's just something Daddy gave me when I said I wanted a gun to carry. Its main virtue, he said, was that if I did shoot somebody with it, it couldn't be traced.''

"Main and only virtue," I said. "Do you want the lousy clunker back?''

"No, but I suppose Daddy'll want to bury it, now that it's killed somebody.'' She hesitated. "I wasn't blaming you for shooting him. He did have a gun. It was what . . . what you did to him afterwards, a dying boy, that was a little hard to stomach.''

I said, "Did you want me to have killed him for nothing? Well, just to save my skin?''

"What do you mean?''

"He had only a minute or two left. If there's a pressure point you can use to check the bleeding when that big leg artery is cut that high, I don't know about it. I could either just stand there and watch him exsanguinate, or I could get something useful out of him while he was still breathing. In order to accomplish that, I had to keep him from realizing what was happening to him; what leverage can you use on a man, or even a boy, who knows he's dying? So I went at him hard and bullied him, threatened him, scared him; and I got a couple of words before he went. What they mean, if anything, I don't know yet, but it didn't hurt him much more than he was already hurt, did it?" I took a fake-alligator wallet out of my pocket and opened it to check the driver's license. I read the name aloud: "Antonio Morelos."

We drove for a while in silence; then she said, "It's *el nombre*."

"What?"

"When you were browbeating him. Your Spanish is lousy. *Nombre* is masculine. *El nombre,* not *la nombre.*"

"Thank you, teacher."

"Just what did he say?" she asked. "He was so weak we couldn't hear."

I said, "Your daddy's probably going to go for a big debriefing scene; they'll have given him a preliminary report over one of the car phones. So let's save the post-mortem until we get there."

She glanced at me sharply. "If you're thinking of holding out on him, please don't. He . . . he gets very rough sometimes."

I said, "Oh, gee, golly, you mustn't scare me like that, ma'am."

Her mouth tightened. "Just because his men have been trained not to behave like movie hoods, just because they say mister and missis and please, don't underestimate what they're capable of."

I said, "What are you trying to do, tease me into tell-ing you how we big, tough characters from Washington eat little fellows like that for breakfast and spit out the bones?"

She laughed, and stopped laughing. "I guess . . . I guess I just don't want any unpleasantness between the two men who are left in my life now that Matthew . . . now that I no longer have a husband. Please don't fight with Daddy if you can help it, Matt." She went on quickly, without waiting for me to commit myself: "That was the bridge across Lake Worth we just crossed. Now we're driving through Richville-by-the-Sea, vulgarly known as Palm Beach. You should really take your hat off to show respect, like in church. If you had a hat."

"They gave you a hard time here when you were a kid, huh?"

"And still do. It doesn't seem quite fair to my mother's family; that half of me is quite respectable. But they act as if my disreputable daddy managed to produce me all by himself. To them, I'm all nasty Varek. Untouchable." She grimaced. "Oh, well, I guess it's good for the char-acter to learn what it's like being a despised minority, or is it?" After a while, as the car slowed, she said, "Here we are, the entrance to the old ancestral mansion."

I looked at the tall gates and whistled. "Not bad for a despised minority."

"It was built by my maternal grandpa, Homer Ganson, back in the gaudy old days when the Palm Beach *ricos* were all trying to outglamour each other . . . . As you can see, we've got security coming out our ears. Don't try to pet these dogs; they hunt people, not ducks."

The ornate old iron gates had been wired for electric-ity; they opened without anybody pushing at them. There was a gatehouse with a guard, presumably the man who'd pressed the button to let us in. Another husky gent stood by with a Doberman pinscher on a short, quick-release

58

lead. The dog was lean and glossy and handsome, brown on black, a good specimen of its breed. It watched us pass but expressed no opinion; it hadn't been told to hate us, yet.

We drove on into the grounds. The drive wound its way through a jungle of flowering trees and blooming shrubs; it was hard for me to remember that this was autumn and the duck season was already open in Texas. I noted that the planting wasn't quite as dense as it looked; there were clever little camouflaged paths to let the guards and dogs slip up on any intruder who breached the perimeter defenses. Then we broke out into the open to see a wide green lawn, a monstrous house, and the Atlantic Ocean.

"Not much protection from seaward," I said.

"More than meets the eye. You wouldn't want to land a boat down there unless you were invited," Sandra said. "What do you think of our little beach shack?"

"You didn't need a wedding cake. All you had to do was cut a slice of that."

"Isn't it awful?" she said. "But I've become very fond of it lately, after all my years of sneering at it. It's got character, unlike the glass boxes people are putting up nowadays . . . . There's Daddy now, and my current stepmother. Number Four, I think, but I could have missed one or two over the years. You'll have to admit he picks them decorative."

The car made a wide sweep, following the paved drive bordered by flowerbeds. It pulled up before the couple waiting in front of the house. The woman was spectacular, dark and slender and moderately tall; but I put off further appraisal for the moment. The man was my immediate concern. He was no taller than the woman: a blocky, middle-aged gent with a deeply tanned face and a head full of white, wiry, tightly curling hair that looked strangely innocent as a frame for his heavy features. I mean, it's hard to accept a racketeer and drug smuggler, even retired, with sweet, white, curly locks. He stepped forward to greet his daughter as the driver opened the door to let her out. There was no kissing or hugging. They faced each other like ancient enemies.

"Are you okay, Sis?"

"Thanks to Mr. Helm I am," Sandra said.

"Well, you don't look it. Go wash your face and put on a clean dress."

The girl's voice was sharp. "If you don't like the way I look, don't look at me. All I need is a couple of Band-Aids and a stiff drink. I think my father-in-law, here, might also accept a drink if you asked him nicely. . . . Daddy, Mr. Helm. Mr. Helm, Daddy."

Alexander Varek hesitated, and decided not to lose his temper. There was a hint of challenge in the way he held out his hand to me. I suppose he'd met occasional moral citizens who'd refused to shake the dirty hand of the notorious Sonny Varek; and I was a government employee from whom such corny signs of disapproval could be expected. To hell with him. Going around disapproving of people is a fool's game; and I'd shaken bloodier hands than his. His grip was a little firmer than it needed to be; but at least it wasn't a macho bone-crusher performance, just a good manly handshake between relatives by marriage.

"I guess, from what Sis says, I owe you one," he said.

I said, "Let's not start adding up the score yet. What's the police situation? Do we need a call from Washington to the local constabulary?"

He studied me for a moment, apparently a little surprised by my cooperative attitude; then he shook his head. "It's being arranged. The fuzz isn't going to lose any sleep over a dead terrorist punk who was part of a dead-fall that didn't work; all they'll regret is that they didn't get to him before you did." Varek smiled thinly. "And

60

they're damn well not going to cry in their beer because I lost a couple of my boys, either. Just so we wipe up the blood and don't keep the honest taxpayers awake nights with all the gunfire. . . ."

"Alex, are you not going to introduce this nice tall man to me?"

It was the stepmother. As Sandra had said, she was closing in on thirty, but fighting every step of the way. Her taut figure was nicely displayed in snug black slacks and a filmy white blouse designed to reveal the pretty, lacy garment underneath—the word that pops into my mind, not necessarily correct, is camisole—and the firm breasts barely concealed thereby. The black hair was drawn smoothly back from the lovely oval face to a comb at the back of the head, Spanish fashion. There was a full red mouth and there were big dark eyes emphasized by a great deal of elaborate makeup; the lashes seemed to be an inch long. Her nails were also very long, and very red; and her shoes had three-inch heels. They brought her up to a convenient height for a man my size. I don't suppose that was the idea. Guys like Varek just like to own, and display, tall girls who attract attention.

She reminded me of someone. It took me a moment to track down the memory, then I had it: our cool computer lady, Dana Delgado, another tall and slender brunette, who'd have been deeply insulted if she'd known I was comparing her to this overstated sexpot. The latest Mrs. Varek's name was Rosalia, but I was given her gracious permission to call her Lia.

"Did you really save Cassandra's life?" she murmured. "You must be very brave, Mr. Helm."

"Matt, please."

"Was it very frightening, Matt?"

"Getting shot at is never fun, Lia. You learn to run like hell." I glanced at Sandra. "We both showed pretty good speed over the short course, wouldn't you say, Sandy?"

The new wife wasn't entirely pleased to have me bring the stepdaughter into the conversation in such a friendly manner, indicating that we shared the special relationship of two people who had faced death together. However, she was smart enough to give the girl a look full of sympathy.

"Oh, my dear, it must have been terrible! And you've hurt your poor knees again. Come and let me put something on them."

The kid said irritably, "God, I'm all right! It's just a little scrape. The way some people act, you'd think I was covered with mud and bleeding to death! Leave me alone!"

I said, "Well, Sandy can suit herself, but personally I'd like to clean up a bit before I have that drink that was mentioned earlier. . . ."

CHAPTER 7

LATER, with night at the windows, I headed towards the gunroom as I'd been instructed. A dinner jacket had been mentioned, but mine was feeding the moths in Washington; I was wearing my slacks and sports coat with a clean white shirt and dark tie. The gunroom had been pointed out to me when we passed it, by the pretty Hispano maid named Maria who'd shown me to the guestroom on the second floor where my suitcase awaited me; but the house was enormous and, trying to find my way back, I made a wrong turn somewhere and got lost. They might have had to send the dogs after me eventually if I hadn't bumped into Sandra in a corridor. She was all cleaned up and wearing a long green silk dress with a high neck and long sleeves. It was a rather severe garment, and somehow it went well with her cropped hair, emphasizing what an attractive young lady she was, even shorn and scarred.

"It's a good thing you're almost a foot taller than Daddy; otherwise he'd have made you wear his spare dinner jacket," she said. She laughed a bit sharply. "What do you bet everybody else in Palm Beach is sitting down to dinner in shorts and slacks and bathing suits; only the Wicked Vareks are dining formally."

I said, "I think it's kind of nice, dressing for dinner. I'd have brought my tux if you'd warned me. I think I remember how to tie one of those ties."

"Well, I think it's silly," she said. "Are you lost or something? We ought to pass out little maps like a Holiday Inn. This way."

The outside of the house was Palm Beach Classic, all tiles and stucco and towers and arches and verandas. The rooms through which she led me were light and airy, with high ceilings and elaborate furniture. The room we finally entered, however, was all dark paneled walls filled with racks of guns and heads of animals. There was no rug or carpet on the parquet floor, just a tigerskin and a bearskin, both complete with heads. The bear, an Alaskan brown, was a good one, over ten feet squared the way the trophy boys measure. The elk rack over the fireplace was also a prize, seven points to the side and very massive; and the mule deer that had carried the nearby antlers must have been the size of a small horse. I had no basis for judging the more exotic stuff, like the tiger. I've never gone in for trophy hunting myself; but if it pleases a hunter to bring in the hide and the head as well as the meat, I can see nothing against it. He's really showing more respect for the animal he kills, and utilizing it more fully, than the gent like me who just goes out for the chase and the steaks.

Varek was standing by the fireplace when we entered, dressed in a black dinner jacket with a ruffled shirt and a black tie that was not the clip-on variety. I thought it was rather touching, the way he was reaching for respectability. What the hell, we all have our dreams. A small man in a white coat waited by the bar in the corner. His manner was respectful and unobtrusive, but there was a bulge under his left armpit.

"I hope they're making you comfortable upstairs," Varek said. "Tell Philip what you want. You, too, Sis. Sit down and take a load off."

"I'd like to look around a bit first, if you don't mind," I said, after specifying a vodka martini, a choice with which Sandra concurred.

There's a certain protocol to be observed when you enter a room like that, if you've ever done any hunting yourself. You're supposed to act interested. As a matter of fact, I was interested. He had a lot of good stuff, and I moved around the walls checking out the display.

Varek said, "I'm a sucker for a good gun. I won't say I've shot them all at game. Some I bought just to look at. Most of my big-game hunting I did with that .300 Weatherby Magnum, except for the really big stuff, of course. . . . God, it's a long time since I've been out in the field. Sis says you got some good duck shooting down in Texas. New dog, she said. Handsome yellow Lab. From Sweden, she said. Why Sweden?"

He was working hard at being the gracious host. Even though our backgrounds made us natural enemies, he wanted me to realize that he was no comic-strip thug. And I must admit that I'm always more favorably inclined towards guys with guns and trophies on their walls, as long as they didn't buy them at auction so they could put on a phony outdoorsman act. I may not love them, but at least I have something in common with them; which is more than can be said for the tender folks, male or female, who faint at the sight of a firearm.

I said, "The pup was a present from some relatives. I've got family all over that country."

"A Svenska boy, eh?"

"That's right." I was tempted to ask about his origins, but a Varek with the middle name of Konstantin just had to have roots somewhere in middle Europe; and I didn't want us to get off on a long and irrelevant discussion of genealogy. I said, "There's only one thing about this room that bothers me, Mr. Varek."

"Alex, call me Alex. What bothers you, Matt?"

"Your daughter."

He frowned quickly. "What do you mean? What about Sis?"

"How can she stand it?" I asked him. Without looking in the direction of the girl, I was aware that she was frowning at me. I went on: "I mean, when we met in Texas, she made a big production about how guns scared her shitless. I even had to get my shotgun out of her sight so it wouldn't frighten her—one lousy little Remington 1100 all dressed up in a stout leather carrying case. But look at her now, totally surrounded by naked firearms, as relaxed and happy as you please! And see what she was carrying this afternoon!" I took the automatic pistol from my pocket and laid it on the mantelpiece beside him, putting the cheap .22 there also. "You may want to ditch both of those. The revolver belonged to the kid I shot and could be hot; and the automatic left some evidence behind, like a bullet and an empty cartridge case. But it's kind of a strange object to find in the purse of a young lady who's terrified of guns, wouldn't you say?"

The small man named Philip had tensed when I brought out the weapons; now he relaxed and came forward with two stemmed glasses on a tray. Sandra took one and tasted it approvingly; I got the other. Varek started to speak, but she interrupted him.

"You're exaggerating, Matt," she said. "I never said they scared me shitless."

"Okay, you just said they made you very nervous. You also indicated that you disapproved of hunting and all other forms of shooting. That was in Texas. But here in Florida, apparently thinking you were in some kind of danger, you asked your daddy to give you a handgun to pack around in your purse. Not exactly the behavior of a young lady who detests firearms and all associated activities. So what was the idea of that phony I-hate-guns routine you pulled on me. . . ?"

"Who hates guns?" That was the seductive Mrs. Varck, entering with a platter of tiny, colorful sandwiches. "Nobody hates guns in this house; they wouldn't dare. Here are some poo-poos for you. That's Hawaiian for hors d'oeuvres, Matt; but don't spoil your appetite. We're having dinner a little early since it's been a harrowing day and young people do get hungry when they get excited." She smiled fondly at Sandra. "I don't know how you'd survive in Mexico, my dear, they never eat dinner before nine or ten o'clock. . . . Philip, would you bring me a margarita in the kitchen, please."

"Yes, ma'am."

We waited politely until she'd left the room. She was wearing something filmy and white that might have looked bridal and virginal on another woman but not on Lia Varek. Her husband waved me towards a deep red-leather chair like the one in which Sandra was already ensconced. He sat down beside me, but it was Sandra who spoke first.

"You must understand, Matt, that my previous stepmother, Barbie, like in doll, went in for interior decoration in a big way—well, you've seen the house. So Lia, poor girl, feels she has to have a specialty, too, and she's picked cooking, even though she's hardly the Aunt Jemima type. She's driving the kitchen help nuts.''

Varek said mildly, ''Now, Sis. Be nice.'' He glanced at me. ''You had a problem, Matt.''

''Two problems, Alex,'' I said. ''In addition to the problem of why my daughter-in-law was kidding me about her fear of firearms, there's also the problem of just how did she know she'd be in danger today—danger enough to justify packing a gun and riding in a bulletproof car.'' I looked from one to the other of them. ''Somebody might get the idea that you folks knew they'd be laying for us in that little street by restaurant La Mariposa to which Sandra had us drive. Somebody might even entertain the wild notion that we were bait for some kind of a trap, or counter-trap, you'd planned there. If so, I guess the opposition pulled a surprise on you with that heavy gun. Clearly you weren't expecting that.''

Sandra licked her lips. ''What are you trying to say?''

I grinned. ''I guess what I'm really trying to say, in my lousy Spanish, is: *Disponos la mierda, amigos.* I hope I got the gender right this time, teacher. In other words, let us dispose of the bullshit.''

There was a period of silence during which I could hear the distant clink of china and clatter of silver as a table was set in a dining room not too far away. Philip slipped quietly out of the room with a tray holding a single stemmed glass.

Sandra spoke stiffly: ''I don't believe that's a proper Spanish sentence, Matt.''

I said, ''Hell, it isn't even a proper English sentence. In fact it's very improper indeed.'' I shook my head, looking at her. ''As I've just said in two languages, let's cut the crap. You didn't go to Washington with Beth just to hold her hand, you wanted to talk her out of her wild idea

67

of finding me and sending me out to avenge our dead son, right? And since you couldn't dissuade her, you followed along and got to work on me with that nonviolent, law-abiding, gun-hating act, trying to keep me from going on the warpath in spite of her urging."

She licked her lips again. "Well, isn't that just what I told you? Why is that so terrible?"

"I don't say it's terrible. I just say the motive you gave me was a lot of bull. You weren't trying to call me off the vengeance trail because you were such a sweet and peaceful and legal young lady. You were trying to keep me from going after these terrorists because you were going after them yourself."

She shook her head. "You're not making sense, Matt. If I wanted them killed, why would I care if you helped?"

"Because you already had all the help you could use," I said. "You have a daddy right here whose homicidal resources are quite extensive, judging by the research I had done on him a couple of years ago. My hunch is that he agreed to put those resources at your disposal on one condition: He wanted you to make sure I wouldn't interfere." I glanced at Varek. "Daddy may have the local law in his pocket, but that doesn't extend to the U.S. government. I think Daddy is violently allergic to having feds in his hair while he kills people for you. Right, Alex?"

"You're telling it, Matt," Varek said.

I nodded, and turned back to the girl. "So, since you were putting on a phony act for me, I put on one for you to keep you happy while I was sorting things out: I told you how I wasn't really the wild man I was cracked up to be, and how I'd never, ever dream of using my gun for personal reasons. But now can we just forget all that nonsense and admit that there isn't a forgiving Christian character in this room? I'm here because my son was killed. Sandra, you're here because your husband was killed. Your pop's here because his daughter was hurt, and in his po-

68

sition he can't afford to have people get away with blowing up members of his family; somebody may think he's getting soft in his old age. So let's face it, we're all nasty, vicious, violent, vengeful people, all three of us, and our common goal is to annihilate the bastards as painfully as possible. And since that's the case, wouldn't it make sense for us to work together instead of playing corny charades for each other. . . ."

There was a knock on the door. It opened to reveal the young girl in a musical-comedy maid's costume, Maria, who'd shown me to the guestroom.

She addressed Varek: "Señora Varek says I am to inform you that supper is served, señor."

"We'll be there in a minute, Maria. Close the door." When it had closed, he turned to me. "So what's your proposition?"

I said, "I have a list of seventeen names, or will have if our computer girl does her stuff properly. I'm not greedy. I don't need to see them die; I just have to know they're dead. You take as many as you want. I'll figure out how to deal with the rest, personally or otherwise. How about it?"

The door opened abruptly to show Lia Varek, looking impatient. "The soup becomes cold," she said firmly. "You can all discuss your very important business at the table. It is very impolite to keep your hostess waiting."

"Yes, ma'am," Varek said humbly. He grinned at me as we rose to follow her. "As they say, you can't live with 'em and you can't live without 'em."

"And you're the living proof of that, Daddy," said his daughter, but her voice wasn't as sharp as it might have been.

CHAPTER 8

THE dining room was impressive, high-ceilinged and very formal. A great crystal chandelier was suspended over the glossy table, the kind that could be extended by inserting extra leaves in the middle. Even now, at its smallest, it was too big for the four of us. With the lord and lady of the house at the ends, and the Varek heiress and the guest of honor, me, facing each other across the middle, we almost needed walkie-talkies to communicate. I wondered who the Vareks found to fill that dining room on festive occasions, with the table fully extended, unpopular as they seemed to be here in Palm Beach. Lia, on my left, seemed to read my mind.

"We were married on the lawn out there, Matt," she said, "right by the ocean. It was rather overwhelming at first for an orphan girl from Key West; but Alex made it very nice for me since I had no people of my own to see me married. We had our wedding breakfast in here, but this table wasn't big enough for everybody; Alex had to have extra tables set up out on the veranda. All his friends and family and business associates came, from all over the country; and Sandra, of course, and . . . and your Matthew." She shivered. "It was such a terrible thing that happened to him. He was such a sweet and polite boy. We miss him so very much."

It wasn't a subject I cared to discuss. "Thank you," I said. "I'm glad he made a good impression, but I can't

70

take any of the credit. After the first few years, I had nothing to do with his upbringing."

"Well, it's the first few years that count, isn't it?" Lia said.

I ate my soup, reflecting that it had been rather sweet of Alexander Varek to make such a production of his fifth wedding—assuming that Sandra's count had been correct, and that she'd had one real mother and four stepmothers. You'd expect that by this time in his marital career, Varek would simply drag the dame down to city hall when he got the urge. . . .

"Seventeen!"

That was Sandra, facing me across the big table. She'd obviously been brooding over what I'd said in the gunroom.

Lia frowned. "What are you talking about, dear?"

The younger woman said sharply, "He's got a little list, seventeen names. And they'll none of them be missed; they'll none of them be missed."

"Yes, dear, we all know our Gilbert and Sullivan. That is from *The Mikado*, isn't it?" Lia frowned, puzzled. "What about a list?"

Sandra jerked her head in my direction "Ask the Lord High Executioner over there!"

Varek spoke, with a glance at the maid removing the soup bowls. "Maybe it would be better to put off this discussion until after dinner."

I said, "No. It's no secret that we're coming for them. If they haven't got their own ways of finding out, and I think they have, we'll take a TV spot and tell them. Let them feel the pressure, Alex; let them know that they're dead, or will be as soon as we get around to it."

"We?"

I shrugged. "With you or without you, it'll get done."

Lia said, "If you are talking about those wicked people who threw the bomb, they deserve anything that hap-

71

pens to them! If I could push a button and make them all dead, I would!''

I laughed. "Unfortunately, it's not that easy. The CLL, the Caribbean Legion of Liberty, claims something like two thousand members. Our information is that they do have a few hundred. It isn't really feasible to track down and eliminate them all, so it has been decided in Washington that we should settle for just the governing council and a few strays. As Sandra indicated, the number we came up with was seventeen.'' I looked at the girl on the other side of the table. "But now she seems to feel that's overdoing it. Apparently her nonviolent act in Texas wasn't altogether an act. How about it, Sandy?''

Sandra shook her head quickly. "Don't pick on me, Matt. I . . . I've never been involved in anything like this before. I hadn't really visualized . . . Hearing an actual number makes it seem more grim and real, sort of.'' She swallowed; but when she spoke again her voice had hardened. "I'm all right. I apologize for the sentimental noises. Seventeen of the lousy creeps is all right with me. Make it eighteen if you like!''

"I probably have," I said. "It seems unlikely that the kid this afternoon was important enough to be on our list, so he becomes an added number. However, I'm authorized to take out any of them who try to interfere; and I classify a gun pointed my way under the heading of interference.''

Varek stirred. "The boys would like to know who told you he'd be there. They said you headed right into the building as if you'd had advance information. Considering that you weren't supposed to know you'd be going anywhere near the place, they thought it was kinda funny, if you know what I mean.''

I said, "Hell, they should have figured it out for themselves. With the ambush set for us on the side street, there was bound to be a lookout posted on the main street

72

to let the guy with the blocking car, and the guy with the cannon, know when we were approaching. And the most likely spot, if they could arrange to use it, was one of those windows facing the T-intersection from which the lookout could see down both streets. Of course, there was a possibility that none of the offices up there had been available and they'd had to post him somewhere else. If so, I'd have lost my gamble and had my exercise for nothing.''

''But you didn't.'' Varek signaled to the maid to refill his wineglass. ''Tell us about the heavy artillery. What the hell kind of a howitzer did they have mounted in that window? They boys said it shot right through armor and bulletproof glass like it was cheese.''

I said, ''I'll have to do some guessing. I just caught a glimpse of the muzzle up there; but of course I saw the results and checked how long it took the guy to reload. I'd say we were dealing with an overgrown and kind of clumsy single-shot rifle, probably on a tripod mount. At least I didn't see a bipod at the muzzle; and even if you could lift it and hold it steady, say, kneeling inside that window, you wouldn't want to fire a piece like that off your shoulder. It would kick you back into last week. I'd say it used fifty-caliber machine-gun ammunition with armor-piercing bullets.''

''Where would one acquire such a weapon?'' Lia asked.

''One would probably make it,'' I said. ''The barrel and ammo can be picked up as military surplus, if you know where to look and whose arm to twist. A clever gunsmith could cook up some kind of an action without too much trouble. I seem to recall that years ago somebody made up a bunch of similar weapons for insurgency use, kind of a poor man's antitank gun.'' I grimaced. ''I'd hate to be a ragged *campesino* lying in the road firing that thing one round at a time at a government tank clanking at me; real tanks have armor that won't quit. However, those AP projectiles took care of the supposedly bulletproof stuff on your family Mercedes all right. Maybe you should take it back for a refund."

"We didn't expect they'd be shooting anything like that at it," Varek said.

I said, "Which brings up the question: Why did you expect them to be shooting anything at it? Or to put it differently, how did they know we'd be coming there to be shot at? They were ready and waiting for us, with all the right equipment." There was a little silence. I looked at Varek for a moment, and turned to Sandra. I said, "Maybe I should tell you what I really came down here for. I wanted to ask you to help us out in a kind of risky way."

Sandra glanced quickly in the direction of her father before speaking to me. "What risky way, Matt?"

I spoke carefully: "My chief and I had a very bright idea. Here was a young lady, you, who'd been involved in the bombing and had actually seen the bombers. Of course she claimed she'd only caught a fleeting glimpse of them through the restaurant window before the world blew up in her face, and that she couldn't possibly recognize them if she saw them again—but that's what she'd naturally say to protect herself. If she admitted to being able to identify them, she'd have been up to her pretty butt in cops and feds and prosecutors, and she'd have faced the strong possibility that the people she could finger would try to silence her."

Sandra licked her lips. "Go on."

I said, "Our computer lady is still kind of short of names to work with; she needs more information. This seemed to offer a possible way of teasing some of those fanatics out of the woodwork and into the open where we could catch them and squeeze them dry. The idea was, I'd come down here and protect you, with whatever man-

74

power I needed—with your permission, of course—while my chief spread the word through some of his underworld contacts that, in spite of her disclaimers, the young widow who'd survived the Mariposa bombing was a secret government witness who, when the time came, would definitely identify the guilty parties. That should give somebody the notion that maybe it would be better if you didn't live long enough to testify in court." I grinned at Sandra. "But I'll have to report back to Washington that we were just too slow with our bright idea. You and your daddy have already used you as bait in just that way, right? That was what it was all about his afternoon, wasn't it?"

She licked her lips. "Yes, and I feel terrible about exposing you to . . . That car was supposed to make it perfectly safe, or I'd at least have told you what we were trying to do. I should have, anyway."

"Forget it. I've been shot at before," I said. "Did you dream it up yourself or was it your pop's plan?"

Varek spoke up quickly: "Sis had the idea. I thought it was too risky, but she insisted on trying it, so I used the bulletproof heap for insurance." He grimaced. "The barge was supposed to be safe against the kind of weapons a gang like that would be likely to use; and we leaked the rest of our plans to them on purpose. To pull them out of the woodwork, as you put it. I've got a few connections, too. I primed them with the phony information about Sis and her photographic memory to get them interested. Pretty soon . . ." He looked around the room, but the maid was in the kitchen temporarily. "Pretty soon, one of the girls we had working here quit very suddenly for no good reason. We guessed that somebody'd leaned on her and got her to move out and recommend a sneak to take her place, great. Of course, we left the new girl strictly alone, just keeping an eye on her while figuring out what information to feed her."

Sandra said, "It wasn't hard. Everybody in the house knew I'd had bad nightmares after . . . after the bombing. I just pretended that they'd started up again, all about La Mariposa. I kept saying that I didn't want to go to a shrink. I didn't need to go to a shrink; all I needed was to face it, to go back to the lousy place again and look at it hard and get it out of my system. Only I just couldn't work up the nerve to do it, after what had happened there. But this morning I suddenly announced at breakfast that I was going to be brave at last and make the lousy pilgrimage on my way home from the airport. Naturally, I waited until Bernadette was pouring the coffee. Daddy says she went out right afterwards."

"She called her boyfriend from the house. Just loveydovey stuff, but there must have been a special word in there somewhere," Varek said. "Afterwards she kept looking at her wristwatch. After forty-five minutes, she went out of the house and slipped out a side gate on foot. The boys had been told not to interfere. A young fellow came along in a commercial van: A-1 PLUMBING CO. They drove back over to West Palm and stopped at a gas station. He used the pay phone. They headed for the freeway south. They took the Miami airport exit. The boys ran them to the curb. They had airline tickets for San Juan, Puerto Rico. It's where you'd normally go if you were heading for Islas Gobernador, or nearby Montego where there's some kind of half-ass invasion force being trained, according to the boyfriend."

I said, "Yes, we've heard about that. Is that where the two of them were heading?"

Varek shook his head. "They didn't have reservations beyond San Juan. You have to switch to a smaller airline to get to the little islands, but there was nothing indicating that they'd been going to. The boys got the idea they were aiming for some kind of a CLL hideout right there in San Juan. It would make sense for a terrorist outfit to have a regional headquarters, sort of, in a big city with good air connections handy to the scene of their current operations. But neither Bernadette or her boyfriend could come through with an address. They'd been told, when they got the word to run, they should get themselves down to San Juan. Somebody'd meet them at the airport and take care of them from there.''

"Where's the loving couple now?"

Varek looked at me coldly. "Don't ask. I might tell you."

Sandra was shocked. "Daddy!"

"She was planted on us, Sis. She set you up for it today, at La Mariposa. She admitted it; she said she was sorry, she liked you okay, but one life was not important in the great forward march of history. Anyway, the way she was after the boys had worked on her awhile, she's better off where she is, along with loverboy." He frowned at his daughter. "I told you it would get rough."

The girl shivered. "All right. I suppose it's all right. I'll just work on remembering how . . . how things looked in La Mariposa right after the blast."

I said, "What about the ambush? Did you pick up anybody there?"

Varek shook his head. "We had a fancy envelopment maneuver, as they say in the military, all figured out; but when they sprung the field artillery on you, everybody was ordered to start shooting and bust straight in, to keep them busy dodging bullets while you got clear. The boys counted five of them, including the guy working the big gun. One was hit hard—he had to be carried away—and a couple of the others were probably nicked, but as far as information is concerned we wound up with zilch, unless that kid told you something."

"He told me something," I said. "How much it's worth, I won't know until it's planted in the computer and watered to see if it grows." I gave him a hard look.

"But we still haven't really settled the big question. You didn't want me on this job; you tried to get Sandy to steer me off it, but I'm here. Are you willing to cooperate with a lousy G-man?" I reached into my pocket, brought out a folded slip of paper, and gave it to the maid to take around the table to him. "Do you recognize that phone number?"

Varek frowned. "Area code three-oh-five. That's right here on this side of Florida."

"A penthouse in Miami Beach. Sixty miles away. The call won't break you."

He hesitated; then he rose and left the dining room.

Lia looked at me curiously and asked, "Who's in Miami Beach, Matt?"

"A man whose name I don't bandy around if I don't have to," I said. "If Alex wants to make it public when he gets back, that's his business."

She made a little face at me. "I was just making conversation; I wasn't snooping. How about some more dessert?"

"Thanks, it's delicious."

Actually, it was some kind of a fruity mixed-up mess; and I'm an old ice cream man from way back, although I'll settle for cake if I have to. Then Varek was returning.

He sat down and drank from his wineglass. "How did a guy like you ever make connections with Giuseppe Velo?"

"I did him a favor once, kind of accidentally, in the line of duty."

Varek frowned. "Hell, Seppi retired from his New York enterprises and moved down here, it must be twenty years ago. He must be pretty damned old by now."

I said, "I don't know his age, but he looks ancient enough, like a lizard that's died and dried out in the sun. But he still keeps in touch, a little."

"I know. Everybody knows. He says . . . Well, to hell

78

with what he says about you. You knew what he'd say or you wouldn't have had me call him. So what do we do next?''

CHAPTER 9

THE phone was an elaborate job with a keyboard, some extra mysterious buttons, and, in addition to the usual handset, a loudspeaker. There had to be a mike in there, too, since you could talk into it as well as listen to talk coming out of it. Philip had to check me out on the controls before he'd trust me to fly it. He was very polite about it, going heavy on the ''sirs.''

I'd asked for a speaker-phone so both ends of the forthcoming conversation could be heard by everyone present. A gesture of good faith. No tricks. No secret messages. Nothing up my sleeve. Call me Honest Helm for short. I punched out the number for the direct line, and Mac's voice came on almost at once.

''Yes?''

''Matt here,'' I said, using my real name rather than my code name, our signal that the conversation wasn't private. Well, honesty and frankness can be overdone.

''Yes, Matt?''

I said, ''We've had some activity down here in Palm Beach—actually over in West Palm—but I'll make my full report later. Right now I'd like to speak with Miss Delgado if she's available.''

"I believe she left the office several hours ago, but she's on call. Just a minute."

It wasn't surprising that the lady had left for home, since my wristwatch read close to eight o'clock. Mac, of course, never requires food or sleep as far as anyone has been able to determine—evidence to support the theory, very popular throughout our small agency, that he's not really human. Evidence against: the fact that he has a lady out west, a fairly powerful businesswoman, with whom he spends some time occasionally. However, he doesn't seem to let this relationship affect the organization, although it can't be an easy thing to manage.

We'd left the dinner table and returned to the gunroom for coffee, because our hostess felt it was cozier than the enormous, formal living room for a small party like ours. As we waited for Mac's voice to stir the speaker into action once more, she came in accompanied by a maid carrying a tray, which was placed, at her direction, on the low table by the red-leather sofa. Lia settled herself gracefully behind the tray.

"Matt? Regular or decaffeinated?"

"I'll just have a touch of brandy if it's available."

"It will be," Lia said, "but right now we're in the coffee business, darling. Sandra, you'll have decaffeinated, won't you?"

Instinctively, the girl started to protest against being protected from real coffee as if she were a child; but she checked herself.

"Yes, Lia," she said. "We wouldn't want to stunt my lousy growth, would we?"

As the maid was carrying the steaming cup across the room, the speaker came alive again.

"Go ahead, Miss Delgado." That was Mac's voice.

I heard Lia say, "That will be all, Maria."

The maid delivered the cup to Sandra and went out, closing the door behind her.

Another voice, female, came through the speaker: "Delgado here."

It seemed unnatural to carry on a phone conversation without holding something to my face, but I spoke to the electronic marvel on the table. "This is Helm. Have you got your screen and keyboard handy?"

"I'm at my apartment, Mr. Helm, but I have a computer terminal here, yes. Do you have some information for me? Just a minute . . . All right, go ahead."

I said, "For your information, present and listening to this conversation are Mr. and Mrs. Alexander Varek, and Mr. Varek's daughter, Mrs. Cassandra Helm. I wouldn't be surprised if we were also being recorded. How about it, Alex?"

Varek said, "The boys tape all phone conversations in the house unless they're told to get off the line. You want me to tell them?"

I said, "Hell, no, let them get an earful. Anyway, we may want a record of some names and addresses. . . . Why don't you start the ball rolling by telling Miss Delgado about the maid who was planted on you?"

Varek shrugged. "Whatever you say. Her name was Bernadette Saiz. Loverboy was Ronnie Juan Jackson."

"Did you get that?" I asked the phone. "Bernadette Saiz. Ronnie Juan Jackson."

"I heard." There was a little pause before Miss Delgado spoke again. "Sorry. We have no data on those names."

I said, "Well, file them and asterisk them, or whatever you do to indicate that they're no longer with us. They helped set up a hit for the CLL, but it didn't work and they didn't get clear."

"Give me the details, please. We never know what information will be useful."

"Mr. Varek will tell you all about it."

While he was relating how the girl had come to be

81

hired as a maid, Sandra put a big round glass into my hand. There was a splash of brandy rolling around in the bottom of it. Very high class, but I'll have to admit that I prefer less glass and more booze. I have a tendency to strangle on that strong stuff, trying to sip it daintily from one of those big snifters. I listened to Varek telling the microphone what little had been learned about Bernadette and her boyfriend.

"Could I have the name of the former employee, please?" asked the speaker. "The one who quit and recommended Saiz."

"Ernestine Jaramillo."

"Jaramillo with a *J*?"

"That's right," Varek said. He'd pronounced it Haramijo, Spanish fashion.

"Go on."

"That's all I have," Varek said. "Except that they were on their way to Puerto Rico when we stopped them. Matt?"

I said, "Okay, I'll take over. Miss Delgado?"

"Yes?"

"Mr. Varek's people got the impression that those two had been promised sanctuary in San Juan somewhere; but apparently they hadn't been given the address. They expected to be taken there on arrival."

Dana Delgado's voice said, "Yes, there are indications that the Legion is operating from a San Juan base convenient to both Gobernador and Montego. It is being investigated. Anything else?"

I said, "Antonio Morelos."

There was a pause. "No data . . . Wait. Morelos? Young?"

"He was well under twenty and he won't get any older."

"I see." The voice was steady. "Another asterisk job, Mr. Helm?"

"That's right. Why did you ask the age?"

"We have no Antonio Morelos, but we do have a Dominic Morelos. This one is on our master list. Member of the Caribbean Legion of Liberty, member of the Council of Thirteen. One reference to a nameless kid brother on record."

"Give me Dominic, please."

"Thirty-three, five-ten, two-ten. A burly, muscular type. Hair black, medium length at last report. Large *bandido* moustache at last report. Eyes brown. Small scar on left side of chin. Nails of left hand missing or deformed—we understand that, as a guest of the current government of Gobernador, our great democratic ally in that island region, Morelos underwent an interrogation involving a pair of pliers. Primitive, brutal, and apparently useless; we understand that the desired information was not forthcoming. Morelos seems to consider himself God's gift to women; and some women seem to agree. The record shows considerable military training. Unarmed combat, expert. Edged weapons, expert. Firearms, average. It is recommended that, if you have to deal with Mr. Morelos, you take him at long range. Don't let him get close."

"Yes, ma'am," I said.

"I know. You're all supermen out there in the field; no advice required. Unconfirmed reports credit Morelos with five kills, two bare-handed. Also . . ." She stopped abruptly.

"Also what?"

"It's highly classified, Mr. Helm."

"Everything's highly classified in Washington, up to and including the location of the public johns." I winked at Varek. "We're all good trusting friends together here, so fire away."

"Very well. The responsibility is yours. But I'll have

83

to report that the information has been compromised at your request."

I started to get annoyed at her stuffy, bureaucratic attitude. Then I detected an undercurrent of amusement in her voice and realized that, guessing what I was trying to accomplish, she was deliberately impressing our audience with the fact that it was being made privy to great government secrets. Bright girl.

"You do that," I said, deadpan.

Miss Dana Delgado cleared her throat in Washington, a thousand miles to the north. "We recently, very recently, came across some evidence indicating that Dominic Morelos may actually be the mysterious chairman of the Legion's thirteen-person council."

"You mean the guy who calls himself, or is called, *El Martillo*, The Hammer?"

"It's only a possibility, unconfirmed."

"An unconfirmed possibility is better than no possibility at all. Any more on Morelos, like a home address?"

"The last fix we had put him in San Felipe, a small village at the western end of Hawkins Island, the main island of the sovereign nation of Montego. Incidentally, I feel obliged to point out, Mr. Helm, that if Antonio Morelos was Dominic's young brother, and you're the one who killed Antonio . . . ."

"I am."

"Then *El Martillo*, if he is *El Martillo*, is not going to like you very much. You might check from time to time, as you proceed with this mission, to make perfectly certain who is hunting whom."

"The thought had already occurred to me, but thanks anyway, ma'am."

"I know, I know, you're all bulletproof and immortal out there. I apologize for wasting your time with my foolish suggestions. Anything else?"

"One more problem, but first, you'd better have the details of Antonio's demise for your hungry computer." I told her how the shooting had come about, and went on: "After he was shot, I tried to get out of him the name of the woman who was seen outside La Mariposa at the time of the bombing. I figured there was a good chance he'd know something about it, working with them like that; and in any interrogation, it's better to ask for the name of a specific person. I figured if we got the identity of the bomb lady we could probably work from that to the names of her two companions, and maybe even get a line on those who'd sent the three of them out with the whiz-bang. Anyway, Antonio was reluctant, but just before he died he said something about an angel. A little angel. Can your computer field that one?"

"Just a minute." Presently Miss Delgado's voice returned. "The Morelos file contains a reference to, among a number of other women, an Angelita Johansen. A small blonde girl. One of several attractive tourist-ladies who were privileged to spend a night in Dominic's hotel room—the Privateer Hotel, Morganville, Montego."

"Morganville, for Sir Henry Morgan. Hawkins Island, for Sir John Hawkins. Those old English sea captains got around, although I never read of Hawkins navigating in that area. But, hell, if local legends can put Leif Eriksson on Cape Cod, I guess they can put Sir John Hawkins in Montego." I frowned thoughtfully; a wasted frown since she couldn't see it. "But I thought you said Morelos operated out of a place called San Felipe."

"Yes, but according to our information he also kept a room in the capital city sixty miles away. Data on Morelos is still coming in, but it seems that he was in the area primarily to observe, and maybe supervise, the progress of the Legion unit of about eighty men training with Heinrich Bultman's strike force, now numbering about four hundred. However, he'd slip away frequently to

Morganville, presumably on CLL business although he often managed to mix it with private pleasure. Usually he went there to meet people arriving by plane.''

"People like Angelita Johansen?''

"Not exactly. Most of the ones he met were new recruits for the invasion force. But Señor Morelos' nights in the Privateer Hotel were seldom spent alone. Apparently, while keeping his hands off the local ladies so as not to arouse hostility among the Montegan natives, he preyed quite successfully on the female tourist traffic. Angelita Johansen came to Morganville by plane, all right, but with an organized tour group. The evening after her arrival, she wandered away from her tour and came into the hotel bar alone, exploring. Morelos zeroed in on her. Our informant states that, from what he could learn without asking too many questions, the contact seemed casual enough. The locals apparently admire Morelos' sexual prowess; they enjoy watching him stalk his prey of the evening. It seems to be a local spectator sport; there's even some betting. Apparently the little Johansen looked proper and ladylike enough that quite a bit of money said she'd brush him off; but in the end she succumbed to the Morelos charm like most of his other targets. Typically, in the morning when she rejoined her friends she was rather the worse for wear, noticeably bruised and rumpled, but glowing in a very improper and unladylike fashion. The local consensus was that there was one little *gringa* schoolteacher—actually she works in an architect's office—who'd go home feeling that she'd got her money's worth from the travel agency.''

"But you say she's a blonde?'' I said, with a glance at Sandra. "Our witness to the bombing states definitely that the perpetrators, as the police like to call them, were neither blonde nor albino.''

The speaker-phone said, "There are such things as hats and scarves, not to mention wigs.''

I spoke to Sandra: "What about it, Sandy?"

The girl hesitated, and shrugged. "It's certainly possible. I don't think I'd have missed a hat or scarf; but I really caught only a glimpse of her, and I wouldn't have noticed if all that dark hair wasn't for real."

"You heard that, Miss Delgado?" I said to the phone. "So Angelita is in the running. You have no other angels, small or large, in your computer?"

"None at the moment."

"Well, she may be our girl. It would be a hell of a coincidence if she wasn't. Dominic sleeps with her down in Montego, Antonio dies with her name on his lips up here in Florida—assuming he was referring to the same diminutive angel." I frowned. "Do we have a home address for the lady?"

"Right down there near you, between Palm Beach and Lauderdale. Pompano Beach. Do you want the street and number?"

"Please."

She gave it, and I said, "Fine. Now drop Angelita."

"Drop her?"

I said, "We'll make the approach from another angle, and I don't want her alerted by too many people asking questions about her. Drop Angelita, but keep on digging the Morelos dirt, and let me know if you turn up any more fat worms. Okay?"

"Instructions noted."

I asked, "Anything else I should know?"

"I have the names of several other people, all probably members of the Legion, two probably members of the Council as well. Do you want them?"

"Read them off, please, with addresses if any. Somebody here may recognize them."

There were a dozen names, both Hispano and Anglo. The Council members, unconfirmed, were an Arthur Galvez and a Howard Koenig. The addresses were all of

87

the reported-seen-in or rumored-to-be-living-at variety. I watched my companions as Miss Delgado read her list, but there were no visible reactions. After the last name. Varek shook his head: negative.

I said, "No bells rung here, Miss Delgado. What about the information I asked you to get for me about the people involved in the previous explosive incidents attributed to the CLL?"

"A courier is on his way with that material, fairly complete. It was all in the official records or in the newspapers, no problem. You know where to make contact and pick it up."

"Right. I guess that's it, then. Sorry to bother you at home."

"No trouble. But I have a bad feeling about that Dominic, Mr. Helm. Keep looking behind you."

Considering the hostile attitude she'd shown me earlier, I was surprised that she'd show so much concern about a lousy field man; but perhaps she felt it would reflect on her professional competence if I went and got myself killed acting on her information.

"I always do," I said.

The line went dead. I pushed the button Philip had shown me, which shut down the speaker and mike and turned the fancy instrument into an ordinary telephone. Sandra came over with the brandy and splashed a little into my empty snifter; she moved on to replenish her father's.

Varek stirred. "So you're poking around in past history, too? Explosive incidents! Bureaucratic double-talk! Why not call a blast a blast?" He sipped his brandy and asked casually, "How many others have you come up with, besides La Mariposa?"

I said, "Just two so far that were definitely the work of the Caribbean Legion of Liberty, although they've claimed a couple of others that we think were set by different crazies. One of the definites was up north in Newport, Rhode Island. The other was down in San Juan. Maybe somebody got too close to their current base down there and had to be taken out. I thought I'd check out both explosions and talk to some of the survivors and see if they can tell me a little more about the gang.'' I hesitated and got to my feet. ''Well, it's getting late and I've got some thinking to do. I hope you don't mind my making a couple of calls from the phone in my room. Sandra had better show me the way so I don't get lost again.''

CHAPTER 10

THE guestroom into which I'd been put was called the Blue Room. It was actually a suite with a large, light bedroom, a small, dark sitting room, and a sizable bathroom with a pale blue tub big enough to swim in. Sometimes you wonder if it's worth it, being honest; the crooks seem to have more fun, or at least more money. There was elaborately old-fashioned wallpaper that reminded me of some I'd seen in a country house I'd stayed in over in Europe, but that had been old and shabby. This was new and immaculate, with a pattern of pale blue flowers. The bedroom furniture was pale, too, pretty and rather spindly; but Varek's previous wife, the interior-decorator lady called Barbie, like in doll, had allowed a substantial, adjustable chair to be placed in front of the big color TV that dominated the little sitting room.

Sandra hit the remote control and watched the picture

form on the screen in a satisfactory manner. She checked the sound, okay, and snapped the set off again.

She said, "If you need anything, that button will get you Maria."

"Sounds good," I said. "A man never knows when he'll need a Maria in the middle of the night."

Sandra grinned. "I guess that sentence didn't come out exactly the way I intended it; but Maria might oblige, at that." We moved back out into the big bedroom, and she glanced at me curiously. "Matt."

"Yes?"

"I don't think your sense of direction is quite as bad as you make out. You could have found this room without a guide."

I nodded. "I wanted to get you alone so I could ask you a favor. I'm going for the closest explosive incident first. Blast, in your daddy's terminology. That's Newport, Rhode Island. I'd like you to come with me."

She studied me for a moment. "Why?"

I shrugged. "Well, I could say I was doing it for your safety. Certain people still don't like you. There's no reason to think they've given up just because they failed this afternoon. I could say that I feel more confident of my ability to keep you alive than of your pop's."

She smiled faintly. "What else could you say, Matt?"

"That I want them. We all want them, right?" When she nodded, I went on: "At the moment we still don't have enough information to track them down; we've got a better chance at them if we make them come to us. Although they probably know by this time that I've been appointed Bloodhound-in-Chief on their trail, they might not make a major effort to eliminate me if I were traveling alone. However, if you were with me the bait should be irresistible."

She grimaced. "Sandy, the sacrificial goat. Or just the goat?"

I said, "I'll have some good people covering us, but I won't try to tell you there's no risk involved."

"Risk?" Sandra laughed shortly. "I'll be running plenty of risk right here, won't I? I mean, if they're really going to be persistent about shutting my mouth. And Daddy's men didn't look too great protecting me at La Mariposa. I'm not forgetting that a couple of them got themselves killed trying; but I'd have been dead right along with them if it hadn't been for you. Anyway, I still have to do something about the house in Connecticut, which is right next door to Rhode Island. Old Saybrook is only a short drive from Newport." She laughed. "All right, you talked me into it."

"I'll make the arrangements and let you know in the morning. Thanks."

"Sure." She started for the door, and stopped, and spoke without looking around. "When I called you the Lord High Executioner . . ."

"Yes?"

"It wasn't you I was mad at," she said, and turned to face me. "I think it was me. I'm just so damned confused these days I don't really know what I think. I hate them, of course I hate them, but the idea of killing seventeen people, any seventeen people . . . And the number is really up to twenty now, isn't it? Your seventeen, and Antonio Morelos, and Bernadette and her boyfriend. That's going to be an awful lot of dead people by the time we're finished, Matt."

I said, "You might keep in mind that the casualty list you just rattled off is a little one-sided. You're just counting their dead, actual and potential. What about ours?"

She frowned. "What do you mean?"

"Six people died in West Palm Beach," I pointed out. "Two in the Newport blast. Another five down in San Juan, including some small children. That's thirteen people that we know about, blown up by these loonies just to show how mad they are; and that figure doesn't include the injured. Who knows how many they'll kill and maim next time, if we let there be a next time?"

"I know," she said. "I know they have to be stopped. That's why I'm going with you, to help if I can. Just don't expect a vengeful wildcat at your side. It isn't as if it would bring Matthew back. If it would, I wouldn't have any qualms at all, I'd mow them all down personally; but nothing will bring him back. Good night, Matt."

Then I was alone. I heard her footsteps recede down the hall, and stop. I heard her open a door and close it behind her. The idea of having her sleeping right down the hall wasn't quite comfortable; and the fact that it wasn't bothered me. I mean, she was a good kid, sure, but I wasn't supposed to be interested in good kids, or even bad ones. Hell, even though she'd been married briefly, the girl was barely out of her teens.

I drew a long breath and walked over to unpack my suitcase. I threw my pajamas onto the big bed—a four-poster with a canopy, no less—and inspected the weapons I'd drawn in Washington. Varek undoubtedly had people available who could open a locked suitcase without leaving a mark; but I saw no indications that anyone had tampered with the contents.

I got into the pajamas—tan with brown piping, if it matters—and looked at the bed, but it was still early and I knew I wasn't relaxed enough yet to sleep; besides there were those phone calls to be made. I reached for the blue phone beside the lamp on the spindly bedside table and thought of Varek's boys monitoring all calls from the house. To hell with them. Let them listen. No secrets between friends and allies, right?

I punched the number and got a man's voice and went through the mandatory identification procedure.

I said, "This number is now compromised. I'll use the first fallback procedure next time."

"Check."

I said, "Termination on command: Arthur Galvez, Howard Koenig. Washington has some data; ask for Delgado. Find them, put them under discreet surveillance, see if they lead you to anybody else. Any contacts you spot, pass the information to Delgado. Extra manpower available if needed. Be ready to take them out at any time, but wait for the word. Repeat."

The man at the other end of the line, whose code name was Louis, read the instructions back to me and gave the sign-off query. I responded with the affirmative and the line went dead. Then I called another number and went through a similar ID routine with a man using the cover name Trask, who'd been assigned to ride shotgun on this stagecoach run. I told him what I needed and he said he'd get it to me as soon as possible.

"There'll be two of us," I said. "I'll try to keep us together so you won't have to split your team to cover us, but if we should separate do the best you can."

"I read you, but remember I haven't got an army to work with. If we have to concentrate on one, who's got priority?"

"Cover the girl. I can take care of myself better than she can. They're more likely to go for her, anyway, given a choice. But, Trask . . ."

"What?"

"When it comes to the main job, nobody's unexpendable. If you get a good crack at them, take it, no matter what. We don't play the hostage game with anybody, or for anybody."

"Yes, I read the instructions." His voice was stiff. Nobody had to tell *him* not to be a sentimental jackass. "Trask out."

It was still too early for bed, so I checked out the entertainment center. The chair was fine, very comfortable after I'd figured out the controls. The TV worked

93

perfectly, as Sandra had determined; but aside from a funny, funny sitcom and a totally implausible cop story, there seemed to be nothing on the air but rock-and-roll. Well, it wouldn't hurt me to know a little more about the younger generation and its taste in music, even though the stuff generally sounds to me like a lot of noise going nowhere; and the slapstick nonsense that usually accompanies it on the screen, supposedly comic, makes a rerun of the Three Stooges look like a Shakespeare festival. . . .

I told myself that we were gaining on the mission, a little. Howard Koenig and Arthur Galvez, with Dominic Morelos, gave us three names out of the thirteen on the Council, leaving us a mere ten to go. Then there was Angelita Johansen. She gave us one name out of the three directly involved in the Mariposa bombing, complete with a local address. We could hope that, caught and properly interrogated, she'd lead us to the other two.

Varek had offered to handle her and I'd told him okay, as if doing him a favor; actually, if he hadn't offered, I'd have suggested it. The age of chivalry was past. Varek's goons probably wouldn't be very nice to little Angelita, any nicer than they'd been to Bernadette Saiz; but there was no reason for me to trouble myself about the fate of a young woman who'd helped murder my son. Was there?

I sat there for a while reviewing the events of the day, and the information received, and the actions taken. At last I got tired of the jerky images on the screen and switched off the set and went to bed. Then I was trying to tune a guitar but the strings kept breaking on me. Sandy kept telling me I was cranking them too tight; but how was I going to get the right pitch with a slack string. . . ? Suddenly wide-awake, I realized that the snapping sound on which I'd built my dream had been the latch clicking home as somebody, slipping into the room, had pushed the door gently closed behind them.

94

I opened my eyes cautiously, only enough to peer through the barely parted lids but not enough, I hoped, to expose a gleaming eyeball. Fortunately, I was lying on my left side facing the door. The window blinds were drawn and the room was dark, but I could make out a white figure over there. An intelligent murderer operating at night wouldn't be likely to wear white; but you can't count on all assassins being smart. I let my hand slip down my leg to the ankle holster in which rested a very small .25 automatic, not the most comfortable sleeping companion imaginable; but if you use the traditional hiding place under the pillow, the weapon stays behind if you have to make a hasty dive out of the bed.

My uninvited guest took a couple of steps towards me and paused to let one ghostly white garment slip to the rug with a silky whisper, retaining another. If I hadn't already guessed the sex of the intruder, the perfume that reached me would have given me the clue—somebody'd got themselves all fixed up pretty and fragrant for this visit. I reminded myself that men have died trusting perfumed ladies; but I thought I had things figured out and I reached down to stuff the little pistol back into its holster. I meant to sit up, after that, and switch on the bedside light; but it took me a moment to secure the automatic. They come out of holsters more easily than they go back in. By the time I'd finished, I had company in the bed.

There was a confused melee for a moment. I don't know what my unexpected bedmate was trying to do except that it was definitely not hostile. I was trying to reach the light switch and illuminate the situation. I touched a warm, satin-covered body and identified a pleasantly shaped breast. I resisted the temptation to investigate it more thoroughly, although I was being encouraged, even helped, to do so.

"Sandy, for God's sake, cut it out!" I said. "Who the hell do you think you are, Mata Hari, Junior?"

Freeing myself, I reached for the lamp again and felt a lock of hair brush my hand. . . . Hair? The girl I'd had in mind had been pretty well shorn when last seen. I sat up abruptly and found the switch at last. I'd had a momentary thought that Sandra had sent me the pretty maid, Maria, as some kind of a girlish joke or test; but in the sudden glare I saw Lia Varek smiling up at me lazily, her heavy black hair spread over the pillow.

CHAPTER 11

THE breakfast room was actually a glassed-in sunporch looking out on a peaceful, sunlit scene: the lawn, the beach, and the ocean. There was a white metal table with a glass top, surrounded by four white metal chairs with colored cushions on the seats. A couple of long chairs of similar design allowed you to recline, after eating, in a nook at the other end of the room, surrounded by enough potted plants, many blooming, to stock a greenhouse. Somehow, although very casual compared to the formal dining room we'd used last night, the room conveyed the message that it was still a very high-class place, infinitely superior to an ordinary sunporch with ordinary sunporch furniture.

The barman of last night, Philip, in his white coat and automatic pistol, was doing sentry duty by the door. Maria, dressed in her cutie-pie maid's uniform complete with frilly apron, was doing the honors at the warming table in the corner. Apparently, due to the size of the mansion, food would get cold if it were carried all the way from the kitchen in individual servings; it had to be brought out and maintained at the proper temperature here for immediate delivery to the breakfasters.

"Ah, there you are, Matt," Lia Varek said. "Did you have a good night's sleep?"

Her expression was beyond reproach: the lady of the house inquiring politely after the health and comfort of a guest. She was sitting at the glass-topped table with Sandra. They had both, apparently, just been served. The younger girl was in jeans and a blue T-shirt. Her step-mother was wearing a scarlet sundress, just a sheath of some linenlike material supported by narrow shoulder straps tied in little bows—it wasn't easy to overlook the fact that if you took the ends of the straps delicately between the thumb and forefinger of each hand and pulled gently, the bows would come untied and interesting things would probably happen.

"Very good, thanks," I said, equally polite. "Your guestroom is very comfortable. I slept just fine."

"Sit down and tell Philip if you want a drink," Lia said. She glanced at the tiny watch on her wrist. "It's only nine and Alex sleeps late; he won't be down for a while. Tell Maria what you want to eat. Bacon and scrambled eggs, or cereal and cream. Toast or warm rolls. And if you'd prefer your eggs done some other way, it could be managed."

"Scrambled is fine, with bacon," I said, seating myself. "It's too early for a drink. Orange juice if available. Toast. Black coffee . . ."

Sandra made a strangled little sound, threw her napkin down, and ran out of the room, her high heels clattering on the tiled floor. High heels and shabby blue jeans still seem like an odd combination to me, but I'm not complaining. From a masculine standpoint, at least my masculine standpoint, it makes for a much better view than sneakers or jogging shoes.

Lia was looking after her wonderingly. "Whatever is the matter with the child?" she asked.

I said, "Cut it out, Lia. She's not a child. She's been married, she knows all about the birds and bees; and she sleeps only a couple of doors down the hall from the Blue Room, as you call it. She's also a very observant young lady."

"Snoopy is the word," Lia said a bit grimly.

I shrugged. "Whatever." I reached out and touched her shoulder. "You do like those bows, don't you?"

Lia gave me a slow smile that was not the smile of a hostess conversing with a guest in the house. "They were very convenient last night, were they not, darling?"

When I came back to the bed last night, gun in hand, after checking the bedroom door and the hall outside, she was still lying there smiling at me, in the shining satin nightie that had the same kind of little bow-tied shoulder straps. I picked up the negligée she'd dropped on the floor and draped it over a nearby chair. Tidy. I regarded her rather grimly, thinking about the fact that the door had no bolt, and that whatever keys had once existed for the old-fashioned lock had gone missing or been removed—one reason why I'd worn the gun to bed in the first place. Somehow, I didn't have all the faith in the world in Sonny Varek's hospitality.

"You're beautiful," I said to the lady in my bed, "you're exquisitely desirable, or desirably exquisite, but I can't help wondering at what point in the proceedings your husband comes charging in with that .44 Maggie I saw on the gunroom wall, and invokes the unwritten law, boom! He doesn't like feds on general principles; I imagine he'd be even more prejudiced against a fed he caught sleeping with his brand-new wife."

Lia laughed and patted the bed beside her. "Relax,

darling. Don't stand there scowling. You're being very silly and naive.''

"Naive about what?''

"Alex and me. You're acting as if I were a respectable matron living with a dull nine-to-five husband in a split-level suburban bungalow, with two and a half children— or whatever is the current average—raising hell in the back of the house.''

"I don't know about your respectability,'' I said, "but your husband isn't dull. He's got a gun. Several guns in fact. No man with a gun is really dull.''

She glanced at the little automatic I still held. "You are wrong about that, my dear. I am finding you very dull at the moment, gun or no gun. Here I put on my prettiest lingerie and my most expensive perfume and the man just stands there! The least you can do is sit down and put away the firearm and listen. . . . Well, all right, hold it if you must, but don't tower over me like a thundercloud. That's better.'' She smiled again. "I think you simply do not understand my position in this household, Matt.''

I grimaced. "Now tell me you're here in the performance of your wifely duties!''

She laughed and said slyly, "Would you rather believe that I am here because women, even married women, naturally gravitate to your bed?''

I shrugged. "Strangely enough, once in a while they do seem to, as a matter of fact. For one reason or another.'' I shook my head. "And mostly the reasons are pretty goddam murderous, sweetheart. No, I don't kid myself I'm so fascinating. No, I don't believe your little heart went pit-a-pat the moment you saw me. I once knew a gent in my line of work who considered himself irresistible. Once. He's not around anymore. Unlike him, I don't take for granted it's my natural magnetism at work when the ladies throw themselves at me. I just wonder which hand has the knife, and who's sneaking up on me from behind while my attention is being drawn so prettily the other way.''

Lia studied me gravely. She said, "You must understand that Alex and I have an agreement. At the end of an unspecified length of time, when he ceases to find me interesting, he will divorce me as he did his other wives, and give me a substantial sum of money in return, enough to keep me in reasonable comfort the rest of my life. Why he feels that marriage must be part of the arrangement, I don't know; but all men have peculiar ideas where women are concerned.''

I said, "I'd say that, being in a disreputable business, he feels the need to be super respectable in other ways. Like dressing for dinner and marrying the girl.''

She shrugged. "Maybe. And I certainly have no objection to a wedding ring. I have spent too many years doing without one. Being legitimately married is a pleasant change.''

It occurred to me that I was learning a lot about Sandra's stepmother tonight, and she could be learning things about me; but Miss Manners would hardly have approved of the circumstances under which we were getting so well acquainted, houseguest and hostess, more or less undressed on a rumpled bed.

I said, "As a matter of fact, Sandra told me about her daddy's standard marriage contract.''

"I doubt that the child knows the fine print in that contract," Lia said wryly. "The unwritten fine print, shall we call it? Alex was very clear about what my duties were to be. I was to share his bed when he wanted me, of course. I was to make a pleasant home for him, and be gracious and decorative at all times, but particularly when we entertained. I was to make friends with his daughter if I could; although he conceded that might be impossible.'' Lia hesitated, and looked away from me, speaking to the windows with their drawn blinds. "There is one more clause, not actually printed but understood by both contracting parties. I doubt that my stepdaughter is aware of it. From time to time I must perform for Alex the kind of task I was doing for him before we were married. An attractive woman can be very useful to a man in Alex's position, in a business way. If you understand what I mean, darling."

I looked at her sharply. I guess I was a little shocked. I said, "In certain Indian tribes, I understand, the host supplied the honored guest with a tepee to keep him dry and a squaw to keep him warm. Hospitality."

She shook her head. "Hardly that, pale-faced stranger. Your comfort is the least of my husband's concerns; he's just worried about your reliability. Of course, old Seppi Velo did say you could be trusted. He said your agency doesn't concern itself with drugs, for one thing; but Alex can't really believe that there's any part of the U.S. government that isn't rabid about drugs."

I said, "My chief says he's not going to waste his time or ours trying to hold back Niagara Falls with a teaspoon." I glanced at her curiously. "Doesn't your husband's business bother you, just a little?"

Lia laughed harshly. "Have you any idea where I grew up, my dear? Fortunately a man noticed that I might be cleaned up to look moderately presentable. He was looking for suitable female material. He had me put through the mill. I was taught to wear clothes properly, to speak reasonable English, to be attractive to men. Never mind how I was taught." Her voice was grim. "When I hear of the terrible sufferings of those poor brainwashed prisoners, I laugh and laugh. And if you think that, coming from where I came from, I am going to concern myself about a little white poison being smuggled by the man who has given me all this, who even condescends to let me feel like a real human being occasionally, you are

101

even more naive than I thought. He doesn't force the stuff on them, does he? If they want to commit suicide slowly, or OD overnight, that is their business. Why should I worry about them? They never worried about me.''

I shrugged. "Sure. I'm not much for saving people from themselves, either.''

She said, "Anyway, there are other things besides drugs. . . . Alex can't help wondering if you could be working some kind of a law enforcement scam, the kind the FBI is so fond of these days. You could be using the fact that your son married his daughter to gain his confidence, while you're really helping out some other government agencies that have been after him for years. They would still like to nail him for something, anything, even though he is retired now.'' She laughed shortly. "He thinks you were a little too good to be true, Matt. Letting him listen to all that information coming over the phone, even ordering your computer girl to break security. And steering him so subtly to that bomb-happy blonde and her two boyfriends. Alex can't help wondering, if he does go for those three, as you obviously want him to, who will be hiding in the bushes to catch him with the smoking gun in his hand.''

She was sitting up now, beside me. Whereas the fragile negligée she'd discarded was quite an elaborate garment, the nightgown was very plain, unruffled and unadorned, like a simple, long satin slip that left her arms and shoulders bare but covered her smoothly and shinily elsewhere. I wondered how she'd known that I don't find instant nudity very attractive; I like the revelations to come gradually. Well, she was obviously an experienced woman; she was also a very lovely one. I noticed that she was wearing no makeup tonight, which was all right with me. She looked better without it, softer and less artificial.

I said crudely, "So your generous husband sent you

here to climb into my bed and fuck me silly and find out what kind of a guy I am and what I'm up to. But why are you telling me all about it?''

She gave me a sideways glance. ''You wouldn't have believed me if I had claimed to have fallen passionately in love with you. Would you?'' She hesitated. ''I rather hoped that, waking from a sound sleep, you would find yourself fully involved, if you know what I mean, before you realized what was happening; but you mistook me for someone else, someone you had no intention of making love to. I find that very interesting, and very sweet of you, my dear. But it left me with no approach but this one; and I am not quite sure what to do next. Just what turns you on, Mr. Helm?'' Her voice was expressionless, but the words came swiftly. ''Do I tease you with a displaced shoulder strap, or just slide out of my nightie completely? I assure you, I am very good at getting out of my clothes gracefully, and I have a very nice body, and no diseases of any kind, and some very special skills. Who'll start the bidding on this healthy twenty-seven-year-old female, five feet eight, a hundred and thirty pounds, clean and attractive and well trained in the arts of love. . . ?'' Her compulsive chatter stopped. After a lengthy silence, she sniffed and said, ''Get me a Kleenex, please. No, never mind, I will use the sheet.''

She started to dab at her eyes. Abruptly, she let out a gasping sob and buried her face in a handful of white percale and huddled there crying desperately. After a little, I reached over and put an arm around her. She turned towards me helplessly and clung to me, crying into the shoulder of my pajama jacket; but suddenly she dug her nails into my back and raised her wet face to glare at me.

''D-damn you!'' she gasped. ''Sitting there looking so smug and superior! Making me feel so cheap and dirty! What gives you the right? You are just another mercenary, no better than those Alex hires! You sell your skill with a gun, I sell my skill with something else, where is the difference? We are all whores together. . . . Hold me, damn you! I don't know what. . . . I seem to be coming all apart inside! Hold me, please hold me!''

I laid the pistol aside so I could do the job properly, telling myself this was the corny way experienced agents got themselves killed; but nothing happened. Well, at first. I just held her and stroked her hair and let her cry it out. It was only gradually that I found myself becoming very much aware that one of the straps of her gown had come untied. I discovered that sympathy for her despair was no longer my primary reaction. There seemed to be a lot of woman in my arms, and very little clothing.

Her sobs had dwindled away to an occasional hiccup. Then I heard a sudden, choked little laugh, but it held no disapproval. ''Ah,'' she whispered, ''pure Sir Galahad you are obviously not, darling. How about Lancelot, who played around with Guinevere behind King Arthur's back. . . ? Here, why leave me only half naked?''

Between the two of us, we'd managed to conquer the other little bow. From there on nature had taken its breathless course, with some expert guidance from her. . . .

I was aroused from my intriguing reverie by the brisk tapping of high heels on the sunporch tiles. I found myself doing very well by my scrambled eggs, while my hostess kept me company with a second cup of coffee. Our conversation, after that one sly reference to the fastenings of her dress, had been very polite, with hardly any double meanings. Now we watched Sandra return. Without looking at us, she carried her cold breakfast over to Maria, who replaced it with a fresh plate holding a warm serving. Sandra marched back to us and resumed her former place at the table. She began eating industriously. When she spoke at last, it was as if she had never left the room.

"Are we still heading for New England, Matt?" she asked. "Have you arranged for our flight yet?"

I said, "We're not flying. That airlines firearms hassle could leave me naked just when I need a gun most; and driving will serve our purpose better, anyway. I'm having my car driven down from Washington; I hope you people can put up with me until it arrives."

Lia said, "Of course you are welcome to stay as long as you wish, Matt."

I heard Sandra draw a quick breath; but whatever sharp remark she'd intended to make, she stifled it. Clearly, she'd come back resolved to be good.

She said, "It's over a thousand miles, Matt, closer to fifteen hundred." When I didn't speak, she shrugged. "Well, all right, but what's so special about your car?"

"Washington is willing to supply normal transportation to its agents; but you should hear the screams if somebody asks for a sports car." I grimaced. "I want us to have a little edge, if they come at us on the highway. Something reasonably fast and agile. My old Mazda RX-7 isn't the hottest thing on the road, but it will get out of its own tracks."

Sandra hesitated. "If you don't mind a suggestion . . ."

"Suggest ahead."

"I've got something faster than your RX-7, and we don't have to wait for it because it's right here in the garage. A Porsche 911. Two hundred horsepower. With a good tail wind it'll break one-fifty. Daddy gave it to me as a wedding present."

"I thought you got a sailboat for a wedding present."

"That was graduation."

I studied her for a moment. "Your wedding present could pick up some dents. Or even some bullet holes."

She grinned. "Daddy was going to buy me a new one when the ashtray got full, anyway."

CHAPTER 12

THE Porsche was blue with black upholstery. It was brought out of the garage for us by the current family chauffeur, Richard, the one who'd driven us away from the Mariposa ambush. He was in uniform today. I wondered if he'd inherited the late Leonard's spare whipcord suit or had one run up overnight for himself. Before putting our suitcases aboard, he gave the car some final touches with a polishing cloth. It gleamed like a jewel; but it wasn't really as flashy a car as I'd have expected a mobster to buy for his only daughter. The color was subdued and there was hardly any chrome. More evidence of Varek's striving for respectability.

The car had power windows, power sunroof, stereo, and air conditioning; and the seats would adjust themselves to the peculiarities of your anatomy at the touch of a button or two or three. It was a considerable change from the last Porsche I'd driven, years ago, a fairly noisy and rugged little beast, but it still carried its engine behind. After giving me a quick briefing, Sandra handed me a pair of keys. For traveling, she'd put on a loose blue shirt over her T-shirt.

"You'd better keep those, they're extras," she said. "And you'd better drive, at least at first, so you'll have the feel of it if things get tricky."

"I'd better drive, period," I said. "We don't know how or where they'll be laying for us, and I probably know a few useful maneuvers, defensive and aggressive, that you don't.''

"But it's *my* car!'' Then she laughed at her own childishness. "Oh, all right. That makes sense, I suppose. Maybe I'll learn something, watching you. Daddy says you're supposed to be a pretty hot wheelman.''

I raised my eyebrows. "An exaggeration, to say the least. Where'd he get that idea?''

She laughed. "Daddy's got his sources, just as you have yours. Apparently you've brushed up against the organization a few times in various parts of the country. They do compare notes, you know.''

I looked at her for a moment. The jeans and the bulky shirt made her look sturdy and not particularly feminine; but we weren't setting out on our honeymoon.

"Are you carrying?'' I asked. "If not, I'd better get one of the spares out of my suitcase.''

"Carrying? Oh, you mean a gun. Yes, I got Philip to get me one.'' She patted the big purse she was holding. "It's right in here.''

"I hope it shoots straighter than the last one you had.''

"I checked it out on our pistol range this morning. It's okay.'' She laughed shortly. "By Hollywood standards, that's the true test of a villain, isn't it, having a shooting range in his house. If a wealthy man likes tennis and puts up a couple of courts on his property, okay. If he likes golf, nobody minds his shelling out a few grand for a putting green; and of course everybody's got swimming pools. But if the guy just happens to like to shoot and installs some soundproof facilities so he won't bother the neighbors, according to the movies he's just got to be a homicidal baddie practicing his murder techniques. . . . Oh, here's Daddy now, coming to see us off. And Lia, too, how nice.''

It wasn't the most comfortable farewell scene I've ever attended. I shook hands politely with the husky, white-haired gent whose wife I'd slept with, and with the lady herself. She patted my hand, holding on to it.

"We just loved having you here, Matt," she said. "Isn't that right, Alex?"

His eyes held no expression whatever; but I got the impression that, while he might have sent his wife on her midnight mission, he didn't have to like the guy he'd sent her to. Not that we'd been bosom pals before that.

"Sure," he said. "Come back anytime."

"Well, take good care of our little girl," Lia said.

She pressed my fingers lightly before releasing them. She was smiling, obviously getting some perverse enjoyment from this face-to-face encounter between two men who'd shared her favors. I had a hunch that, instead of moaning about the terrible humiliation to which he'd subjected her by sending her to make love to another man, she was punishing her husband by acting as if she'd enjoyed every minute of it and wouldn't mind a return engagement. Sandra gave her father a peck on the cheek and turned away, ignoring her stepmother.

"Come on, Matt, we'd better put it on the road."

I followed her to the car, helped her in, and walked around to slide behind the wheel. I realized that the little heap was fancier than it looked; the upholstery was real leather. The seat wasn't adjusted properly for a man my height. I played with the levers and buttons until I was comfortable; then I took us away down the winding driveway. In the mirror, I could see Lia waving good-bye to us, standing in the sunshine in her bright sundress. I could see her husband, too. He wasn't waving.

The iron gates opened to let us out. I must say I drew a breath of relief as we left old Homer Ganson's estate behind. It occurred to me that I hadn't thanked my host and hostess for their hospitality, but they might have wondered just what they were being thanked for. Well, Lia wouldn't have wondered. She'd have known.

"At least you're brave," Sandra said at last. Her voice was cold.

"A veritable lion, that's me," I said. "But what made you think of it now?"

"I told you Daddy was a dangerous man. To make love to his wife right there in his own house. . . ! That takes real courage, in a kind of sneaky way."

"Talking about sneaky, you seem to have been peeking through keyholes, little girl."

She glared at me. "Don't *you* start that little-girl routine! And of course I was peeking. Well, listening, long enough to find out who you had in there. My timing was great. I caught her big God-am-I-lousy scene." Sandra laughed scornfully. "I'm surprised at you. An experienced man like you falling for a tearful act like that!"

I said, "An experienced man like me always figures that when a normally well-painted female comes to him with all her makeup removed, she's expecting to have to do some pitiful weeping pretty soon and doesn't want to be caught with a smeary face afterwards."

Sandra stared at me, shocked. "You mean, you knew . . ."

I said, "Sweetheart, you've been reading mushy novels about sweet, sensitive love and perfect passion. This was strictly a business transaction between professionals; but we never like to be crude about it. I thought she did a very smooth job of getting herself into my consoling arms so the rest could follow naturally, didn't you?" I hesitated, but the kid had to grow up sometime. "Incidentally, it was a three-cornered deal. Your pop was one of the pros involved," I said.

She frowned. "You mean, he knows that she went to you last night?"

"I mean, he sent her," I said.

"You're crazy! Even . . . even Daddy wouldn't do a thing like that!"

I said, "Oh, for Christ's sake! She admits herself it's what he hired her for in the first place, to find out certain things he needed to know about certain people—well, certain male people—with whom he was dealing. Or influence them in certain ways. Only after employing her like that for a while and getting to know her, he decided, being between wives at the time, that he liked her well enough to keep her around on a slightly more permanent basis. But that didn't mean he wasn't willing to use her in her old capacity if a situation required it." I shrugged. "I don't think she'd mind my telling you; she was perfectly frank about it."

Sandra licked her lips. "I think that's horrible!"

"You're entitled to your reaction. It's pretty routine stuff in my line of work, and your pop's, but go ahead and be shocked if it makes you feel better."

"So cold-blooded!" she breathed.

I said, "Yes, I must admit I like to wrap sex in a little sentiment and romance when I can, it's more enjoyable that way; but as I told you, this was strictly business. I needed to have your daddy trust me, and the only way I could do it. . ."

"Was by sleeping with his wife? That's nuts, that's positively perverted!"

I said patiently, "Look, if I'd turned her down, kicked her out of bed, your pop would have figured I just had to be the kind of high-principled government freak who couldn't bear to contaminate himself by screwing the wife of a criminal he was planning to trap and arrest. Now he has pretty convincing evidence that I'm not one of those fine, honorable federal agents who've been trying to nail him for years. He's even got a little something on me. At least he can understand me. I'm not an incomprehensible, self-righteous, law enforcement prick in a three-piece suit; I'm just a normally larcenous and lascivious guy who'll steal anything that's lying around loose, including

110

wives. Okay. He knows me now. Maybe he can even trust me enough to believe what I tell him—well, what I told Lia to pass on to him, afterwards. You must have heard me.''

Sandra shook her head quickly. ''I just caught part of the prelims, I didn't stay for the main bout. Ugh! I said to hell with both of you and ran back to my room!''

I said deliberately, ''Actually, it was rather nice. She's a nice, sexy lady—''

''Lady!''

I was getting a little tired of the kid's attitude. I said, ''What the hell have you got to be so proud of, small fry? Here you are, educated with dirty mob money, sailing a boat bought with dirty racketeering money, driving a car paid for by dirty drug money, feeling superior to someone who's had to make her own way with her own talents. . . .''

''Talents! That's a new word for it, *talents*!'' Sandra's voice was choked. She drew a long breath, cleared her throat, and spoke in a different tone: ''You cross U.S. 1 up ahead, and drive on until you hit the Florida Turnpike going north. It'll swing northwest up around Fort Pierce. That's where we switch to I-95, which will take us all the way up to New England.''

''Check.''

We drove along in silence for a little. I followed the turnpike signs to the on-ramp; soon we were rolling northwards along the interstate at a cagy sixty-four. I didn't want to make it hard for anybody, friendly or hostile, who was following me; and I didn't want to get into a hassle with any cops. They'll usually give you ten miles over the idiot limit, even in a sports car.

''Matt.''

''Yes.''

''I'm sorry.''

I glanced at her. "Let's both be sorry together. I shouldn't have said that about your dad's money."

She shook her head quickly. "I had it coming; I was acting like a disillusioned little juvenile ninny. Daddy can take care of himself and it's none of my business whom you sleep with. It isn't as if she were my real mother. And you're perfectly right about Daddy's money. It's bothered me for years, but I've never had the guts to refuse it, so what makes me so great?" She gave me a tremulous grin. "How's that for an apology? You want sackcloth and ashes, just ask. It's the little-sister syndrome, you know."

I frowned, watching the highway come at me smoothly. The Florida freeways take you through the green countryside inland, where you can see that it must have been a pretty state once, before they loaded it with all that condo crap around the edges.

I asked, "Are you trying to say that you don't like to see me misbehaving because you want to think of me as your noble and stainless big brother?"

"No, that's not exactly what I was trying to say." Her voice was carefully devoid of expression. She went on: "It's a well-known fact that, if a man loses his wife after a happy marriage, he's very apt to turn right around and marry her kid sister, if available. It makes sense. He's looking for something as close as possible to the marvelous girl he lost. Well, Matthew's kid brother wasn't handy, and he's a little young for me, anyway; and there was no marvelous older brother available. But Matthew did have a kind of . . . kind of intriguing daddy; a tall, sinister-looking, romantic-looking, secret-agent type. An older man, sure, but hardly ancient."

"Thanks for the flattery," I said dryly. "But, Sandy . . ."

"Shut up and let me finish!" she snapped. "I don't normally go around listening at bedroom doors. I . . . I

112

didn't sneak down that hall in my sexiest nightgown to *listen*, damn you! Do you understand?'' When I didn't speak, she said harshly, ''You really had them standing in line last night, didn't you? Lia, and I; and maybe our pretty little Maria was waiting on the stairs in *her* best negligée! What is this strange power you have over women, Mr. Helm?'' She swallowed hard, and went on: ''Anyway, when I got there on my tippytoes, all breathless and scared, asking myself how could I be doing such a crazy, shameless thing . . . when I got to your door, I heard voices inside. Lia's voice! Lia's theatrical sobbing! It was like having a bucket of ice water dumped on my head. I didn't really mean to eavesdrop, but I simply couldn't move at first. Then I fled, very happy that I hadn't opened the door and made a complete fool of myself.''

It seemed better not to embarrass her by looking at her, so I concentrated on passing a long semi. The little sports car tracked nicely; but with only our suitcases up front holding down the tires that were doing the steering, it was a bit more wind sensitive than my old front-engine Mazda, although it had a lot better acceleration. Sandra stirred beside me.

''So now you know. Don't say anything. I mean, just tell me what it was that Daddy sent Lia to find out from you.''

I hesitated, but it wasn't my place to tell her she was a silly girl with a juvenile crush on an older man; and it seemed likely that last night had cured her of the aberration, anyway.

''It's very simple,'' I said. ''There are a lot of sentimentalists in this country. Even now, when terrorism is unpopular enough that people will support military action against it, we'd get some backlash if it were known that a government agent like me had been sent out with orders to arrange for the demise of seventeen or more

113

people, no matter what kind of ruthless murderers they may be. Well, look at your own horrified reaction. It seems to be all right to blow them up wholesale with military boom-booms—men, women, and children, innocent and guilty together; but if you pick your terrorist targets carefully, and shoot them neatly through the head one by one, it's considered too brutal for words and you could get your wrist slapped. At least that's the current thinking in Washington.''

She said, ''But you are going after all those people, regardless. Aren't you?''

I didn't answer directly. ''That's the situation as far as *governmental* action is concerned,'' I said. ''But there's a double standard operating here. If an *individual* fights back, even if he's pretty ruthless about it, he generally gets forgiven, like that gent in the New York subway who was the most popular guy in the country for a few days. By God, somebody'd turned the tables on Them at last! So here's your dad, his son-in-law killed by a terrorist blast, his daughter cruelly injured—and They won't even leave the poor young widow alone to heal her heart and body in peace! Driven by fear of exposure, They're still coming after her! Can this loving father be blamed if he tracks down the bomb-throwing creeps and punishes them appropriately, even if his reputation isn't all it might be? Hell, Sonny Varek may even be hailed as a hero for a change!''

Sandra threw me a sharp glance. ''I see. You're asking Daddy to take the rap for . . .''

''No rap,'' I said. ''First of all, as I've just explained, nobody's going to complain too much, these antiterrorist days, about what a private citizen does to save his daughter from a bunch of blast-happy fanatics. And, second, if he should happen to run into a little legal trouble, we'll back him all the way. Well, I told all this to Lia last night.''

"Must have been quite a little postcoital conversation," Sandra said dryly. "But why pass the word through Lia? Why didn't you just tell Daddy yourself, when you were talking with him earlier in the evening?"

"He wouldn't have believed me then," I said. "He was too suspicious of me; he thought I was pulling some kind of a scam, or setting some kind of a trap for him, using our vague relationship to help out my government colleagues. But I'm hoping that, now that we've got a lady in common, his lady, he'll accept my motives even though he hates my guts. Now he can believe that I'm a conscienceless, calculating jerk who's just figuring out a sneaky way of getting other people to do my dirty work for me. And he'll probably do it, since he's just as mad about the bombing as I am, now that I've assured him the ceiling won't fall on him if he does. The official ceiling." I glanced at the rearview mirror. "Incidentally, we've got company astern."

She started to turn her head, and checked herself. "Your men?"

"Well, they're back there somewhere, too. They're just covering us loosely with instructions to stay out of sight and not spook the game. Our reserves, so to speak. But that maroon sedan behind us, I think it's a Chrysler of some kind, isn't ours. It not likely to be the CLL opposition either. At least I don't think they'd go in for open surveillance like that; they'd just hit and run."

"Open surveillance, what's that?"

"It's when you don't hide the fact that you're tailing the subject or subjects. You let them know they're being followed. It's supposed to make them nervous."

She grimaced. "It's a big success. I'm nervous."

I grinned. "Cheer up, they wouldn't show themselves like this if they were planning immediate action; they're working up to something gradually. We'll have a bit of fun with them in a little while; but first we'll give our

115

protection a chance to spot them and make suitable arrangements.''

"I hope they're good. The arrangements, I mean.''
After a moment, Sandra went on: "Matt, you're not really going to Newport just to get information on that old bombing incident, are you? You're looking for somebody else like Daddy who's mad enough to do your work for you. Carry out your executions. Aren't you?''

"Smart girl,'' I said.

"Matt, let me come with you.''

I said, "You're here by invitation. You're sitting right beside me, moving northward at a discreet nine mph over the lousy limit.''

"I mean, all the way, when you investigate these people. I want to see . . .'' She cleared her throat. "I have to see how others have dealt with this kind of violent bereavement, people who've had more time to adjust than I have.''

I said, "I wasn't planning to leave you behind. But we might as well discuss the ground rules. Is your gun loaded?''

"Yes, but not in the chamber. Philip said that with a . . . a hammerless automatic it isn't safe to keep a round up the spout—his words—since safeties aren't all that dependable. He said that only if I anticipated trouble should I jack the slide back once and set the safety. And then I should put the cartridge back into the top of the clip when the crisis was over; he showed me how.''

I said, "Sounds as if Philip knew his stuff.''

"About guns, all Daddy's boys know their stuff.''

I said, "Okay, I'll tell you when to chamber a round, and when to shoot. Don't get independent. And if I do tell you to shoot somebody, you shoot him dead. None of this movie marksmanship, hitting the shoulder or the leg or, God save us, shooting guns out of people's hands! They're always getting guns shot out of their hands and

116

coming out of it with a full set of functioning fingers. Jesus! Forget that nonsense. Shoot for the chest or, if he seems to be wearing too many thick clothes, blow his head off to teach him not to try to fool people with that lousy body armor." I glanced at her. "Are you still with me, or should I leave you off in Connecticut to do some housecleaning?"

She smiled faintly. "You can't scare me off that easily."

I grinned. "Well, let's play some games with our shadows and see how good this glamour buggy of yours really is. Buckle up your sissy-straps and hang on."

I latched my own harness. It was a pleasure to drop down a gear and put the hammer down and feel the Porsche dig in with the weight of the engine back there holding the tires in firm contact with the pavement, unlike the newfangled front-drive jobs where the driving wheels lift and spin if you try for too much acceleration. We were passing the hundred mark before the driver behind woke up and tried to close the gap, but this was not sedan country, and either his power or his nerve gave out at a hundred and twenty. We'd passed one off-ramp almost too fast to see it; I eased off a bit, looking for another.

"Chicken!" Sandra shouted over the uproar. "Oh, don't slow down; take it all the way. Go, man, *go!*"

She was laughing with excitement. I grinned at her, hit the brakes hard enough to throw us against the webbing, and cut across in front of a thundering semi, almost losing it as I swerved sharply to catch the exit—all that weight in back tends to come around if you overdo things. That's known as oversteer and I love it because it's predictable with a rear-engine car; you know it's going to happen. What I can't stand is a car full of strange surprises, that sometimes breaks loose at one end and sometimes at the other.

Off the interstate, I made some fast turns on the small

roads below. Then I pulled into a roadside joint and bought coffee for both of us, black for me, cream and sugar for her.

"If the cholesterol doesn't kill you, the carbohydrates will rot your teeth," I said.

"Judging by this morning, I'm not going to live long enough to have to worry about it," she said happily.

CHAPTER 13

SAVANNAH, Georgia, is a little over four hundred miles north of Palm Beach, Florida. That's not a great day's run, but it's where you get if you drive conservatively after a late start. It's a nice old city pretty well buried, as most nice old cities are these days, inside a not-so-nice new city. However, when you penetrate to the pleasant sections near the river, you can imagine what Savannah looked like before the internecine conflict I grew up calling the Civil War.

They have a lot of picturesque, old, tree-lined streets. I didn't spot any Spanish moss, but Savannah would be a good place for it. The shady thoroughfares run one-way around a series of pretty little parks that'll throw you if you're trying to get somewhere. I wasn't, really. That is, we had a reservation in a motel near the water-front, but I wasn't in a hurry to reach it. First I wanted to determine how many lice we'd picked up along the way.

"You should have kept straight on around that last square."

Sandra had Rand-McNally open to a sketchy little city map in the corner of a larger state map. She was navigating conscientiously. I jerked my head towards the rearview mirror.

"That's what he did," I said. "The guy in the little green Ford. He took the correct route and let us go. But Car Number Two moved up to replace him. That beat-up four-wheel-drive Nissan."

Sandra looked at me quickly, startled. "I thought we'd lost them!"

"We had," I said, "but they picked us up again after we returned to I-95."

"Wasn't that kind of stupid?" she asked in her forth-right way. "I mean, no disrespect or anything, Mr. Helm, sir, but we could have stayed on the little side roads where they couldn't find us, couldn't we?"

I said, "Hell, if we lost them permanently, we might hurt their poor little feelings." I grinned. "You don't understand how this game is played. The moves are all cut and dried, like the standard chess openings. First, they place us under open surveillance to show their interest and study my reaction. Second, I lose them to show that I've suddenly discovered, surprise, surprise, that we're being followed; and that I disapprove. Third, they pick us up again with a full team—not just one lousy, conspicuous Chrysler—to show that they mean business and to hell with my disapproval."

"But who are they?"

"Anything I'd tell you right now would be a guess." I shrugged. "People who don't like me? You won't believe it, a sweet guy like me, but there are some. People who don't like you? People who don't like your dad? Or any combination of the above. Until we learn more, we'll just continue with the standard moves. Are you clean?"

She was a little startled by the question. "Well, I took a shower this morning, if that's what you . . . Oh!" She looked at me indignantly. "That's a lousy question to ask me, Matt!"

I said, "I do most humbly beg the young lady's pardon. Her pop used to deal the stuff, but I'm not permitted to ask if she's got a little something stashed away in her luggage or purse or clothes. Or her car. Excuse me all to hell, ma'am."

Sandra spoke stiffly: "Maybe that was a little stuffy of me, but I've never in my life. . . . Daddy would have beat me with a baseball bat if I'd so much as taken a whiff of somebody's secondhand smoke, that kind of smoke." Then she shook her head quickly. "No. I won't lie to you. I was curious; I wanted to know what all the fuss was about. I suppose most kids do. So I did try it a few times in college, different things people offered me, but I didn't like the out-of-control way they made me feel." She made a face. "That official propaganda about how you take one snort and you're hooked for life, that's a lot of bull; I didn't have any trouble turning it down, afterwards. The social pressure was much worse than the biological pressure, if you know what I mean."

"It wasn't a big problem in my day, everybody was more concerned about booze, but I get the general idea."

She said flatly, "Anyway, it was rough enough being Cassandra Varek without taking that risk. All my life, off and on, some creep with a badge has been watching me and harassing me, hoping to get something on me, like drugs, so he could use me against Daddy. I wasn't going to make those bastards happy by letting them catch me out that way."

I spoke without expression: "So if somebody shakes you down now, and triumphantly discovers a little plastic bag full of white stuff, I'm justified in blowing him away for planting it on you? I won't be executing an honest

120

law enforcement officer unjustly because you're too shy to admit that you do have just a bit of happy-powder hidden away—strictly for medical emergencies, of course?''

She glanced at me sharply. ''Do you think it's those people? They won't be happy until Daddy's dead; and then they'll dig him up to make sure he didn't take something with him in the coffin!''

I said, ''Let's not worry about your poor persecuted pop; he's been making it for a good many years. The point is, I don't know who's behind us, but the people you mention are certainly one possibility, and we should be prepared for them.''

The girl beside me drew a long breath. ''I don't know how to convince you, Matt. You're welcome to search me if you like.'' When I didn't speak, she cleared her throat and said, ''I guess it sounds ridiculous, these cynical days, to talk about words of honor—although I don't see why it should—but all I can say is that you have my word of honor that I have no illicit substances in my possession.''

I said, ''It doesn't sound ridiculous to me, and your word of honor will do just fine.'' I felt her relax beside me, and went on: ''Well, it's obvious that our unidentified friends are making a point of showing their muscles this time, using at least three cars to keep us covered. We'll let them think we're suitably impressed. Now tell me how to find Bay Street and we'll proceed to the motel to find out what they've got planned for an encore.''

She licked her lips. ''What do you think they'll do, Matt?''

I said, ''I won't kid you. If they're one of the outfits I think—we both think—they'll probably come on pretty strong. Can you keep your temper if things get unpleasant?''

She nodded. ''Yes, I think so.''

''Okay, we'll play it as it lays,'' I said. ''Keep your

gun but don't use it, don't even chamber a round, it's not that kind of a game at the moment. They'll probably try to tease us into giving them an excuse to really push us around; don't give it to them. Let them take the piece and do what you're told, no matter how crummy it gets. The situation is under control and things will work out if you'll just let them.''

Our refuge for this first night out of Palm Beach was an old-fashioned-looking hostelry just half a block from the river, which didn't mean it was actually ancient. They're all built to look old-fashioned down there, where the city has been restored along the waterfront. Our rooms were at the back, ground floor, we were told. The connecting door that had been specified gave the lady behind the desk some interesting ideas about wicked men, no longer very young, who got their kicks from robbing the cradle. To hell with her.

I took the keys, and we drove around to park in one of the designated slots in front of the doors with the correct numbers. They didn't wait for me to use the key I'd picked; suddenly they were all over us like a swarm of bees. I acted too surprised to defend myself; and I was glad to see that Sandra gave up her purse without a struggle.

"Inside, both of you!"

This was a big, handsome, blond gent in white designer jeans and a knitted blue sports shirt. Steely blue eyes; at least he obviously hoped so. Short hair, which scared me a little. It used to be that long hair was a statement of rebellion and nonconformity; but the rebels and nonconformists never hurt anybody much. All they wanted was to be left alone to do their long-haired thing. Now everybody wears it fairly long except a few and it's these short-hairs who are making the statement. Decently shorn, a self-righteous minority in a shaggy immoral world, they want to impose their short-haired standards

122

of decency and morality on everyone around, no matter who gets hurt in the process.

Blondie said, "Don't even dream of resisting, Helm. We know all about you, and you don't scare us a bit. You're covered every way; make one false move and you're gone. Inside!"

Somebody'd already got the door open with the key that had been snatched from me. Somebody else gave Sandra a shove so that she stumbled into the room; but they let me walk in under my own power. There seemed to be a lot of threatening firearms on display, but they always seem more numerous when they're pointed at you. I made it four by actual count.

"Frisk them!" Blondie said, kicking the door closed behind him.

I saw Sandra grit her teeth as one man patted her down, a little more intimately than necessary. Another got the pistol from her purse, an old Colt .380. Kind of a museum piece now, it had been a good enough gun in its day if you didn't require a really potent cartridge. Listed as .380 ACP, for Automatic Colt Pistol, it's also known currently as 9mm Kurz, to distinguish it from the 9mm Luger Parabellum, a much hotter round.

A third man managed to locate the snub-nosed revolver I'd worn inside my waistband for him to find. If I'd been found weaponless, everybody would have worried; on the other hand, it hadn't seemed advisable to confuse the boys with exotica like sleeveguns, ankle holsters, crotch rigs, or neck knives. They were clean-cut, simpleminded, college-educated government thugs in jeans and sloppy shirts of one kind or another. A couple had even passed up shaving for a day or two so nobody could possibly guess that their paychecks were signed by Uncle Sam—but the guns were all the same, standard .38 Special revolvers like mine, except that theirs had four-inch barrels where mine was a two-incher.

That went for the troops; Blondie was fancier. He packed a heavy, stainless .357. Well, I would have bet that he'd be one of the Magnum boys. It was too bad they didn't let him tote a .44 and really make some noise.

"Over there, both of you!" he snapped, waving his big revolver towards a blank wall. When he had us posed properly against it, he came forward. "Now let's make this official. I'm in charge here. I'm a senior special agent—*the* senior special agent—of the President's Task Force for Illicit Substances, the PTFIS. Just in case you haven't been officially informed, Helm, I'm notifying you now that our authority supersedes that of all other government agencies including yours. Washington wants a final solution to this vicious problem; and we've been given the power to go for it regardless of costs or consequences."

I reflected that a final solution had been all Hitler had ever wanted, but I didn't say that. It was low-profile night in Savannah, Georgia.

Instead I said mildly, "Do you have a name, Mr. PTFIS?"

"Tallman," he said. "Robert Tallman."

"Well, that figures," I said, although he wasn't really so tall. I had at least an inch on him in height, although he had more breadth and weight. I went on: "If you've got all that superseding authority, why the hassle? We're both on the same side, the government side. All you had to do was ask."

"Maybe." Tallman's voice was sharp. "And maybe not. One of the things we're here to find out is why you're still in government service."

"Why wouldn't I be?"

"After your son married into the Varek family; and Sonny Varek is reliably known to be associated with the Chicago Mob? We're looking for soft spots in high government places; and your hush-hush chief and his little secret agency have been treated as sacred cows much too long. Clearly, the kindest thing that can be said is that security must be pretty lax around your shop for you to still be working there, a man related by marriage to a known underworld figure, a man who drinks cozily with Sonny Varek, spends the night in his house, and sleeps with his wife and maybe even his kid, or what's that connecting door for?'' Robert Tallman made a gesture of distaste. ''My God, the idea of going to bed with any of that female Varek slime would turn a decent man's stomach; and if my boy ever so much as looked at a drug dealer's brat I'd shoot him dead on the spot.'' He turned, as a man who'd left the room came back in. Tallman asked, ''Anything?''

''Not in the car.'' The man was short and slight and dark, with sharp brown eyes and slender, long-fingered white hands. He was proud enough of those hands to keep them carefully manicured—his one claim to beauty, perhaps—although he didn't seem to be particularly fastidious in other respects. He qualified his first statement. ''At least I couldn't find anything without trashing the heap, Mr. Tallman.''

Tallman shrugged. ''Maybe we'll get to that if we strike out here; it's got to be somewhere. She wouldn't travel without it, not a little tramp like that brought up in that decadent family. A few million unearned bucks on Mama's side; and you know what those society dames are. And we know about Papa, too, don't we? You can't tell me she isn't using. Check out her suitcase. His, too, he might be packing it for her, thinking we'd be too petrified by his reputation and his government ID to look there. . . . Go on, Vance, go on, you're supposed to be the expert. The way you're acting, anybody'd think you'd never searched a piece of luggage before!'' Tallman looked sharply at me. ''You said something, Helm?''

''Not a word,'' I said. ''It's your show. No comment.''

"What, no threats of governmental reprisals, no promises of deadly retribution? Clint Eastwood would be ashamed of you! What about you, girlie? Aren't you going to tell me how your high-powered papa will sic all the godfathers on me with their little Tommyguns?"

Sandra looked to me for help, got none, and remained silent according to instructions. Good girl. The fact was that Tallman probably wasn't quite the blowhard he was making himself out to be. As I'd suggested earlier, he was probably hoping to goad us into angry action of some kind, if only so he could assert his authority and maybe put "resisted arrest" on the report.

"Nothing in the suitcases, except he's packing a lot of spare firepower," reported the little man called Vance. "At least, if it's there, I'm not going to find it without using a knife. And they weren't in here before us, so she couldn't have tucked it away in a chair or something for safekeeping."

I sensed that they were all getting tense now, two of them covering us from different angles while Tallman, in front of us, handled his shiny Magnum with phony negligence. Clearly, the big scene was coming up; and I had a pretty good idea what it would be. I hoped the kid wouldn't find it too distressing.

"Last chance, Miss Varek," Tallman said. "Oh, excuse me, I meant to say Mrs. Helm. Tell us where to find it and we won't have to resort to a body search, very humiliating."

Sandra threw me another questioning glance; but I gave her no help. She started to speak, checked herself, and shook her head. Tallman snorted angrily.

"All right, you little bitch, if that's the way you want it! Strip her, Vance! Cut them off her if she resists."

Sandra, still watching me, let her hands move towards the buttons of her shirt, obviously thinking that if it had to happen she'd much prefer to undress herself. I shook

126

my head minutely. She let her arms fall and stood quite still while the little man with the slender white hands unbuttoned her shirt and unfastened and unzipped her jeans. Then he slipped the shirt off her and pulled the T-shirt over her head.

He made a point of examining both garments carefully, letting her wait, bare to the waist. You had to give the kid credit. She made no silly, September-morn attempts to cover herself; she didn't even clutch at her insecure trousers. She just stood there. Vance tossed the shirts onto the nearest bed and turned back to her, making it clear that he was aware, like every man in the room including me, that she was a nicely developed young lady. He prodded each of her breasts with a forefinger in an exploratory way.

"Pretty," he said. "Very pretty, and all her own. I got one lady, once, a society lady no less, who'd added a little something plastic there so cleverly you could hardly tell by looking, hollow inside, of course. Made her look real good in sweaters for a while, but she's back to A-cup now, sweating it out behind bars. Kick off the shoes, sweetie, and drop the pants and step out of them."

Sandra obeyed, her face expressionless. She was wearing white nylon panties and no socks or stockings. For a girl who'd recently been hurt and hospitalized, and hadn't had much chance to recuperate on the beach, she retained a nice tan; but the five-inch scar down her thigh had not had time to fade. It was red and angry-looking against the smooth brown skin. After examining the jeans and tossing them aside, Vance picked up the high-heeled white shoes.

"I wouldn't say those heels had ever been off," he said judiciously. "Well, we can check them out later if we have to. Come out from the wall a little, honey, and we'll slip those panties down. . . . Ah, what have we here?"

He'd placed his hand low on her back to urge her out

into the room. Now, abruptly, using both hands, he dragged her last garment down her hips. He reached behind her again, right-handed, to grasp something, and pulled hard. We heard the hissing sound of adhesive tape releasing its grip on human skin; then Vance was displaying his trophy triumphantly and tossing it to Tallman. It was a wide strip of flesh-colored tape, to the sticky side of which adhered a small, flat, white package.

When I looked at Sandra, the shock that I'd expected to see on her face wasn't there. Instead she looked wryly amused. She was watching Tallman as he examined his find—well, Vance's find—with the tolerant expression of someone watching a very bad stage performance. Then she winked at me. It was, I realized, a sign of trust and confidence. She was saying that, well, we got these clowns to commit themselves and it wasn't fun; now let's lower the boom on them, please. Hard.

But her voice was shy when she spoke to Tallman. "Please, is it all right if I put my clothes on?"

The blond man looked up. "For now, you can put your own clothes back on, but we'll have some other clothes for you shortly, not so fashionable but nice and durable, provided by the state. Everybody's been pussyfooting around Sonny Varek and his whore of a wife and his jailbait daughter; but I'm going to put them all away where they belong, beginning with you, sister. Unless . . ."

"Unless what?" Sandra asked quickly.

"Unless you can convince your boyfriend here to help us out."

I decided that Mac was definitely not going to like this man. Mac has a strong prejudice against having his agents coerced by anybody but him; but more important, he can't stand people who use the word "convince" when they mean "persuade."

I asked, "Help you out how?"

Tallman said harshly, "You've got the inside track with Varek. Your son married his daughter, and more recently you saved her life. I'll make a deal with you: You cooperate with us to nail that slippery bastard and we'll forget about your security problem and, if the little bitch means anything to you—your late son's wife—we'll let her go, too. She's not important; Varek is. Otherwise she faces a lot of years in the pen. We've got the goods on her right here, and don't think it won't stand up in court even if she does yell frame-up. People have heard that I-wuz-framed routine too many times before. They're sick and tired of seeing criminals and their families and associates go free on legal technicalities. They're not going to look too hard at the evidence in a cocaine case where the accused has been living in luxury all her life on the money provided by drugs and racketeering. . . ." He stopped as the telephone rang. "You take it, Helm. Be careful!"

I shook my head. "Waste of time. There won't be anybody on the line. That's just my associates out there, telling me I've got exactly five minutes to figure out how I'm going to grab the girl and roll under the bed when they smash the doors and come in shooting."

CHAPTER 14

THE phone stopped ringing, leaving the room in silence. After a moment, Tallman laughed contemptuously. He walked to the nearest door, the one leading

129

into Sandra's room, that she'd not yet had a chance to see. He knocked a certain way. International Morse code. Soft for a dot, hard for a dash. Dot-*dash*-dot. *Dash*. RT for Robert Tallman. Cute.

"You're bluffing, Helm. I have men covering both doors of this room."

I shook my head. "Not any longer, or that phone wouldn't have rung."

We waited. There was no response to the identifying knock. Tallman's face was flushed with anger when he turned on me.

"If your gang of secret assassins has attacked agents of the U.S. government, you'll regret it!"

"Says the man who's pointing a large revolver at an agent of the U.S. government," I said dryly. "Hell, with one exception, we're all feds here, Mr. Tallman. You might remember that the President authorizes quite a few operations. What you forgot to ask was who'd authorized my operation."

"Operation?" he sneered. "What kind of an operation could you be conducting, gallivanting around the country with that little gangster-bitch."

"Who happens to be my daughter-in-law, as you just pointed out yourself; and I'm getting a little tired of hearing her badmouthed," I said. "But never mind that. The fact is that you and I both draw authority from the same source, the White House. We've both been instructed to treat our missions as imperative and to deal ruthlessly with any opposition or interference we encounter, correct? Unfortunately, the White House doesn't always co-ordinate these things very carefully. The authorization I was given was just as strong as the one you seem to have received. There's apparently no machinery for deciding a conflict between our two imperative operations, so we're going to have to work it out between us. I'd say the decision we reach will depend largely upon which of us has the clout, wouldn't you?'' He started to speak, but I went right on: "Do you read western novels, Mr. Tallman?"

He allowed himself to be distracted. "I wouldn't waste my time on that melodramatic trash; and the way it's being dirtied up with pornography these days, it shouldn't be allowed on the bookstands!"

I hadn't know westerns had gone pornographic. It was an interesting idea. I'd have to pick up a copy or two and find out just what could be accomplished on horseback.

"That's too bad," I said. "Then you've never come across the wonderful old line they often used to put on the covers: *No man is bigger than the bullet from a .45.* How big are you, Tallman?"

He laughed scornfully. "Don't try to frighten me, Helm."

I said, "The old .45 Colt is almost obsolete these days; so let's discuss instead the 9mm Luger cartridge as fired at the rate of about eight hundred rounds per minute from an UZI submachine gun. I believe that's the weapon our kill team is equipped with, out there, and I'd guess they'd have at least four of them. Plus other assorted hardware. Can you beat that for clout?"

"Man, you must be mad!" he said. "You can't really be threatening to use armed force against . . ."

"Against whom?" I asked gently. "You don't understand the situation, man. My people outside don't know what sterling characters you are, all personal buddies of the President. They're operating under a serious misapprehension. They think you're a bunch of political fanatics who call themselves the Caribbean Legion of Liberty and don't like Mrs. Helm and me very much. They made one attempt on us yesterday. Today we set a trap for them, hoping they were still in the mood. The lady and I were the bait. Well, somebody took that bait. You did. Now the trap is snapping shut, and there's no way for my

131

friends out there to know that they've caught themselves a quartet of purebred heroin hounds instead of a pack of shabby terrorist mongrels. And let me remind you that we're not in the arrest business. If you arrest a terrorist, all you get is more terrorism, as his pals try to free him. The boys outside have their orders, and those orders are very simple: *Exterminate!*''

Tallman said harshly, ''You're lying! You can't tell me you'd deliberately set up a situation that would leave you and the girl at the mercy of . . .''

''They killed my husband!'' That was Sandra. She was stepping into her shoes, fully dressed again. She didn't look up, and her voice was very soft as she went on: ''I can't speak for Mr. Helm, although it was his son who died. but if I can decoy a reasonable number of them to their deaths, I'll feel it's worth anything that happens to me; I'll die happy.'' None of the reservations about this vengeance mission she'd expressed earlier showed now; she was very convincing.

I glanced at my watch. ''Make up your mind, Tallman. You're cutting it very close. Do you want a shoot-out or don't you? I guarantee that you're outgunned and out-numbered. Unless I show Mrs. Helm and myself, un-harmed and unthreatened, within the next ninety seconds, the fireworks start, irreversibly. Do you and your men want to be dead heroes fighting a bunch of fellow em-ployees of our great government, who'll be rushing this room under the impression that you're dangerous activ-ists with homicidal intentions? I suggest you put that Magnum away, and tell your troops to holster their pieces, and let me take my daughter-in-law out the front door where they can see us. . . .''

Tallman started to speak angrily. He stopped, looking around as a rustle of movement caught his attention: the little man, Vance, had holstered his .38. Without looking at their leader, the other two followed suit. I walked forward slowly, took Sandra by the arm, and led her towards the door. The man standing there stepped aside for us. As I reached for the knob, I was very much aware of that big, shiny .357 behind me. Then we were outside in the fading daylight.

For a moment nothing moved out there. Nobody showed. The rear of the motel was now lined with parked vehicles nosed in towards the building. Almost all the spaces were full; apparently the hotel/motel business was pretty good in Savannah, even this late in the year. I had time to wonder if the phone call had been a coincidence; maybe the boys had lost us or been driven off somehow. Then a man rose from behind the hood of a small white pickup truck with a camper top, parked three slots off to the left. He was holding a machine pistol I didn't recognize. Well, they come out with new ones all the time. I'd only used the UZI name for effect; everybody knows the UZI.

"*Ciao*, Eric," he said.

"And *salud y pesetas* to you, Trask," I said, completing our fancy all-clear nonsense. Why a transplanted German—his real name was Miller, derived from Muller—should be giving an Italian greeting, to be answered by a Spanish phrase badly pronounced by a transplanted Swede, was a minor mystery of a kind often encountered in our melting-pot nation. Trask came forward to join us. I didn't take time to perform any introductions. I said, "Watch out in there, a little. Those heroic drug sniffers can get awfully peevish if they're not treated with the respect appropriate to their glorious crusade against chemical evil. Don't be overcome with brotherhood just because we're all working for Uncle Sam, is what I mean."

"No chance, I never had a brother."

"Don't try to disarm them; the top man's got a bad case of Magnum jitters. Just cover them and hold them,

133

but don't hesitate to shoot if they act up. We can't help it if people blunder into our operations and get themselves killed, can we?''

Trask was a rather stout, pale man without too much hair; the last man in the world you'd pick as a dangerous secret agent, and don't think he didn't work at it. What there was of his hair was black. He was two hundred pounds of competent operative on a hundred-and-seventy-five-pound frame, wearing a green sports shirt, a black windbreaker, and baggy black pants. I knew him to be fast in spite of his bulk, and good with the hand-to-hand stuff and the shining blades, maybe better than I am. At least I'm sure he thought so. However, on the record, I was better with the guns, particularly the long guns. Also, I'd been around a bit longer, which wasn't necessarily an advantage except that it did give me the experience and the seniority.

"Wait out here with the young lady, hero," he said. "Give us a minute or two to wrap it up for you. I'll whistle."

Moving away, he made a minute hand signal, and a couple of men appeared from nowhere silently, one on each side of him. They made the standard wide-apart approach to the open door. As I led Sandra aside to a spot where we were out of the line of fire and had some cars for shelter, I was aware of a backup sniper with a scoped rifle on the roof of the low building across the alley, apparently a garage of some kind.

"Sorry you had to go through all that," I said to the girl beside me.

"I hope they fight back," she said. When I glanced at her quickly, she went on: "I hope they resist and your men shoot them down, every last lascivious one of them! But you weren't much help; your eyes were popping out just like the others. What's the matter, haven't any of you miserable studs ever seen a naked girl before?''

I said, "Don't look now, but your nonviolence seems to be slipping." After a moment, I said, "You did swell."

"Yes, didn't I?" Her voice was bitter. "Maybe I've found my profession. Sandra and Her Dance of the Seven Veils. Oops, six veils. Five veils. Four, three, two, one, and bingo. . . . What are they doing in there, anyway?"

Then Trask showed in the doorway and, by God, stuck a couple of fingers into his mouth and let out a real blast. I was jealous; I never could master that two-finger whistle technique as a kid, and it wasn't for want of trying. It was almost dark outside now; and when we reentered the room all the lights were on. Our recent captors were sitting down, Tallman and Vance in the room's two armchairs that had a cocktail table between them. The other two men, still unnamed, were seated on the side of the nearest bed. Trask had two competent-looking young characters covering them with the unidentified rat-a-tat guns. His own weapon wasn't too far off target as he closed the door and took up a position just inside it.

"According to instructions, they have not been disarmed," he said.

I said, "If we have to shoot one, we want him to be found with a gun on him, don't we?"

"Listen, Helm . . ." That was Tallman.

I said, "You've done a lot of talking, now let somebody else take a crack at it." I looked at the four of them. "There's a new Smith and Wesson revolver missing, and an old Colt automatic."

One of the men on the bed, very cautiously, produced my weapon and, at a sign from me, walked forward to lay it on the low table. He resumed his seat beside his colleague. Vance groped in his coat pocket with a thumb and forefinger and gingerly brought out Sandra's automatic. He leaned forward to place it beside the revolver. I stepped over there, holstered my own piece, and

135

checked the .380 ACP—chamber empty, magazine full, okay. I tucked it into Sandra's purse, which was lying on the table.

Tallman said again, "Listen, Helm . . ."

I said, "We don't see you, Tallman."

"What?"

I said, "Not one of the people associated with me will recognize any of you again. That goes for Mrs. Helm and me, also. You're perfect strangers to us from now on. Understood?"

Tallman said angrily, "No, I don't understand! What do you mean, you won't recognize . . ."

"You've had your break," I said. "You should be dead now. What I'm saying is that next time you interfere in our operations you will be. We won't know you, and we'll treat you as hostile strangers, meaning that we'll shoot you dead." I looked from one to another of them. "In other words, stay the hell out of our hair from now on. You've probably loused up this part of our mission completely. The chances of the people we want coming in the way we wanted them to are nil, now that you've sprung our little trap and shown everybody out there that we're ready for them, waiting for them."

"Dammit, you can't give me orders, Helm. My authority . . ."

"Let's not go into that authority nonsense again," I said. "Is your authority bigger than a bullet from a 9mm Luger cartridge? Because that's what you'll get, or a .38 Special, or any damn caliber that's handy, if you try to barge in on my business again." I stared at them hard. "Let me repeat myself so that there can be no misunderstandings. I've been given a clear directive: If anyone obstructs me while I'm carrying out my orders to break up this terrorist outfit, I'm to assume he's involved with the opposition, and I'm to take him out, too. That goes for you and your bunch, Tallman."

Tallman snorted. "You can't sell that in Washington, Helm! You can't hope to make them believe that I and my men were working on behalf of . . ."

"But you are," I said. "You've already done the CLL a big favor and helped them avoid the deadfall we tried to set for them here tonight. I'm not going to let it happen again; and I don't intend to risk my life every time I spot a threatening shadow, making sure before I shoot that it isn't some eager cocaine chaser sticking his long nose where it doesn't belong, instead of a dangerous, armed political fanatic. I'm not going to lose good agents because they hesitated before using their guns, checking that the target wasn't one of you creeps. I repeat, we've never seen you; we don't know you; and we'll wipe you out for terrorists anytime you make nuisances of yourselves." I turned my head. "Do you copy, Trask?"

"I'll pass the word."

Tallman protested, "Goddamn it, Helm, I've also got a job to do, stopping this dirty traffic. . . ."

"There's no dirty traffic around here except yours," I said. "Don't threaten me with investigation again. I have a full tape of what went on in here tonight. If that's not enough, I have a hunch it isn't the first time you've tried to use that kind of crooked pressure to achieve your purposes. We've got some pretty good investigators; you don't want them turned loose on you to see what they can dig up . . . . Trask."

"Yes?"

"Are we holding any of Mr. Tallman's people?"

Trask went to the connecting door. He spoke his name and gave an order. The door opened, and a couple of sheepish men marched in, shepherded by a submachine gun in the hands of another of Trask's silent young heroes.

I said, "Give them back their toys and turn them loose. All right, Tallman, take your army to hell out of here."

Tallman started to say something and thought better of

137

it. His super-steely blue eyes glared at me murderously for a moment; then he turned sharply and marched out the front door of the room. His men followed. The motel unit seemed suddenly much larger with all of them gone. Trask started to tell his own team to withdraw.

I said, "No, those jerks went out mad and trigger-happy. Give them plenty of time to get clear. We don't want a replay of Tombstone's O.K. Corral in the middle of Savannah."

"We're going to have trouble with that one, hero. He's not going to pay any attention to your warning."

I shrugged. "His choice," I said. "However, I've got a little distraction planned that may keep him busy elsewhere. Have you got that tape handy?"

Trask gestured towards the young man who'd just come in from the adjoining room. That one took a cassette from his pocket and gave it to me. I was slipping it into my own pocket when somebody knocked on the front door of the unit. Trask stepped over there, asked a question, and got an answer. He opened the door a crack, cautiously.

A man's voice said, "Somebody wants to see Mr. Helm. He says his name is Benison."

I said, "Let Mr. Benison in."

The man who came in was very pretty. He wasn't big, a compact gent in his thirties with smooth brown hair and a smooth tanned face. He was wearing a smooth brown suit, all three pieces of it, a starched white shirt, and a maroon silk tie. His brown shoes were polished to perfection. If I hadn't been used to looking for guns, I'd never have spotted his under the carefully tailored suit coat, high on the right hip and tucked in close to the body.

"Mr. Helm?" he said. "I saw Mr. Tallman's forces withdrawing, so I thought you might be ready for me."

"Mr. Tom Benison?" I said. "We've got it right? Not Mr. Denison?"

The man smiled thinly. "Thomas Benison is correct. Benison, as in blessing. A little identification is indicated, if these well-armed gentleman will permit." When I nodded, he took a leather folder from his inside pocket and handed it to me. I opened it, glanced at it, and gave it back. He said, "The chief of your organization telephoned the chief of mine earlier today. He said you'd called in from somewhere along Highway I-95, saying that you had company astern which had been identified as belonging to people more or less in our line of business. Of course, we have no authority over a presidential task force, you understand that."

"We didn't expect you to pull them off us; we just thought you might want to know something about their operations."

Benison gave me his limited smile once more. "As you said, we are in the same line of business as Mr. Tallman, dealing with the same problem, as well as we can with the funds made available to us. I will admit that we are not overjoyed when we see some of those funds thrown to a wild man who's been disciplined several times for what a tolerant person would call overenthusiastic law enforcement efforts. We don't feel quite so tolerant. We try to adhere to certain legal standards. We feel that drugs are a serious threat to our society; but so are ambitious empire builders who use that threat to establish themselves in positions of power, and proceed to abuse that power."

I said, "I have a tape here that may interest you. I hope it'll help you make trouble enough for Mr. Tallman to keep him off our necks."

Benison took the tape and looked at it. "I won't accept this under false pretenses," he said. "While we do feel that Mr. Tallman's antics tarnish the professional image

139

we would like to present to the public, keeping him off your neck is not a high-priority item with us."

I grinned. "Hell, take it. But watch yourself. Tallman knows it exists; and he's not a very scrupulous character."

Benison nodded. "I will keep it in mind. I have had some experience in dealing with unscrupulous characters. Thank you, Mr. Helm. Good night."

We watched him go. Trask closed the door and said, "A neat little fellow. I've met a few of those. They're usually tougher than they look."

I said, "I think the lady and I are pretty well washed up as decoys, at least for the time being. All the milling around tonight will have told the CLL we're ready for them. They'll either give up on us altogether, which we can't count on, or they'll pull back and wait for a better opportunity up north. You may as well dismiss your commandos for now. Just keep the phone manned and have somebody trail us around to keep an eye on the Porsche; I don't want to have to search it for whiz-bangs every time we stop for coffee. People who've used explosives once tend to get hooked on them, just like heroin."

"Check. Take it easy, hero."

I watched them file out of the room, feeling that a little speech of appreciation would not have come amiss. However, I'm not a great leader of men; and I don't know how to tell a bunch of trained specialists that they're good at their jobs without sounding patronizing. I locked the door behind them, and turned to the girl who'd been sitting quietly on the farther bed during the final proceedings.

"Okay, you can lose your temper now," I said.

CHAPTER 15

NORTH of Savannah you get a lot of pine forests. You also get a lot of torn-up freeways—well, we'd already encountered those down in Florida. Apparently the whole U.S. interstate system is falling apart and they're trying to stick it back together, causing innumerable single-file detours, all plastered with slow-down signs to make certain no opportunity is missed to create a mile-long traffic jam.

I found myself remembering a detour I'd hit in France some years ago when I was trying to travel inconspicuously, never mind why. I made the mistake of slowing down for the construction area like any good little defensive American driver, thereby incurring the wrath of the French *gendarme* on duty. Just how stupid could I get? Did I not comprehend simple logic? Clearly, when the road is reduced by half its width, monsieur, automobiles must proceed at twice the velocity in order to maintain the same volume of traffic! *Vite, vite . . .*

"What's funny?" Sandra asked as we crawled around a culvert under construction, or reconstruction. "Please share the joke, Matt. I need a good laugh."

We hadn't been on very good terms since last night. She'd obviously been brooding over the insults and indignities to which she'd been subjected, and blaming me for not preventing them—or at least for not meting out dramatic punishment to those responsible, afterwards.

141

Dinner had been a silent meal, after which she'd retired to her room, emerging for a wordless breakfast of bacon, eggs, and a sizable stack of hotcakes. My dad always told me not to worry about a puppy as long as it was eating well.

I said, as we inched our way through the last of that detour, "Well, the French have a different attitude towards these things." I told her about my experience, finishing: "Fortunately, it didn't jeopardize the mission, but it could have."

I was glad to hear her laugh. "I won't ask what your mission was; but we could certainly use a few *gendarmes* to speed things up around here. Instead of the characters we've got with the fluorescent vests and the red flags, who are just overjoyed whenever they can bring the whole U.S. highway system to a screeching halt. Matt."

"Yes, Sandra."

"I wanted to kill them. That big creep with the nasty blue eyes, and the little rat with the wandering hands."

"I know," I said, "but the whole point of the exercise was to get them off our backs without killing them. My chief's got enough homicide-related public-relations problems with this assignment already, without my handing him a pickup-truck load of defunct presidential drug agents to explain away."

Sandra made a wry face, and said, "Of course you know I'm just talking big. Even if you'd put my gun into my hand with a cartridge in the chamber and the safety off, I couldn't have pulled the trigger." She shrugged. "You did get that tape to where it would do the most good, I ought to be satisfied with that. I guess I just overreacted. Little Miss Modesty, that's me. Dumb! So I've got a body and some men saw it, big deal!" She giggled abruptly. "But you're really a devious monster, aren't you?"

"Meaning what?"

"Your men all knew perfectly well who was in that room with us. They didn't think for a minute we'd been taken prisoner by the Caribbean Legion, like you told Mr. Tallman."

I said, "Sure they knew; they're the ones who identified Tallman's people in the first place, when I spotted them following us. But Tallman would have thought I was bluffing if he'd been aware of that. He wouldn't have believed my men would attack if they knew whom they were attacking."

"Would they have?"

I said, "Hell, yes. Trask wouldn't have cared. He'll take on anybody he's told to take on: he doesn't give a damn whether it's the KGB or the CIA or points in between. His boys are trained to go for any throat they're aimed at, without hesitation. Does a Doberman stop to ask silly questions when he gets the eat-'em-up command?"

Sandra shivered a little. "And they look like such nice boys—all except the fat man, he looked tough. And you look like such a nice man, too!" She gave me a sideways glance. "Matt, why did you bring me along, really?"

It was a complete change of subject, and it seemed to surprise Sandra as much as it did me.

I said, "Hell, we went all through that a couple of nights ago. You're bait for the trap."

"But Tallman spoiled the trap yesterday, and it seems unlikely they'll fall for it again very soon. That's what you told Mr. Trask last night. But you haven't said anything about sending me home. Sure, you kind of promised to take me along when you interview those people in Newport, but you're not running a guided tour for young ladies, and I'd probably let you out of your promise if you asked nicely."

I said, "Maybe I don't want to send you home because I don't think you'd be very safe at home."

She was watching me closely. "But why should you care, Matt? I mean, you're not in the bodyguard business, you've got important work to do, and there's no real blood relationship or anything. If they blow me up again, or shoot me down, what's it to you, really?"

I glanced at her. "What are you plugging for, small fry, a declaration of undying love?"

She made an impatient gesture. "Please stop that. I get a very strong impression, not a very flattering impression, that you have no designs on my . . . my affections or my young white body, even though you weren't above ogling it when you got the chance. It's some kind of a lousy sense of responsibility, isn't it, although there's absolutely no reason why you should feel responsible for me."

"You're wrong there," I said. Then I said, "Oh, God, here we go again. Another detour."

We were silent while I guided the car into the proper lane, as the freeway traffic piled up for another bumper-to-bumper procession between the big red plastic hats indicating the part of the roadway we were permitted to use while they beat the other part to death with jackhammers. The vehicle ahead was a large motor home the rear of which let us know that it was the rolling residence of Dot and Harry from Duluth. There was also a sticker reading: GOD SAVE AMERICA—AND HE'D BETTER HURRY UP!

"How am I wrong?" Sandra asked. "Ex-father-in-law isn't much of a relationship. There's no real obligation, Matt."

"Maybe not to you," I said. "But I have an obligation to my son. I didn't do much for him when he was alive. From what you tell me about him, he wouldn't have appreciated being avenged, so that's something I'm doing just for myself. But he loved you very much, and I can do one thing for him that I'm sure he would have liked:

144

I can do my best to see that you make it okay, that nobody kills you, and that you get all the help you need to see you through to a good life, even though it has to be a life without him. You're an independent kind of girl, and I didn't tell you this before because you might have objected to having a nursemaid; but I hope very much that you'll accept me as a kind of beat-up guardian angel until things settle down.''

She was silent for a little, and I couldn't tell what she was thinking. "Some guardian," she murmured at last. "Some angel! The first thing he does is let me in for an involuntary striptease!"

Then she grinned at me, and I knew everything was all right. We made it through the detour, and some other detours, and spent that night in Richmond, Virginia. The following day we battled our way past Washington, D.C., and made an end run around New York, taking the Garden State Parkway to one of the upper bridges crossing the Hudson, and then cutting east and south to pick up the Connecticut Turnpike which is no longer a true pay-as-you-go turnpike. The big trucks kept misjudging their brakes and crashing into the cars lined up at the tollbooths and killing people. You'd think they'd do something about the trucks; instead they tore down the tollbooths. Who says we aren't a permissive society?

"Old Saybrook ahead," I said at last.

"What?" Sandra sat up beside me, making the standard feminine gesture of pushing her hair into place, even though she still didn't have enough hair to worry about. "Oh. I must have been asleep. You must be dead after all this driving. Old Saybrook?"

"Next exit."

"Do you mind just taking me past the house? It's not very far."

I switched on the turn signal and cut over to the right; a few minutes later, under her direction, we were driving

145

along a shady street—well, it would have been shady in the summer. We were far enough north now, in New England, that most of the leaves were off the trees. The houses were smallish and set back from the roadway on grassy lots; there were no sidewalks.

"The white cottage on the right. Can we stop?"

"Better not," I said.

"I know, it's getting late."

"It's not that. Somebody may have found out that you own it. They could have figured you'd be checking it out about now if you were heading for this area. They could have prepared a welcome for you."

"Yes, of course. It's hard to remember that we're at war. Thanks for letting me look at it. We . . . we were very happy there." After a moment Sandra cleared her throat. "I'll have to get somebody to tie down that boat cover and clean up the lawn."

Just before dinner time we checked into a large frame hostelry overlooking Newport Harbor. We'd had to cross a couple of bridges, one quite high, to get there, since Rhode Island is cut up by a lot of water and Newport is on a large island—bearing the same name as the state, incidentally. There was a small marina on the seaward side of the hotel and a large parking lot to landward. Our rooms were on the second floor looking down on the parked cars.

While Sandra did whatever girls do before going out to eat, I made a reservation for dinner; then I called the control number. I got hold of Trask for a change—usually I did my daily talking to the phone watch—and learned that we'd picked up a flea when we drove past the house in Old Saybrook; a human flea, as yet unidentified, in a green Toyota two-door. Smart people. Scared off by Tallman in Savannah, they'd figured out where we were going, as I'd thought they might. They'd waited for us to come to them rather than chase us along hundreds of miles of freeway.

I said, "That's fine. I was hoping they'd reestablish contact. Observe but don't disturb. That won't leave you much manpower for us, so concentrate on keeping the Porsche free of loud presents. I'll try to survive without a chaperone, away from the car. Anything else?"

"Yes. Have you read any Florida papers recently?"

"No, why?"

"Vicious drug wars. Two pushers executed gangland style in Pompano Beach for trespassing on the wrong territory. At least that's the public version. Actually, the cops have pretty well established that the victims were the two men involved in the Mariposa bombing. They're not pursuing the murder investigation too energetically, on advice from Washington."

"So Varek's people got the men; what about the Angela girl?"

"It didn't work out quite the way it had been planned. The Delgado woman in our office came up with some new information; that gal wields a mean computer. She had the two men pinpointed. Varek was supposed to hold off to give their female accomplice a chance to join them; but I guess he's the impatient type. He moved too soon and all he got were the men. He's still looking for the blonde. However, Louis reports that, with help from Washington, his team has located Arthur Galvez and Howard Koenig; the boys are waiting for the word to close in."

"Good enough. We do seem to be gaining on it a little. . . . Just a minute, somebody's at the door."

"That's the report. Watch your ass, hero. Trask out."

Replacing the phone, I heard the knock again and realized it was Sandra at the connecting door. "Come in, I'm respectable," I said. "Well as respectable as . . . Hey, what's the matter?"

147

I jumped to my feet and hurried to her, where she stood in the doorway a little uncertainly. She was wearing high-heeled white sandals and clean white slacks, a change from the scuffed jogging shoes and grubby jeans in which she'd been traveling today. She was wearing nothing else except the Colt .380 automatic.

"I don't know," she said. "I really don't know if I'm making a big fuss about nothing."

"Tell me!"

"Maybe I'm overreacting, but when I came out of the bathroom a maid was putting some flowers on the dresser. The crazy thing is, she looked just like. . . . I'm almost sure she was the girl outside the Mariposa. . . . Matt!"

I guess I'd grabbed her hard enough to hurt a little. I kicked the door closed behind her. I hauled her across the room and shoved her down behind the farthest of the two beds, and held her there, lying flat beside her. Nothing happened.

Sandra started to raise her head. "I guess I did over-react. Sorry to be so chicken. . . ."

I pushed her down again as the room she'd just left exploded with a flat, hard bang that blew the connecting door open again and shook a picture off the common wall. A little whitish smoke drifted in through the open doorway. I held Sandra long enough to make sure she wasn't going to break down; but Matthew had picked a good unhysterical type.

"We'd better find you a shirt," I said. "It looks as if we might have company."

CHAPTER 16

HE was moderately tall, a lean, sandy man in tweeds with a thin, sandy moustache that he liked to stroke with the middle knuckle of his right forefinger. He was doing it now.

"Beautiful!" he said. "Simply beautiful!"

Well, there's no accounting for tastes. I've seen a number of wrecked rooms and I found nothing in this mess that made it lovelier than any of the others. But the local blast genius, whose name was Colonel Farnham, was studying the holes in the walls and ceiling with admiration.

"Note the even distribution," he said. "A really fine little antipersonnel device employing number four buckshot."

"Yes, well, what do you think, Colonel?"

This question came from the uniformed gent who'd brought us the tweedy bomb specialist. He was standing by the splintered hall door. High-ranking policemen have the same look of bulletproof perfection as high-ranking military men; you can't imagine them bleeding on those immaculate, snug-fitting cop suits, or soldier suits, even assuming there's human blood inside them. This one carried all the right cop hardware in all the right places and you knew you'd never find a speck of rust or dust on it anywhere. He was a stocky character with a square brown face and thick, glossy, black hair—not a strand out of place, of course.

He spoke again, when the man addressed didn't answer immediately: "Just a preliminary opinion, Colonel?"

Farnham turned to face him. "I can tell you nothing with certainty, of course, until I've had time to examine all the evidence. But the signature is the same, if you know what I mean."

"The signature?"

"The technique. The approach. What we sometimes call the handwriting. Yes, the people who constructed this device could very well be those responsible for the bomb employed at the Silver Conch Restaurant a few months ago. That was a different type, of course, designed to be effective over a larger area; but like this one it was no bigger than necessary. Economical. Usually they go for overkill in a big way. They have fifty-megaton dreams even when it's merely a question of blowing up a small hotel room."

Waiting beside Sandra for the top cop to get around to us, I put in my dime's worth. "There have been two other bombings that might interest you, Colonel. The restaurant La Mariposa in West Palm Beach, Florida; and the Howard Johnson Restaurant in San Juan, Puerto Rico. If you'd like to compare some more signatures."

The uniformed man by the door gave a short bark of laughter. "Who'd blow up a Howard Johnson? That's kind of like staging a full-scale SWAT operation to shoot Smokey the Bear."

I said, "Nevertheless, five people died, three of them children."

Colonel Farnham said, "I'll check the incidents you mentioned. Thank you."

The shiny policeman said, "While the colonel looks around in here, maybe we can move into the other room and be comfortable while I go over the young lady's evidence with her."

It was the usual cop interrogation; they don't know how to ask a simple question without sounding as if they're accusing you of murder. Sandra had to describe the maid again: a smallish girl with shoulder-length blonde hair, wearing a gray cotton uniform, dark stockings, and gray canvas shoes. She'd brought a vase of flowers. She said it was courtesy of the management. She put it on the dresser and fussed with it a little. Sandra'd had an uneasy sense of recognition, but it wasn't until the door was closing that she realized where she'd seen this maid before. . . .

The cop took her through it repeatedly, the way they do; then he worked me over a bit, mostly to indicate that he didn't really like having wolves from other lairs, even from that big wolf-hole in Washington, prowling around his territory—we had, of course, gone through the ID routine with the first officers on the scene. Finally we got the usual cop lectures on "Firearms, the Local Legal Aspects Thereof," and "Interagency Cooperation, a Two-Way Street." He hoped. He put away the notebook at last, picked up his cap, and departed, name and rank still unknown, after assuring us that the damaged doors of the next room, particularly the connecting doors, were being secured properly, and that there would be a man on duty there all night.

Sandra made a face after him. "That makes me feel warm all over," she said as the door closed. "Having a pig watching over her is just what it takes to make a girl sleep soundly. Particularly if she's a girl born with the name of Varek."

"Now you sound just like a gangster brat," I said. I studied her for a moment. "We've got a problem with the arrangements. You can't sleep in *that* room, and they have no other connecting rooms available; the only vacancy on this floor is way down the corridor.''

She grinned. ''Could you be leading up to the fact that there are two big beds right there? Are you being shy about it? Your virtue will be safe with me, honest.''

''It wasn't my virtue I was worrying about.''

''Oh, goody, the man finds me irresistible!'' She laughed, and shook her head. ''If it's my reputation that concerns you, Sonny Varek's daughter never had one, so forget it.'' She shivered suddenly. ''I don't want to be at the far end of any corridor tonight, Matt. I don't even want to be next door. I want to be right in here with you watching over me, not some lousy cop. And if you don't take me out and pour some drinks into me, double-quick, you're going to have a basket case on your hands. That blast reminded me of too many ugly things. How long does a girl have to be brave and sober around here, anyway?''

We walked to the restaurant. Newport isn't a big city, and most of the action takes place in a fairly limited area around the waterfront. In years gone by there was a lot of glamorous social life in the big mansions out along the shore where the millionaires spent the summer—as opposed to the big mansions in Palm Beach where they spent the winter. It must have been nice work when you could get it. But that glittering world is gone and nowadays the dock area is the big attraction, with its marinas and boat yards and America's Cup yachts and ship chandleries, not to mention its quaint little shops and picturesque eating places, all housed in colorful frame buildings that reminded me of the restored section of Savannah's riverfront, except that the style here was Olde New England instead of Olde South.

''Kind of cute'' was Sandra's verdict. ''Matthew and I . . . we were always going to visit Newport, it was so close, but we never got around to it.'' She was silent for a moment as we walked; then she spoke in forced, bright tones. "Where are you feeding me? Could it be the Silver Conch?"

"I hate smart-ass broads," I said. "How did you ever guess?"

"If it got blown up only a few months ago, like the man said, they must have done a fast job of patching it up."

I said, "Only half of it got blown up. They haven't quite finished repairing that part yet; but the other half is still in business. All we have to do is find it."

It was only a couple of blocks by the direct route; but we'd slipped out a back entrance of the hotel to avoid any reporters who might be lurking around the lobby. That threw my bearings off, so we did a little more hiking than necessary in that maze of narrow streets and alleys before we found our way to the right pier. The restaurant was a long, low, unpretentious gray building perched over the water. It had recently been repainted, presumably so the new construction, or reconstruction, at the seaward end would match the rest.

There was a sign displaying a shiny, spiraling seashell on a black background; pretty, but I couldn't help wondering what a conch was doing up here in New England. In my experience, it's a Florida shellfish, and it's so tough you have to beat it with a club to make it edible, and even then it's never going to run clams and oysters out of business. At least not out of my business. A movement nearby made me throw out my right arm to shove Sandra behind me, while the little .25 sleevegun—well, I'd shifted it from ankle to forearm for daytime wear—slipped into the palm of my left hand.

"Mr. Helm?" It was a woman's voice. "Mr. Matthew Helm? And Mrs. Cassandra Helm?"

She stepped out of the shadows, a tall, trousered female with short dark hair and large spectacles. A miniature camera with a motor drive hung around her neck. I think they still call them miniatures although they've grown considerably since my photographic days. The camera had a flash attachment on top. Those have shrunk; some of the ones we used when I was a kid working for a newspaper were the size of searchlights. Well, as they say, what you lose in the curves you gain on the straightaways.

"Bennington," she said, "Laurel Bennington, of the *Newport Free Press.*"

Sandra took my arm and started to pull me away. "Please, we don't want . . ."

I said, "Hold everything. I guess a little publicity won't hurt, if you can stand it, Sandy."

She said, "Oh, I suppose so, but I got so sick of having those things go off in my face, last time; and every time I'd jump a foot thinking I was being blown up again."

I'd turned aside so I could slip the little automatic back into its clip without attracting attention to it.

I said, "I'm sure Miss Bennington won't fire hers without warning. You do want pictures, Miss Bennington?"

The tall woman grinned. Nothing was going to make her craggy face beautiful, but the grin made her look like a nice, bright person who might be fun to know.

"We call it visual enhancement nowadays," she said. "Yes, I'd like some visual enhancement for my story on your daughter-in-law's narrow escape from death, Mr. Helm. Her second narrow escape from death, if the police had it right."

It was actually the third, of course, counting the antitank gun at the high window, but I saw no need to correct her.

I said, "Let's do our talking inside with some drinks in front of us, and maybe even inside us; but first why

154

don't you shoot your visual enhancements out here, if you don't mind. Anybody who pays the current price for a good restaurant meal should be allowed to eat it in peace, without having his digestion ruined by man-made lightning.''

Going inside after a brief photographic session—the lady knew what she wanted and went right for it—we were seated right away although we were late for the reservation I'd made by phone when we first checked into the hotel. It was a large, pleasant, rather rustic room with wooden tables and chairs; but there were white table-cloths and napkins, the waiters were in dark suits, and there was a sign near the door to the effect that gentlemen were required to wear jackets. I was way ahead of them. I even had a tie on. The younger generation of males seems to be terribly intimidated by neckties, but they don't scare me.

We were seated at a table for two. The restaurant was full and there was no larger table available; but an extra chair was brought for Laurel Bennington, who said she'd already eaten, thanks, but she could probably choke down a Scotch-and-water. Sandra and I both voted for vodka martinis. Twists, no olives.

"Let me see if I have it straight, Matt," Laurel said after we'd talked for a while. We were on a first-name basis now. "Sandra was married to your son, who was recently killed in a terrorist atrocity down in West Palm Beach. So now the two of you have come up here to Newport to investigate our local atrocity of last spring. You're interested because it was perpetrated by the same gang, called the Caribbean Legion of Liberty—at least they claimed the credit, if that's the right word—and you hope it will lead you to them somehow. Apparently they agree with you, or they wouldn't be trying to stop you. Am I right so far?"

"Not quite," I said. "I don't think they're worrying

about the older Silver Conch bombing, at least not yet. They think Sandra can identify the team of terrorists that was actively involved in the more recent Mariposa bombing—that's the one down in West Palm.''

"Yes, I know," Laurel said. "Can she?"

I nodded. "She was actually kind of doubtful until a couple of hours ago; but then she found that she did recognize the phony maid who planted the loaded flowerpot in her room as one of the bomb-throwers she'd seen when her husband, my son, was killed.''

"There were three altogether, weren't there? The woman and two men?''

"We don't have to worry about the men," I said. "They were killed down in Florida, in some kind of a drug hassle, just a day or two ago. At least the police seem to think the identification is positive."

There was a little silence. Sandra was looking at me in surprise; I hadn't got around to telling her what I'd learned over the phone just before the explosion. Laurel Bennington was watching me shrewdly. A good reporter, she knew that while I might not be lying to her, I wasn't telling her everything. She was guessing hard about the things I was keeping back.

" 'Some kind of a drug hassle,' " she quoted dryly. "Isn't that a bit of a coincidence, that they should die violently like that within a few weeks of the bombing?''

"Violent people die violently." I grinned. "Sandy and I didn't vigilante them, if that's what you're thinking. We were several hundred miles away, driving north up I-95, at the time they were killed."

The reporter lady wasn't satisfied. "But the idea isn't altogether repulsive to you, is it? What do you plan to do if something you learn here leads you to the girl who's been planting these bombs, or any of the other members of the terrorist organization responsible for your son's death? What will you do if you get your hands on them? Shoot them?"

I gave her a look of hurt innocence. "Do I look like Charles Bronson in one of those massacre-the-miscreants movies?"

She didn't smile. "As a matter of fact, Matt, you do, a little. Different physical type, of course, but the same . . . well, mental attitude, I'd say. I think you're probably a mean man to meet in a dark alley. But let's keep it simple for my sentimental readers; they just want to hear about the bereaved young wife and her desolate father-in-law, two innocents bravely tracking down the villains responsible for their grief, so dedicated to their pursuit that even bombs can't stop them. Let me fill in the picture with a few more questions, if you don't mind. . . ." At last she sat back and drew a long breath. "And now, what can I do for you? You didn't give me all this information without wanting something in return. Like information?"

I laughed. "You guessed it. First of all, tell us about the bombing that took place here. I gather it was in that other room down the hall beyond the bar and kitchen and rest rooms."

"That's right. That was their formal dining room, at the other end of the building, open only for dinner. This end was more a casual saloon-type eating place serving lunch and drinks and dinner. While they're rebuilding, they're compromising: they keep this room casual during the day, but flossy it up for dinner as you see it now."

I said, "Blatant discrimination, I call it. Men have to wear coats but women don't have to wear skirts. What we downtrodden males need is an Equal Rights Amendment."

Laurel laughed. "Anyway, it was an attractive young honeymoon couple. Obviously splurging happily before settling down to matrimony. The boy in ice cream pants and a blue blazer, the girl in a fluffy pink dress. All dolled up for a special dinner in a high-priced restaurant selected from the guidebook sticking out of his coat pocket. He was carrying a couple of packages from local stores that are open late. The cute little blonde thing was so proud of the rings on her left hand, even though the solitaire wasn't going to make anybody wear dark glasses as protection from its blinding brilliance. The handsome, tanned young fellow was so proud of her. Champagne, of course. And more champagne. Dinner ordered at last. She had to go. He had to go. Nobody thought anything of it; champagne does that to you. It was a table for four. The packages were on one of the vacant chairs. Boom. Two dead, seven injured. Nobody knows whether they slipped out of the johns before the blast or waited for the smoke and confusion afterwards to make their getaway.''

Sandra, who hadn't been saying much, spoke up at last: ''She must have a lot of nerve, to come back to Newport. A good many people must have seen her, in much better light than I had down in West Palm Beach; and she was wearing a wig then. Still, I managed to recognize her, although it took me a minute or two.''

''Of course, our excitement was way back last spring,'' Laurel pointed out. ''People forget with time. She's probably gambling on that, and on staying out of the places she'd been back then.''

I said, ''Those seven people who were hurt, did they get over it?''

Laurel thought for a moment. ''I'd say so. Of course there are a few scars. But no dreadful disfigurements, no crutches or wheelchairs or permanent hospital beds. Yes, I'd say they're all pretty much back to normal by this time—with a few unpleasant memories, of course. But I haven't heard of any of them requiring the services of a psychiatrist.''

I said, ''Okay, tell us about the dead ones.''

"Pirate Williams took the worst of the blast. He was at his usual table by the window, the one he always got when he came in to celebrate one of his boat deals. Would you buy a secondhand boat from a man who called himself a pirate? People did, like they buy secondhand cars from men who call themselves Cheatin' Charley or Sneaky Sam."

"Oooh, what you just said," I said. "Don't you know they aren't secondhand cars anymore? They're pre-owned cars. Like a silencer isn't a silencer anymore; it's a sound suppressor. As a journalist, you'd better keep up with the language, baby."

"I'm not a journalist, I'm a crummy reporter," Laurel said. "Anyway, the Pirate was one of our local characters, always looking as if he'd just come ashore after a month on a trawler, complete with whiskers and sea boots. He'd put on an old tweed jacket to comply with the rules when he came in here; and he didn't mind a bit when the tourists asked about the picturesque old seadog by the window. A phony in a way; but he was supposed to run a pretty good boat yard, and he was a hell of a seaman, and loved it. He'd take that old Hatteras of his out in any weather and laugh at the landlubbers who were scared of a lousy little force eight. He wasn't what you'd call a sweet, warmhearted guy; but Newport misses him."

"And the other victim?"

"Well, she's missed, too. Again, not what you'd call a sweet, warmhearted person; but God she was beautiful. Linda Anson. The campus-queen type, if you know what I mean." Laurel cleared her throat. "Talking about dreadful disfigurements, I didn't like her, but you don't want to think about anything like that happening to a girl as lovely as that. It's probably just as well she only lasted a couple of days after they got her to the hospital; she wouldn't have wanted to live like that. The Pirate didn't

159

last any time at all, of course; he was practically blown to pieces.''

"Were they together?''

Laurel laughed. "God, no, Linda wouldn't have given old Williams the time of day. She liked them young and handsome and rich. Not that the Pirate was a pauper. That boat yard of his was apparently a growing concern, and he seemed to do all right chartering the *Montauk Maid*. At least that's what most people thought, but there were some rumors. . . .''

"Go on.''

"Well, if you've got something a little shady going for you, you've got two choices. You can either act so straight nobody'll suspect you, or you can go around telling everybody what a terrible crook you are—figuring that they'll think you'd never call attention to yourself like that if you were doing something really illegal. Some people thought the Pirate overdid his piratical act.''

"What would he be covering up?''

She said a bit impatiently, "Come on, Matt! An old master seaman with a legitimate place of business on the water and a moderately fast boat he takes out at all hours, not always with charter parties on board? What would he be doing out there, admiring the sunset over Rhode Island Sound?''

"Did he ever have trouble with the Coast Guard? Or any of the land-based drug busters?''

Laurel shook her head. "Not that I know of. They may have been keeping an eye on him as a possibility, it would be surprising if they weren't; but it's the IRS that's been doing the digging since his death. They aren't happy about his books. It seems that maybe the old guy didn't make as much profit on his boat sales as he claimed, and that the boat yard actually ran at a loss; so where did the money actually come from?''

160

"You'd say he was conducting a small-scale laundering operation on the proceeds from his smuggling?"

"I didn't say it. You did." She laughed, and reached for her camera. "Anything else I can tell you?"

"Relatives, friends, people I can talk with?"

"Williams didn't have any relatives that I know of. The boat yard closed down after he was killed. Nobody came forward to inherit it or run it, so if you want to talk with the handful of workmen he employed, you'll have to track them down. Check the other boat yards and the marinas. The Pirate didn't have any friends, to amount to anything."

"What about the girl?"

"That's different. Everybody loved her, now that she's dead. As a matter of fact, quite a few of them loved her when she was alive. Miaow. But she did play the field, although don't suggest that to her parents if you talk with them. They remember her as an immaculate angel, of course. The address is in the book, Walter Anson. As for the men in her life, if you need names, I can probably give you some if you call me at the paper tomorrow morning. The one she was with on the fatal night was a typical specimen, good old New England family, good old New England money, and handsome enough to make any girl's heart go into sexy spasms. Jerome Elliot, of the Elliot Manufacturing Company Elliots. He's in the book, too, I believe."

"Good enough." I changed the subject. "After they blew up this place they sent notes to the local papers and TV stations to claim credit?"

"That's right. Another victory for the brave soldiers of the Caribbean Legion of Liberty in their heroic war against Yankee imperialism. Pasteups. The letters were cut from newspapers and stuck to cheap bond paper. Any good suspense-novel reader knows that can't be traced, unlike typewriters and handwriting."

161

I nodded again. I'd already got all that from the material dug out for me by Dana Delgado and our research people. I didn't really know what I was groping for. Laurel got to her feet, and hesitated.

"Look," she said, "look, when it's a question of a girl with a face like Linda Anson's, you shouldn't ask a girl with a face like mine, because the answer you get is bound to be prejudiced. Actually, the girl had plenty of brains, and a wonderful personality when it was worth her while to turn it on. . . . God, there I go again! Bitchy Bennington! Thanks for the drinks and the cooperation."

Watching her make her way out of the crowded dining room, Sandra chuckled. "Would you say the beautiful campus queen stole a man from the plain reporter lady at one time or another?"

"Seems likely. What about some coffee?"

"Why spoil this nice buzz I have? Matt."

"Yes, Sandy."

"So Daddy did two thirds of his job. Or your job," she said a bit tartly. "You didn't tell me about the two men being killed."

"We had a few cops in our hair, remember?"

"That's five down so far. Are you happy?"

I said, "Cut it out, small fry. You worry about your conscience and I'll worry about mine."

"The trouble is, there's no evidence that you really have one."

When we returned to the hotel, there was a policeman stationed in the hall outside the wrecked room that had been Sandra's; but I put more faith in the telltales I'd rigged, leaving. They told me nobody'd entered my room from the corridor—our room now. Inside, while I checked the connecting door, also unopened since we left, Sandra took her gun out of her purse, slipped out the clip, and jacked the slide back to eject the chambered cartridge.

I'd had her ready the weapon when we left the Silver Conch, just in case. She fed the round into the top of the clip, rammed the clip home, and checked that the chamber was really empty before replacing the gun in her purse. Well, it was nice to meet a young lady who'd been brought up properly; instead of being taught just to swoon gracefully at the sight of a firearm.

"Who gets the bathroom first?" she asked.

"You do," I said. "I've got a couple of calls to make."

Trask was still available. He'd already heard about the latest bomb atrocity. We decided that he'd better increase our cover, under the circumstances. He made the usual moaning noises about lack of manpower; but there never was a cover man yet who didn't moan about lack of manpower. Then I got Louis on the line.

"Take them out," I said.

"Galvez and Koenig? The boys will be happy to oblige, they're getting tired of trailing them around."

"The boys tire easily, it's only been a couple of days. But their ordeal is over. Hit both targets. We've had a little trouble here. To hell with playing cagy. We'll let the opposition know this isn't touch football; we tackle for keeps."

I put down the phone. Sandra came out of the bathroom wrapped in a thin blue silk dressing gown, and I went in. I took longer than she had since she'd already had her daily shower, earlier. When I came back into the room, she was sitting cross-legged on her bed watching TV. The room was full of rock-and-roll. I watched the gyrations on the screen until the piece ended, and she snapped the set off with the remote control that was bolted to the table between the two beds so nobody'd run off with it.

I said, "It's a funny thing. The TV characters who're paid a few hundred bucks to tell you all about Perfectodent toothpaste or Sweetiepie candy bars, they speak so clearly you can't miss a word; but the gents and ladies who make thousands, maybe millions, shouting songs into those mikes can't enunciate for shucks. Can anybody understand those lyrics?''

Sandra had shed her dressing gown. She was wearing blue cotton pajamas, rather crumpled. She looked about six years old, except for her eyes, which were adult and wise and knew exactly why I was prattling about TV performers.

She didn't answer my question. Instead she said calmly, ''You don't have to be afraid, Matt. If I were going to rape you, I'd be wearing my passionate silk nightie, the one I had on the night I came to your room and found that Lia had beat me to it. But your virtue is safe from me tonight. Sleep well.''

Surprisingly enough, I did.

CHAPTER 17

AWAKENING with daylight in the room, I lay for a while debating whether to rouse my roommate or let her sleep a little longer. She solved my problem by slipping quietly out of the other bed and tiptoeing into the bathroom, clearly doing her best not to disturb me. I heard the door close gently. The john flushed. A toothbrush went into action.

It seemed like a good opportunity for me to get out of my pajamas and into a T-shirt, shorts, and pants. I mean, it wasn't as if we'd spent the night in each other's arms;

and I didn't want to embarrass her, or myself, with any suggestions of intimacy, like zipping up my trousers in front of her. I was sitting on the edge of my bed pulling on my socks when the telephone rang. I reached for it and put it to my ear.

A low contralto voice I recognized said, "Delgado."

Sandra appeared in the opening to the dressing alcove. She was holding her blue silk robe more or less closed about her with one hand. The toothbrush was in the other. There was toothpaste on her lips.

"Oh, you're awake," she said.

"It's for me."

"Okay, okay, I can take a hint," Sandra said, and vanished.

I spoke into the phone. "Helm."

"Communiqué from Louis: 'Targets terminated. No repercussions.' "

"Good for Louis. What else."

The Delgado said, "There's an interesting development—a possible development—but I'd like to make my report in person, if you're up and receiving visitors."

I remembered the cool, dark, hostile lady in Mac's office, and decided not to give her the satisfaction of hearing me go into a surprised my-God-how-did-you-get-here routine.

"Anytime," I said. "I'll have a pot of coffee sent up."

"I already have one, and some extra cups," said our efficient computer lady. "I'll bring the tray. I'm right down the hall from you."

Socks on, I stuck my feet into my shoes and crossed the room. I spoke to the closed bathroom door: "Visitor coming on business. Female."

"Okay, thanks."

I considered putting on a shirt for the benefit of Miss Dana Delgado; but if she didn't know what a man looked like in his undershirt, it was time she learned. I was a high-powered field operative. I didn't have to dress up for the office help. I heard footsteps in the hall and went to the door and opened it in the way the manual prescribes for times of crisis; but it was the right lady and nobody was behind her holding a gun on her. I let her enter and checked the hall outside. It was empty except for a different policeman guarding the room next door. Nobody but a real cop could have achieved that look of limitless patience. I stuck the .38 Smith and Wesson into my waistband, took the coffee tray from the Delgado, and carried it to the cocktail table in the corner.

"Have a chair. When did you get to Newport?"

"Late last night. Very late last night. It wasn't urgent enough to wake you for."

She was looking around the room with its unmade beds and noting, I hoped, that there were two of them. Not that my sex life, or Sandra's, was any of her business. She was just as handsome as I remembered her, slender and moderately tall in wine-colored slacks, and a matching sweater with a turtleneck that made her look more sporty and less severely efficient than the mannish shirt and tie in which I'd last seen her. But she still wasn't what you'd call the cuddly type. The dark hair was drawn smoothly back from her face, which was discreetly but carefully made up. Her well-groomed appearance reminded me that I wasn't fully dressed and hadn't shaved yet. The woman had given me an inferiority complex since the first day I'd met her, perhaps because computers are a closed book to me. I always feel that anybody who can talk to those machines can't possibly talk to me, at least not in a language I can understand.

"I don't mean that it isn't important," she said, seating herself and reaching for the insulated coffee jug on the tray. "If it develops the way I hope, it could be very

166

important. But it may be a few days before I can confirm. . . . Cream or sugar?''

"Black, thanks."

"What about Mrs. Helm?" She glanced towards the bathroom.

I called, "Sandy, do you want some coffee?"

After a moment, Sandra appeared in her dressing gown but this time, I noted, there were no pajamas underneath. She made it easy to note. So much for embarrassing suggestions of intimacy. She gave me a sweet smile.

"Did you call me, dear?" she asked.

"Miss Delgado, Mrs. Helm, and vice versa," I said. "Dana, Sandra, and vice versa. Do you want some coffee, Sandy?"

Sandra nodded. "Yes, darling, I'll drink it in there and finish dressing while you two transact your secret business. . . . Black, please. Thank you so much, Miss Delgado."

We watched her go holding the cup, the unrestrained robe fluttering around her.

"An attractive child, even with her hair like that," Dana Delgado said.

"Cut it out, Computer Lady," I said. "Patronizing her will get you nowhere; and I'm a little tired of this female infighting. Last night I had to listen to a presumably intelligent woman reporter making snide remarks about a dead beauty who'd offended her in some way. This morning I have a normally sensible young lady playing femme fatale in a peekaboo dressing gown just because you've turned up. Now you're making with the catty comments. Ugh!''

Dana Delgado laughed. "Poor man, does he have a hard time with his women?"

"None of them is exactly mine at the moment, including you." I looked at her and went on deliberately: "Of course, I'm always open to suggestions."

167

"I'm sure you are." She smiled coldly. "Let me see, if you've refrained from having relations with your daughter-in-law—in spite of her sexy antics, and this cozy room, neither of you has that blissful look—your last confirmed conquest was her stepmother, am I correct? Do you really think I'd want to follow in the footsteps, if that's the right word for it, of that overpriced callgirl?"

I started to make a sharp retort and checked myself. It was ridiculous to feel protective about Lia Varek. After all, it had only been a business transaction of sorts, even if it had been conducted in a bed; and the pretty lady in Palm Beach with the dubious history would be the first to laugh if I went charging to her defense like a latter-day Galahad.

"Well, it was just an idea," I said.

Miss Delgado gave me some more of that edged smile. "Oh, don't dismiss it too hastily," she said. "If my theory develops as I expect it to, we will be traveling to the beautiful islands of the Caribbean together, under orders, fairly soon. You can work on your ideas on the way. Judging by your record, I'm sure you will."

I stared at her. "Whose brainstorm was that?" I asked.

"You're not pleased?"

I said, "You're undoubtedly terrific with computers, Delgado, but that's not much help out here on the firing line. I'm already responsible for one untrained female; but at least she seems to know something about guns. Do you?"

"No, but I speak fluent Spanish. Yours is rudimentary, if I'm not mistaken. I'm also well acquainted with the little island nations we're to visit, in fact I was born down there; and it's my understanding you've never been there. I have local contacts that will be of value to us. I think, even if you have to handle all the firearms chores yourself, you will find me useful."

I'd taken the other big chair. I leaned forward to push

my coffee cup towards her and she refilled it; then I drew a long breath and leaned back to study her for a moment. She was really a very good-looking woman. She even had brains, or she wouldn't be working for Mac in her present capacity. I don't usually react unfavorably to handsome and intelligent ladies. There had to be a reason.

I asked, "How are you on apologies?"

She glanced at me sharply. "Giving or taking."

"Taking."

"Oh, I accept them if they're reasonably sincere." After a moment, she asked, "Are you offering one?"

"Yes. Reasonably sincere. My attitude has been reprehensible. I'm sorry."

"Apology accepted. May one ask the cause of this reprehensible attitude?"

I said, "I'm one of those sensitive people who love to be loved, and hate to be hated."

She smiled thinly. "That isn't exactly the reputation you have around the shop, Mr. Helm. You're supposed to be one of the best-hated men in the country, in certain undercover circles at least. And I never heard that it bothered you greatly."

I said, "Oh, that. I don't mind a little hatred in the line of business. But when a lady I've never met before, who's supposed to be on my side, offers me undisguised hostility . . . I thought at first it was just the natural antipathy between office people and field people, but it's stronger than that. When I opened that door for you just now, that first look you gave me was like the ice wind pouring off an Antarctic glacier. I guess my own attitude was an instinctive response to yours; besides, I thought if I was objectionable enough you might get mad enough to give me an answer. What have you got against me, Delgado?"

She said calmly, "My dear man, you're imagining

things. Just because I'm not in awe of your fierce reputation or your homicidal talents . . ."

"No, that won't do!" I said sharply. "Hostility is my business, lady. I can smell it, like a retriever smells ducks. It's a sense that has saved my life more than once, and it tells me that antagonism is coming off you in waves. Why? Did I take a boyfriend of yours out on assignment and lose him? Not likely, since I gather you're a recent acquisition as far as the agency is concerned; I get the idea you were drafted for this particular operation because of your computer skills and your special knowledge. So it isn't very probable that you'd have established a close relationship with any of our people, earlier. Well, did I ever damage a relative or lover of yours, in the line of business? I've never worked down in the Antilles, that I can recall, except for Cuba; but I have worked in Mexico and the Bahamas. Just what did I ever do to you or yours?"

She licked her lips. "I think you're confusing one emotion for another. It isn't hatred that I feel for you."

"It certainly isn't love."

"How about fear?"

I laughed at that. "Yes, you look like the timid type!"

She said, "You don't understand. As you said, I was engaged for my special qualifications with respect to the people you're after. I . . . I made myself available because they must be stopped. The Legion must be destroyed! But I was brought up very gently, Mr. Helm, and suddenly I find myself working with men, and even women, whose whole outlook is so different from the humanitarian attitude I was taught as a girl. . . ."

"You find yourself in a den of snarling wolves, is that it?"

She smiled faintly. "Yes. And who, by reputation, is one of the most wolfish of the senior canines of this killer-pack with which I find myself associating? Can you blame me for treating you with, let's say, a little reservation?''

I looked at her grimly. "If that's a little reservation, I'd hate to be around when you really put the chill on somebody, Delgado. But okay, let's say my apology and your explanation are both accepted. On to business. What's the big news that's so important that you couldn't pass it over the phone, you had to bring it here yourself?''

"The Caribbean Legion of Liberty is probably planning to hold a full-scale Council meeting very soon. Do you find that interesting?''

I whistled softly. "Yes, indeed. Where?''

"Probably in San Juan, Puerto Rico. They seem to have a command post of some kind there. I can't give you the address yet, I don't have all the data, but more are coming in all the time.''

"The purpose of this gathering?''

"I don't know that, either. Maybe they want to plan their next atrocity. Or maybe you're making them nervous. Two of the three people involved in the Mariposa bombing died the other day. Two members of their Council died last night. That's too recent to be reflected in my figures, but they could be getting together to plan effective countermeasures. Of course I'm just guessing.'' She shook her head ruefully. "I'm not even certain the meeting will take place; I'm extrapolating from very skimpy data at the moment. But it's statistically enough of a possibility that I thought you'd like to know so that you could make some contingency plans.''

"Plans including you?''

"Yes. It is felt in Washington that you will need my local knowledge.''

I shrugged. "Actually, there's nothing I like better than having a pretty girl guide show me the sights of a foreign land. But you're going to have to get along with Sandy.

171

She's still the only person on our side who knows the bomb-throwing blonde by sight; and I've got private reasons for wanting to keep an eye on her until things settle down."

Dana Delgado smiled faintly. "It should be an interesting *ménage à trois*. Very well, I promise to be good."

"What are the indicators pointing towards a meeting?"

She said, "Several Council members I've been tracking on the computer have disappeared from their usual haunts; a couple have already turned up in Puerto Rico. Dominic Morales has also been seen there recently—well, a week ago. I hope to have the date and the meeting place for you fairly soon. With that information, you *lobos* should be able to make a very good killing."

For a girl who claimed to have been brought up gently, she showed a lot of satisfaction at the thought.

CHAPTER 18

OUTSIDE, it was a modest white frame house with a green roof, set under some large trees—I identified the big one shading the walk, tentatively, as an oak—in the middle of a lawn that had only a few dead leaves on it, meaning, at this time of year, that somebody'd been doing a lot of conscientious raking. Some of the neighboring lawns were pretty well littered.

Inside, it was a shrine.

"Come in, come in," said Mrs. Anson. She was a

thin woman in her sixties with blue-white hair carefully arranged about her head. She was wearing a flowered cotton dress and low white sandals that looked comfortably worn and showed the reinforced toes of her stockings. She ushered us into the living room. "You are the Mr. Helm who called? And this is the young lady who was married to your . . . Oh, my dear. I see that you suffered more than a bereavement; you were badly hurt yourself!" She was looking at the scar almost hidden by Sandra's growing hair.

"I'm all right now," Sandra said. "Yes, I'm his daughter-in-law."

"And those devils won't let you alone? It isn't enough what they did to you the first time?" Mrs. Anson raised her voice and called up the stairs. "They're here, Wally. Wally, did you hear me? They're here."

"Coming."

"He's a little deaf. You have to shout," Mrs. Anson said to us. "Oh, yes, that's our Belinda. Isn't she lovely? She liked having her picture taken. We are grateful. It helps. It's as if she's still with us, a little. We keep her room upstairs like it was when she went away to college. Afterwards, you know, she went to New York and did modeling for a while, but she was a good girl and you know how they are in New York. She wouldn't put up with any of *that*, I can tell you, so she came back and took the job with the insurance company and got that little place of her own although why she wanted to pay all that rent—aren't rents *awful* these days?—when she knew we'd be so happy to have her living at home . . . Oh, there you are, Wally. Here they are, the ones who called. Mr. and Mrs. Helm. I showed it to you in the morning paper. She was married to a boy who was . . . was murdered like our Belinda; and Mr. Helm was the boy's father. And they're still after her, they almost killed her again last night, isn't it awful?"

"Yes, I read the story."

It took me a moment to focus my attention on Mr. Walter Anson; I had a hard time looking away from the endless collection of photographs that hung on the living-room walls and stood, in expensive frames, on every available piece of furniture including the coffee table, the end tables by the sofa, and the upright piano at the end of the room. They ranged from tiny amateur snapshots to giant professional enlargements and traced the development of Linda Anson from a crawling baby in diapers, to a blonde and blue-eyed little girl with very long straight hair and braces on her teeth, to a startlingly pretty teenager, to a real beauty. A little too knowing, perhaps, a little too skillful at presenting herself to the camera, but still so lovely it was hard to stop looking.

I shook the hand of the rather short man who'd entered the room. "It's good of you to let us come here and bother you, Mr. Anson."

It was hard to see how the two of them could have produced a Linda Anson, but you never know what those genes and chromosomes are going to do. Still, the thin, plain woman and the small, bald man weren't the dam and sire I'd have picked if I'd been breeding for beauty. He was wearing a white shirt, dark trousers that looked like part of a suit and bagged at the knees, and well-worn black shoes that needed polishing.

Mr. Anson spoke abruptly. "No," he said. "No, it is not good of me. You will find no help here."

Mrs. Anson said, "Wally, please . . ."

Her husband said, "No, I must speak. Normally I would not have wanted to meet with you, Mr. Helm, or your daughter-in-law, even though you have both felt the same hurt as we have. It is not a pain that can be shared. But I read the newspaper, and I read between the lines of the story, and I know what you are trying to do. I know because of course the same evil, angry thoughts came to me, right after Belinda . . . right afterwards. I suppose it comes to everyone in such a situation. So I told myself, *Walter, you must see these poor misguided souls. You must try to save them from the sin from which you, yourself, were saved only by the Word.*'' He drew a long breath, looking up at me. His eyes were very bright behind his horn-rimmed glasses. He went on harshly: "Vengeance is not for us, Mr. Helm. Do not seek it for yourself, and do not lead this innocent young girl into a vain search for a retribution that is not hers or yours to bestow. It must come from Elsewhere. It will come, that I assure you, but it is not our place to deliver it. We cannot usurp such powers. Leave them to the One to whom they belong. . . .''

Outside, as we made our way down the walk, a single leaf came drifting down from the great overhanging tree. I stepped aside and caught it. Definitely an oak. Not bad for a man brought up in piñon country. I might even recognize a maple leaf if you handed me a good specimen. I laid the oak leaf gently on a small pile that had been raked together but not picked up yet. Halfway up the block, a young man in jeans was fiddling with the windshield wipers of an undersized white Chevrolet. He made a certain gesture as he got into his car, letting me know that the Porsche was still safe to drive.

"Phew!" said Sandra. "Well, you're not going to get any recruits in that house!"

"The trouble with people who're going to wait for God to do the job," I said, "is that we always seem to wind up having to do His work for Him."

"That's awfully close to blasphemy, Matt."

"I know. I never finished Sunday school and I guess it shows. But Mr. Anson wouldn't be calling you an innocent young girl if he'd seen you with that flop-open dressing gown this morning. And what was the idea of all those dears and darlings?''

175

Sandra giggled. "Did I embarrass you, I hope? That's what you get for serving up beautiful brunettes for breakfast. Where do we go next?"

"I thought we'd take a look at Pirate Williams' boat yard."

The Pirate's Lair Marina and Boat Yard was out of town; we had to drive well up the island to reach it. Located in a cove and surrounded by summer homes, it was a forlorn sight. Somehow there's nothing as deserted-looking as a marina without boats. Well, almost without boats. A waterlogged wooden rowboat that had once been painted green was tied up at the dinghy dock, and a white cabin cruiser in the thirty-five- to forty-foot class was secured at the end of one of the piers; it carried outriggers so perhaps you'd call it a sportfisherman. The seagulls had taken it over and staked their claim in the usual way. Otherwise the docks were empty and looked as if hungry marine organisms would have the supporting pilings eaten up fairly soon.

To one side was an enormous metal boatshed for smaller boats, the kind that are launched when they're wanted and picked up again and stuck on a shelf or rack when the owner is through boating for the day. An oversized forklift was rusting outside the big doors. A neglected Travelift stood over the rectangular basin where the big boats had come in to be picked up with slings and parked on the nearby concrete for bottom work or trundled off into the outdoor storage area. A few shabby hulls still rested over there inside the chainlink fence. A low, unmarked building was presumably the machine shop; another one was marked OFFICE at one end and SHIP'S STORE at the other. A fairly complete facility; it seemed a pity to let it fall apart.

"The way this fence looks," Sandra said as we stood by the gate, "we can probably find a place to crawl under it if you want a closer look."

"You'd get those nice white pants dirty," I said. "Anyway, I don't want to look, I just want to be seen looking."

"What does that mean?"

I reached up to give a friendly pat to the faded sign overhead, which showed a cheerful rascal of a buccaneer with a black eyepatch and a cocked hat. I led the way back to the Porsche parked at the side of the access road; the marina's parking lot was inside the fence.

Driving away, I said, "Look, we're not detectives; we're just going through the investigative motions while we wait for our presence and Laurel Bennington's story to stir things up around here."

"You mean, you're not really interested in Mr. Howard 'Pirate' Williams and his possible drug connections?"

"Frankly, I don't give a hoot about his connections, if any. As I told friend Tallman, the happy stuff is not my business. Oh, I suppose if I stumbled onto a neon-lit clue, I might pass it onto Tom Benison, the guy who dropped in after Tallman left, the other night in Savannah. He works for a real law enforcement agency, unlike Tallman's half-baked panty raiders. But I'd do it only if I felt that having Benison's people snooping around here wouldn't interfere with my own mission Frankly, I consider terrorism a much more important threat than drugs; and I'm not going to jeopardize my chances of wiping out the people I'm after just so Benison, or Tallman either, can get a few lousy pushers off the street. There will always be more where those came from."

"There will be more terrorists, too."

"Maybe," I said, "but I'm cynical enough to think that terrorism can be contained if we make it too risky, because there's no money in it. The number of people, these days, who'll die for a cause, good or bad, is much smaller than the number of folks who'll stick their necks way out for a profitable business like drugs." I shrugged.

"Anyway, I don't think we're going to get much closer to the CLL by digging up dirt on Pirate Williams, or Linda Anson, either. It's just a way of staying visible while we wait for things to break."

Sandra frowned. "I don't quite understand what you're trying to say, Matt."

I grinned. "Maybe I don't quite either. Except that we've got to keep our priorities straight. What we're after is the Caribbean Legion of Liberty, not the solutions to a lot of local mysteries, real or imaginary. Delgado has her computer working on a promising lead. If her microchips come through for us, I want to be ready."

Sandra grimaced. "Ready with a scapegoat like Daddy?"

I said, "So far, I've heard nothing to indicate that what he did for us, and himself, has got your pop into any trouble. Angelita Johansen's two sidekicks are listed as unmourned casualties of the Florida drug wars and there's no reason to think they won't stay that way." I glanced at her. "Incidentally, the game now stands at seven to thirteen."

She frowned. "Game?"

"We figured that they'd made thirteen points in three bombings, right? Deads a point apiece; woundeds don't count. And you toted up our score yesterday and made it five. Well, you can add two to that. Arthur Galvez and Howard Koenig were taken out last night on my orders."

She started to ask a question and stopped. "Oh, those were the two members of the Council. . . ."

"Right. So we're still behind, but gaining. And I haven't had the slightest protest from my conscience, not a twinge."

"Which just goes to prove that it doesn't exist, as I told you." Sandra shivered. "To call it a game is disgusting, Matt. Like those body counts in Vietnam."

"If they're dead, they're dead. Counting won't hurt them. And your problem is that you've got the strange idea these are people we're talking about. We're People, honey. Those are Enemies. A different species entirely. Open season."

"That's a convenient way to think, if you can manage it. I can't." She grimaced. "But I can't forget La Mariposa, either. What does that make me, a schizo?"

I said, "No, just a normal human being, unlike some. But in answer to your original question, yes, I'm looking for a scapegoat, somebody to carry the ball while I run interference. Let's find out if this scion of New England nobility, Jerome Elliot, fills the bill. Maybe he'll see us at his office."

CHAPTER 19

WE never got to see the offices of the Elliot Manufacturing Company. After keeping me on hold for several minutes, a secretary came back on the line and informed me that Mr. Jerome Elliot, Jr., would meet us for lunch at a place called the Chowder Hut. Noon sharp. She didn't say if he planned to pick up the bill. If he was a real chip off the old block, he probably wouldn't; those old New England merchants and manufacturers didn't get rich buying meals for nosy strangers.

From the gas station phone I could see Sandra giving the Porsche tender loving care, filling the tank, cleaning the windshield and rear window, and even opening the engine compartment back there to check the oil. She was wearing a black silk blouse, and her white slacks fit her nicely—no fashionably baggy bloomers for Mrs. Helm, Jr. I told myself I liked tall blondes and to hell with sturdy little females with shorn black hair. I made a second call, to the contact number, and asked to have the rendezvous covered. At this stage of a mission dealing with folks who got their kicks blowing up restaurants it seemed unwise to keep a lunch date without taking a few precautions.

"All set?" Sandra asked as I returned to the car.

"Check. Linda Anson's dream man is meeting us for lunch. I wonder why."

Sandra frowned. "What do you mean?"

I said, "We have no official standing that Elliot knows about, and he must be pretty damn tired of people asking him about last spring's explosive incident. Why should he give us the time of day? Even if he's a little curious about a fellow victim and wants to see you, why make a lunch of it? He could have had us in his office, answered our questions politely, and got rid of us in ten minutes."

"I don't think you understand." Sandra was very serious. "It's like a club, a very exclusive club."

I said, "I've seen things go boom a few times myself, ma'am."

"It's different for you, it's your business," she said. "You play games with . . . with death all the time. For us peaceful citizens to get that kind of a look into hell is a very significant experience. It changes everything. I think maybe Jerome Elliot wants to talk to somebody who's been there, too." Sandra hesitated. "Let me handle him, Matt. I have a hunch, after looking at all those glamour shots at the Ansons'. . . . Let me ask the questions, please."

180

"I never argue with anybody's hunches. Carry on, as they say in the navy."

We killed a little time sightseeing; then Sandra looked up the restaurant in the guidebook and navigated us to the address given, but we had a hard time finding a place to leave the car—the parking problem is no closer to being solved in Newport than anywhere else. The Chowder Hut turned out to be a self-consciously gloomy saloon-type establishment with a long, old-fashioned bar and butcher-block tables that would have looked more authentic if they hadn't been sealed in plastic.

Although we were right on time, noon sharp, there was no Elliot there to greet us. He had a table reserved, however, but I didn't like it. Even though Trask's people were supposed to be covering us, I didn't like it. I had us moved into a corner where I could put my back against a wall. Wild Bill Hickok had once, just once, made the mistake of sitting with his back to the door. I'd hate to make him feel, wherever he is, that he'd died in vain. Even sipping slowly, we had time to reduce the liquor levels in our glasses significantly, and watch the place fill up, before a blow-dried young businessman came marching in briskly, consulted the headwaiter, and was directed our way. I rose and shook hands with him and was told that he was Jerry. I told him that I was Matt and that Sandra was Sandra.

Along with his breezy, first-names-only style, Elliot had some other informal habits; and we got to watch him strip for action, removing the coat of his expensive gray suit and arranging it neatly on the back of his chair, unbuttoning his vest and shirt collar, pulling his tie down to half mast, and finally sitting down with a sigh of relief. To me, it always seems like a weird performance, undressing in a public restaurant, but more and more of them are doing it. A gesture of rebellion against the three-piece suit, I suppose. It must be nice to find an easy

181

revolution, one that can be won just by sitting down to lunch bravely in your shirtsleeves. A waiter placed a drink before him. He helped himself to a healthy slug, eyeing Sandra with interest.

"So you're the girl who almost got blown up last night," he said. There was an odd intentness in the way he looked at her, and I remembered her remark about an exclusive club; I guess he was searching for signs of the trauma they shared, beyond the obvious scar. He went on: "That's twice for you, the paper said. Well, once was enough for me; but we both carry the terrorist brand, don't we? My right shoulder looks as if somebody'd played tic-tac-toe on it with a sharp knife."

Sandra said, "At least we're still alive. That makes us the lucky ones, I guess. So far lucky, anyway. Maybe they'll get me next time, the bastards. I'd like to tie them all into chairs, the whole lot of them, in a nice circle, and put a big bomb in the middle of the circle, and let them sit there watching the fuse burning down very, very slowly while I look on from a safe distance, laughing fit to kill as they mess their pants and scream for mercy. Mercy? After they killed my husband like that? Well, you must hate them as much as I do, after what happened to your girl."

Her savagery startled me; it was out of character. She saw me looking at her and closed one eye minutely. I realized that she was playing her hunch. Something about the dead Linda Anson or the live Jerry Elliot made this approach seem promising to her.

I gave him a sharper scrutiny. He looked pretty stock to me, right off the young-executive shelf. There was quite a bit of hair, so meticulously arranged it made me remember Tallman's tough, no-nonsense crew cut with nostalgia. It was light brown with chestnut glints that might or might not be real. The face it framed so carefully was boyish with a cute little cleft in the chin and a slightly upturned nose. Whatever the origin of the hair color, the freckles were genuine. If he could have played a guitar, he'd have made his fortune as a rock-and-roll idol of the wholesome, as opposed to the degenerate, variety. But the hazel eyes were uneasy, he was a little too hasty with his Scotch or whatever, and his response was a little slow.

"Hate? Well, naturally I hate those SOBs; but you've got it wrong about Linda. She wasn't my girl. I mean . . ." Elliot grimaced. "We used to go together, certainly. But that was back when we were all kids together. That night at the Silver Conch was, well, just a friendly date for old times' sake. I was getting married the next month." He made another wry face. "Hell, the way everybody acted afterwards, you'd think getting blown up with a girl was the same as being caught in bed with her!"

"What happened?" Sandra asked. "About the wedding, I mean."

"Oh, it went through on schedule." He gave his boyish grimace again. "Rally around the flag, boys and girls, even if the groom's picture just hit the front pages alongside that of the town tramp and he has to march up the aisle with his arm in a sling to remind everybody of his indiscretion. Janet is a very loyal girl."

"That's your wife?" Sandra asked.

"Yes. Janet Whiteley as was. Very fine family, the Whiteleys, but the old Puritan blood pumps strongly through their arteries." He took a sip of his drink and looked down at the glass and shook his head ruefully. "I'll have to do penance for this, I'm supposed to have rejected the Demon Rum, but I couldn't face talking about . . . about it cold sober."

"About the bombing?" Sandra asked.

"That's what you came here to hear about, wasn't it?" His voice was a little sulky. "Well, I've told everybody else, why not you? As far as I was concerned, the whole thing took only a second or two. We were sitting there talking and sipping what was left of our wine, waiting for dessert, when something hit me in the back and right shoulder. There was a kind of wave of heat and sound, not really a noise, if you know what I mean, just a great, deafening, numbing shock.''

He glanced at Sandra and she said, ''I know.''

''It was like a nightmare,'' Elliot went on. ''I mean, it was *unreal*. One moment we were talking politely over our wine; the next, I was feeling my shoulder and back blasted by this incredible force and watching bug-eyed as Linda's face and dress . . . well, they were simply ripped right off her. At least that was the way it seemed: shreds of flesh and rags of cloth—and blood, lots of blood—kind of streaming away from her like when one of those creatures disintegrates in a horror movie. And glass, lots of glass. I remembered wondering where all that glass was coming from, even as I was being hurled on top of her along with the table and everything on it. The next thing I knew, I was in the hospital.'' He glanced at Sandra. ''Well, you know what it's like. You've been through it.''

She said, ''Yes. I try not to remember.''

He shrugged. ''Why bother to try? It's there like the scars. It may fade a bit, but we'll never get rid of it completely. I can still see . . .'' He stopped and gulped down the last of his drink and signaled a waiter for a refill. He went on: ''What really happened was, there was one of those serving stands behind me and a little to the right, you know, one of the folding jobs with a tray on it. There were some dirty dishes and stuff on the tray, and a big glass pitcher of water. Well, the explosion picked it all up and threw it at us. I got chopped up by the flying china and they tell me I had a fork sticking into my shoulder like a spear. Linda took the heavy water pitcher right in the face; it kind of exploded when it hit.

It fractured her skull in addition to all the superficial damage, if you want to call *that* superficial. They kept her alive for a couple of days, but she never regained consciousness. Perhaps it was just as well she never knew what had been done to her.'' He was silent for a moment; then he shivered slightly and reached out for the fresh drink that had been placed in front of him. He tasted it and set it down. ''Maybe we'd better order. I've got to see somebody at the office at one. They have chowder, chowder, and more chowder. Oyster, clam, fish, you name it. Very substantial; one bowl is a meal and a half. But if you can't take chowder, they serve a pretty good hamburger.''

Everybody settled for clam chowder. It turned out to be very good, the creamy New England product rather than the thinner Manhattan variety; and we didn't talk much as we shoveled it out of the outsized bowls.

''Reminds me of picnics on the beach when I was a kid,'' Elliot said at last, sitting back with a sigh of satisfaction. ''We'd dig the clams ourselves at low tide and steam them in seaweed.''

''Was Linda a picnic girl?'' Sandra asked.

Elliot laughed shortly. ''Not so you'd notice. Janet was—we all grew up together—but Linda! Gripe, gripe, gripe. Sand in her shoes. Bugs in her hair. But, God, she was pretty even way back then!''

Sandra spoke carefully: ''If somebody showed you how to get a crack at this outfit, the Caribbean Legion, to pay them back for what they did to her . . .''

He laughed again, short and sharp. ''You don't know how ridiculous that suggestion is!'' Then he realized that he'd betrayed more than he'd intended, and he went on hastily: ''I mean . . .''

''You mean she was blackmailing you, don't you?'' Sandra said.

There was a long silence. At last Elliot licked his lips and asked, "How did you know?"

"I saw her pictures at her parents' house. Lovely, but quite immoral and unscrupulous. Ordinary standards of human behavior were not for her." Sandra shrugged. "Besides, why else would you jeopardize your impending marriage by allowing yourself to be seen in public with a woman you yourself just called the town tramp? You wouldn't have called her that if you were still fond of her, so it could hardly have been the friendly farewell date you claimed. She must have twisted your arm in some way to make you buy her a dinner in one of the best restaurants in town."

Elliot shook his head. "You're a smart girl, Sandra, and you've got the basic idea all right, but you missed a little on the details. Linda actually wanted us to meet at a shabby little roadhouse she knew; but with my wedding only a month away I wasn't going to get involved in any sneaky, back alley assignations with a girl Janet detested. If I had to see Linda—and she made it sound imperative—it was safest doing it right out in the open in the Silver Conch."

Sandra said dryly, "Not so safe after all, as it turned out; but you couldn't know that a gang of Caribbean fanatics would join the party."

Elliot ignored that. He said, "You've done some pretty good guessing; you might as well hear the rest. It was something that happened a good many years ago. Linda got pregnant. It could have been mine. She said it was. I hit my folks for enough money to pay for the abortion without telling them why I needed it. I went with her to where it was easy and legal, never mind where. Linda had the evidence, all the bills with my name on them. And Janet is pretty straitlaced—I told you about those puritanical Whiteleys—and she's always felt strongly

186

about all that right-to-life stuff, even before they started calling it that. She knew about Linda and me, of course, it must have been pretty obvious at the time; but a long-ago love affair was one thing. A secret pregnancy and abortion might have been harder for her to accept. At least Linda thought I'd be willing to pay to have the information suppressed."

"What did she want the money for?"

"Thirty-five thousand was the figure," Elliot said. He glanced at me when I whistled, and smiled thinly. "Yes, Linda was never a piker. She didn't say why she needed it, exactly, but I got the impression that she'd played one of her gold-digger games with a gentleman in New York who wasn't a true gentleman. Few of them are, in New York. Just what he'd been buying and she'd been selling wasn't quite clear—beautiful as she was, I can't see anybody paying thirty-five grand just to sleep with her, but she'd held out on him in some way, and he wanted his money back, the cheapskate."

"Could it have been a gambling debt?" Sandra asked.

Elliot shrugged. "I suppose so. It wasn't one of her vices back when I was going with her, but she picked them up fast." His voice was bitter, the disillusioned voice of a man remembering an angel with shop-soiled wings. He went on: "Of course she'd already spent the money. The man apparently told her that if she didn't pay up by a certain date, he'd send some of his friends around to see her with brass knuckles. That's why she fled from New York and came back here hoping he couldn't find her. However, he tracked her down; she'd just got a call from him reminding her that her time was almost up. So thirty-five grand, please, or Janet learns the worst about the man she's about to marry." He grimaced. "Of course, with Linda, you never knew. That menacing gentleman in New York, who was no gentleman, could have been quite imaginary. She could just have developed a compulsive desire for a sable coat.''

He swallowed the last of his second drink and looked around for a waiter, but changed his mind and shoved the glass away from him. People were leaving now, finished with their meals.

''I've got to get back,'' Elliot said with a glance at his watch. ''I told her no deal, of course. I mean, I couldn't let it get to be a habit. That long-ago abortion I paid for was all right; she'd been entitled to all the help she needed under those circumstances. But now . . . I couldn't have her thinking she had something on me and coming around with her hand out every time she wanted a fur coat, or more gambling money, or whatever. Anyway, I said no. I told her I'd see Janet myself that very night and tell her all about it; and Miss Linda Anson would be smart to settle for a good dinner and forget the whole thing.''

''I bet she didn't like that,'' Sandra said.

''She didn't.'' Elliot's voice was grim. ''I hadn't realized what kind of a person . . . I think she must have been on something. She hadn't drunk very much, just the wine, but maybe it reacted with something she'd taken earlier to prepare her for the interview. Anyway, she started in on me in a nice, low voice, smiling at me fondly across the table, and telling me things about myself and herself. . . . She made it all dirty, everything we'd shared when we were younger. I'd been very much in love with her, and she told me what a prize sap she'd thought me, mooning around her like an affectionate puppy. Then she got to work on Janet. I suppose she was jealous, she never liked losing a man to another woman even if she didn't want him anymore; and she said some pretty vicious things. By the time she was through . . . well, as far as I was concerned, that New York hoodlum

188

could have her if he made it quick; otherwise I'd do the job for him.''

"Really?" Sandra asked.

He stared at her for a moment; then he grinned boyishly. "Well, probably not really. But I was pretty angry; angry enough to tell myself I'd like to kill her. And she knew I was thinking it. She was laughing at me because she knew I'd never have the guts. I can still see her sitting there with her head thrown back, laughing, when the blast . . . happened. She must have died thinking that in some weird way, angry as I was, I'd managed to do it after all. Get Elliot mad enough and he blows right up like a bomb. Unreal!" He shook his head. "But you can see why I'm not burning to join your crusade against this Legion outfit. Somehow, that bomb of theirs straightened out my life and blew away the secrets that could have wrecked my marriage—I told Janet everything after I woke up in the hospital. She didn't like it, of course, but she got over it, and we're getting along fine." He rose and started buttoning his vest. "Well, it's been nice talking to someone who's been through the same violent experience, even if she's too damn good at worming secrets out of people. Good-bye, Sandra . . . Matt.''

We watched him go, pulling on his jacket and settling his tie as he crossed the restaurant to the desk, paid, and disappeared out the door. I apologized silently for my earlier thoughts about stingy New Englanders.

CHAPTER 20

SANDRA sipped her coffee thoughtfully, still watching the door through which Elliot had vanished.

"Poor guy," she said. "He's still in love with her."

I stared at her. "Then I'd hate to hear him talking about a girl he hated. Considering that the wench is dead, he sure didn't pull many punches."

"That's what I mean. He's trying to prove to everybody, including himself, that she never really meant a thing to him. But he's not doing a very good job, at least not on himself." She finished her coffee and set down the cup. "Well, aren't you going to tell me what a great interrogator I turned out to be?"

"You were terrific. All you need now is to be checked out on the rack and thumbscrews, and the needle full of scopolamine or whatever they use nowadays."

She made a face at me. "Who do we tackle next?"

"I don't know. I was hoping somebody'd make a move that would give us a lead to follow. . . ."

"Mr. Helm?"

I looked up to see the headwaiter. At the moment he wasn't looking at me but at Sandra, checking up; clearly he'd been told to look for a gent escorting a young lady with a damaged scalp.

"Yes?" I said.

He turned his attention on me. "You're Mr. Helm?

There's a phone call for you. You can take it at the desk.''

"Thanks." I went over there and accepted the phone the cashier offered me. "Helm."

A voice I didn't recognize gave me a code word I did. Then it said, "Call Control. Repeat, call Control."

"Check." I gave the phone back to the cashier, thanked her, and returned to the table. I put down some money, not knowing whether or not Elliot had taken care of the tip. "We're on our way," I said.

"Trouble?" Sandra asked, rising.

"Probably. I've got to find a pay phone. Let's go see what the man has to say."

Ten minutes later I was standing in a corner of the lobby of a motel just outside town listening to Trask's voice giving me the latest news: There had been a violent explosion in a small house in Old Saybrook, Connecticut. Listening, I had a view of the motel parking lot through a nearby window, but I couldn't see the shady corner where the Porsche was parked.

"I suppose it's the house I think it is."

"That's right."

"Damage?"

"Total. Fire helped. The police are trying to determine whether or not the dead bodies found in the debris are those of the owners of record, a certain Matthew Helm, Junior, and his wife Cassandra. Washington says we'd better straighten them out before they put out too much wrong publicity."

"How many dead bodies?" I asked.

"At present they've only got enough pieces to tell it wasn't dogs or cats and that there were more than one of them since few people come with two left hands. It was quite a blast. A long Ford van, black or navy, with the dark windows you can see out of but not into, has been hanging around; the neighbors had seen it several times

191

and thought about calling the police. It was parked half a block away before the explosion; it wasn't there afterwards. A witness thinks it had an out-of-state license plate, but she's uncertain how far out of state. In other words, all we know is it wasn't Connecticut, and I wouldn't be too sure about that. You know how witnesses are.''

I said, "We drove by that house yesterday."

"Yes, I read the report of the agent covering you."

"We didn't go inside. Officially, if the cops ask, we didn't go in because it was getting late and we had about sixty miles left to go to Newport to pick up our hotel reservation. Unofficially, just between us, we stayed clear because we'd just headed over there on the spur of the moment, without giving you a chance to have the place checked out. Maybe we were smart; maybe the house was already boobytrapped at that time. Or maybe, seeing that we'd only had a quick look at the outside, the CLL figured Sandra was bound to have us go back for a thorough inspection tour, later. After all, it was her honeymoon cottage, more or less; and she'd been away for weeks. So they sent somebody to leave her a belated wedding present, but he got careless with it and blew himself up, along with a friend. Or she did; it could have been Angelita Johansen again. That blonde gets around. That's one possibility. Another is that, regardless of when the whiz-bang was put there for us, presumably by the CLL, it was set off by unauthorized visitors of some kind, maybe just unlucky burglars. After all, a house left standing empty that long, these lawless days, is asking for a break-in. A van would be just what they'd be driving to carry away the televisions and microwave ovens."

Trask said, "Well, it'll take the authorities a while to put the human jigsaw puzzles together and make the identifications, assuming that they can find enough pieces. Meanwhile, Washington feels that, since she's in the area, Mrs. Helm should make an appearance, terribly distressed by the destruction of her home, of course, giving you a chance to find out more about it.''

''Check,'' I said. ''In the meantime, keep an eye on our Newport hotel room; we don't want that to go up in smoke and flames when we get back tonight and open the door.''

When I returned to the Porsche, Sandra had the windows open and her seat reclined; she seemed to be asleep, but her purse was on her lap. She reached for it when she heard me come up, slipping her hand inside. In spite of the nonviolent attitude she tried to maintain, the kid displayed a nice sense of self-preservation, unlike the movie heroines who never dream of reaching for a weapon even when they're being chased around a haunted house by a slobbering maniac with a cleaver in his hand and murder on his mind.

''Oh, it's you,'' she said, closing the purse and raising the back of her seat. ''This business of hush-hush phone calls is making me jumpy. . . . What's the matter?''

I hesitated, not knowing how much the Old Saybrook house had meant to her. Then I told her. She was silent for a long time. At last she gave me a crooked little smile.

''Well, that's one way of getting out of a housecleaning,'' she said. ''I suppose I do have to look at it. What's left of it. Let's go.''

Pretty soon we were off the Rhode Island islands and back on the Rhode Island mainland. We picked up good old I-95, the highway that had brought us clear up from Florida. It took us back into Connecticut, where we drove past Mystic where they keep the tall ships and New London where they keep the submarines. Connecticut has a weird law: You can't pass on the right on a four-lane

193

highway. Any slow jerk who feels like holding up all traffic in one direction can just amble down the left lane, legally blocking that half of the highway; and lots of them do. Approaching the Connecticut River with Old Saybrook, on the far bank, almost in sight, we ran into a traffic jam: The bridge was under repair. We were pretty well hardened to highway-construction zones by this time, but this was a prize specimen and held us up for twenty minutes.

As we picked up speed again west of the river, Sandra looked up abruptly and said, ''Oh, you should have taken that exit!''

I said, ''I know but—don't look around—we have a big black van with dark windows about four cars back.''

She glanced at me sharply. ''The one you told me about? The one they told you about?''

I shrugged. ''The world is full of black vans, but let's check him out. I guess all roads to the left here just go south a few miles to Long Island Sound. We need more room. You've lived here, think hard. Give me a nice little twisty road to the right without too many towns and houses on it. Preferably one you remember pretty well so you can call the turns.''

''Twisty little secondary roads are what Connecticut does best.'' She thought for a moment. ''Three exits up the line . . . no, two, now. There's a stretch of little suburbia near the turnpike, but then you get into some fairly empty woods for a while. . . . There, up ahead.''

''I see it. Don't worry about the guy behind unless I tell you; I've got him in the mirrors. Just watch the road ahead, and try to remember what's coming next, and keep me posted.''

''Take it easy going down the ramp; there's a stop sign at the bottom. It's a blind intersection and they come through fast.''

''Check. Here we go.''

I did it by the book, using the turn signal and slowing down cautiously in the deceleration lane before heading down the ramp to a complete halt at the stop sign. The driver of the van, following, had no choice but to pull up behind us. I kept an eye on the mirrors, but no windows rolled down back there and no weapons appeared. The dark glass gave the vehicle a blind look, as if there really wasn't anybody inside, as if it were just a piece of malevolent machinery tracking us of its own evil volition. I used my turn signal again like a good boy, waited for a pickup truck with local plates to pass, and headed north along the two-lane asphalt road behind it. The van followed.

I said, "Looks as if he's our man. He's coming right along with us."

"How did he pick us up?"

"He must have figured we'd be called to the scene once the house went bang. There's only the one bridge we'd be likely to use across the Connecticut River, coming from Newport; the next one's way upstream. All he had to do was wait somewhere along the approaches for a flashy little sports car to come zipping by."

"Watch out for kids and dogs along here. . . . Okay, now you can goose it a bit if you like."

It was a scrubby little hardwood forest with a few houses spotted along the road here and there. The asphalt seemed to have been laid right on the original wagon track winding through the trees. I took the speed up a little. The van followed suit. The pickup ahead turned off into a narrow lane, leaving the road to us.

I said, watching the mirrors, "Brace yourself for the old movie routine. You know, the one where the car behind goes bang into the car ahead. . . . Here he comes, hang on now."

I watched the square black front of the van coming up fast in the mirrors. Double clutching out of old habit, I

195

dropped down a gear and waited until his heavy bumper was almost into us before I hit the accelerator. The Porsche squatted under the surge of power, the tires chirped, and we jumped clear with a few inches to spare. I made it look jerky and panicky, with a lot of fishtailing. I eased off as soon as possible as if those high speeds—I guess we hit all of sixty at one point—frightened me terribly on that narrow road.

Sandra asked calmly, "Who do you think it is, Matt?"

I shrugged. "I'd say somebody who doesn't like us."

"Funny!"

The guy behind, whoever he was, started gaining once more, really pushing the heavy van after us. It was angry driving and it was bad driving; he was abusing the tires, brakes, and drivetrain unnecessarily. In the bends he had the big truck heeling over like a sailboat in a high wind. I knew that in his mind he was seeing the way it always worked on TV: the car astern charging repeatedly into the bumper of the car ahead until the victim up there lost control and went flying off the road, bursting into flame in midair. Just what's going to set a car on fire before it even hits the ground, I've never figured out, but they do it all the time on the screen. Why the helpless victim never puts his foot to the firewall and gets the hell out of there, or at least gives his pursuer as good a race as he can, is another riddle I've never solved. Those movie heroes always just sit there, passive and despairing, waiting for the next big bump behind.

"What's coming up?" I asked, watching him gaining in the mirrors, letting him gain. "Cue me in."

"Wiggly stuff like this for another mile or so, then a sharp left turn at the lake. . . . Well, it's just another swampy pond, they've got dozens of them around here, but I remember this one because there are usually a couple of swans on it."

"I don't think we're going to have time for much bird-watching today. . . . Oops, here he comes again!"

We went through the routine a second time. I was kind of slow in the head, it appeared, it wasn't until the last moment that I discovered, surprise, surprise, that the nasty man was still trying to hit us. Desperately, I crashed some gears and pumped the gas pedal and got out from under, swerving all over the road in my panic. Then the gradual deceleration again as I retreated from those fearful speeds. . . .

"How far to the lake?"

"I can see the curve sign now."

"Hold tight. I'm going to try to dump him up there. . . . Come on, baby!" I whispered, watching the van grow larger in the mirrors once more. "Come to Papa, that's a good boy!"

"I can see the lake through the trees. It's a *very* sharp curve, Matt."

"Let's hope your car is as good as you say." I spoke to the image in the mirrors: "Come on, come *on*, what are you waiting for back there? Don't chicken out now!"

He came in straight and true, like a young Canada goose to a good caller with a convincing spread of decoys. I crossed my fingers, mentally; if we met traffic on the road at the wrong moment, it could get awkward. I could now see the gleam of water through the trees ahead. The curve-warning sign flashed past.

"*Now* you look back!" I said. "I'm going to be too busy to keep an eye on him. Call it out: Tell me how close he is and how fast he's gaining."

She turned in her seat. "He's coming up fast. . . . that's better," she said as I fed more gas to the Porsche mill. "But he's still gaining. Three car lengths. Two. He's getting very close, Matt. . . ."

The curve was a sharp one, all right. I held my speed as long as I dared, still praying for a clear road.

"Matt!"

I was already well down in the gears. I hit the throttle hard and cut the wheel over. The rear tires broke loose and the little car swung sharply left like an opening gate, leaving the van nothing to hit, although I thought I heard or felt a slight bumper-to-bumper contact as it plunged past us. Then the road was full of Porsche, but we were lucky, nothing came the other way as I brought it back from the left-hand ditch, and got it under control beyond the curve.

CHAPTER 21

I PULLED off onto the shoulder of the road and braked to a halt. We sat there for a minute or two catching our breaths, although I don't know why we should have needed to. The car had done all the work.

"He went right out into the pond," she said.

"Frightening the swans all to hell, no doubt."

"Well, I wasn't exactly looking for swans, but I did see a flash of white off to the side as he hit the water. Matt."

"Yes?"

She was watching me. "You've done that before, haven't you?"

I said, "They always get so obsessed with killing the guy ahead that they forget about saving the guy behind. Them." I could see that she was still feeling a certain amount of reaction, so I kept talking to steady her—and maybe myself as well. "The last time, we were in my Mazda, heading down a mountain road in New Mexico. The opposition of the moment sent a big semi after us. Their boy got overeager just like this one. He took a hundred feet of guardrail with him as he went off the cliff."

Sandra shivered. After a moment, she said, "We'd better get back there, hadn't we?"

"Why?"

"The man in the van. He's probably hurt."

I said, "I was just giving him plenty of time to drown. I hope it's a good deep lake."

But when we got there, leaving the Porsche parked well off the road and making our way down through the brush, we found that the van had by no means sunk out of sight. It had plowed its way about twenty feet out into the pond before lying down to rest, on its left side, like a tired horse. It must have thrown up a junior-grade tidal wave when it hit; mud and weeds were still oozing off it, but it was less than half submerged at the rear. While I looked for signs that somebody had waded ashore nearby, a car went by on the road behind us; but you couldn't see the wreck from up there, and the damage to the vegetation could have occurred at any time during the past day or two.

"Looks as if he's still on board," I said. "Unless he swam across the lake. I see no indications that he came out here. . . . Where are you going?" I grabbed her arm as she started down the bank.

She gave me a shocked look. "We've got to get him out, don't we? The way it's lying, he could be underwater, unconscious and drowning!"

"And it couldn't happen to a nicer guy. The sonofabitch was trying to kill us, remember?"

199

"Let me go!"

She gave a sudden lunge that, when I hauled her back by the arm, swung her against me. I grabbed her by both shoulders, intending to shake a little sense into her. I'd underestimated the power of the Florence Nightingale syndrome. I hadn't taken the precautions I'd have used instinctively struggling with a man, or a woman, I considered dangerous. She had a clear shot and she took it, kneeing me in the groin, not hard, but it doesn't take much down there. The pain was as shocking as always. I was only vaguely aware of her pulling free. I was wondering dimly how the hell I'd ever managed to get mixed up with a screwball kid who'd castrate a man who'd saved her life in order to rescue a man who'd tried to murder her.

When I managed to straighten up, she was wading out into the muddy pond, heedless of her nice white pants. I had my .38 in my hand by this time, but it was too late. She was in the line of fire and moving so erratically, as she fought her way through the muck and weeds, that I couldn't take the risk of shooting past her. Otherwise I'd have riddled the van systematically to make sure the occupant was harmless before she reached him. Of course, I could have gone charging out there bravely to drag her back to safety, but if she was right about the poor helpless victim inside, I'd be getting wet for nothing, and if I was right about the murderous bastard, I'd be dead right along with her. Mac doesn't run any suicidal agents.

I picked up the purse she'd dropped at my feet. Apparently I'd been a little premature when I'd admired her fine sense of self-preservation: She hadn't even taken her gun along on her idiot mission of mercy. After pocketing the automatic for extra firepower, and the spare clip she carried with it, I tossed the bag down the bank to join the high-heeled shoes she'd kicked off before entering the water. I took cover behind a tree from which I could rake the van from rear to front whenever I got a clear field of fire. Sandra was getting close, almost hip-deep now, working hard against the drag of the mud and the resistance of the water. I resisted the impulse to yell at her to come back; why waste the breath? She'd already made it painfully clear what her response would be.

Reaching the van, she paused a moment to catch her breath. Then she tried the handle of the big rear doors, but they were locked or stuck. After straining at the handle for a minute or two, she gave it up, and moved over a bit, and bent down to peer through the smoky glass of the right rear window. The left one was pretty well submerged.

I saw her suddenly throw herself sideways. Apparently she'd seen something hostile inside. The sound of the shot was muffled, but her gasp was not, as she clapped her hand to her left arm. She tried to run, but the gluey mud betrayed her and she fell headlong—her only sensible move since she'd put her knee into my testicles. There were two more muffled shots from inside the van, but both missed her. One made a starry hole in the black glass of the door, the other punched through the black-painted metal a foot away, near the exit hole of the first shot, the one that had winged Sandra.

I'd switched guns, since pinpoint accuracy wasn't needed here: I had no real target to shoot at. The .38 was the best weapon I had and I wanted to save it for a final showdown, if any. I used Sandra's automatic, therefore, and emptied half a clip of .380s into the van's rear doors, crouching low to send the bullets almost parallel to the water and angling them to search the interior thoroughly. This was a better gun than the last one I'd borrowed from Sonny Varek's little girl; at least it shot pretty much where it looked. It wasn't very powerful, but I had a square shot at the van doors and even a .22 will perforate car metal at that angle.

Of course our mystery murderer had a bulletproof hideout in there. All he had to do was duck under the water that partially filled his vehicle and no slug could reach him, but unless he had finny ancestors he couldn't stay under very long. For the moment, however, he wasn't shooting, as Sandra surfaced, dripping and spitting.

"Keep down!" I shouted. "Head over to your left. Work your way clear, but stay low."

There was another muffled report inside the van, and a bullet came screaming out through the already riddled doors; a hope shot that hit nothing but made a very nasty sound as it passed overhead. I gave him the rest of the .380's first clip to cover Sandra's clumsy withdrawal, spacing my shots deliberately to make it last longer.

As I was reloading, a movement in the trees made me swing around quickly. A sandy-haired young man in jeans, T-shirt, and windbreaker was heading towards the water, stripping off his jacket as he ran. Well, it was about time Trask's agent joined the battle even though his current duties were technically confined to merely following us so he could keep the Porsche from being sabotaged or boobytrapped whenever we left it. He dropped the jacket on the bank and waded out towards the floundering girl. I gave him covering fire, putting the metal-jacketed .380 slugs where I felt they would do most good, varying my aim and timing to keep the van's occupant ducking. Trask's boy helped Sandra ashore. He half led, half carried her into cover, and knelt beside her to examine her wounded arm.

That situation seemed to be under control. It was time

to put an end to this nonsense, before the neighborhood got ass-deep in cops. I moved cautiously along the shore to the right and waded out until I had a clear view of the underside of the van, exposed as it lay on its side. The gas tank was an obvious and easy target. I used Sandra's last two bullets to perforate it neatly low down, and saw the volatile fuel come spurting out of the holes. The water of the pond had already acquired a limited rainbow sheen around the wreck; now it started to spread rapidly.

"Hey, in the van," I shouted. "Come out fast before I burn you out."

There was no answer, but he could smell the stuff as well as I could—better, since he was closer. I saw the vehicle shake as he moved around in there. Then he was at the rear, working at the double doors. He had to lift one a little—the right-hand one when the van was up-right—in order to open the other. It flopped down with a sudden crash, like a station-wagon tailgate. A dark object came flying out to make a splash in the pond: a large automatic pistol. Great, but who'd guarantee he didn't have another, large or small?

I was ready with the Smith and Wesson as he came rolling out of there, picked himself up painfully, and waded ashore, a husky dark man in jeans and a gray work shirt. I hadn't wasted all the lead I'd thrown at him. He was limping and one arm hung loose. Attaining dry land, he went to his knees, first, and then fell on his face and rolled over on his back, lying there with his arms spread wide in an attitude of total helplessness. He wasn't much better as an actor than he'd been as a driver. I sloshed ashore, avoiding the spreading film of gasoline, and moved over cautiously to cover him as he lay there.

At first glance, his face was totally unfamiliar, and I

wondered who this angry stranger was and why he'd been so eager to murder me. Then I realized that I had, after all, seen this dark Latin face before, twice: once in a fuzzy photograph supplied by Trask, and before that. . . .

I remembered a boy named Antonio Morelos bleeding to death from a bullet hole in the leg. He'd had the same face fifteen years younger.

"Señor Dominic Morelos," I said. "*El Martillo*, The Hammer."

He licked his lips, but it took him a moment to work up strength enough to speak. I could see the deformed fingers of the left hand, where the Gobernador torturers had done a job on the nails. Sometimes it's hard to know who the bad guys are. And the good guys. I don't qualify, that's for certain.

"You murdered my little brother, señor," he whispered. "The woman was present also. . . ."

Hatred was in his eyes; then it was replaced by a look of shocked surprise. He coughed twice, rackingly, and a thick dark stream of blood poured from his mouth, while his eyes went blank and his body went slack. After a moment I bent down and found the hideout weapon he'd been trying to conceal from me when he rolled over on his back like that: a businesslike knife sheathed at the nape of his neck. I found that he'd actually been hit or nicked five times. The one in the lungs had done the job. Another asterisk for Dana Delgado.

When I got over to where Sandra lay, I found a situation I hadn't expected. Instead of one man watching over her, there were two.

One was the sandy-haired fellow who'd pulled her out of the pond. Wet and muddy now, he was standing against a tree with his hands in the air, peering through big horn-rimmed glasses at the other man. Fortunately, I recognized that one, or there could have been an awkward misunderstanding. I'd seen him in Savannah, one of Trask's lean young men, tanned and tough, wearing khakis and holding a .38 revolver.

"Gregertsen, sir," he said. "The recognition code is . . ."

"Never mind that crap, I recognize you," I said. "What goes on? Who's this character?"

I had the chilly feeling you get when you've taken things for granted. I'd assumed without checking that the sandy-haired boy was one of ours running to my assistance, when he could just as easily have been racing to help Morelos. Well, it was a good antidote to the cocky superagent syndrome that often hits in the wake of a victorious firefight.

Gregertsen said, "My orders were to follow you and just keep an eye on the Porsche so nobody'd tamper with it; but I saw this guy tail you from Newport. Then the van picked you up at the bridge. You were handling that okay, nice driving, but when you and the lady headed down here, and the fireworks started, and I saw this punk sneaking after you, I figured I'd better forget about watching the sports car and see if you needed a hand. Incidentally, he's clean. No weapon."

Sandra stirred weakly. "Matt, it's a big mistake. Let him go! I don't know who he is, but he helped me in spite of all the shooting. See, he even used his handkerchief to bandage my arm."

I looked down at her for a moment as she lay there, even wetter and muddier than the young man who'd rescued her, with a bloodstained cloth around her left arm.

I said, "Nobody'd know you were a respectable widow lady, the way you keep making a mess of yourself."

She seemed to take that as a statement of forgiveness, and maybe it was. "I'm sorry if I hurt you," she whispered. "But I had to do it; I couldn't let you stop me, even if it went wrong. But tell your man to put that gun away, please.''

"Sure." I made a sign to Gregertsen and he holstered his piece. I turned to the other. "We're grateful for your help," I said. "But who the hell are you and why have you been following us?"

He licked his lips. "I'm Lester," he said. "Lester Leonard. I read about you in the newspaper. I wanted to talk with you."

He was having a hard time finding a piece of dry shirt on which to wipe his spectacles. Without the glasses, his eyes looked wide and innocent. They were an indefinite gray-green color; a cowlick of the damp sandy hair fell down his forehead. His face seemed unformed, as if his mother hadn't quite got around to finishing him, before giving him birth. Pale and a little pudgy, he was clearly not a trained outdoor type like Gregertsen; I should have seen at a glance that he couldn't be one of ours.

"Who's Lester Leonard?" I asked.

"I am . . . was a friend of Linda Anson's." He put his glasses back on. I guess they helped him recognize my doubtful expression; he wasn't exactly what I'd judged to be Linda's type. "Well, not really a *friend*," he corrected himself hastily. "She hardly knew I existed, although we went to high school together. But I . . . I *admired* her, I admired her tremendously for years. When she was killed like that . . ." He stopped and cleared his throat. I saw that his weak eyes were wet behind the big glasses. He said hoarsely, "I understand from the newspaper story that you're hunting the people responsible. I want to help you. I want to help you kill them!"

Well, I'd been hoping for that kind of a break, hadn't I? That was why I'd come all the way to Newport to investigate the Silver Conch bombing, wasn't it? The fact that what I'd got was a nearsighted kid nutty enough to spend years worshiping a tramp like Linda Anson from afar was beside the point. I reminded myself that the boy might be helpless-looking but he wasn't gutless. He'd waded after Sandra when guns were firing and bullets flying, when a lot of Herculean heroes would have been lying flat in good cover and keeping their heads down. He was an odd avenging angel, but he'd do.

The swans came in at the far end of the pond and swam around for a few minutes, but then the police sirens flushed them out again.

CHAPTER 22

WE walked through the hotel parking lot and made a dash across Newport's busy main drag, proving that we were braver than a lot of visiting small-boat sailors who've merely crossed the Atlantic Ocean.

"It's up that street," Dana Delgado said, pointing, as we reached the other shore in safety against all odds. "The White Horse Tavern. I made reservations. You could say I'm celebrating. I was wondering how to get rid of the brat. Since she's a relative of yours, even if only by marriage, I thought you might object to strangulation."

It was a beautiful evening. The evening of any day in which someone has tried to kill you and failed is always beautiful, simply because you're still alive to see it; but this was really a pretty good specimen for damp and misty New England. As we climbed the steep side street, the setting sun spotlighted a large, carefully restored, old hip-roofed frame house ahead of us. I couldn't read the discreet signs at the distance, but I had a hunch they marked our destination. Delgado wouldn't have chosen to walk to the restaurant, in her high heels, if it had been much farther away.

I said, "I thought you were looking forward to our little *ménage à trois* in Puerto Rico."

She laughed. "My dear man, no woman wants to share a male with another female, even in the line of business." After a moment, she went on: "I don't really wish young Mrs. Helm any harm, but I'm just as glad they're keeping her in the hospital for a few days. She'll be safe there, and it disposes of her temporarily. . . . Reservation for Delgado," she said to the somberly dressed gent who came forward to greet us as we entered the restaurant.

"Yes, madam. This way, please."

The place had once been a comfortable residence. The big, high-ceilinged downstairs rooms were now filled with tables boasting white tablecloths and—those not yet occupied—intricately folded white napkins. Following Dana Delgado as she followed the headwaiter, I had the half-proud, half-jealous feeling that comes to a man in the company of a truly handsome woman who's being favorably appraised by all the other men present, and also by the women—although perhaps not quite so favorably.

She was wearing a dark red wool dress expensive enough to do nice things for her figure, not that it needed things done for it. The skirt was calf-length in response to the dictates of current fashion, a pleasant compromise, long enough to be dignified and graceful without concealing too much of the view. The dress had long sleeves and was quite severe in its simplicity. Well, she'd always been severe and businesslike in her dealings with me; the fact that she'd unbent enough to call my hotel room when I finally got back to Newport and invite me to dinner had been a pleasant surprise. I'd have expected her to adhere to traditional man-woman protocol and wait for the suggestion to come from me. Her dark hair was as smoothly arranged as always.

"We'd like to see the wine list," she said after we'd been seated. As the man went away, she smiled at me. "Are you thinking how terrible it is to be the guest of a managing woman? Should I let you choose the wine to make you feel masculine?"

"I feel fine. Carry on."

We went through the formalities of ordering and it took a while. She held a rather lengthy consultation over the wine list, after which the relative freshness of the various fish on the menu came up for discussion. I've eaten too many questionable meals off my lap in too many oddball places, and accompanied them with too many strange libations, to be very critical of my food or drink; but it seems to be a popular indoor sport. Although she played it well and obviously enjoyed it, I had a hunch she was also getting a kick out of putting me in my place, hinting that I was just a clumsy peasant with a gun who had to be shown how civilized people live.

Well, she was nice to look at, and I've been snooted by experts; she didn't really bother me. But I must say I missed the kid, and worried about her a little. Although she was in good hands, the wound had been a nasty one. The bullet had apparently been deformed and upset by its passage through the van door, and it had ripped things up a bit rather than just drilling a neat round hole. The doctor had also had to prospect around in there for flakes of paint and scraps of bullet jacket; and he wasn't quite sure he'd got them all, which was one reason he was keeping Sandra in the hospital for observation.

"Wouldn't you know?" she'd whispered, looking up at me from the hospital bed in New Haven, where she'd wound up after a twenty-mile ambulance ride that couldn't have been much fun. Her face was pale against the short dark hair. She'd been given enough painkiller that her eyes had an unfocused look and her voice was a little slurred. "I just get one lousy sling off and now they're going to put me in another!"

I said, "That's what you get for being a sentimental slob. Next time maybe you'll have sense enough just to let the bastard drown." I looked at the floral display on the dresser. "Who's been sending flowers?"

"Not you, that's for sure." She grinned weakly. "Lester sent them. Are you jealous?"

"Lester? Oh, the boy with the glasses."

Her grin faded. "Are you still mad at me?"

"Who's mad? It isn't my arm that's got a hole in it. This way, I get to travel to Puerto Rico all alone with a dame who's got all her hair, for a change."

"She won't have it long if I get hold of her." Sandra stared at me resentfully. "So you're going to run off with your glamour agent and leave me lying here crippled and helpless to be blown up by any stray bomber who comes along!"

"You'll be protected, day and night."

There was a little silence, then she whispered, "Take care, Matt."

"You, too."

I stood there by the bed a moment longer. There was something between us: the fact that there was nothing between us, in the popular sense of the phrase. Even if she'd written me off as an object of romance after the night she'd found her stepmother in my room, she

210

couldn't help but wonder why, if that was the kind of man I was, I hadn't at least made a try, considering the opportunities I'd had on our long trip together. Of course I'd told her I'd felt an obligation to look after her for Matthew's sake, but that didn't necessarily involve a vow of chastity. However, she was a well-adjusted young lady, and she wasn't about to go into a decline because a certain lecherous character had failed to make a pass at her. . . .

"Matt?" Delgado's voice was a little impatient.

"What? Oh, sure. Salmon is fine."

She'd brought me back to Newport, R.I. I knew that we'd already settled on some kind of a Blanc de Blanc, if I have the name straight, at thirty dollars a bottle. Now I'd given my okay to salmon prepared a special way with certain special fixings. When the negotiations had been completed, and the final waiter had gone away, Delgado raised her wineglass to me.

"Pretentious is the word," she said softly.

"What?"

"That's what you were thinking, isn't it? A pretentious bitch showing off her social graces."

"To a bloodthirsty roughneck who ought to be fed out in the barn with the other livestock, right?"

She laughed. "When we come to know each other better, we'll undoubtedly discover that we're both very fine people. So Morelos came after you to avenge his brother, as we expected."

"Yes. I guess he was hanging around waiting for me to walk into the Saybrook house and blow myself up. He wanted to see it happen. But the wrong people sneaked onto the premises and set off the fireworks prematurely. . . . Has anybody yet figured out who they were?"

Delgado nodded. "Yes. It hasn't been released yet, but

211

I got the information, to be passed to you, just before you knocked on my door back at the hotel. There were three of them. Their names were Vance, Johnson, and Spearman.''

I whistled softly. ''Vance . . . You mean that Presidential Task Force for Illicit Substances? They're the ones who blew themselves up with the CLL bomb meant for us? Tallman's little gang of snoops?''

Delgado nodded. ''Yes. Very embarrassing for certain people in Washington. They're having a hard time trying to explain what Tallman thought he was doing, breaking into your daughter-in-law's house without a warrant. They're trying to figure out what he expected to find there.''

''Find, hell!'' I said. ''He tried to plant something on the kid once before. Why should he stop with just one try? Oh, I'm sure his boys were instructed to search the premises thoroughly first in the hope of finding something. Tallman has the idea Sandra's just got to be a drug-using degenerate because of her parentage. However, in case they came up empty-handed, I'm willing to bet he gave them a little chemical evidence to hide in a not-too-obvious place so it could be discovered later under the proper incriminating circumstances. Only somebody else had been ahead of them and left something louder, and they tripped the trigger when they broke in and started poking around. . . . Tallman's got a thing about Sandra's dad, and he doesn't care who he has to frame if it gives him leverage against Sonny Varek.''

Dana Delgado hesitated. ''You have to understand something, Matt. Robert Tallman has a special reason to hate drugs and the people who deal in them, particularly Alexander Varek. A few years ago Tallman's daughter Elissa disappeared. A lovely young girl by all accounts. She was just finishing college; but suddenly

212

she dropped out of school and vanished. He found her months later, in dreadful shape, dying. He traced the drugs she'd been taking back through the pusher and dealer to the importer. Varek. He was still in business at that time."

It was such an old story, these days, that I found it hard to work up much sympathy for an Elissa Tallman who'd died because she'd chosen to play with stuff she'd been warned was dangerous. After all, Tallman wasn't the only one who'd lost a child. My son was just as dead as his daughter; but Matthew had been offered no choice and given no warning.

I said, "Seems like everybody's avenging somebody. Tallman wasn't blown up with the rest?"

"Not unless he was totally vaporized, which they say is unlikely. They could only make three bodies out of what they found in the debris." She made a little face. "Not very pleasant dinner-table conversation!"

I said, "So I don't have to look over my shoulder any longer for Dominic Morelos; but I now have Mr. Tallman to worry about seriously. Before, he was just a potential pest. I hope he doesn't have some cracked notion that I somehow arranged for his boys to wind up in little pieces, but I wouldn't bet on it."

Delgado said, "That's pretty farfetched, Matt."

I shrugged. "That's how I'm still alive, by figuring out the farfetched possibilities. But let's hope you're right. I don't want any more intramural conflicts; they raise hell in Washington."

She said, "Well, Morelos was a greater danger; at least you're free of him."

I grimaced. "Sure, but we're losing ground, statistically speaking."

"What makes you say that?"

"Yesterday, the body count was six for our side as
213

against thirteen for the Legion. Today we made one point, Morelos, but they made three: Vance, Johnson, and Spearman. So the game now stands at seven to sixteen. They've gained on us, a little.''

''Ugh, I don't like thinking of it as a game.''

I grinned. ''That's exactly what Sandra said. You girls have something in common at least. Weak stomachs.''

Delgado said firmly, ''That is enough business talk. I will now change the subject. This is the oldest operating tavern in the United States. It was originally built as a residence, in 1673. . . .''

When we came out of the White Horse Tavern, it was cooler than it had been, quite chilly in fact, and late enough that all light had gone from the western horizon. Delgado took my arm to steady herself on her narrow heels as we walked down the hill towards our hotel. The sidewalk wasn't as smooth as it might have been and the streetlights could have been brighter. I found myself very much aware of her beside me. I thought she knew it and, perhaps, intended it; but I didn't know if it was a case of mutual attraction or if she was merely building me up so she could slap me down. I didn't trust her very far. I could still feel the aura of antagonism that I'd sensed at our first meeting in Mac's office.

I said, ''In certain societies I would now burp loudly to indicate my appreciation of a very fine meal.''

Delgado laughed. ''Words will suffice,'' she said. ''Polite belching is not required. . . .''

She'd been walking on my left. Being right-handed, I always prefer to have the lady over there for the same reason the Three Musketeers made a point of keeping their sword arms free for action; but it put her on the street side, between me and the white van that suddenly drew up alongside us. It seemed as if everybody was driving those bulky heaps today, but this one was much shorter than Morelos's elongated vehicle, with no side windows except in front. It was elderly and kind of beat-up looking.

Reaching for my gun, I saw the gleam of something metallic inside the open window as the van stopped abreast of us. I slung Delgado around behind me and heard her stumble and fall. I took a long step to the side to draw any return fire away from her, and looked for a target as my weapon came up. The boy, Lester Leonard, stuck his head out the window and looked shocked when he realized he was looking into the muzzle of a .38 Special. I realized that what I'd seen gleaming in the darkness hadn't been metallic after all; it had been the glass of his spectacles.

He spoke apologetically: "I'm very sorry, sir, I didn't mean to startle you."

I drew a long breath, holstered my piece, and turned to Delgado. She was sitting on the sidewalk in a rather undignified manner, legs wide apart. They were nice legs. A wisp of dark hair had come loose and was falling over her left eye. She brushed it aside, checked her nylons for runs as she sat there, and let me help her to her feet. She reached around to rub herself behind, craning her neck to see if she'd incurred any damage back there.

"Damn you, Helm, I'm going to be black and blue for a week! And if you've made me ruin the only good dress I brought along, I'll sue you!"

Well, you can't win them all.

CHAPTER 23

ALTHOUGH its interior volume was greater than that of most sedans, Leonard's van had only limited seating accommodations: two bucket seats up forward. There was considerable space between them, presumably so the driver could get through to the stuff he was hauling in back without walking clear around the outside of the vehicle and wrestling with the rear doors.

Being bigger, I got the outer two thirds of the right front seat; Delgado perched on the inner third and managed somehow to fit her legs past the console up forward that encroached badly on the footwell space. I had to hang on to her to keep her from sliding off into the walkway between the seats whenever Lester Leonard made a right-hand turn. She made no complaints although she must have been thinking ruefully that she'd put on a smart dress and sheer nylons and high heels to eat dinner in a good restaurant, not to take pratfalls on the street and get jounced around in a hippie van.

"It's at my folks' house, where I live," Leonard had said, asking me to accompany him. "It's some things I've been working on. That's why I've been following you and trying to get in touch with you, Mr. Helm. I'd like you to see them. It's only a little ways out of town. If she wants, we can drop Miss Delgado off at the hotel."

But Miss Delgado would have none of that, even

though it was obvious that we were going to travel in something less than limousine luxury. The van was old enough that it must have turned the clock at least once, but I noticed that all the instruments worked and the motor sounded healthy enough. A couple of square buttons, black and red, a toggle switch, and a small keypad displaying numbers from one to six had been neatly installed on the dashboard. I couldn't begin to guess what purpose they served.

However, the body metal was dented and the white paint had been touched up here and there with pigment that didn't match, clearly not for cosmetic reasons, just to keep the body from rusting through in the damp New England climate. The vinyl upholstery was cracked and split. The dark rear of the van behind the seats seemed to house some kind of laboratory or workshop.

"Oh, that," Lester Leonard said as we drove. "I just set up my old Atari back there when I got my new IBM-PC; that way I didn't have to do all my work at home. There's some other electronic stuff. . . . But you wouldn't be interested in that."

"Miss Delgado might be," I said. "Those were computers you mentioned, weren't they? She's supposed to be a computer whiz, although you can't prove it by me. I have to take off my shoes to count to twenty."

Leonard asked politely, "What kind of computer work do you do, Miss Delgado?"

"Just routine office stuff," she said, clinging to me as we turned a corner. Again I tried not to let her nearness bother me, without much success. She went on: "Not very interesting, I'm afraid. I'm just the girl who pushes the buttons. Is that what you're going to show us, computers?"

"Oh, no. No, it's something I've been working on ever since . . . ever since Linda was murdered in that horrible way. What kind of animals would . . . Oh, oh!"

217

The radio had suddenly let out a beep-beep sound and the tuning dial began to flash on and off. Leonard reduced speed hastily and glanced at a police car that appeared ahead, parked a little off the road. He drove past it at a discreet velocity and grinned. "Our friend the fuzz."

Delgado said, "That radio. It's really a radar detector?"

"Yes, I don't drive very fast, myself; but a friend who's into souped-up cars kept complaining about the laws they were passing against those devices, so I made him one they wouldn't spot. That's the pilot model; his was much more elegant, you could actually get AM stations on it." He shrugged. "Of course I never listened to it anyway. Just the tape deck. Classical music. Strictly a square." He came back to the previous subject of conversation. "What kind of . . . of animals would do a pointless and vicious thing like bombing a restaurant full of people thousands of miles from the country they're trying to change?"

"Vicious but not exactly pointless," Delgado said. "There are a lot of wild beasts out there these days, who don't care who they destroy if it brings them a little closer to their political goals."

"Well, it's time somebody turned the tables on them! That's what I've been working on, but I'd rather show you than tell you about it, if you don't mind. Otherwise you might think I'm some kind of a kook. Lots of people do."

I said, "I can't imagine why."

He grinned boyishly. "I guess I am a bit abnormal, at that, Mr. Helm. I never know who won the World Series, and I can't ever tell you who's playing in any of those bowl games. But I do have a B.S. in physics with a minor in chemistry, and I'm pretty good with computers if I do say so myself." He laughed self-consciously. "They were just a hobby until . . . Well, they kind of took over and now I'm with CCI, that's Computer Communications, Incorporated, up in Providence. I'm kind of their resident brain, junior grade, if you know what I mean; and they're going to send me back to school for some advanced work pretty soon. Just about every company in the field has its tame juvenile genius nowadays, ever since it was discovered that kids seem to catch on to the stuff faster than adults, maybe because they aren't hung up on traditional ways of thinking. It's an entirely new field and it demands entirely new thought patterns. . . . Well, of course you know all about it, Miss Delgado. Sorry. Didn't mean to run on like that. Here we are. The old homestead.''

Déjà vu is the term, I believe, that describes the feeling you get when you've played the same scene before. Less than a week ago, a thousand miles south of here, I'd accompanied another young person through the gates of the drive leading to her old family residence, to which she'd referred with the same self-conscious mixture of embarrassment and pride. Here there were no guards. The ornate iron gates stood open. The lighted drive curved up across the wide lawns to the massive three-story gray-stone house, with lights at many of the lower windows. The structure was as impressive in its way as the late Homer Ganson's sprawling Palm Beach confection, now the retirement retreat of his mobster son-in-law.

"That is quite a mansion, Lester," said Delgado.

"Yes, isn't it a monstrosity? I keep trying to live it down." He glanced at me. "I see my folks are home. I . . . I'd rather not have to explain you to them, if you don't mind, sir. I often bring friends to the stables to discuss computers and stuff; they don't expect me to touch base with them every time."

219

Delgado said, surprised, "The stables? Surely you didn't bring us here to admire your horses!"

He grinned. "No horses have been kept here since the horseless carriage came along, Miss Delgado. When I got a job and started looking for a place where I could, well, spread out my work a little, my folks had the old stables remodeled for me. They said it was a shame to waste all the space they had here. I pay them rent. . . . Yes, both cars are there."

We drove past a sporty Mercedes and a brand-new Ford station wagon, the kind with phony wood paneling. As we followed the driveway around the corner of the house we could see the lawns sloping down to the rocky shore beyond. If I remembered my geography correctly, the water was technically Rhode Island Sound, but the demarcation line between that and the Atlantic Ocean seems to be pretty fuzzy. I figured that if you headed straight out over the dark horizon you'd eventually hit Bermuda, six hundred miles away on the far side of the Gulf Stream. A moving cluster of lights, white and colored, not too far out, indicated a boat of some kind.

"Commercial fisherman," Leonard said, deciphering the light pattern with the casual glance of an expert.

"Do you have a boat?" I asked.

"Dad keeps a thirty-five-footer at the yacht club; he likes to wrestle with tuna and such. I run it for him when I can—Mom's a pretty good sailor, too—but I don't fish much myself, except to please him. He likes to think there's *some* sport I'm not too awful at." He glanced at us quickly, clearly afraid that we'd take the remark wrong. "Oh, he's not compulsive about it like the dads of some boys I used to know in school, who were always after them to make the team, any old team, and raised hell when they didn't." Leonard guided the car around a sharp curve that took us away from the ocean. He brought us to rest in front of a long, low building that showed black

220

against some dark trees. "Wait while I turn on the lights and cut off the alarm."

He pushed the square black button on the dashboard and illumination flooded the area. Then he touched the toggle switch. The red button lighted up. He pressed it and, holding it down, punched a combination on the nearby keypad. When he released the button, its light went out. He hit the little switch again, and nodded to us.

"All clear. It makes a terrible racket when I forget."

I got out and helped Delgado disembark. It was a long step down and she couldn't make it without a nice display of stockings and lingerie—I noticed that there was pretty lace around the hem of her slip. She went through the usual feminine routine of smoothing her dress and patting her hair. Leonard came around the van to join us.

"Do you really need that much security?" I asked.

He laughed. "The lights? I'm always hauling stuff in and out of here I wouldn't want to trip and fall with. The other's just a system I worked out for one of Mom's friends whose husband died. She was petrified of coming home alone; she was always sure a rapist was waiting in her bedroom. A simple burglar alarm wouldn't do; somebody could have outwitted it and turned it off in her absence; she wanted to be able to check it from her car. If the red light doesn't come on, that means the system has been tampered with. I wouldn't call her a promising candidate for sexual molestation, she's over seventy, but I guess rapists aren't much more selective than terrorists."

He shrugged as we walked towards the door. "Actually, I'm kind of glad to have it. Not that I'm afraid anybody's going to steal things, but it guarantees that nobody'll enter the lab when I'm gone, even with the best intentions in the world. As long as I was just working on the electronic projects it didn't matter, but when I started

221

on this other stuff . . . Well, some of it was pretty sensitive in the early experimental stages. I wouldn't want Mom to get hurt, for instance, because she happened to bump into something in the lab when she was just looking for a beaker to use for a vase to put some surprise flowers in my apartment.'' He laughed again. "She's used to it, of course; they both are. I was a secretive kid. When I lived in the main house, I always locked my rooms when I went out so nobody'd disturb my important experiments. My folks were nice about it, once I convinced them I wasn't doing drugs in there; but they've been wondering ever since how a nice normal stockbroker and a nice normal debutante managed to beget a nut like me.''

There was a kind of tolerant affection in the way he spoke of his parents; clearly he considered them okay people but not really very bright. Still, the affection was there; pleasant to encounter these days when the battle of the generations is often pretty savage—witness Sandra and her parent. Leonard unlocked the door for us and turned on the light inside; we entered what seemed to be the living room of a small apartment. It looked as if his mother had furnished it with the advice of her interior decorator, all pale wood and light upholstery and beige carpet; but he had it cluttered up with computer readouts and piles of books. Mysterious odds and ends of equipment were parked in various corners. A picture of Linda Anson in living color hung on one wall; as I came closer I realized that it was a magazine page, carefully framed.

Leonard went over to a small, pale bar on which stood a tapering Pyrex flask of the kind my college chemistry teacher called an Erlenmeyer—and don't ask me how I remember that after all these years. The flask, plugged with a black rubber stopper, was filled with a pale green liquid that looked like something nasty out of a sci-fi movie that would kill you if it touched you or turn you into a zombie or werewolf.

"Would either of you care for a drink?" he asked. "I'm a Gatorade man myself; but there's some stuff Dad brought over. He said the booze I'd been serving my drinking friends was a disgrace and gave the place a bad name. He gave me a funny-looking bottle of Scotch he said was okay. Pinch?"

Delgado said, "I've never been know to turn down Pinch. Yes, I'll have a little, thanks."

"I'll second that," I said.

"You do it while I get the ice, please, Mr. Helm." He set out the bottle and showed me the glasses. When he came back with the ice bucket, he said, "Are you really a government man?"

I nodded. "I work out of Washington, yes."

"It puts me on kind of a spot," he said. "I thought when I read that newspaper story that you were here on personal business. I mean, about your son, who was also, I understand, the husband of the girl in the hospital."

"Well, personal feelings are certainly involved," I said. "My chief selected me for the assignment for that reason. Incidentally, the girl in the hospital thanks you for your help under fire. And for the flowers."

He turned slightly pink. "It seemed like the right thing to do. I mean, she was so brave. It must have hurt terribly, but she didn't make a sound even when they were lifting her onto the stretcher. I'm a sissy; I know I'd have screamed my head off. Mr. Helm, if you came across something slightly illegal, would you feel obliged, because of your government position, to report it to the police?"

I said, "I shouldn't commit myself without asking a few questions, but I will. The answer is no."

"I debated a long time after seeing that you seemed to be authorized to carry a gun, there at the lake. And the way you talked with the police. I almost decided not to approach you. It was different when I thought you were a private citizen; I thought I could give you something you needed for your, well, mission. But if you're connected with the government, you can get everything you need, can't you? Guns or . . . or anything else.''

"It doesn't necessarily follow," I said. "And it seems that you decided to change your mind. Here we are, at your invitation."

He nodded. "Yes. I've worked hard on this. I can't see anybody else to offer it to, and it must be used. Maybe, as an employee of the U.S. government, there are some things you can't bring yourself to do or aren't allowed to do. There's absolutely nothing I won't do, Mr. Helm, to make those fiends pay for their crime."

It was very still in the cluttered living room. The big spectacles were aimed at me steadily. I remembered that I'd thought the boy's eyes kind of muddy and indefinite in color when I first met him, but they were clear and fierce now.

"That statement covers a lot of territory, Lester," I said. "It could get you into serious trouble."

He said, "You must have some kind of a plan. Can you use a helper who's dedicated, reasonably intelligent—and expendable?"

"It means that much to you?" I asked softly.

He said, "You don't know what it's been like. I keep her pictures to remind me. . . . Well, there's one. They keep reproaching me for not . . . Well, there was never anything I could do for her while she was alive, but I can do something for her now she's dead; and I have to do it. Then, maybe, if I survive, I can take down the pictures, all except maybe the best one for remembrance, and start living again." He drew a long ragged breath. "The project I set myself is finished. I'm pretty good with my hands, I have the material, and I know how to use it. I'm a quick study, I know some chemistry and physics, and it's really not a very complicated subject. But I don't know where to start! I haven't any idea of how to go about finding them. If you can show me, you'll be doing me the biggest favor in the world, no matter what happens to me as a result.''

I didn't speak at once when he'd finished. Now that I'd found exactly what I'd come here to Newport to search for, I didn't like it. He was a nice boy even if he was a bit far out; and I could very well get him killed. I told myself that he'd just given me absolution, if that should happen. Conscience isn't a commodity we deal in much in the business, anyway.

I said. ''Okay, it's a deal. Let's see what you have to show me.''

''This way.''

It was quite an establishment, off the side of the little apartment, one room leading into the next, railroad-car fashion. There was a crowded computer-electronics room with banks of mysterious screens and switches and dials that presumably meant something to Delgado, but were just sci-fi to me. Then there was what looked to be a rather well-equipped little machine shop. Beyond was a chemistry laboratory complete with sinks and stone-topped lab tables. There were ventilating hoods to suck out dangerous fumes, and racks of reagents, and shelves of chemical glassware like the Gatorade flask; there were also several ovens and furnaces set into one of the walls. Beyond that was what Leonard called the assembly room, with a couple of large workbenches, three scales that would weigh anything from a horse to a mosquito, and a large chest of tools.

Leonard stopped at the final door. ''It's all in here,'' he said. ''It's perfectly safe, but you'd better not smoke. I got most of it from the computer. You'd be surprised what sources are available if you know how to access

225

them. And there are books available that would shock some people. You know the kind of people who think certain kinds of knowledge should be hidden from other people."

Dana asked, "What kinds of knowledge, Lester?"

He grinned boyishly. "Well, sex, for instance. And of course they'd want to make a secret of, for instance, the fact that diesel fuel combined with certain kinds of fertilizer makes a very powerful explosive—they'd like that to be kept out of print even though everybody knows the Irish have been using it in their car bombs for years. They don't want anybody to know that aspirin can be made to yield picric acid, which can be employed in homemade detonators, but it hardly comes as a surprise to anyone who glances at the chemical formula. Anybody who wants to know how to make old-fashioned gunpowder—black powder—only has to reach for a history book; the pioneers manufactured their own and it's no secret how they did it." He shrugged. "I robbed Mom's compost pile for a source of nitrogen and used wood ashes from the fireplace and made my own charcoal; sulfur was a little more of a problem. . . . Well, you're not interested in the details, and black powder isn't such a great explosive anyway. I just started with that because it's a simple process and I wanted to get the feel of working with these materials." He gave us a rather shy and apologetic grin as he opened the door. "Sorry for the lecture, but it was really a very interesting project and, well, for obvious reasons I haven't been able to discuss it with anybody else. Go on in."

It was a small, windowless room, with a chill like that of a cave, indicating that the temperature was controlled thermostatically. I heard a ventilating fan whirring somewhere. There were shelves along the walls. He had it all neatly displayed and labeled like a school assignment, and it was all there, from the little ones that would blow off your foot to the big ones that would bring down your condominium—well, the working parts of the latter with the bulky missing ingredients neatly listed. It was the warehouse of a one-man bomb factory.

He spoke from the door, softly. "I thought . . . I thought it was time those terrorists learned a little about bombs from the other end," he said. "I thought it was time a few of them got blown up, for a change. Just tell me who, Mr. Helm. Just tell me where."

CHAPTER 24

THERE were half a dozen big cars parked and double-parked carelessly in front of the hotel doorway. An undoubtedly significant comment on our society, although I don't know what it signifies, is the way a guy with a cheap Honda or Volksie is generally pretty careful how he parks it, while the gent with the expensive Caddy will just go off and leave it sitting in the middle of the street.

Leonard squeezed past the pile-up and let us out on the sidewalk a little farther on. We watched the van drive away through the big, lighted parking lot and join the stream of traffic on the four-lane boulevard. Delgado started to speak, perhaps to comment on what we'd been shown; but I silenced her with a warning hand on her arm as two figures came towards us from the bright hotel entrance in a purposeful way.

I couldn't identify them against the light. With the .38

ready but hidden, I threw a quick glance around, something I'd learned long ago while duck hunting: You concentrate too hard on a bunch of teal approaching the decoys from across the lake in front of you, and a pair of mallards will slip in from the marsh in back of the blind and almost knock your hunting cap off, and be gone before you can lift your shotgun. But nobody was sneaking up behind us at the moment.

Delgado said calmly, "If you want me down, just say 'down.' Please don't hurl me to the pavement as you did . . . Oh, it's Trask. I don't know the man with him."

"Benison," I said. "Drugs."

I holstered the gun again, feeling a little foolish. It was the second false alarm of the evening. Maybe I was getting a bit paranoid. Well, better a warm, paranoid body than a cold, well-adjusted corpse.

Delgado said, "Oh, one of those. I wonder what he wants."

"Drugs, what else?" I said. "That's what they all want these days, and it's getting to be a pain in the ass for those of us in other lines of endeavor. I'm not saying it isn't important. I'll admit it's a nasty problem; but the way one bad habit's become a national obsession scares hell out of me. When we're finally invaded by hostile aliens from outer space, they'll meet no opposition at all. The army, the navy, and the air force will all have been sent off to chase drug smugglers. . . . Miss Dana Delgado, Mr. Thomas Benison. Hi, Trask."

"You were gone awhile," Trask said. "The man I had watching said you entered the van voluntarily, but we were beginning to wonder."

"The kid had something to show me," I said. "What can I do for you, Mr. Benison?"

The compact, brown-haired man spoke deliberately: "You've been displaying some interest in the late Mr.

Pirate Williams. Is he, or his marina, connected with your present mission in any important way?''

I shook my head. "Not that I've been able to determine. I was just being thorough, checking out both victims of the Silver Conch bombing. The man is dead and so, by the looks of it, is his boatyard complex. Why do you ask?''

Benison said, "Because I'd appreciate it if you'd leave it strictly alone from now on.'' I must have shown some kind of adverse reaction because he shook his head quickly. "Don't get touchy, Helm. I'm not giving orders; I'm asking a favor. That marina and boat yard aren't as dead as they look. We think they'll soon be revived with money that comes, in roundabout ways, from a source that interests us—if said source isn't scared off by signs of official curiosity. We've been after him a long time. We thought Williams was going to lead us to him, but Williams had dinner in the wrong place at the wrong time and got killed by terrorists. Now it looks as if Mr. Big may show his hand a little, taking over where Williams left off in order to maintain his pipeline.''

"You mean that boat of the Pirate's? It looked like a barnacle farm to me.''

Benison laughed. "That was just a diversion, the boat and the pointless trips offshore. Williams figured that if we were watching him, we'd sooner or later show some interest in his minivoyages. He'd be stopped and searched and nothing would be found; but it would be an early-warning signal of sorts, letting him know he'd better cool his operations, at least for a while. But as long as the *Montauk Maid* was left alone, he reasoned, in spite of her curious offshore jaunts, it meant that nobody was suspicious of him and he could safely keep the stuff coming through—cunningly built into private boats that entered his yard for repairs. You can do practically anything with fiberglass, you know; and short of breaking up a

229

hull with a sledgehammer, and that isn't easy, there's hardly any way of finding something that's become an integral part of the structure.''

"Tricky," I said.

"Yes. So we prefer not to have our man worried by people poking around that harbor, particularly government people of any kind. We want him to feel safe in resuming operations. I'd be grateful if you'd just forget the dead Pirate and his dusty lair completely.''

I studied him for a moment. He was being surprisingly tactful and diplomatic. Tallman would have told me to lay the hell off or else, and I'd probably have jimmied a couple of boathouse locks just to show him that he wasn't the guy from whom I took my instructions. But this smooth, carefully dressed character—he was wearing another three-piece suit, charcoal gray this time—didn't throw his weight around unnecessarily, which didn't mean he didn't have any to throw.

I said, "Unless something compelling turns up pointing that way, which I don't expect, I'm out of your hair. And if something should turn up, I'll get in touch before I make any moves. Okay?" He nodded and I said, "You're very polite for a drug agent."

"Maybe I'm frightened, Helm," he said gravely. "It's quite terrifying, the things that happen to people who try to push you around, even people working for the same government." He was watching me closely.

I said, "Don't look at me, I haven't blown up anybody lately. Those snoops of Tallman's just couldn't keep their feet out of other people's bear traps. First they sprang one of ours, in Savannah, and now they seem to have stepped into one of the opposition's, in Old Saybrook. Except it went bang instead of snap.''

"I know," Benison said, relaxing a bit. Apparently he hadn't been quite sure until he heard me say it. He went on: "But does Tallman know? If not, if he blames you

230

for setting him up, directly or indirectly, he could cause you trouble. He's not a very stable personality, and he took a lot of pride in his little task force. Under his leadership, that quartet of politically appointed amateurs was going to solve the dreadful problem of illicit substances that has baffled hundreds of us pros for years. Only it seems that they broke into one house too many without a warrant; and their high-handed and illegal methods backfired on them, quite literally. Some people in Washington are laughing, but not too loudly. After all, the appointments came from fairly high up.''

"But you're not laughing," I said.

"No. Any more than a policeman laughs when other cops get killed, even if they weren't too bright and their commander is an arrogant loudmouth who nobody likes. So I'm glad to hear that you're not responsible.'' The threat implicit in his words wasn't strong but it was there: He didn't think I'd been lying to him, but if I had been, I'd regret it. He said, ''Good night, Helm. Miss Delgado. Trask.''

He walked out into the parking lot and unlocked an inconspicuous medium-sized car two rows back. Watching him drive away, I said, "It's nice to meet a guy who doesn't have to talk tough just because he is."

"It's still a goddamn crusade; and crusaders bug me.'' Trask shook his head, dismissing the subject. "I've got your plane tickets. Kennedy, American, tomorrow at twelve-thirty P.M. They want you there an hour early. The hotel serves breakfast at six-thirty. Pack ahead of time and eat fast, because there'll be a car outside at seven. It's a hundred and fifty miles and something; and with all the highway construction, the driver likes a bit of leeway. Leave your weapons with him; you'll get others in San Juan. No sense going through all that firearms red tape if you don't have to. Lunch on the plane; I think it's a DC-10. You get in at four, but that's Atlantic time, an hour ahead of us. Check with Avis at the airport for your car. Hotel El Convento downtown. Two rooms adjoining. Couldn't get you into the Howard Johnson over in Condado on such short notice, or any of the nearby resort hotels, but there's not much to see in that restaurant anyway, they've had most of a year to clean up the bomb mess. Your contact goes by the code name Modesto. Miss Delgado knows the contact procedures; she's been in touch with our people down there. Modesto will have the information you wanted on the blast victims. He'll supply arms, and arrange cover for you if you need it." Trask took three travel-agency folders from his inside coat pocket, glanced into them, and handed me two. "I'll take care of canceling this," he said, pocketing the third one.

"What's the word from the hospital?"

"Mrs. Helm's asleep, under sedation. Vital signs strong and positive; no unfavorable symptoms noted."

"Watch over her carefully, please, *amigo*," I said. "We don't want to lose her. A safe house would be best when they kick her out of her hospital bed. Tuck her Porsche away somewhere for the time being; here are the keys. And put somebody on the boy who just dropped us off. I've been in touch with Washington about him. We'll be using him shortly, so keep him safe, too. I'll probably be asking you to ship him down to me, complete with some toys that the airlines won't like."

"Sure. I'll see if Air Force One is available."

"Do that. Well, we're all still breathing, in spite of some efforts to the contrary. There would undoubtedly have been more without your nursemaids in attendance. Tell them thanks from me."

"Keep your nose clean, hero."

Delgado took my arm as we moved on down the walk and into the hotel. We didn't speak until we were in the elevator. I'm not usually affected much by perfume; in

232

fact when there's a lot of it I always find myself wondering if the lady's trying to conceal the fact that she hasn't bathed recently. But this was just a faint, intriguing fragrance and I found myself very much aware of it—and of her, but I'd been in that painful state of awareness most of the evening.

She broke our silence. "Do you think Mr. Benison checks his nice silk necktie in the mirror and combs his nice brown hair before he pulls out his gun and shoots a dope pusher?"

I said, "Don't kid yourself. It's an act. He's taking advantage of the fact that a lot of rugged gents in grubby jeans can't believe that a fancy chap with a necktie and a crease in his pants can possibly be a threat to them. They judge the amount of danger in a man by the amount of whiskers on the chin and the quantity of dirt under the fingernails. I have a hunch a lot of grimy fellows have found our Mr. Clean a very unpleasant surprise."

"Well, we certainly met a couple of odd ones tonight," she said. "That Lester is also quite a specimen."

"Cross a stockbroker with a debutante and you never know what you'll get."

I found the casual chitchat hard to manage. The elevator stopped, and the doors slid open. I followed her out into the corridor, feeling like a high school kid on his first date wondering if the girl expects to be kissed, and how to find out without offending her, and how to go about it if she does. I mean, the signals weren't clear. She was being very polite and pleasant, but I still sensed a small residue of her old hostility, a little reserve, as if she found it a strain to be friendly with a homicidal type like me. At least that was the explanation she'd given earlier. I wasn't sure how far I believed it.

She stopped at the door of her room and turned to face me. The events of the evening had left no marks on her except that, somehow, she didn't look quite as severe and untouchable as she had. Nevertheless, I half expected her to send me on my way, and she knew it. She smiled faintly.

"I have a little silver flask in there," she said. "Chivas Regal. Just enough for a nightcap. I mean, two nightcaps."

"Wow, we're really doing ourselves well in the Scotch department tonight," I said. "In that case, I won't even mention my old workhorse bottle of J and B. You've got yourself a customer, ma'am."

She unlocked the door and preceded me into the room, which was a duplicate of the one down the corridor that Sandra and I had shared platonically the previous night. There was a suitcase open on the nearer of the big beds. Delgado got a small shiny flask out of it and turned to look at me.

"This is rather silly, isn't it?" she said quietly. "You don't really want a drink, do you?"

I said firmly, "No one shall ever claim that Helm entered a lady's room under false pretenses. I'll choke down a drink if you want me to."

She laughed, and dropped the flask back into the suitcase, watching me. "That little girl has got you in a bad way, hasn't she?"

"I was hoping it didn't show."

"It shows. But it's not very flattering, Matt. I mean, it's not as if you were overwhelmed by my unique grace and beauty. After a chaste week on the road with that nubile child, including a night spent in the same bedroom, you'd react the same way to any reasonably presentable female, wouldn't you?" There was nothing to say to that, so I remained silent. She went on, looking at me curiously: "You're an experienced older man. I'm sure you could have . . . persuaded her, if you'd really tried."

234

"Seduced her, you mean?"

Delgado shrugged. "Whatever. But you didn't try?"

"That's right." I cleared my throat. "In an old-fashioned costume movie, I'd be saying nobly that I'd sworn an oath on my son's grave. Well, I don't have the sentimental feeling for graves that some people do, and I haven't even seen that one; but when I learned that Matthew was dead I found myself remembering that I'd never done much for him although he was my son. Then it occurred to me that there was something I could do for him now. I could see to it that his young widow made it all right."

Delgado said dryly, "A very interesting project, as Lester Leonard would say."

"Don't be snide, Delgado," I said. "I'm quite aware that my young-widow resistance is very low. I was also quite aware from the start the last thing the girl needed was to get mixed up in any important way with a superannuated veteran of the undercover wars, particularly one who was related to her by marriage and looked a little like the husband she'd lost and probably had a few of the same mannerisms. Even if you couldn't call it incest, technically, the weird kind of relationship we'd have, with Matthew's ghost between us, would tear her apart, and maybe me as well. Hence Iron Man Helm."

There was a little silence, then Delgado said: "You'd better not let it get around that you're really kind of a nice person, Matt. It would ruin your reputation around the shop." She turned and moved to the dresser and, with the aid of the big mirror above it, started pulling the pins out of her hair. Standing there with her back to me, she spoke to my image in the glass: "A woman taking down her hair is supposed to be very sexy. Am I?"

I said, "You're teasing me."

She didn't turn her head. "What do you expect? A

young girl gets you all wound up like a clock, and you come into my room with fairly obvious motives; and I'm not allowed to tease you a little? You're lucky I don't take it as a deadly insult and slap your face." She shook her head and dark hair came tumbling down over her shoulders. There was more of it than I'd thought. She reached back with both hands and lifted it all to expose the zipper down her back. She spoke, still without turning her head: "Now you may help me off with my dress. Please don't get impatient and damage it. It's survived a number of indignities tonight, including a tumble on the sidewalk; it deserves to be removed with care and hung up properly."

I moved closer in order to operate the long zipper. Bending over her, I said, "I don't know if I can bear this dreadful penance. You're a cruel, sadistic bitch, Delgado."

"I'm a woman and my name is Dana." Standing there in front of the mirror, she helped me work the red dress down from her shoulders and arms. She stepped out of it. "Now hang it up, please."

"Yes, Dana."

"No, not on a hook. I said properly. Use a hanger."

"Yes, Dana."

With the dress properly stored away in the closet, I returned to her. She was the loveliest thing in the world in her lacy slip with her dark hair loose on her shoulders. She was smart enough to know that it's difficult for a woman to look severe and untouchable half undressed; she'd settled for looking breathtakingly desirable.

She said, "That's better. That's much better, my dear. I wanted you to *see* me. Now you're looking at me as me, not just as a convenient substitute for the little girl you've forbidden yourself to touch."

I said, "I see you, Dana. You have my full attention."

236

She smiled as she came forward. "Not quite, but I will have."

She did, too.

CHAPTER 25

I AWOKE in the night to hear her crying. It surprised me; I hadn't judged her to be a crying girl. It wasn't a violent paroxysm of grief or regret or whatever, just an occasional quiet little sniff or stifled sob.

Lying beside her in the dark, I said, "Whatever it is, I didn't mean it."

"There's K-Kleenex on the table beside you. Please?"

"Light?"

"I don't m-mind."

I switched it on and gave her a wad of tissues, and watched her while she mopped and wiped and blew.

I asked, "Anything I did?"

"No."

"Anything I can do?"

"No. I'm sorry I woke you."

"It's all right. I ought to get to my room pretty soon, anyway. Got to get showered and packed."

She was a tidy weeper and didn't look as destroyed afterwards as they sometimes do. A lovely lady who had problems. Well, who doesn't? I remembered another dark-haired lady who'd also cried in bed, although Lia Varek had shed her tears before the act rather than afterwards. It wasn't a comfortable memory. It made me

237

feel disloyal, although I couldn't say to whom. Maybe myself. Don Juan Helm. I consoled myself with the fact that at least I'd kept my hands off the kid. I didn't seem to have much resistance, but at least I'd had that much.

Aware of my regard, Dana pushed away a lock of hair that clung damply to one cheek, and retrieved an escaping shoulder strap of the slip she still wore. After making certain that her dress had been removed to safety, she'd relaxed and let the rest of her costume take care of itself. The pumps she'd kicked off were presumably undamaged, but I wasn't so sure about the panty hose. Removing them had, I recalled, been a community effort accompanied by breathless laughter—she'd called them a ridiculous garment—and afterwards the situation had become quite urgent, so we'd wasted no time on the slip beyond displacing it as far as necessary.

"It's too bad," Dana said, tugging the rumpled garment straight about her as she lay there. "I brought a beautiful nightgown along, just in case I should meet somebody irresistible; and here I wind up making love in my underwear!"

"Well, it's pretty underwear." I kissed her lightly. "Are you all right now?"

She nodded. "I'm sorry. It was really very nice. A little . . . well, desperate, but nice. I don't know what I woke up feeling so sad about. Just the well-known *tristesse*, I suppose. Yes, I'm fine now. Do you *have* to go?"

Under those circumstances, there's only one acceptable response to that question, put that way; and it took me awhile to make it. Later, after reawakening in my own room, shaving, toothbrushing, showering, dressing, and packing, I transported my single bag to the lobby and found that starvation had got me down ten minutes early. Some people get sad afterwards; others merely get hungry. However, there was a coffee urn for early risers

238

in a corner, complete with Styrofoam cups, packets of sugar, and little plastic pots of the soluble talcum powder that's supposed to whiten your coffee and make your eyes believe it's actually got cream in it even as your taste buds say no. Fortunately, I mostly drink it black.

By the time I got all the hot, brown, wake-up liquid down without burning myself too badly, they were letting people into the breakfast room. I established myself at a table for two. It was a glassed-in veranda that reminded me of the Vareks' sunporch—and of Lia Varek herself in her scarlet sundress with little bows at the shoulders. I wished she would go away and stop bothering me. I guess I'm just not comfortable with promiscuity. Then Dana appeared, slender and lovely in the wine-colored slacks and sweater I'd seen before; and I found my high-principled guilt feelings evaporating.

"I brought my suitcase down," she said, after I'd done my gentlemanly duty by her chair. "It's beside yours in the lobby."

"That's cozy," I said, sitting down to face her. I was surprised to see her blush like a young girl, as if I'd said something very intimate.

She licked her lips. "Matt."

"Yes, Dana."

"Don't . . . don't let's allow it to become too important."

I looked at her for a moment. I said, "Sure. Hell, it was just an act of mercy on your part. My endocrine balance was all loused up and you generously restored it to normal, for which I thank you. Okay?"

"Yes," she said, smiling faintly. "Yes, okay. I'm very glad to hear that your balance is normal." She went on rather hastily: "It looks like a good day for flying. Of course you can't tell how it'll be down where we're going. Regardless of what the travel folders say, they're not islands of eternal sunshine. I was in Santo Domingo once when it didn't stop raining for a month.''

"Is it diplomatic to ask what you were doing in Santo Domingo?''

She shook her head. ''No.''

"I get the impression that you're a little more than a computer jockey, Dana.''

"More? Or less?'' She shrugged. "I'm not a trained agent, if that's what you're asking. Well, you know that. You complained once that I was so helpless I didn't even know how to shoot a gun, and you were going to have to look after me and hold my hand when we get down there.''

I said, "Somehow my attitude seems to have changed. It will be a pleasure, looking after you and holding your hand. But it isn't fair.''

"What isn't?''

"Since Mac sent you here to work with me, he probably told you as much about me as he thought fit for public consumption. But he hasn't told me a damn thing about you.''

"There's very little to tell,'' she said. "I was born down in the islands, I got to know them pretty well as I grew up, I became acquainted with a few useful people, and I learned a few useful things like how to run a computer, so when the job came up of correlating information on a terrorist group based down here, I was the top choice among those available.''

"That doesn't tell me how you came to be applying for a job in that crazy-house—or were you recruited? Most people don't know we exist.''

She smiled serenely. "No, it doesn't tell you, and I'm not going to. Nobody's told me how you came to be working there, either, and I'm not asking.''

I grinned. "The old whore answer is: Just lucky, I guess.''

She said, "Let's leave it at that, Matt."

"Sure." Actually, it was bad form, as the British say, to question a colleague about his, or her, origins and motives. I saw the waitress heading our way with a laden tray, and glanced at my watch. "Well, here it comes. We'd better gulp it down. Our limousine will be at the door any minute." I grimaced. "I don't like making the trip naked, even just from portal to portal, or airport to airport."

"Naked?"

"Unarmed. I get very unhappy without my little thirty-eight-caliber security blanket. Well, let's hope our friend Modesto, whoever the hell he may be, is on the ball down there in San Juan and doesn't let us get shot before giving us something to shoot back with."

Dana said a bit reprovingly, "I know the man they call Modesto. He's a very reliable person. I'm sure he won't let anything happen to us."

I said, "Only God is that reliable, and we haven't been able to recruit Him yet. But it's not for want of trying."

It was a good thing Trask had given us plenty of lead time because we had to run a gauntlet of construction zones on our way to Kennedy. When we got there, it was the same madhouse as always, it doesn't matter which airline building you're sentenced to. After checking our bags and receiving our boarding passes we still had the better part of an hour to waste, having arrived as early as ordered in spite of the driving delays.

We wandered around a bit. I picked up a couple of hunting-fishing magazines at a newsstand. Dana, more intellectual, settled for a news magazine and a journal of opinion a little to the right of center; well, everybody's going conservative these days, except me. I've learned to remain apolitical since Mac never asks our opinions; he's just as apt to send us after a rabid rightist as a wild-eyed leftist. I led Dana along the concourse to a wide-open coffee bar where she had coffee, and I had coffee and a very gooey cinnamon roll.

After we'd sat there for a while on our stools, sipping and chewing as appropriate, she glanced at me curiously. "Why are we stalling?" she said. "Why don't we just go to the gate and read our magazines comfortably in real chairs, until they find us a plane? I don't think you really wanted that sugary mass of dough. We'll be having lunch on board shortly."

"Shhh," I said. "You're interfering with extrasensory perception."

"What?"

I said, "Somebody's interested in us. I've been catching activity out of the corners of my eyes, movements that don't fit the crowd pattern. Somebody's following us closely; several somebodies, in fact. After enough years in the business you learn to sense it, even if you don't quite see it or hear it. But I haven't been able to pick out a face. . . ."

Then I saw him, shuffling along with the crowd with the slow movements of the sick or aged: a bent old man with a cane. He was wearing a shabby black suit and hat, and carrying a worn, old-fashioned black-leather valise. The cane was also old-fashioned, also black, and I wondered if the two feet of steel inside would show up on the airport scanners.

At least, when I'd last known him, I'd classified him as a potential sword-cane type. It seemed unlikely that, in a getup that demanded a walking stick, he'd be satisfied with just a wooden stick. However, the face I was seeing now was not quite the face I remembered. It was lined with suffering, and it was noticeably emaciated as was his body—he looked like a cancer patient who was beginning to show it, although it probably wasn't cancer. Of course, some of it could have been makeup and acting; but we'd suspected illness when he'd ceased operations after that Costa Verde business. Herman Heinrich Bultman, known as the Kraut, one of the best exterminators-for-hire in the business. The man who intended to change the map of the Caribbean because somebody'd machine-gunned the old German shepherd bitch he'd named after Marlene Dietrich.

It wasn't my job to stop him. I'd refused that job. As far as I was concerned, Bultman was free to remodel or totally demolish the sovereign nation of Gobernador in any manner that pleased him, as long as he didn't interfere with my job of demolition directed at the CLL. That was the deal I'd made with Mac: I'd only go after the Kraut if he came after me. But here he was.

I shook my head as Dana started to speak. "Drink up your coffee and act natural. Then pick up your purse and magazines and come along to the gate, chatting brightly all the way."

She drained the cup and slid off her stool. "That old man with the cane?" she asked, laughing as if it were a big joke.

"He's the one, and a deadlier gent you'll seldom encounter. Yours truly excepted, of course."

"Modesty," she said. "That's what I like about working in that place. You meet so many shy and unassuming gentlemen. . . . But he didn't look very dangerous."

"It's got to be mostly a disguise. I mean, at last report he was training a tough commando unit in Montego; he'd hardly be up to that if he were as decrepit as he looked just now. However, we know he was badly hurt on one of his last jobs and while he seemed to have recovered pretty well, aside from the loss of a foot, something else could be going bad on him. Now I'm saying something very funny, ha-ha."

She laughed obediently. "Bultman?" she said. "That's the name, isn't it, Herman Bultman? I remember, it came

243

up on the computer screen several times in connection with that military nonsense in Montego to which the CLL has been contributing men, ninety-three the last I heard." She glanced at me. "Funny, funny, funny. Your turn to laugh."

"Laugh, laugh, laugh," I said, and laughed. "Why do you call it nonsense?"

"What?"

"You don't think Bultman's invasion force is a real threat . . . ?"

"Don't be silly," she said. "Haven't you done any checking at all? Your friend the Kraut has only a few hundred men. Perhaps they're very dedicated, perhaps he's trained them well; but the President of Gobernador, that Yankee-lover whom they hate, has a home guard of several thousand, also well trained, with plenty of arms and equipment courtesy of Uncle Sam. And it's not inconceivable, these aggressive days, that if he really gets into trouble, the U.S. Marines will bail him out. Washington considers the installations on Isla del Sur of vital importance." Dana grimaced as we walked. "It's nice to think that the heroic spirit of the patriots reclaiming their country will inevitably carry them to victory over the cowardly oppressors who have stolen it, and that the people will rise up to help them. It's undoubtedly what Bultman's men are telling themselves, but it didn't happen at the Bay of Pigs, and it won't happen here in miniature, unless Bultman has a secret weapon up his sleeve that nobody knows about. Otherwise he'll simply be leading a lot of brave men—I suppose even the rabid CLL contingent doesn't lack for courage—to their deaths."

It was a new view of the situation, but there wasn't time to consider it now. I said, "Here we go through the idiot scanners. Brace yourself. They're going to scream as usual at my change and keys and belt buckle."

"Well, if you weren't so rich and didn't wear those Texas-sized buckles. . . ."

We went through the routine and stepped aside to let others pass while I threaded the belt I'd had to remove back through the loops of my slacks.

"The long-haired one in jeans and ripped T-shirt is our personal escort," I said.

"Which long-haired one in jeans and ripped T-shirt? You've just described half the passengers."

"The tall, dirty-blond one, male, carrying a denim jacket and a big paper bag that probably holds an UZI and half a dozen loaded magazines. The scanners wouldn't worry about little things like that. Just belt buckles."

Actually, the machines had seemed to be operating at fairly sensitive settings, and I'd sweated a little walking through the arch the second time with all my legitimate metal piled on the plastic tray.

"You think he's with Bultman?" Dana asked. "Why?"

"No sign of annoyance when I held up the line; no expression of amusement or sympathy when he passed the funny tall man struggling to put his belt back on. Just deadpan, eyes front; and in spite of his hippie getup, if they still call them hippies, he couldn't help showing that he'd had military training somewhere. Anyway, when you've been in the business as long as I have, you can kind of spot the killer types, even the young ones. That boy has homicide on his mind." I laughed heartily. "Joke, joke, joke."

She laughed a bit uncertainly. "Ha-ha, ha-ha. What do you think he'll do?"

"Improvise. I don't think he was meant to carry the ball. He was just a backup in case things didn't work out inside the airport as planned. Now the responsibility is on his shoulders and he's trying frantically to figure out

245

what to do. Well, he knows what to do; he's just got to come up with a way to do it.''

She shivered. ''What do you mean, if things didn't work out. . . ?'' Then she frowned suddenly. ''Aren't we walking right into a trap? Once we're on the plane . . . What if they've put a bomb aboard?''

''And sent a guy along to be blown up with us, just so we won't lack for company?''

''A hijacking, then? They'll just take over the plane and . . .'' She stopped talking as we entered the waiting room.

I said, ''We'll sit over there where he can keep an eye on us. No sense making things difficult for the poor fellow; he might think we've got him spotted.'' Seated, I said, ''This is where a cigarette would come in handy, or particularly a pipe, to help us look peaceful and unsuspicious. I quit way back when I was a half-baked photojournalist because it fogged up the darkroom, long before they made a religion of it; but there are still times when I miss being able to fiddle with the old pipe and tobacco and matches. You could really make a career of those matches. . . .''

''Matt! Stop chattering like an idiot. What if they hijack the plane?''

I asked, ''Did you ever really look at the seating plan of a DC-10?''

''No, why?''

''It's a hell of a big plane. Sure, determined men and women could take one over; determined men and women probably already have, or other planes just as big. I haven't kept track of which brands of flying machines have been hijacked and which haven't, if any. But it's a major operation, like taking over a good-sized theater full of people; and while Bultman's quite capable of organizing it, what would he gain? He just wants two people, us; actually he just wants one person, me. And presumably Sandra, but she's not here. If he grabs a whole DC-10 to get me, what's he going to do with the other three hundred and some passengers, assuming a full load? Not to mention the crew?''

''He and his friends haven't shown much regard for innocent bystanders so far, Matt.''

I shook my head quickly. ''You're talking about the Caribbean Legion of Liberty. Sure, they're a bunch of ruthless publicity hounds, anything to intimidate folks and attract attention to their sacred cause. They seem to have concentrated on restaurants so far, as the public gathering places most suitable for bombing, but I doubt if they'd pass up a plane if it came easy. But Bultman's a hound of a different breed entirely. He's a pro, he's got invasion on his mind, and the last thing in the world he wants at the moment is to be publicly connected with an air atrocity. That could make his sanctuary in Montego too hot to hold him and louse up his plans before he's ready to make his assault on Gobernador. But your reaction is exactly the one Bultman was hoping for.''

''I don't understand.''

I said, ''I told you, this is an expert we're talking about. I can give you a long list of dead men: Bultman's hit parade, if you'll pardon the pun. So, with that in mind, tell me what's odd about the performance you just witnessed. What's the first thing that comes to mind?''

Dana hesitated. ''Well . . . well, wasn't he a little clumsy? First he let you spot his men following us; and then he marched past us himself. To be sure, he was in disguise; but it wasn't a very good disguise. At least you managed to penetrate it. That doesn't seem like very expert behavior to me.''

''You're wrong,'' I said. ''It was very expert behavior. He alerted me by having a few too many of his people tailing us a little too closely. That was so I wouldn't miss the real show: Herr Bultman himself doing his senior-citizen walk-by act, in costume. How was I supposed to respond to that? I figure I was supposed to react just as you did: *Oh, my God, it's the sinister Kraut himself and he's got us surrounded; if we get on that lousy plane we'll be trapped and killed!''*

"But why . . . You mean, he doesn't really want us on the plane?"

"We'll make an agent of you yet," I said. "That's right, he wants us anywhere but on that airliner, if I have him figured correctly. When they closed in on us like that, so obviously herding us toward the gate and the plane, I was supposed to forget all about flying to Puerto Rico and think only of self-preservation. I was supposed to panic and make a run for it like a steer crashing out of the chute that leads to the gent with the big mallet. Remember, Bultman likes *big* operations involving lots of manpower. What probably happened was that the CLL asked him for help; they weren't getting anywhere with killing Sandra and me. We escaped their ambush in Miami Beach, Angelita's bomb missed Sandra in her Newport hotel room, the bomb in her Old Saybrook house blew up the wrong people, and Dominic Morelos died trying for the two of us in the Connecticut woods nearby, leaving his dead brother unavenged. Meanwhile, other members of the Legion are dying mysteriously elsewhere. Sonny Varek's people blew away the two men who were Angelita's partners in the Mariposa caper; and even though we're really not supposed to figure in this punitive operation—it's supposed to be strictly private citizens rising up to take vengeance on their own hook—I took a chance on getting Louis's hit team to take care of the two members of the Council you fingered for us, very discreetly."

Dana shivered slightly. "Yes, I suppose I did put the finger on them. Well, that's my job, isn't it? All right.

The Koenig and Galvez killings came in on the computer and you'll be pleased to know that the perpetrators, as the police like to call them, remain unknown and there seem to be no repercussions in our direction."

"Louis's perpetrators always do a nice clean job. Of course the cops probably have pretty good information about Arthur Galvez and Howard Koenig—if they didn't have it before, I'm sure Mac arranged for it to be passed on to them—and they aren't going to worry too much about how two top terrorists got dead." I shrugged. "Anyway, as far as we're concerned here, the way it probably worked was something like this: The CLL top brass started to feel the pressure, so, as I said, they took their problem to Bultman. Although he'd probably have preferred to concentrate on his military business, he couldn't afford to refuse them because he needs the recruits he's getting from them and, probably, the information they're supplying him about conditions in his target area on Gobernador. I'd be surprised if he wasn't using them as a source of intelligence as well as manpower."

Dana said, "Yes, that's correct. But hasn't there been a change of, well, let's call it emphasis? The Caribbean Legion started out simply trying to eliminate a certain embarrassing witness, Mrs. Helm. You were endangered only because you were her escort. Now the CLL seems to have instructed Bultman to forget her and concentrate on you. At least he isn't hanging around her hospital in Connecticut; he's here at the airport in New York giving you his personal attention."

I grinned. "That's Bultman's change of emphasis, not the Legion's. It's a compliment. He knows me. He knows that if I'm around, and there's homicidal trouble around, it's not a coincidence; and I should be disposed of, fast. Furthermore, I got the better of him once; and although we wound up working as allies on that operation, he's not forgetting the defeat. If he's got to take time out from his invasion project to soothe his panicky associates, he's not going to waste time on Sandra when he can get a crack at me. He has a personal score to settle. He'll worry about minor details like girl witnesses after I'm dead.''

Dana said dryly, ''Proving he's the fastest gun east of the Hudson, I suppose.''

I said, ''What's wrong with wanting to be the top expert in your field? Competition is the lifeblood of America, right? You just disapprove because the field happens to be homicide.'' I shook my head sadly and went on: ''Once he'd agreed to do the job, Bultman presumably rounded up a bunch of his toughest commandos and flew them up here, planning to take care of me and Sandra as fast as possible so he could get back to his real business in Montego and Gobernador. As I said, he goes in for large operations. I'll bet there's a gunner or two of some kind covering every exit of this building I'd be likely to use. He stationed them there, warning them to lounge around casually, of course, and not attract the attention of airport security. Then he went inside with his deliberately clumsy surveillance team, and his old-fogy act, to scare me off the plane and flush me out of the building and into the sights of his waiting marksmen. A gangland-style killing on the ground, or even two if you got caught in the cross fire, wouldn't attract nearly as much attention as something that happened in the air. Then he'd go for Sandra to wind up the job; but I'm gambling that as long as I manage to stay alive he'll give me top priority, if only for old times' sake.''

Dana didn't seem too interested in the question of Sandra's safety. ''So the only way we can get out of here, without shooting our way out, is to take the plane.''

I nodded. ''If I have it figured right, there's only one

safe place for us at the moment, and that's our long-awaited DC-10.''

"And if you have it figured wrong?" She grimaced, rising. "Well, we'll soon know. Here we go; they're boarding us now."

There was the usual delay on the ground; then we were airborne. Dana gripped my arm as the jets rammed us back into our seats; I felt her fingers tighten convulsively at the small rumble and jolt as the wheels came up. Four and a half hours later we were landing in Puerto Rico.

CHAPTER 26

IT wasn't Kennedy or Heathrow or Orly, or even Stockholm's Arlanda, but San Juan's Isla Verde International Airport wasn't any little boondocks airstrip, either. Inside the sizable modern building, we found immigration no problem since we were American citizens arriving in U.S. territory; but we had to retrieve our luggage and that involved the usual endless wait at the snakelike conveyor belt that wound its way through the baggage-claim area. Even though the room was a large one, a DC-10 load of passengers filled it almost to capacity.

I noted our shadow lounging in a corner of the crowded area. He was now wearing his faded denim jacket instead of carrying it, perhaps to alter his image slightly; he was still, however, lugging the same brown shopping bag. Although of heavy paper, it had got slightly ripped in transit. He was in his late twenties, a tall young man, over six feet, with bony masculine features that contrasted oddly, and rather unpleasantly, with his long feminine hair. I mean, if the pretty boys want to look prettier it's understandable; but for a gent with a face like Mount Kilimanjaro to go in for greasy golden locks was incomprehensible to me and therefore disturbing.

He wasn't very good at discreet surveillance. He'd spend long intervals ignoring us; then he'd throw a sudden panicky glance our way to make sure we hadn't vanished. That figured. Bultman would have had plenty of tough jungle fighters to choose from but few if any trained and experienced undercover operatives, when he'd picked his hit team hastily way down there at his training camp in Montego—well, it wasn't really so far from where we now were in Puerto Rico.

The baggage conveyor rumbled into action at last, and we moved forward for a better view of the stuff gliding past, as did everybody else in the room.

I said to Dana, "Try to keep an eye on our long-haired friend and see if he's met by anybody. Also . . . Do you know what Modesto looks like or do we have to wait for him to identify himself?"

"I know him."

"Okay, when you spot him, give him the signal for immediate contact and never mind being cute about it. I want a gun. I'm not one of your fastidious undercover heroes who disdain crude implements like firearms and do it all bare-handed or maybe with silk gloves on. That's a big guy and chances are he's just had some intensive combat conditioning, while all the exercise I've been getting lately is sitting on my butt behind the wheel of a sports car. He's working himself up to something. I'd like to be armed when he decides what it is."

She asked dryly, "What are you going to be doing while I'm watching out for all these people?"

"Looking stupid and unsuspicious," I said. "So that when I unleash my secret powers it will come as a terrible surprise to him."

"There's my bag now. It's the gray one. . . . Well, you saw it earlier."

It took a while for mine to arrive; then we were emerging in the concourse after passing through a fairly dense crowd of people waiting to greet arriving friends.

"There he is up ahead. . . . Matt!"

"What?"

"Have you ever heard of a self-healing grocery bag?"

I glanced at her sharply. "You're sure?"

"I'm sure that the paper bag he was carrying, one of those heavy ones with cord handles stapled to it . . ."

"Yes, I saw it."

"It had a noticeable rip near one of the handles. He had to carry it carefully by the bottom to keep it from splitting open; but I'm almost certain it isn't torn now. I got a good look at it when he set it down to get into that big backpack he got off the carousel. . . . Now he's going around the corner. Going. Gone."

I was busily studying a gaudy tourist map of the island, as if deciding how we should get where we wanted to go. "Modesto?" I asked.

Dana shook her head. "I can't be absolutely sure, of course; the place is full of short, dark, middle-aged, Hispano-type men; but if he were here he'd have spotted us by this time; he'd be trying to attract our attention inconspicuously."

"Well, we'll just have to do without him," I said. "Blondie's either got somebody watching me, or he's sneaked back to keep an eye on me himself; he can't afford to lose me. I'm going into that john down the way. That'll give him a chance, if he wants it, to corner me without the whole airport watching. You stand guard over our luggage, right here. I think you'll be safe alone since it's me they want. Keep your eyes open. Somebody might come by carrying a torn paper bag. Of course the guy who brought the undamaged one could already have jettisoned the ripped one he got in exchange; it probably contained nothing but Blondie's dirty laundry. But maybe not. I'd kind of like to know what their local contact looks like.''

Dana frowned. ''Matt, be careful. You said you needed a gun to handle him.''

''Let's have a little accuracy here. I said I *wanted* a gun to handle him. I want a gun, period. With Modesto missing, I'll have to get one elsewhere. Wish me luck.''

''Luck, darling.''

I was aware of her watching me in a concerned way as I headed for the men's room. Well, it's always nice to have somebody who cares. I found the place empty for the moment. It was fairly new and quite clean. The plumbing seemed to be in good shape. I picked the urinal farthest to the right, taking my time about my business. If I stood back a little, peeing at maximum range, I could see the door out of the corner of my eye, the door through which Blondie had to come.

It was a gamble, of course. He presumably had a gun now or the paper-bag switch made no sense. It was a gun I intended to have since my own source of supply seemed to have dried up, but first I had to keep it from shooting me. It wasn't going to be easy, in this shiny tiled room without any cover but the booths, which weren't bullet-proof, and the slab of marble beside me separating the urinals from the lavatories, which might be if it was real stone. They can do some very deceptive things with petroleum nowadays. In my favor, of course, was the fact that he was not a pro. He'd hate me for saying so, protesting what a tough mercenary soldier he was, but this wasn't soldier business. I was betting that, like any amateur, he'd shuffle his feet a little before he got to work, instead of simply stepping inside, firing three aimed shots, and stepping out again.

The door opened, but the man who entered was small and dark. He came over to stand beside me. Then the one I was expecting came in and paused by the door. He saw me, but he didn't have a clear shot because of the marble divider, and he wasn't ready to take it, anyway, with a witness standing beside me. He just came forward slowly, waiting for the one beside me to finish and go off to the lavatories. There was a nervous moment as Blondie passed behind me, but he wanted us alone, and he just stepped up beside me to claim the vacated urinal.

He was stripped for action, I noted. The backpack and paper bag had been left somewhere, along with the denim jacket. The T-shirt, which had been tucked in all around, now hung loose over his jeans. Standing there beside me, he was slow about opening his pants, presumably for the same reason I was fast about closing mine: it's embarrassing to go into battle hanging out. The little dark man with the well-washed hands went out, never to know the excitement he was missing.

The door closed automatically behind him. As if it had been a signal from the range master in charge of the combat course, we moved simultaneously. Blondie reached up under the concealing T-shirt and went for the gun tucked into the front of his jeans. I already held concealed in my right hand, open, the little Gerber knife I'd once more got past the airport sensors, although at Kennedy they'd had me sweating. I reached out with my left hand. . . .

My intended tactics were practically flawless. Grab the long convenient hair behind and yank hard; that would throw him off balance and keep him from pivoting towards me and bringing his weapon into action. I'd determined earlier that he was right-handed; and I'd carefully placed myself so he'd have to attack from my left. The hair-pull would also tip his head back and expose his throat to the blade. The mark of the true professional is this kind of meticulous planning. There was only one catch. The hair I grabbed wasn't his.

It came off in my hand. The lack of the resistance I'd expected threw me off balance instead of him. I was saved only by my position on his right. I had a moment to pull myself together while, catching the gleam of the knife, he was swinging his left arm over to cover his throat and at the same time attempting to turn the pistol barrel towards me—the weapon was a silenced .22 automatic that had a familiar look. It was a relatively feeble assassination weapon, but one that would certainly do the job if I let it.

For a moment, the situation bordered on the ridiculous: Two armed men trying to kill each other with weapons that were both pointing the wrong way. I was crowding him so he couldn't bring the gun around to bear; but I'd been holding my knife for an upstroke at his now protected throat and I knew I didn't have time to reverse it for a downstroke at his gun wrist. I struck anyway; to hell with the blade. I drove a hammer blow with my fist down at his gunhand. The hilt of the knife gave it authority and knocked the weapon from his grasp.

He knew about guns. He knew too much about guns for this situation. He couldn't help an instinctive little pause, waiting to learn if the falling weapon was going to discharge when it hit. I had a moment in which to strike again—we're trained to ignore things we can do nothing about, like bouncing firearms—and I went for the chest as the best target available to me, although three inches of steel there, although it may kill eventually, isn't likely to disable anybody promptly except the kind of person who faints at the thought of being cut anywhere.

I managed to miss the breastbone and, with luck, the ribs. The blade went in all the way, but I almost lost it when, undisturbed by the fact that he now had a perforated lung, Blondie, who wasn't blond any longer, dove for the gun that had clattered away across the tiles without going off.

I managed to give him a helpful shove with my left hand and stick out my right foot to trip him, so he went down harder than he'd planned. Too bad for Blondie, who'd been taught to take firearms too seriously. If he'd stood fast to slug it out, he'd have had a chance, even with a hole in his chest. Flat on the floor, reaching desperately for the pistol, he had none. I landed on top of him hard, slammed his face into the tiles, and drove the point of the pear-shaped blade into the neck between the proper vertebrae. There was a kind of general convulsion under me; then he was limp and still.

There's supposed to be a moment of regret or something afterwards, but that's for the amateurs. When they come to kill me I have no regrets when they die. Sometimes I've known a sense of accomplishment when the task has been a difficult one and I've executed it well, and a certain pleasure at being alive afterwards; but there was nothing like that here. All I felt was disgust at my own immense stupidity. My subconscious mind had been telling me right along that there was something wrong with all that hair; my God, this was one of Bultman's commandos! When, since the age of the Vikings, had men been sent into battle with shoulder-length locks?

Lying there now, he looked the way he should, considering where he'd come from: a tough man with crew-cut brown hair. There wasn't much blood from the chest wound and hardly any from the neck wound. I hauled him into the nearest booth and sat him on the pot and hurried out to retrieve the gun and the wig. The door to the concourse was opening and I couldn't take time to clean up the small gory smears on the tiles; but somebody's always bleeding in rest rooms.

I ducked back into the booth. I hoped that nobody'd count the number of feet showing under the partitions; but I didn't want to leave him alone in case he'd fall over. A man came into the place, and then another; for a while the traffic was brisk, but it was all urinal business and soon completed. When the room was empty again, I braced him in place as well as I could. I started to put the wig on his head but left it in his lap instead. He was a warrior who'd tried hard to play a deadly game with which he was unfamiliar; and he'd lost. Why make him look ridiculous?

There was no way of locking the cubicle from outside, but I rolled up the handkerchief I found in his pocket and jammed it in the crack to hold the door closed. I made sure the pistol I'd inherited was secure inside the waistband of my slacks, and buttoned my jacket over it, and got out of there.

CHAPTER 27

DANA was leaning against the wall beside our luggage. Obviously tense and worried, she was trying hard to look like a bored lady traveler just wondering what the hell was delaying her gentleman companion in the john, Montezuma's revenge? When she saw me she straightened up abruptly and took a couple of quick steps to meet me.

"Matt!" she breathed. "It took so long. . . . I saw him go in there after you! I thought I'd die waiting to see who . . . Are you all right?"

"Never mind all that," I said. "Did any damaged paper bags go by?"

"Yes, she went around the corner over there, where he came from."

"A woman?"

"A girl, not much over twenty. Spanish or Latino or Chicano, whatever it is they want to be called today, I don't bother to keep track. They'll change it tomorrow anyway. Not Pachuco, that's derogatory. Hispano? Matt . . ."

"Description?"

Dana showed some resentment at my persistent questioning, but shrugged and said, "She was rather pretty. Olive skin, good complexion. Considerable makeup, but pretty well done. Black hair, careful hairdo, rather short, blow-dried. Not as tall as I am, but not tiny." I'd asked for a description and she was by God going to give me one, every detail. "Good figure but just a little too female, if you know what I mean; or maybe it was the jeans she was wearing. Fashionably faded. Fashionably threadbare. Fashionable holes at knee and rump. And tight, my God; you wonder how they get into them and why they don't split when they do! But clean, and she was wearing a clean white fiesta blouse, you know the fancy ruffled ones, cut down to hither, or maybe yonder. Décolletage, they used to call it; *mucho* décolletage. High-heeled white shoes. She was definitely holding the bag, if you'll excuse it. The right bag with the rip in it. Is that descriptive enough for you?"

"It's fine," I said. "Now . . ."

"Matt, what *happened* in there?"

I said impatiently, "This is no time for an instant replay, sweetheart. You're the liaison girl. Find a phone and get some gravediggers here fast. Tell them he's sitting on the potty, last cubicle to the left, up against the wall. The door isn't latched, just jammed shut; a hard push will do it. Tell them to take him out and bury him deep. If they're too late, if he's already been discovered when they arrive, they'll have to get somebody heavy to lean on the authorities for us. When you've finished briefing them, call Washington and report that Bultman has intervened, so I guess I'm going to have to take care of him before I'm through. That should warm the cockles of Mac's heart, if any. He said the Kraut wouldn't leave me alone to do this job and he was right as usual, damn him. Give him all the details. Then hie yourself over to Avis and collect our car. Where can you pick me up around here?"

"So you killed him." Dana's voice was flat.

It had been a pretty close thing in that tiled rest room; and I found that I didn't have much tolerance for bleeding hearts and girls who couldn't make up their cotton-picking little minds. First there had been Sandra who'd bounced like a tennis ball between her humanitarian impulses and her thirst for vengeance; and now I had this handsome lady who couldn't seem to decide whether she loved me for staying alive or hated me for making the other guy dead.

"Better I should have let him kill me?" I asked sourly.

Dana grimaced. "I know. I'm sorry, I guess I'm just not used to it, Matt. I guess I'm just an office girl at heart; but I'm really very glad you didn't let him kill you." She smiled crookedly. "I'll pick you up over there at the loading zone behind the car-rental booths. Don't get impatient. They keep their cars on a lot half a mile away. I'll have to use their bus to get out there, whenever it decides to come along, unless I can bribe a taxi driver to make that short a run." She hesitated. "What are you going to do?"

I said, "I'm going to see if I can find Blondie's girlfriend. I want to ask her how she managed to get hold of one of our special toys to give him." I patted my jacket at waist level. "Device, termination, sound-suppressed, twenty-two-caliber. I think that's the current Washington jargon. They're great on 'devices' these days; they wouldn't dream of using a nasty word like 'weapon' or 'gun' in one of their spec sheets. Actually it's a Ruger, not to be confused with a Luger. It's what Blondie was packing. Almost certainly one of ours."

Dana frowned. "Do you think . . . Modesto?"

"He's the most likely answer, yes. Either he sold out . . ."

"Modesto wouldn't betray us!"

I looked at her curiously. "You know our contact that well, huh? Okay, say he didn't sell out. Say they just grabbed him and took away from him the weapon he'd intended to bring here for me. That probably means he's either lying dead somewhere or being held alive somewhere, and I'd better find out which and where. But first I'd better find this tight-pants chick you saw, if she hasn't vanished completely by this time."

But the girl hadn't disappeared. I spotted her at once over at the side of the concourse when I reentered the building at the far end after making a wide, fast detour outside, passing the loading area where Dana was to pick me up and the taxi stands and bus stops. It was obviously the vantage spot from which Blondie had watched me go into the john, a shallow alcove formed by a convenient jog in the wall. His backpack was there and she was sitting on it. She had both paper bags—one torn, one whole—on the floor beside her, along with his jacket.

I studied her briefly from a distance before making my approach, wondering at the inconsistency of her getup.

261

She was a classy young lady from the meticulous dark hair to the immaculate white heels—with the glaring exception of the jeans, faded and ripped and frayed, that made her look like a bum from waist to ankles. Well, I guess I simply don't understand the modern denim mystique, having worn out too many pairs of Levi's as a boy on my parents' New Mexico ranch. They'll always be just post-hole-digging, shit-shoveling pants to me.

She didn't notice me coming up behind her; she was too busy staring in the direction of the rest-room sign, willing Blondie to appear. It seemed likely that she'd seen me emerge alive and healthy; but she'd continued to wait there among the missing man's belongings, clearly hoping that, although he'd obviously failed in his murderous mission, he'd at least managed to survive it.

"He won't be coming back, señorita," I said softly. She started, and turned to look at me. I said, "No, sit still, please, and keep your hands off that purse."

She was staring at the gun I was pointing at her, concealed by my body from the passersby. "He is dead? He must be dead for you to have his weapon!"

It was no place to go into the question of whose weapon it really was. Presumably, they'd got it off Modesto, and presumably that meant they knew Modesto was working for us. But I didn't want to gamble too much on presumably and ask the wrong questions, about the weapon or anything else. I didn't want to betray to this girl any information she didn't already have. She was glaring up at me angrily. She was quite pretty, with wide cheekbones, white teeth, and big brown eyes emphasized by the careful makeup noted by Dana. The black, curling eyelashes were as spectacular as those Lia Varek had sported when I'd first seen her. The eyes were luminous with hatred.

"The man in there was something special to you?" I asked. "If so, I'm sorry. He gave me no choice."

Her mouth was ugly with the same emotion that made her eyes lovely. "They are all special to me, all our brave soldiers of liberation, you imperialist pig!"

I didn't know real people said things like that. I said, "Let me have your purse for a moment, please."

She started to refuse, but shrugged elaborately instead. I took the purse left-handed and checked it out: no weapon. If she was packing anything but herself inside those pants, she could never pry it out in a hurry. The loose, low-cut, white blouse didn't even do a good job of concealing her unsupported and quite admirable breasts; I was fairly sure it concealed nothing else.

I returned the purse and picked up the paper bag that wasn't torn, still left-handed. It contained some clothes and, as I'd hoped, since I'd found nothing of the sort on Blondie, a couple of hard objects that turned out to be a spare ten-shot magazine for the Ruger, loaded, and a fifty-round box of .22 ammo, better than half full. Remington, if it matters. Fifty .45 cartridges will pretty well fill your pants pockets and make you walk bowlegged, but fifty .22s fit into a container hardly larger than a matchbox. I pocketed the gun items and put the bag of clothes down beside the girl.

"You'll carry those bags," I said. "I'll carry the pack and the jacket. We're going out to the loading area. A car will pick us up there, but we may have to wait for it. Please don't get any ideas while we're waiting. Don't think I'll hesitate to shoot because there are people around. The pistol is silenced. I'll drop you dead before you can take two steps and everybody'll think the poor girl just fainted."

"I will not give you the pleasure of killing again, you bloodthirsty fascist murderer!"

"All right. Here we go."

I draped the jacket over my gun arm and hoisted the pack to my left shoulder. It wasn't a real backbreaker, but I wouldn't have wanted to tote it up any big mountains. We walked across the concourse and out under the flaring concrete roof that sheltered the passengers who were waiting to pick up their ground transportation from the bright sunshine beyond. It was a tropical view out there, complete with palm trees. I stopped the girl by a big round pillar near the curb and set down the pack.

"You can sit on it again," I said. "That's an order, sweetie."

"I spit on your orders!"

I didn't know real people said that, either; but after saying it she settled down where she'd been told. I stood beside her, reviewing in my mind everything that had happened, very carefully. I'd missed that damn wig. I couldn't afford to miss anything else. Like maybe a pretty female fanatic putting on a phony Spanish-spitfire act?

"What's your name?" I asked.

"I am La Margarita."

"That's not a girl, it's a drink." I grinned. "Okay. A beautiful drink. A dangerous drink. Too much La Margarita makes a man helpless—with love or alcohol, same difference. Right?" She gave that elaborate Latin shrug again and didn't answer. I asked, "Are you from Islas Gobernador?"

"Ha, those two little spots in the sea!" she sneered. "They are not the only victims of Yankee oppression. I am a member of the FFPR."

"More idiot acronyms," I said. "Translate, please. What's an FFPR?"

"You *Norteamericano* swine don't even bother to learn about an island you claim to own! We are the Freedom Force of Puerto Rico. Like the liberty-loving people of Gobernador, we are being assisted in our fight for independence by the CLL. You do know what that is, I hope!"

"Yes, I know. So the Caribbean Legion of Liberty has

264

been helping you, and now you're helping them. Helping them do what?''

''We are helping them bring to revolutionary justice a government assassin guilty of brutal crimes against the people. You!''

I laughed harshly. ''That's me, all right, sweetie. I'm guilty as hell. Guilty of brutal crimes against the people who murdered my son. Did they tell you that? Did they tell you how they blew up a restaurant full of innocent people, including my older boy?''

She looked momentarily disconcerted, and licked her lips. ''No, I didn't know. . . .'' She caught herself, and made a quick recovery. ''But there are no innocent Yankee people! You are all responsible for the oppression suffered by my poor, captive country!''

I said, ''Have it your way. If you're going to hand out blanket responsibility . . . If we're all responsible, then so are all of you. Responsible for my Matthew's murder. All you two-bit pseudopatriots. What are you griping about, anyway? You got your big bang, or your CLL did. Do you expect it to be free? Do you think you can claim the right to blow up my kid with a bomb without conceding to me the right to come after you with a gun?''

''But you are an agent of the imperialist Yankee government!''

I said, ''I was retired, baby; I'd quit. I was a peaceful citizen—and then your CLL friends set off that blast in West Palm Beach, and Washington called me back. And now I'm going to wipe out your fucking Legion, all of it that matters; and if any of your lousy FFPR members get in my way I'll take them out, too. . . . Here's our ride. Be careful. Keep in mind that one way or another, directly or indirectly, I've already accounted for seven of your half-baked revolutionaries, eight counting your friend in the can. If you want to make it nine, just try to run. Or let your friends try to jump me or get the drop on me. You'll be the first to die. That's a promise."

I hoisted the heavy pack to my shoulder again and herded La Margarita towards the little brown two-door that had just pulled up with Dana at the wheel. La Margarita! Maybe I should call myself El Vodka Martini, hey? I hoped I'd made some impression on her. You can go about it two ways: soft-spoken or loudmouthed. The soft-spoken menace bit is often effective, but you do run the risk of having them get the idea you're as soft as your voice, incapable of really hurting anybody. Of course, if instead you choose to go with the blowhard routine I'd just used, there's always a risk of overdoing it and causing them to think you might be bluffing.

I hoped she wouldn't. As far as I knew, she wasn't on any list of ours, and I had nothing against her except the revolutionary clichés she kept spitting at me, not a capital offense. Well, as I'd tried to make clear to her, her survival depended on her behavior and that of her friends. I hoped they'd all done their homework and knew enough about our brand of government assassins—government counterassassins, we like to call ourselves—to know how we're trained.

On second thought, I did have something against her. Knowing how it was to be used, she'd supplied the weapon with which Blondie was supposed to kill me. But I still hoped she and her friends would be sensible and remember that I'd been at this business since long before most of them had learned to tell the boys from the girls. I hoped none of them would try anything stupid.

266

Chapter 28

Dana drove the little brown car skillfully and smoothly—well, as smoothly as the automatic transmission allowed. It kept shifting on her unexpectedly, each time with a startling clunk, as the feeble engine asked its controlling gremlins for gear relief. She talked as she drove, following my instructions. There wasn't really much to discuss, but there's nothing more nerve-racking than somebody chattering away at a time when you want to contemplate your fears in silence, so she prattled compulsively for our prisoner's benefit, ostensibly giving me information she thought I should have about Puerto Rico.

She told me that the island had been discovered by Columbus on his second voyage in 1493. She said that it was settled by the Spaniards under Ponce de Leon, presumably before he wandered off to Florida in the search for the Fountain of Youth that killed him. She informed me that it was taken over by the U.S. in the Spanish-American War of 1898, and that Puerto Ricans became American citizens in 1917. She said Puerto Rico is roughly a hundred and ten miles long and thirty-five miles wide. It has an area of approximately thirty-five hundred square miles and a population of a little over three million people, half a million of whom live in the capital city of San Juan. The smallest of the Greater Antilles, it lies just east of Hispaniola, which lies just east of Cuba, which lies just south of Florida. On the other side of Puerto Rico are the Virgin Islands and the rest of the long chain of the Lesser Antilles curving down to South America.

The girl with whom I shared the cramped backseat said nothing, although some of Dana's political observations must have offended her revolutionary principles. I had her on my left with the muzzle of the automatic pistol—actually the end of the silencer—touching her ribs, not the safest technique for transporting a prisoner, and I wouldn't have used it on a strong man or a trained one, but she was a small girl and I thought I could handle her if she tried to make a break. She obviously had no doubts as to my intentions and she was sweating it out, her careful hairdo beginning to straggle a little, her face shiny, her elaborate makeup starting to melt with perspiration in spite of the car's air conditioning.

I'd asked Dana to find us a quiet place where we could stop for a while undisturbed. She brought us at last to a little seaside park, a green oasis surrounded by tall buildings, at least a couple of which were hotels. She found us a space at the curb of a park drive lined with other cars. I noticed that they were all in pretty good shape, often quite new like our rental unit. There were none of the rattletrap automotive relics you find, for instance, in Mexico. From the stopped car, we could look out over a grassy expanse and see far out over the Atlantic Ocean, but we couldn't see the nearby beach because of a raised retaining wall that kept the sand from encroaching on the shore road over there.

It wasn't an ideal place, but there wasn't a great deal of traffic, automotive or pedestrian, and you learn to make do with what's available. Dana had informed me that the agency maintained no interrogation teams in this area. With Modesto's life perhaps at stake, there wasn't time to have one flown in, so I'd have to do the dirty work myself. Well, it wasn't as if I hadn't performed similar chores in the past, but I prefer to use the I-teams, not because I'm particularly queasy, but because they're more skillful than I am and have drugs that permit them to pump a subject dry without leaving him, or her, in too bad shape. If the kid beside me was a typical stubborn fanatic, ready to die for her cause, I might have to get very rough.

Dana opened the door on her side and cleared her throat. "I think I'll take a little walk," she said. She was still keeping up the act I'd asked of her, but it wasn't entirely an act now. She looked a little pale. "I have a very weak stomach," she said, getting out.

"Stay within hearing," I said. "Come back when I beep the horn three times."

"Check."

We watched her walk away, tall and slender in her wine-colored slacks and sweater. Then I switched hands on the gun and took out my little knife and flipped it open one-handed, quite legally. Like most of the laws that are supposed to protect us from inanimate objects, the switchblade regulations were soon circumvented by ingenious chaps who figured out how to open an ordinary folding knife one-handed. All it takes is an easy-opening knife like my Gerber, a little lubricant, and a flick of the wrist. It's a handy stunt and it impresses people. The girl who went by the fool name of La Margarita stared wide-eyed at the small, pear-shaped, stainless-steel blade I'd produced so cleverly. She didn't overlook the traces of blood on it. I'd given it a hasty swipe with a piece of toilet paper, but I'd missed a few smears.

La Margarita licked her lips. "Where did you . . . He said you were unarmed!"

"A real hero!" I said. "Carefully equipping himself with a gun to deal with an unarmed man!"

She had no answer to that. She just gave her big Latin

269

shrug again and said resentfully, "That woman of yours, she talks too much!"

"These things always make her nervous. Sick to the stomach even. But my nerves and digestion are in great shape, sweetheart." I poked her with the Ruger. "Where did you get this gun?"

"It was given to me to give to Raoul." When I frowned, she said, "Raoul Bonnette, the man you just murdered. I was selected to pass him the weapon because I knew him by sight. In fact I . . . I knew him very well, before he left for Montego to train with the army that will free Islas Gobernador from the Yankee yoke. It will be a beginning. Eventually we will liberate the entire Caribbean from the imperialist oppressors and their slavish puppet regimes and form a new nation, a great oceanic federation of free islands."

"Make up your mind," I said. "They're either slaves or puppets; they can't be both." She glared at me without speaking. I went on: "So the guy in the airport john was a friend of yours, after all. Sorry about that. Bonnette. That's a French name, isn't it?"

"Yes, we are all together in this, whether our origins are French, Spanish, Dutch, Portuguese, British, or even American. We are cutting the umbilical cord of imperialism. The Caribbean will be a sea of liberty, not an ocean preserve for capitalist exploitation!"

"Who's going to organize this sea of liberty, the Cubans or the Russians?"

"Ah, you Yankees see wicked commies under every bed! And if it should be Fidel, at least he is one of us, an islander like ourselves."

There was a certain amount of irony in the fact that Bultman, who'd lost a foot and his health trying to terminate Fidel Castro on contract, was now engaged in recruiting and training a military force for an operation that might just possibly lead to an island empire under the domination of that self-same gent with the beard. I remembered that Dana hadn't thought much of Bultman's chances, but the feasibility of the grandiose plan didn't really matter. Terrorists and fanatic patriots are seldom in touch with reality. And if they kill you following an impossible political dream, you're still dead. Like Matthew Helm, Jr.

"Given to you by whom?" I asked.

"What?"

"Who gave you this gun? All this is very fascinating, but I still want to hear *how* you got it."

"I have no more to say to you, you murdering Yankee pig!"

She faced me stubbornly in the cramped backseat of the little car. Next time, I reflected, I'd order a limousine. Awkwardly, I stowed the pistol away in the right-hand pocket of my coat, the side away from her where she couldn't grab for it, and brought the knife up close to her face, remembering that I'd done the same menace bit before, quite recently. Talking about heroes, I seemed to spend most of my time frightening children: the Morelos boy in West Palm Beach, and now this young girl in San Juan. I watched her eyes cross in a way that might have been comical under other circumstances, as they focused on the sharp blade only a few inches away.

I said, "One of the Indian tribes out west had a pleasant trick. The punishment for adultery was, they slit the squaw's nose. Of course, in some other societies, I gather, they cut it clear off, but that seems pretty drastic and we'll reserve it for a real emergency."

La Margarita licked her lips. "You should have worked in Auschwitz with the other Nazi animals! But you can't make me talk. . . ."

They always say that unless they're really tough, in which case they don't say anything. In spite of her spitfire routine, she turned out to be not so tough. In fact I was surprised at how quickly she yielded. All it took was a little blood and some further threats, building up to the promise of nasal amputation. I'll admit I was relieved. I have my sexual kinks like most men—I won't venture to speak for women—but whittling on pretty girls isn't one of them.

Still, it bothered me a bit that, after all her brave defiance, she hadn't put up a better resistance before breaking down and answering my questions tearfully. I reminded myself that I'd had another surprise today that had almost killed me; and that I'd better keep in mind the fact that things weren't always what they seemed. Nevertheless, Dana hadn't been gone a full ten minutes when I gave the recall signal on the horn. She came back across the park lawn and approached the car warily, gasping when she saw the red spots on the younger girl's blouse, and the tear-streaked and blood-smeared face.

"Relax, she's just got a couple of little nicks," I said. "You seem to be kindred spirits. She can't stand the sight of blood, either; at least not her own blood. But don't forget this is the same little girl who was perfectly ready to pass her boyfriend a gun so he could spill my blood. Give me some Kleenex so I can wipe her face a bit, will you?"

"Don't touch me!" That was the kid. Before I could start cleaning her up, she'd hauled up the loose front of her blouse and mopped herself off with it, making a gory mess of the ruffles. It seemed to please her in a masochistic way. "There, that's good enough for a dead body, isn't it?" she said triumphantly. "You've got what you wanted, now finish your filthy job. Kill me!"

"You're not going to die at my hands unless you behave stupidly, or your friends do," I said. I handed her the tissues Dana had given me. "Here, hold this to your nose. It'll stop in a little while. It's all inside the nostril, in case you're brooding about it; it won't show. Now we'll check to make sure the address you gave me is correct. . . . 427 Pacheco Street,'' I said to Dana. ''Do you know where it is?''

''No. Pacheco Street? I never heard of it.''

''Tell her how to get there,'' I said to La Margarita, and listened to some Kleenex-muffled directions that meant nothing to me. Then we were driving away from there. After a while I spoke to the back of Dana's head: ''There seems to be a local businessman named Paul Encinias. Big in ladies' clothing. A refugee from the current regime in Gobernador who managed to slip out with enough money to settle here comfortably some years back. Apparently Gobernador had a good reason to run him out, although they weren't aware of it. He was secretly a member of the Caribbean Legion of Liberty, even a member of the Council of Thirteen. However, recently his terrorist colleagues have begun to suspect that he's been passing information to someone in Washington. They don't know to whom, but they're trying hard to find out.''

Dana didn't turn her head. ''Go on.''

''Naturally, suspecting him of double-crossing them, the CLL has been keeping a discreet eye on Paul Encinias with the help of La Margarita's people, the FFPR. Today an FFPR member shadowing Paul saw him make contact with a known American agent and receive a package. The FFPR checked with the CLL—God, their alphabet soup is as thick as Washington's—and were told to grab the lousy traitor. They did, and found that his package contained a fancy silenced weapon complete with spare clip and ammo. They got out of him the fact that it was meant for a U.S. operative who'd soon be arriving in San Juan by air. Me. Then they received a phone call from the U.S. Kennedy International. Herman Heinrich Bultman on the line. Bultman said he had a man on my plane tailing me, Raoul Bonnette, who'd need a

gun when he got here so he could deal with me permanently; meet him and arm him, please. ETA. Paper-bag
routine. The kid, here, got the delivery job since she
knew Bonnette by sight and vice versa. They gave her
the weapon they'd just confiscated from Encinias to pass
along. Guns aren't easy to come by and why waste a
freebie?''

Dana continued to look straight ahead, driving. "What
about Paul Encinias?''

''She says he was alive when she last saw him, but not
in very good shape. I gather they're saving him for further interrogation. They think, from the information that's
been compromised, that he must have accomplices elsewhere in the movement, a whole network. They hope to
weed it all out, like crabgrass, with his reluctant help.''

''But he still hasn't betrayed his contact in Washington?''

''Not yet, but they're hoping.''

''We've got to get him out of there!''

''We don't gotta do nothing, baby. And we certainly
don't gotta discuss it in front of a prisoner. If you tell
her too much, you'll have to shoot her. I promised I
wouldn't if she behaved, but I didn't say anything about
you.''

''Tie her up and I'll see if I can find a park bench
where we can talk.''

CHAPTER 29

OLD San Juan is a walled city defended by several ancient forts. There have been numerous sieges, the first being the 1595 siege of El Castillo de Felipe del Morro, known as El Morro, by Sir Francis Drake. As we came up to the fort on the shore road, Dana was trying to remember whether Queen Elizabeth's favorite sea rover—well, I guess Sir Walter Raleigh actually had the inside track there—had made it or been beaten off, she thought the latter. She said that, as I could see, the old city was located on a peninsula that was almost an island; causeways and bridges connected it with the mainland, if you want to call Puerto Rico a mainland.

She said that "morro" simply means headland or bluff; and she hadn't meant to take us clear out to the point on which El Morro was located, but it had been a while since she'd last driven here and she'd missed the turn for which she'd been looking. To rectify her mistake, she followed the shore around and then chauffeured us into a maze of very narrow one-way streets between shabby buildings several stories high, little urban canyons at the bottom of which the streets were only two cars wide. Parking was permitted on one side, leaving only one lane for traffic. When somebody stopped to make a delivery or chat with a friend on the sidewalk, everything came to a halt, but that's par for the course in any Latin country. I'd lived long enough in New Mexico to know that it never occurs to a driver of Spanish descent that someone behind him may be in a hurry, since he never is.

In the meantime, I'd bullied our prisoner into cleaning herself up a little better, telling her that if she insisted on looking like a battlefield casualty she'd have to ride on the floor where she didn't show, with my feet on her. Fortunately, Dana had a couple of those little plastic-wrapped soapy washcloths in her purse. Even clean, La Margarita's face wasn't as pretty as it had been; there was a certain amount of swelling and inflammation. It wasn't permanent, it would heal, given time, but it made me feel guilty nevertheless. I told myself to hell with it; chivalry was obsolete and these days they didn't even want it, right? If she'd been a man, the state of her face wouldn't have bothered me a bit, right?

I made her struggle into the late Raoul Bonnette's jacket and zip it up to cover her stained blouse. It was much too big for her, of course; but if they arrested women for wearing baggy clothes these days, half the female population would be in jail. Then I lashed her wrists with my handkerchief, and buckled my belt around her ankles, hoping my slacks would stay up without it.

"All set back here," I said to Dana. "Where are we heading?"

"I'm looking for another park I remember, complete with benches," she said over her shoulder. "It's not too far from that address she gave us. . . . There it is; and it looks as if a car's just pulling out across the way. Let's see if I can grab the space before somebody else gets it."

She could; and a couple of minutes later we were sitting side by side on a bench under the trees. All we needed was a picnic basket. The little oasis of green measured one long block in one direction, and two short blocks in the other. There was a small department store facing the park from one corner, and various other retail establishments all around including a hardware store and a dress shop. They looked very much like their small-town U.S. counterparts. I wondered if the dress shop was the one, or one of the ones, owned and operated by Paul Encinias. It was called The Fashion and the window featured a skinny mannequin in a shiny blue jersey dress with an uneven hem that the designer probably hadn't planned on, but that's jersey for you.

We didn't speak at once. Instead we watched a lady policeman stroll by. She was quite handsome in her broad-brimmed hat and snugly fitting tan uniform; but you'd never mistake her for a male officer although she was wearing pants. A polished Sam Browne supported all the usual cop paraphernalia including a big automatic pistol.

"Relax," I said to Dana, who kept throwing apprehensive glances at our parked car. "The kid isn't going to beat on the car windows and scream for help; she doesn't want fuzz any more than we do."

"You keep telling me to relax."

"In this business, you'll wear yourself out if you don't. Just tell yourself it'll all be the same in a hundred years. Okay, the council of war is now called to order. This captured clown Encinias, I suppose he's our missing Modesto."

"Yes, but he's not a . . ."

"Not a clown? Any agent who lets himself be spotted making an important contact is a clown in my book. If he then lets himself be taken alive with important information in his head that can threaten the whole operation and endanger other agents, he's a real comedian. Hell, even if he didn't have a capsule, he had a gun, didn't he?"

She said hotly, "You can't judge Paul by the brutal rules under which you operate! He's not a trained agent, any more than I am. We're both volunteers, Matt. The man who came down here to recruit us—your Mr. Trask, as a matter of fact—knew perfectly well that we knew very little about guns and violence; and I'm sure he never expected us to commit patriotic hara-kiri.''

I said, ''So Encinias/Modesto is our man inside the Caribbean Legion, and you're his Washington contact.''

''That's right.''

''Then it's a simple turncoat operation, after all? Where does all your well-publicized computer expertise come in?'' I shook my head quickly. ''Don't tell me, let me guess. I'll bet your Paul Encinias had his clothing business pretty well computerized, right? Rather than be entirely dependent on the hired help, he'd learned what buttons to push. So when he decided to come over to us, for whatever reason, it was arranged that he should use his office setup for transmissions, working after hours when nobody was around—he was probably in the habit of staying late, anyway; most successful businessmen put in a lot of unpaid overtime. He'd pass information through normal commercial channels, Compuphone or Telecomp or whatever they call it, using some kind of an innocent-looking code or cipher. Say he'd order from a certain supplier in the U.S., who happened to be you, so many pairs of panty hose for his stores, and so many pairs of jeans; and it would mean that the redcoats were landing on Omaha Beach at midnight. Then you'd send back Mac's instructions the same way.''

She smiled faintly. ''Well, it wasn't exactly like that, it was more complicated than that, but you have the general idea.''

Something stirred in my mind. ''What kind of instructions did you pass along? Did Mac ever order Modesto to use his influence to have the CLL bomb a specific target?''

Dana looked shocked. ''Heavens, no! Mac wouldn't . . .''

I said, "There may be something Mac wouldn't do, but I haven't come across it yet. If he needed somebody taken out, and didn't care to make it official by using a regular agent, and had a bunch of gullible terrorists available, he wouldn't hesitate to make use of them by pointing them that way."

"Well, he never passed any orders like that through me." Then she hesitated. "I mean, that I knew about. Of course there was the B-code."

"What's a B-code?"

"Usually we used the A-code; and I'd encode the message for transmission myself. Once in a while, though, when security was very tight, the B-code would be used and I'd be handed the message ready to go and told to send it off exactly as written and not to get curious."

"Did that happen often?"

"Three times since we started operations. The last was a few weeks ago, I can't recall the exact date." She made a face. "I didn't like it. It made me feel . . . untrusted, being bypassed like that, as if Mac and Modesto were ganging up on me."

"Join the club," I said. It was time to drop what was, after all, pretty much a personal matter between Mac and me, and get to the business at hand. I went on: "How do you think I feel, learning that you've had a plain old human contact on the Council of Thirteen right along. Here I thought you were producing all that fine information out of thin air with that computer of yours."

She laughed. "I doubt very much that you really believed that, Matt."

"Well, it was the impression you and Mac were working very hard to put across, wasn't it? That you were some kind of a mad electronic genius who just had to play a few tunes on the keyboard to come up with a detailed picture of what the opposition was doing. It made a cover of sorts, and it may actually have kept some people from getting too curious about your source of information; but I kind of figured there had to be an input somewhere to make an output in Washington. Computers don't construct information from nothing. As they say: shit in, shit out.''

Dana said primly, "We prefer the word 'garbage.' "

"I know. GIGO."

Dana said uneasily, with a glance at the car, "While we're talking, that girl could be freeing herself."

"Stick to your computers," I said. "Let me worry about the kid; that's my line of work. But talking about feeling untrusted: If Modesto is a member of the Council, he must have given you the names of the other members, unless they meet wearing masks and using aliases. Like Señor Primo, Señor Segundo, Señorita Tercero . . . Tercera?"

Dana laughed. "She'd hardly call herself that. It's slang for madam, as in whorehouse." She shook her head. "No, they don't go in for that kind of conspiratorial nonsense much. Just the explosive kind. What makes you feel untrusted, Matt?"

"If Modesto knows all the names, and you know all the names, and Mac knows all the names, why don't I know all the names? I'm supposed to be the guy who's going to take care of the guys who wear them; but you've been hoarding them like the last cup of drinking water in a lifeboat drifting under the tropical sun. I twisted your arm once and got Dominic Morelos out of you, and Angelita Johansen and her two fellow bomb-freaks. . . ."

"Angelita is a Council member, but the two men were just rank and file."

"Whatever," I said. "Actually, you never did give me their names, but apparently you entrusted the information to Sonny Varek since he managed to make the hits successfully. Then you reluctantly fed me Galvez and

280

Koenig, later removed by Louis on my orders. But why hold back any of them if you know them all?''

She hesitated, and said reluctantly, ''I'm afraid you have the reputation of being something of a hothead, Matt; and after all, they did kill your son. It was feared that if you had all the names, you'd lose control and charge off blindly to hunt them down, one by one. That didn't seem very efficient; there were better ways of doing it. So it was decided to give you enough names so you could put pressure on the Legion, to be sure; but only enough to make them take you seriously and call a meeting of the Council to figure out how to deal with you. Not enough to make them scatter and take cover. Not enough that they'd suspect a leak in their own ranks.''

''Complicated,'' I said. ''Scare them enough to bring them together; not enough to blast them apart. I know where that intricate idea came from; I've seen enough of his ideas. But when their people started falling by the wayside, wouldn't those fanatics inevitably figure that somebody'd fingered them? Outfits like that are paranoid as hell.''

Dana shook her head. ''The names released to you were carefully selected. Young Mrs. Helm had got a good look at Angelita and her gofers, or it was spread around that she had, so anything that happened to them could be blamed on her, not Modesto. We picked Arthur Galvez and Howard Koenig to give you because they were heavy drinkers who frequently talked too much in the wrong places; if they were killed, the other members of the Council would assume they'd simply betrayed themselves while drunk. And you were smart enough, as expected, to let Dominic Morelos come to you instead of going after him. That gave the CLL no reason to suspect a traitor. But if we'd given you more names, if more Council members had died, the survivors would have started looking at each other warily, wondering which one was the snitch. We didn't want that. Modesto had to stay in place, unsuspected, until he could give us the date, time, and place of the proposed Council meeting. So you were left to investigate the Newport bombing and follow the dynamite trail to Puerto Rico by easy stages. As it turns out, your timing is perfect. You're here just when you're needed. We have to get Modesto out, wherever he's being held.''

I said, "He's still a clown to me, but okay, tell me about this Marvelous Modesto. God, he sounds like a circus aerialist!''

She didn't speak at once, and I went on grimly: "Come on, let's have an end to all the mystery, Dana. Who is this guy you have such faith in, such tender concern for, your husband, your father, your brother, your lover. . . . Oh, I see,'' I said, watching her face.

She said stiffly, "I don't think you do, Matt.''

I said, "*That's* why you cried in the night after doing me a great big favor. It was necessary to keep me happy because I'm a handy guy with a gun and you might need me—as you need me now—but it broke your heart to think how you'd betrayed your wonderful man in San Juan.''

"It wasn't like that!'' she protested. "I cried because . . . Oh, forget my silly tears. I seem to have turned into an ever-dripping human sponge lately. Matt, hadn't you better take a look at that girl, it's been quite a while?''

I said irritably, "Don't teach me my job and I won't tell you yours. The kid will keep, take my word for it. The subject is still Modesto, Miss Delgado.''

She said, "No.''

"What do you mean, no? Modesto . . .''

"I mean I'm not Miss Delgado. I'm Mrs. Delgado. Mrs. Roger Joaquin Delgado. I look a little Hispanic, but I'm not really. My maiden name was Dana Kingsbury.''

I looked at her for a moment. "I see. So you were married to Delgado but slept with Encinias."

"Yes." Her voice was expressionless.

"Well, it happens. It's an immoral world full of immoral people. But you gave me the impression Modesto was a little, dumpy, middle-aged gent. . . ."

"I didn't say dumpy. And while you may find it hard to believe, at your altitude, there are some nice men who don't have to duck to go through doors. As for his age, well, after being married to Roger too long, I was ready for an older man, a grown-up man who knew how to be tender and considerate instead of . . . Oh, God, this is getting to be a real encounter session, isn't it?"

"The usual line is that you committed adultery because your husband was a brute."

She shook her head. "I could have endured being married to a brute, if he was an adult brute. But instead I found myself married to a little boy. A peevish little boy, if I didn't mother him properly. Oh, he was good to look at, and pretty good in bed if he was humored and flattered and given the adoration he felt entitled to. And he was good at selling things; we weren't poor. An ideal husband by some standards. We got along reasonably well as long as I understood clearly that I existed only to serve him, as his mother had. But if I showed signs of independence . . . Well, for instance, I'd been very good at mathematics at the university. When I decided that I wanted to learn more about computers, when I said I might even take a job as soon as the baby could be left with somebody, when I did get a good position after I'd finished my courses . . . How would you like to spend several years with an advanced case of the sulks, Matt?"

"There was a child?" I asked.

"Yes. The only good thing to come out of my marriage. Dolores. I hadn't wanted to call her that, think of condemning a girl to spend her life being called Dolly, but it was his mother's name and that was that. A sweet and wonderful child; and after I started working, he retaliated by staging a deliberate campaign to alienate her from me, spoiling her rotten and telling her what a meanie I was to insist on a few house rules. Telling her how I neglected both of them and it was him and her against the world. Making a point of taking her to church and proving what a heathen I was, pretending to be so tired I had to stay home after merely playing at my silly job all week. That was how . . . how it happened.''

''It?''

I was beginning to have a pretty good idea of what she was leading up to, but she needed a little help to get there.

Dana licked her lips. ''It was some kind of a special religious observance, I still don't know exactly what. I'm supposed to be a Catholic, but I don't work at it, except around Easter and Christmas. You know. But they got all dressed up for whatever it was and Dolly was happy and excited because there was going to be a lunch party after church, children and parents, at . . . at . . .'' She faltered.

I said, ''At the restaurant of the Howard Johnson Hotel?''

She nodded dumbly. There was a little silence. At last, she said, ''It's open on Sunday and it was handy, I guess. Anyway, they didn't come home. They didn't come home. They didn't come home. At last somebody called to tell me. . . .'' She drew a long, shuddering breath. Then she went on mechanically: ''Later, after I'd gone to . . . to identify, but there wasn't really anything to identify except a little party shoe and a little purse, and a man's wallet, later I took a big knife out of the kitchen of our apartment, and it wouldn't go into my purse so I fastened it to my leg with some tape, under my slacks, and went to kill him. Paul. My lover. My tender, considerate lover. A big shot in that wonderful, patriotic organization that blows up children!''

''He'd told you about the CLL?''

She nodded. ''I'd met him when we helped install his office system. He wanted some lessons in how to use it. The girl he'd hired was quite competent to run it but impossible as a teacher. On the last day he took me out to dinner to celebrate and . . . well, he was a sweet man, a widower, and I'd had another battle with Roger; and afterwards we said it was a beautiful accident but it mustn't ever happen again. But of course it did. And that second night, since it was obvious we weren't going to stop there, he said there was something he had to tell me about himself, and he told me about the brutal regime in Islas Gobernador from which he'd had to flee and the brave band of patriots to which he belonged, working to free their country from the Yankee-supported dictatorship. . . . Well, the world is full of people trying to free something, you meet them everywhere. I just thought it was kind of intriguing, having a lover who was a secret revolutionary. But when the police told me that Paul's noble Legion of Liberty was claiming credit . . . *credit!* . . . I felt totally betrayed, and I charged out blindly to avenge my daughter; but my vengeance turned into a farce. I had a hard time getting the knife loose from the tape, and Paul stared at me as if I'd gone crazy, which of course I had. He grabbed for it and cut his hand; the blood just poured out. It made me so sick I had to run in the bathroom and throw up, still holding the bloody knife. It was just a ridiculous mess instead of high tragedy.''

I said, ''I suppose, since you still seem to be fond of him, he convinced you that he hadn't known what was planned.''

Dana said, ''Yes, when I came to my senses, and told him why I'd wanted to kill him, told him about Dolly, he was terribly shocked. He hadn't known that any action had been planned in San Juan. He explained to me that strike decisions are not made by the Council of Thirteen as a whole. A small group of Council members, picked for experience in the field, makes those decisions in secret and doesn't reveal them to the Council, or the membership at large, until it's time to announce another great victory for the cause of Caribbean liberation, in this case a victory over three little children and two parents. This small secret group calls itself the Executive Board. Its chairman is *El Martillo*."

"Clever. Executive as in execute, ha-ha. Did your Paul give you the identity of *El Martillo*?"

She said, "I told you that. Dominic Morelos. But now Paul thinks that *El Martillo* is really an elective office, so to speak; so probably by this time, with Dominic gone, they've picked somebody else to be their chairman. The Hammer. The Chairman of the Murder Board!" Her voice was bitter. "Anyway, I asked Paul if he intended to remain a member of an organization that makes war on children. He said he'd been finding it harder and harder to go along with the CLL policies of random terrorism; but it wasn't a social club from which one could resign at will. I said, well, maybe he shouldn't resign. If he really loved me, maybe he should stay in and, from inside, find a way of helping me strike back at them. In the meantime I looked around for a U.S. contact. I didn't want the FBI or the CIA; they're too big and have too many rules. I wanted a small government agency that wasn't bound by rules. I heard that a clever reporter from one of the Miami papers was down here doing a piece on the Puerto Rican freedom movements. It occurred to me that he might know of such an agency. I managed to get to talk with him and he said a tall, skinny gent from just such an outfit sometimes called him for information."

"Spud Meiklejohn. *Miami Tribune.*"

"Yes. He said you seemed to be a pretty effective character, probably tops in your organization, which wasn't really a recommendation if I was interested in sound morals and fine citizenship. However, if I was involved in something rough, I couldn't do much better. Mr. Meiklejohn said your agency didn't go in for public relations and I wouldn't find the number in the Washington directory, but he just happened to have come across it a while back and he'd jotted it down in his little black book. He said in return it would be nice if I gave him a head start on the story when and if it could be released." She drew a long breath. "So I called the number and I was afraid I'd get the crackpot treatment, but the man I talked to sounded interested and the very next day Mr. Trask was down here. By this time I'd, well, persuaded Paul. . . . Anyway, we set it up the way you know, using his office computer; but I couldn't stand it if anything should happen to him because I twisted his arm and made him help me. . . ."

I was flattered by the thought that Spud Meiklejohn thought enough of me, or at least of my abilities, to recommend me to troubled ladies. I glanced at her, sitting beside me on the park bench, and decided I knew very little about women; I hadn't sensed the fierce fires that must be burning inside her to make her set up this elaborate scheme of vengeance.

I said, "Okay. Superagent Helm to the rescue. We'll give it a try, at least. The question is how. Is that the right address the girl gave us?"

"How would I know?"

I said, "Cut it out. If Modesto is on the Council, he sure as hell knows where the Legion's San Juan headquarters is located, and there's no reason he wouldn't pass the information along."

"I'm sorry. All this intrigue . . . I can't keep track of

287

who's supposed to know what; I just instinctively go into a spasm of security whenever . . . Yes, Pacheco Street is correct.''

"Why hasn't the place been hit, if everybody knows where it is?''

"Not everybody. Mac has been holding the information until the thing could be done properly.''

"Properly? You mean by me?''

"No, by irate citizens demolishing the terrorist stronghold in revenge for their dead. These fanatics have had a certain amount of popular support throughout the Antilles. If they should be wiped out by government action . . . Well, Mrs. Gandhi destroyed the Sikhs' Golden Temple and India has been in an uproar ever since. Nobody wants to set the whole Caribbean on fire. That's why you were instructed to find some plausible scapegoats in the private sector. You've done very well. They're very pleased, in Washington.''

"Thanks for the pat on the head,'' I said sourly. "Everybody's being so clever I can hardly stand it.''

Dana glanced uneasily towards the car. "I can't see her. What's she doing in there?''

"Waiting,'' I said. "Just waiting to do her job. Don't worry about her, Dana. She's being clever, too. She's not going to run away. She wouldn't dream of going anywhere without us.''

Dana frowned. "I don't understand. What are you trying to say? What job does she have to do?''

I said, "Hell, it should be obvious. She's a tough little girl pretending to be a softy, our La Margarita. She's waiting patiently, accepting humiliation and abuse, so that she can decoy us into a nice little trap her friends have arranged for us on Pacheco Street.''

CHAPTER 30

WHEN we returned to the car, La Margarita was half reclining on the rear seat, as comfortable as she could make herself in the cramped space. There was no indication that she'd tried to escape her bonds. She pushed herself up to a sitting position and held out her wrists. They were tied in front since I'd been fairly sure she had no Houdini ambitions at the moment. I shook my head.

"We'll leave that hanky on you; but if you'll swing your feet this way, I'll take back my belt." Retrieving it, I ran it through the loops of my pants and buckled it. "Okay, move over."

"Ready?" Dana asked over her shoulder as I settled in back there.

"Not yet. Let me talk to this kid for a minute. I don't think she knows what her friends are getting her into. She doesn't look like kamikaze material to me."

The girl beside me laughed harshly. "You can't frighten me, Yankee pig!"

I said, "I promised you that you'd live if you behaved yourself. And if your friends behaved themselves. But they aren't going to, are they?" I regarded her sadly for a moment. "Look, I'm going to give you a break. I'm going to tell you exactly what will happen when you lead me to that address your friends had you feed me—I didn't really scare you with the knife, did I? You just held out long enough to make it look plausible; then you told me exactly what you'd been told to. But what your friends didn't tell you is what's going to happen to you when we get to 427 Pacheco Street and start inside.''

She glared at me. "So tell me what will happen, fascist dog!''

I said, "I can't wait to hear what I'm going to be next, a Nazi worm perhaps? When we get to the place, I'll have my gun in your back, of course. Bonnette's gun. Encinias's gun. And whose before that? It's traveled a long way, that pistol, and it's getting hungry for action. Well, when you get me inside 427, one of two things will happen. Either your friends will shoot me in the back, in which case I'll die pumping bullets into *your* back. That's the way we operate. There are very few marksmen who can drop a man so fast and so dead that he can't pull a trigger; and I'll pull it, believe me. And keep pulling it as long as there's a breath left in me. I'll be very much surprised if I can't get two or three into you before I die.''

The girl stared at me in a puzzled way. "But why? Do you hate me so much? Why would you make such an effort to kill me?''

I said, "I don't hate you; and while I've got orders concerning the CLL, nobody's told me to go after your FFPR. But we never die alone, baby. That's the rule in this outfit. It's supposed to discourage people with homicidal intentions. Often it does, if those people have done their research and know what they're up against, which you people don't seem to. We aren't bulletproof. We aren't immortal. But nobody gets one of us free. We always take company to hell with us; and in this case you'll be the logical candidate. So if your friends take me, I'll take you, and we'll make the long, black journey together, Señorita Margarita.''

She hesitated. "My friends do not shoot people in the back!''

I laughed scornfully. "No, they only blow up people in restaurants. But say you're right. Say they don't shoot me. Say they just tell me to drop my gun and put my hands up, the old TV gambit. That's the second possibility. In that case I'll pull the trigger once and dive and roll whichever way seems most promising, and hope to get at least one of them when I come up. But you'll have one of my bullets in you and maybe one or two of theirs because the boys do get excited when the shooting starts." I looked at La Margarita. "Well?"

"Well, what?"

"Last chance, sweetheart. Have you nothing to tell me? No way to make it easier? No way for me to get into the place and release Paul Encinias without a lot of fireworks in which people will be killed, one of whom will certainly be you? Once the guns start, you're dead, honey. I'll see to that if I see to nothing else. So if you know any way for me to slip into the place and do my job without being caught . . . Otherwise we march in the front door and see how far we get. You won't get very far, but I've shot my way out of tougher traps than I think a bunch of sneaky, bomb-throwing creeps can dream up. Well, we'll see. Or I'll see. You won't be around to see anything. What's your real name, anyway?"

The girl hesitated, and shrugged. "Margarita. That is true. Margarita Bustamente. Rita, it was before. But I chose the other when I joined the FFPR." After a moment, she said a bit defiantly, "Perhaps I do not want to die. They did not tell me how it would be. What is it you need to know?"

"I need to know an unlatched skylight and a way of getting onto the roof. Or an unprotected cellar entrance. Or an open window, an unlocked back door, any way of getting in without being spotted. And I need to know where in the building they're holding Encinias." I waited, but she didn't speak. I shrugged. "Okay, Rita Margarita. It's your funeral. Let's go, Dana. . . ."

"Wait!"

There was a long pause. At last I said, "She's stalling, Dana. Take it away."

"No!" The girl licked her lips. "At 427 Pacheco, your friend is in a small room, a closet, I do not know its purpose, on the second floor at the rear. You open the street door and there is a corridor and a stairway. You ascend the stairs and you are in the upstairs hallway. You continue towards the rear of the building, and the door is the second to your right."

"Locked?"

"There is a padlock. I do not know who keeps the key, but I should think it would not be difficult to pry away the hardware, it is a very old building."

I said, "That's coming in from the front. Is the street door locked?"

"No, not at this time of day. It is only locked at night."

"Any other way of getting into the building?"

"I do not know about skylights or cellars, but there is a rear door from the courtyard behind. You have to reach that from the next street, San Remo. The alley is very narrow, no vehicles, just a walkway, you must go on foot. The courtyard is not very big. As you cross it, the entrance you wish is farthest to your right. It will take you into the downstairs hall, right by the backstairs."

"No fire escape?"

"No."

"Rear door locked?"

She shook her head. "Again, only at night."

"Trusting souls, these Puerto Ricans."

"Perhaps we have nothing left to steal. Perhaps it has all been stolen from us already by greedy *Norteamericanos*."

I grinned, and stopped grinning. I said, "Dana, please pop over to that hardware store and buy a hank of clothesline. No, on second thought, make it a roll of that silver duct tape, if you can find it. Otherwise the clothesline. Otherwise a couple of electric extension cords. And a small crowbar, not one of the big brutes for demolishing houses. Something for dealing with that lock, reasonably short, that I can tuck inside my pants. A big screwdriver if you can't find the right size wrecking bar. You've got money?"

"Yes. I'll be right back."

She got out and walked across the little park, and disappeared inside the store. Rita Bustamente stirred uneasily beside me.

"What will you do to me?"

"Fasten you up so you can't give her any trouble while I'm away checking what you've told me. For both our sakes, I hope it's the truth. The lady who just left us lost her husband and little girl in a CLL bombing, right here in San Juan. She's got a particular hate for the Legion; but she's not very fond of terrorists in general, even if they call themselves patriots or freedom fighters. She'll have orders to kill you if I don't get back within a reasonable time, because that'll mean you lied to me."

The girl protested: "That is not fair! If you are stupid and get yourself shot or captured . . ."

"Then you die anyway, it's too damn bad. What happened to my son Matthew wasn't very fair, either. Or Dana's daughter Dolly. The husband wasn't much of a loss, I gather, but she doted on that kid. All you can hope is that you've given me enough correct information that I can make it safely."

She was silent for a little; then she said, "They will be waiting for you inside the front door. Waiting to kill you."

"Yes, I figured that," I said.

Then Dana was back with a paper bag. I laid aside the miniature crowbar temporarily, and got to work with the silvery tape on the kid's ankles. When they were secure, I took the handkerchief off her wrists and turned her around—not easy in that narrow space—and taped her wrists behind her. Finally, I used the handkerchief as a gag and wedged her into the space between the seats. Fortunately she was a small girl.

Dana said, frowning, "I don't understand. Before, you didn't seem a bit worried about her getting away."

I said, "Before, she hadn't told me everything she wanted to. She wasn't going to run away until she had. But now she's got nothing to stick around for." I held out my little knife, which I'd got out to use on the tape. "Here. It opens normally, but you have to pull back this little bolt to close it."

"What am I supposed to do with it?"

I said, "You told me this park is pretty close to the address she gave us."

Dana indicated a direction with a nod of her head. "I think the street is three or four blocks that way; but you may have to go over a block or two to find the right number."

"Okay, you wait here with the car. I understand this island's got some pretty wild spots inland. If I'm not back in an hour, take the little bitch back there somewhere and haul her off into the bushes and cut her throat with that knife, because it'll mean she double-crossed me." I winked at Dana as I spoke; but I was watching the prisoner's back for some sign that she was having useful afterthoughts. I saw none. I went on, "After you've disposed of her, you're on your own; and it's been nice knowing you."

"It'll be a long hour," Dana said. "Be careful, Matt."

"Sure. Always."

It wasn't much of a street. Five blocks long, it ran

from a busy boulevard to a small church and died there. In front of the church was a statue of a hooded friar or priest in long robes. When you've figured out how the religious boys managed to survive the sun in these latitudes all wrapped up in thick scratchy wool, you can tackle the problem of how their military counterparts escaped heatstroke in their iron vests and tin hats. I guess they just grew a tougher breed of men back in those days; and the women enduring those multiple petticoats in this tropical climate were obviously no sissies either.

After locating the street, and determining where 427 had to be without getting too close, I scouted the nearby San Remo Street and spotted the walkway described by Miss Bustamente. This was a shabby, out-of-the-way corner of Old San Juan, but nobody seemed to pay me any attention. Strolling tourists were clearly a dime a dozen.

It was an interesting problem, I reflected, pausing by the church again to put my thoughts in order. It was kind of like guessing which walnut shell hid the pea. The question was how tricky the kid was, and how tricky she thought I was. I'd waved a knife at her and she'd told me certain things. Then I'd threatened her with death and she'd told me some additional things. The big question was, had I managed to break through to a little truth in the end, or was everything she'd given me merely what she'd been told to give me. . . .

I frowned as a question popped into my mind belatedly: What reason did I have for believing that Rita Bustamente was a simple little errand girl following other people's orders? Or that her name was Rita Bustamente? I'd assumed the one and she'd told me the other. Ha-ha. Certainly she'd given a pretty good impersonation of a lowly, and slightly dumb, girl soldier of the underground army of freedom mouthing corny catch phrases from badly printed activist manuals, but I hadn't really found her act convincing, any more than I'd believed in her

295

abject capitulation to my threats. So what did I believe? Assuming that the little girl was more clever than she appeared, and more important, who was she really?

"Oh, Christ!" I said softly. Then I glanced at the nearby statue and said, "Excuse me, padre."

I mean, dammit, how long does it take a man to wake up to what's right under his nose? A smallish girl had been seen in Montego making contact with Dominic Morelos as a susceptible young tourist lady. A smallish girl had been seen in West Palm Beach helping blow up the restaurant called La Mariposa. Sandra had seen a smallish girl in a maid's uniform leaving a bomb in her room disguised as a vase of flowers. And now a smallish girl had brought an assassination weapon to Raoul Bonnette, along with murder instructions, and allowed herself to be captured so she could feed me misleading information.

We'd assumed in the earlier instances that the blonde girl in Montego had worn a dark wig in West Palm, and been her natural blonde self again in Newport; but it was high time I stopped making casual assumptions about people's hair. One had almost killed me. We could just as easily be dealing with a dark girl who donned a blonde wig upon occasion. Angelita Johansen didn't have to be blonde just because her name was Scandinavian. If it was her name. Maybe she was really Margarita Bustamente. Or maybe her true name hadn't surfaced yet. It was no time to be wasting time on names, anyway.

I was already hurrying back towards the little park where I'd left Dana—left an inexperienced agent to guard a prisoner who was much more dangerous than she knew. When I reached the place, the curb was filled with parked vehicles, but the brown two-door was not among them. I walked forward slowly. Something shiny lay on the sidewalk, a strip of silver duct tape, actually several layers, neatly cut through with a sharp knife. Another, similar strip lay in the gutter. Still retaining something of the shape of the wrists and ankles they'd bound, they put me in mind of the husk shed by an insect. A deadly insect.

CHAPTER 31

I CONSIDERED waiting until after dark to solve the tactical problem on Pacheco Street, but I decided against it. I didn't have a clear picture of the enemy dispositions yet, and it was their city, not mine. In the dark, the advantage would be all theirs. Besides, I only had a .22 to shoot with, a gun with no knockdown power whatever. To compensate for the small caliber, accurate marksmanship would be required, hard to achieve at night.

Furthermore, I didn't want to wait for sunset. It was still a couple of hours away, and I didn't want to wait at all. I had those scraps of duct tape in mind. As a matter of fact, I'd even found the roll itself discarded under the car that had taken the space formerly occupied by our rental. I remembered that, when I was immobilizing the girl, I'd cut off the last strip I'd needed with my knife and then smoothed down the remaining tape neatly for storage; but more tape had been ripped off since and the last few inches loosened and stuck themselves back onto the roll all wrinkled, with a ragged edge.

All of which was a message to me from Margarita Bustamente, or Angelita Johansen, or whatever her real name might be. It read: *I've got your woman all taped up,*

Yankee pig; did you really think a pretty lady like that could hold me?

Well, at least Dana was still alive; nobody'd bother to secure a dead captive. What Rita/Angelita's plans for her might be, I didn't care to think about; nor did I waste time speculating about how the girl had managed to free herself and gain the upper hand. It happens when you leave untrained people in charge of dangerous prisoners, and it was entirely my fault. I'd been criminally slow in realizing who we had there.

It was possible, of course, that Angelita, as I decided to call her, now expected me to proceed to the hotel where we had reservations—if she didn't know our arrangements, she could learn them from Dana—and wait for her to call proposing some kind of deal; but we don't deal. The hostage question is one every organization like ours must face, and Mac had found a simple, one-word answer: *Disregard*. We don't play that game, ever, in any of its variations. However, we are permitted to try to liberate the hostage or hostages, preferably with maximum casualties among the opposing forces.

But first I had to learn where. With my computer lady incommunicado, I'd have to get my CLL information elsewhere, say from the terrorists currently residing at 427 Pacheco Street. It seemed to me that I had no choice but to go there, and knock on the door politely, and ask the boys nicely where Angelita might have taken Dana.

I found myself back at the little church. Passing the tall stone friar, or priest, or whatever the hell he'd been, I gave him a salute, thinking that it must have been nice, facing danger in a strange land, to know that God was right there beside you. My religion is as indefinite as my politics, but I've never been conceited enough to kid myself that, with a few billion other souls to worry about, the Deity takes a special interest in my affairs; although

298

it sometimes does seem that the other guy likes to hang around making things difficult.

I glanced down the length of Pacheco Street as I strolled along the church sidewalk. I could see the heavy traffic passing on the boulevard at the far end, five blocks away. It was a run-down street, mainly residential—I don't know the exact point at which an apartment house becomes a tenement, but these buildings were getting close—with a couple of corner shops. There was also a small restaurant in the middle of the third block on the right-hand side, my landmark. I'd already determined that number 427 was right across the narrow street from it. Both buildings were three stories high. I moved along without pausing, but I retained the image of the shabby, distant doorway; the door Angelita had told me was kept unlocked; the door inside which, she'd told me, they'd be waiting for me.

And if I believed all that, we'd have to try me next on the tooth fairy. If she said unlocked, the door was presumably not only locked but bolted. If she said inside, they were bound to be waiting for me outside. If she said in front, they were undoubtedly laying for me at the rear. Or were they? The old shell game. How clever was she; and how clever did she think I was? She'd told me the front was covered. Did that mean that she expected me to take her word for it and hit the presumably unprotected rear? Or would she think I'd think it was a double bluff and go for the front door she'd warned me against, on the assumption that she'd lied?

I grimaced. A man could drive himself nuts trying to figure it out that way. So forget about Angelita's information, true or false, forget about the walnut shells and the pea; use the brains. Remember that Bultman had been on the horn from New York, getting the boys and girls to set this up for my benefit. Well, if you had a tall, kind of stupid, but armed and dangerous, gringo to eliminate,

299

and wanted to do it with reasonable certainty and safety, how would you go about it? You most certainly wouldn't try to take him indoors, at close range, in a narrow dark hallway where your CLL gunners would get in each other's way and he'd be bound to put a few bullets into somebody before he went down.

There was also to be considered the welfare of the Yankee's female prisoner, an important person, a member of the Legion and even of the Council of Thirteen. There was no possible way of ensuring her safety in a wild melee in a dusky corridor. Of course, this consideration no longer applied; but it had undoubtedly been a factor influencing the way the plans had been made. Even if the boys covering 427 had received notification of Angelita's escape, it probably wouldn't cause them to make any drastic changes in their arrangements now.

The significant thing about what Angelita had told me, I decided, was what she'd refrained from telling me. She'd given me a detailed description of the interior of the building, complete with front and rear stairs and padlocked closet. She'd practically taken me on a guided tour along San Remo Street in back of the place, and through the narrow walkway, and across the small rear courtyard to the entrance farthest to the right. But there had been no mention at all of the street in front, or the building across that street with its restaurant, or the street behind that. . . .

Having come a short block over, I found myself opposite the street in question. It was hardly better than an alley, a skinny, dark thoroughfare called Sebastian's Lane. About to cross and explore it cautiously, I found myself continuing to walk straight ahead: There was something wrong. The little red light was flickering uncertainly at the back of my mind. The sensors weren't getting a clear reading, but they'd picked up hostile emanations of some kind, and they were warning me that conditions down that alley might be unfavorable for survival. In retrospect, I realized that I'd got the same disturbing sensation looking down Pacheco. I kept on walking, therefore; I've been in the business too long to ignore that vague unease. It had saved my life too many times in the past. I decided that I'd better make a wide swing around the whole target area to get the feel of the neighborhood, and to see if everybody seemed to be acting naturally and if there was any significant concentration of parked vehicles anywhere.

Sebastian's Lane; and who the hell was Sebastian and who cared? They couldn't have all the manpower in the world, I told myself. Concentrating on the Pacheco Street place, front or rear, or both if they belonged to the belt-and-suspenders school of assassination, they probably wouldn't have people to spare for guarding all the nearby streets and alleys. Not just for a simple ambush. And still . . . and still, when we'd been riding through Old San Juan on the way here, I'd got an impression of bustling vitality; but this part of town felt dead, dead, dead. The few pedestrians visible had a frightened, scurrying look, as if they wanted to get away from the area as fast as possible. In a city like this, at least in the less well-to-do sections, the people would have their own early-warning signals, and apparently the quiet word was going around: *Stay indoors or get clear!*

It was what had alerted me, of course, although I hadn't recognized it at once: the emptiness of the streets I'd been looking down, and the electricity in the air; the eve-of-revolution feeling. Everybody was waiting for the guns to start firing. It would have been flattering to think it was all for me; but it seemed unlikely that a whole section of San Juan was holding its breath waiting for one lousy little murder, even mine.

I made a wide circle, completing it four blocks in back of the church. Then I closed in a little and circled again, zigzagging through the little alleys and walkways cautiously, working my way around the address on a radius of roughly three blocks. Two vans parked together, one new and blue, the other old and white, held my attention briefly, maybe because the blue one reminded me of Dominic Morelos's elongated heap; but if they were getaway vehicles, they'd be guarded, so I stayed clear. I didn't know what I was really looking for until I found it: a familiar little brown two-door sedan backed into a narrow space between two buildings. Angelita hadn't driven very far with her prisoner. Apparently she'd come right here to report her escape, so the boys would know that when I appeared they could fire at will without endangering one of their own.

The area was still unnaturally quiet. I moved forward cautiously with the usual feeling, down there between the buildings, of having eyes watching me from above and maybe even cross hairs steadying on my spine. I consoled myself with the thought that the CLL had exhibited no long-range expertise to date. They'd used their homemade minicannon at point-blank range to deal with Varek's armored Mercedes, and Morelos had brandished a handgun without much skill; aside from that they'd stuck strictly to high explosives.

I kept those explosives in mind as I approached the rental car, and made no attempt to open it. I didn't even touch it. I simply determined by looking that there were no bodies inside—it was one of the new ones without a real trunk. There was just a space behind the rear seat, cover missing. The only blood I could see was a few spatters resulting from my interrogation of Angelita. . . .
A sound behind me made me whirl with the silenced Ruger in my hand.

"Matt, no! It's me. Don't shoot!"

I stood staring at the sturdy young woman facing me, dressed in white slacks and a big blue shirt belted outside the pants. Blue high heels gave her a little more height than she was entitled to, but she was still a short girl. Although it had only been a day since I'd last seen her, the shorn black hair seemed to have grown significantly, so you were hardly conscious of the fading scar; but now she had her left arm in a sling. I seemed to recall that the right was the one that had been immobilized when I'd first met her. Accident-prone. But an attractive young lady nevertheless.

I could allow myself to appreciate how attractive, now. I no longer had to keep telling myself firmly she was just a chunky little kid, bright and pleasant but not really very pretty, and my daughter-in-law. Another woman had ensured that there was no longer any danger of my making an awkward mistake in that direction.

"Sandy, you're supposed to be in the hospital. What the hell are you doing here?" I asked.

CHAPTER 32

YOUNG MRS. Helm led me two blocks over and three and a half blocks back, meaning away from the target area. The door at which she paused looked no different from any of the doors I'd passed elsewhere in that rather down-beat area, but a small dark man in grimy jeans and a torn T-shirt was squatting against the wall nearby, smoking a cigarette. I didn't know him; but I knew that he wasn't the local bum he was trying to impersonate, and I sensed that he was armed. He had that look. Sandra glanced his way, he gave her a nod; and we went up two steps and inside.

"It's the third floor," she said over her shoulder, leading the way up the stairs.

"I think I can make it if I get to stop and pant occasionally," I said.

"I hope I can," she said. "I don't seem to have got much strength back yet."

"You're doing well to be standing on your feet at all," I said. "It's only in the movies that people get shot and go rock-and-rolling next day."

"Pulling on my pants one-handed is the really hard part," she said.

I hadn't asked where she was taking me and she hadn't volunteered the information. Of course she could have been leading me into a trap. There are ways of putting pressure on just about anybody, to do just about anything. But I didn't think there was any way of turning this girl into a good enough sneak to make it convincing. Besides, hell, you have to trust somebody.

"In here," she said, opening a door.

The hallway had been shabby, but the apartment we entered, while far from new, looked clean enough if a bit cluttered. There was a man guarding the door whom I recognized.

"Willard," I said, to let him know I remembered his code name. We'd worked together once, quite a while ago.

"Go on in, Eric," he said. "The living room. The door to the right."

It wasn't a bad living room, if you went in for strong colors and statuettes of Mary and Jesus and lots of knick-knacks and ornate, overstuffed furniture. I'm not being ironical. It wasn't my taste, but it looked like a lived-in room in which people had been happy and comfortable among their souvenirs and mementos, and might be again, as soon as somebody removed the compact walk-ie-talkie, antenna extended, that rested on the bathtowel that had been spread to protect the low shiny table in front of the sofa, and the two machine pistols beside it, and the four extra twenty-round magazines. In order to be really happy and comfortable, they'd also have to get rid of the man on the sofa. He's one of the least comfortable characters I know.

The weapons were the smallest of their type I'd seen. I like to keep up with the new ones, and I'd read up on the Yugoslav Skorpian when it made its appearance years ago. However, although its compactness has made it fairly popular, I'd never met one before. I remembered that, while it's offered in several calibers, the best-known version, which this seemed to be, shoots the .32 ACP cartridge, a gutless old round that has only about a third the muzzle energy of an ordinary police .38. The revival of this weak and obsolete cartridge is in line with the modern weapons theory stating that with a fully auto-matic firearm you don't need a powerful cartridge for short-range social functions since you can put several of the feeble bullets into the target. If you just keep plug-ging, pun intended, the multiple impacts will eventually add up to a greater shock factor than can be achieved with a single powerful slug.

The truth is, of course, that nowadays they pass out these squirt guns just so they won't have to be bothered with teaching people how to put one bullet where it counts.

"Be careful, Eric," Mac said as, entering the room, I brushed against a flimsy little table by the doorway that held some souvenir ashtrays, a tricky vase with artificial flowers, and a small statuette, perhaps a saint. "Don't knock anything over. The nice people just lent me this place to use as a temporary command post. I don't want any of their treasures broken."

I looked at him for a moment. I suppose I should have been surprised to see him, since he doesn't get out into the field much. However, nothing he does ever really surprises me.

"What's a B-code, sir?" I asked. "Our B-code?"

"We have no such thing as a B-code," he said.

"I was told differently."

"Then you had better check with your informant."

"I will if I can reach her," I said.

I had no idea whether or not he'd given me a truthful answer. He hadn't seemed surprised by the question; but he doesn't give much away. I regarded him a moment longer. We'd never really been friends in spite of working together so many years; but there had been times when we'd been friendlier than now. I found that, rather to my surprise, I regretted this. I remembered that it had all started with an argument about a dog, for God's sake! How ridiculous could you get? I turned and pulled up a chair for Sandra.

"Better sit down. You look a bit shaky."

"I'm all right." But she sat down.

I turned back to face Mac. He wore one of his customary gray three-piece suits, perhaps a little lighter in weight than the last one I'd seen, in Washington. He picks them to match the climate. His hair was as gray as ever, his eyebrows as black, and his eyes as bleak.

He said, with a gesture towards the portable two-way radio, "I've been getting reports of you circling this neighborhood for over an hour, like a lost dog looking for a home."

I said, "Sandra should be in bed. That arm is hurting her."

"It was her choice to discharge herself from the hospital and come along to help us."

"And roam around without protection? They're already holding two hostages, assuming that both still live. Do we want to give them a third?''

''There was little danger,'' he said. ''I knew you would find that car eventually, so I stationed her there. I wanted you brought here, and I had nobody else to spare whom you knew by sight. Willard was needed here. I didn't think it advisable to send a strange operative to slip up on you; you tend to get a bit trigger-happy under stress.''

''Thanks for the testimonial.''

He smiled thinly. ''I have no objection whatever to trigger-happy agents, Eric. Some people would say we specialize in trigger-happy agents. I am merely cautious about approaching them. Anyway, Mrs. Helm was reasonably safe because most of the Caribbean Legion's Council of Thirteen, what you've left of it, is pretty well forted up in their headquarters at 424 Pacheco, along with some rank and file to perform sentry and guard duty while they're getting things organized and holding their meeting. Modesto managed to get the word out before they took him. It's scheduled for tomorrow.''

I made a silent apology to Paul Encinias, alias Modesto, the man I'd never met although we had a lady in common. I'd said some harsh words about him, but you can forgive an inexperienced operative a few blunders if he gets his job done before he gets himself caught.

I looked at Mac, frowning. ''You said 424? The number I was given was 427.''

''That's the building across the street. It's standing empty and I don't think they have anybody in it, although there may be a lookout we haven't spotted yet. This is a depressed area, and the building on this side of the street is also supposed to be unoccupied. The restaurant on the ground floor, Café Ernesto, has supposedly gone out of business. As you may have noted.''

''I never got that close,'' I said. ''I just saw the sign from a distance.''

"Actually, the derelict café is their meeting hall," Mac said. "They are camping out in the empty rooms and apartments above it. The whole building is theirs. I suspect they have it pretty well guarded. I hope so."

I glanced at him sharply. "Hope?"

He nodded. "I want them to feel safe in there. The fact that they are still there even though they're aware of having been betrayed by Modesto indicates that they consider San Juan, and particularly this section of it, a sanctuary of sorts. They feel they are in friendly surroundings, among people sympathetic to their cause, the cause of freedom for little Gobernador now, larger Puerto Rico later, and finally the whole Caribbean with the exception of those few areas already free enough to suit them—like liberated, democratic Cuba." He grimaced. "These self-styled patriots always tend to overestimate the popular sentiment in their favor. They persuade themselves that their fanatical beliefs are universal. They expect a great popular uprising whenever they wave a flag."

I said dryly, "As we did at Bahía de Cochinos."

"Precisely. Overoptimism is common phenomenon not confined to terrorists." He shook his head, dismissing my irrelevant comment, and went on: "At any rate the Legion did have considerable local support until last year, when they murdered those children. Now even the people who believe strongly in Puerto Rican independence have little sympathy for this particular gang of baby-killers. And there have always been those who prefer to remain Americans, like the family that has given me the use of this apartment." He regarded me for a moment. "Dolores was seen being taken from your rental vehicle to the Café Ernesto."

"Dolores?"

"Miss Delgado's working name. She chose it herself; insisted on it, in fact."

It gave me an uneasy feeling to learn that Dana had made a point of conducting her mission of vengeance under the name of her murdered little girl; it hinted again at depths of emotion that belied the image our cool computer lady had been so careful to project. I didn't ask why an attempt had not been made to liberate her while she was still out in the street and fairly available. Whatever he had planned here, Mac wouldn't consider betraying his presence, and his operation, for the sake of one lousy agent.

"Did you notice her escort?" I asked.

"A small, dark-haired young lady with a knife, was the description received here."

"It was probably my knife, sir," I said. "I'd lent it to Dana, I mean Dolores. My knife, and my goof. I overestimated our girl a bit, I guess; but mainly I underestimated the kid we'd grabbed. At least I thought she was just a kid, somebody expendable they'd picked to deliver a message and a gun to the guy who'd tailed me from Kennedy. Now I think she's maybe a bit older than I thought, and certainly much brighter and more important."

"Explain."

I gave it to him in detail, from my glimpse of Bultman at Kennedy to my belated realization that our young female prisoner must be a more significant figure in the CLL than I'd assumed; and my hasty return to the little city park to find our vehicle and the two girls missing.

"The girl left the tape she'd been bound with lying there to let me know she was free and it wasn't Dana who'd driven the car away for some mysterious reason. A threat or a warning, you might call it."

Sandra stirred. "I don't understand. How could she have got free, all taped up like that?"

I said, "No problem. Dana obviously cut her loose."

309

Sandra looked shocked. "You mean . . . you mean that Miss Delgado is on their side?"

I grinned. "Hell, no. But cute little Angelita held her breath until her face turned black, or went into dramatic convulsions, or just moaned and groaned into her gag and maybe even puked a little, strangling spectacularly on her vomit, until Dana couldn't bear to let her suffer any longer and made with the blade. Don't get proud, small fry. You'd have done the same thing."

"I would not!"

I shrugged. "Maybe you're right, but I doubt it. I hate to say it, since it was my fault she escaped, but this is probably the young woman responsible for the West Palm Beach bomb that killed Matthew, not to mention the Newport bomb, and quite possibly even the one here in San Juan."

Mac said, "I see. You are reasonably certain, then, that the same girl was behind all these incidents, or at least involved in them, and that this is the girl?"

I shrugged. "It's a guess, but it doesn't seem likely that they'd have a collection of lethal young ladies that size and a collection of wigs to put on them. It's too bad I didn't have Sandra with me when I grabbed her at the airport. Sandy could have said for sure if she was the bomb-planting maid in our Newport hotel. But I don't think there's much doubt about it. Of course, if she'd thought there was a risk of being recognized, she wouldn't have come; but she was aware that neither Dana nor I had ever seen her." I frowned. "But what I don't quite understand, sir, is why she'd give me that address right across from their terrorist fortress. If she could have been sure I'd go there alone, okay, but what if I stopped at a phone and called for reinforcements? They could have found themselves surrounded by a Puerto Rican SWAT unit, if there is such a thing. Or the U.S. Marines."

Mac said, "You forget, she knew that the location had already been compromised by Modesto; she didn't do any additional damage by giving it to you. And she undoubtedly also knew that we don't often ask for police or military assistance." He shook his head. "You give these people credit for too much caution and common sense, and too little arrogance. As I have pointed out already, in spite of discovering an informant in their midst, they haven't scattered; they're still stubbornly inhabiting an address they know has been betrayed. They are reckless and violent activists, remember; they've had a good deal of success to make them overconfident; they consider themselves clever and powerful and invincible; they are even associated with a daring military operation they fully expect to be victorious. . . . What is it, Eric?"

"About that invasion," I said. "Dana/Dolores feels it's going to be a fiasco. She doesn't think Bultman's little force has a chance of effecting a successful landing on Gobernador; and even if the boys make it that far, they'll never break out from their beachhead. It'll be a Bay of Pigs junior grade. Unless the Kraut has a secret weapon of some kind, or something very tricky up his sleeve like massive reinforcements we don't know about, Dana says, he's going to be slaughtered along with his CLL allies."

Mac frowned. "That's odd. I took for granted . . . Bultman is no self-deceiving fanatic. It didn't occur to me to have a military expert check the feasibility of his project. He spent a good many years as a mercenary before embarking on his kill-for-pay career. He has seen a large number of wars. I assumed that he wouldn't embark on a military venture that had no possibility of success. Why didn't Miss Delgado mention this to me?"

"Bultman's little army was outside the scope of her duties, sir, except insofar as it was partly made up of CLL volunteers. Her business was with the Legion, and whatever information Modesto could give her about it.

311

She probably thought you were aware of the military situation. But she knows the area, and she knows roughly what kind of defensive forces are available on Gobernador; too great, she feels, to be overcome by Bultman's few hundred men and their limited equipment." I shrugged. "I think she simply assumed that the Kraut was just another visionary hothead specializing in glorious lost causes. When I told her that he was a tough professional soldier, she was surprised and disturbed, wondering by what sort of military miracle he expected to get his pocket-sized task force ashore and inland in the face of the government's greatly superior manpower and firepower." I frowned. "Has there been any indication that he's preparing some kind of a surprise?"

Mac hesitated. "Well, the LCT is missing."

"My God, are there still some of those World War Two relics around?"

"He has a number of boats of various kinds," Mac said, "some of which have been used quite openly along the shores of Montego for practice landings. The Landing Craft, Tank was one of the largest vessels of the little fleet, close to one hundred and twenty feet. Normally it would be crewed by one officer and a dozen enlisted men. Range seven hundred miles, top speed eight knots."

"Not exactly a speedboat," I said.

"No, but it can carry five thirty-ton tanks, or three fifty-tonners. So far no tanks have been seen, but delivered at the proper moment they could give the defense forces an unpleasant surprise. However, Bultman's LCT has apparently been plagued with mechanical problems, not surprising considering its age. Recently, our local man reported that it was no longer in Montego. His assumption was that Bultman had either given up on it as too unreliable, or had it taken somewhere for expert mechanical attention. We are checking all shipyard facilities he might possibly be using, so far without results. Of course, he may simply have taken the nautical antique offshore and let it sink, to get rid of it.''

"Maybe," I said. "And maybe it's picking up a load of clanking metal monsters to spring on the Gobernador home guard at the psychological moment." I shrugged. "Well, it's not the immediate problem. I'd like to know what is, sir."

"What do you mean, Eric?"

I said stiffly, "I thought I had a simple assignment. Ambitious, but basically simple. I thought I was supposed to run down and eliminate, or arrange for the elimination of, the thirteen members of the governing council of the Caribbean Legion of Liberty, plus the three individuals involved in the Mariposa bombing. I was supposed to take care that said terminations were not attributed to the U.S. government. In the interest of public relations they should, wherever possible, be laid at the door or doors of vengeful private parties. It was considered desirable to let these terrorists, and all terrorists, know that driven far enough, ordinary people do bite back. Anyone who intervened was also fair game, particularly Herman Heinrich Bultman—as I recall, the rules for attribution were somewhat relaxed where Herman was concerned, since he's been wanted a long time by folks who shall remain unnamed. Have I described my mission guidelines accurately, sir?"

Mac said, "We both know what your instructions were, Eric. There's no need to recapitulate. . . .''

"Apparently there is, sir," I said grimly. "Let me report the present status of my mission. The Kraut has declared himself in as you expected, but he'll keep until I get around to him. Two of the assigned Mariposa bombers are dead. Unfortunately, as just reported, while I had a crack at the third, there was an identity problem and I lost her; but she's here and I was planning to rectify my error shortly. Three of the assigned Council members are

313

dead. After learning of the proposed meeting, I formed certain plans for dealing with the rest, but I thought I'd better come down here and scout out the terrain before I put my ideas into action. However, upon arrival, I find a number of our people already on the ground, including the bossman himself. So with all due respect, I ask: Whose goddamn mission is this, anyway?''

''There's no need to be upset, Eric,'' Mac said. ''Checking back through the CLL's old atrocities was a good idea; and you have done a fine job of putting enough pressure on them to cause them to call this emergency meeting. I would have continued to let you carry on alone, but Modesto's message indicated a need for haste, and it seemed clear that you would need immediate reinforcements. . . .''

He was interrupted by the walkie-talkie: ''Trask calling Control.''

Mac picked up the instrument. ''Control.''

''In position. Respectfully suggest you commence diversion as soon as it gets a little darker. Will report when planting is complete. Confirm E-hour, please.''

''Execute hour confirmed. Diversion shortly. How is the boy doing?''

''Having a ball, sir. Wickerman says his gadgets are a little crude but really very ingenious. They should present no problems; so we're using them as planned instead of the stuff Wicky brought for backup. Any further instructions?''

''None.''

''Trask out.''

Mac returned the set to the protecting towel, beside the ugly little firearms. He looked up at me. ''In case you don't remember him, Eric, Wickerman is our explosives specialist.''

I grimaced. ''I remember him. Somehow I never seem to get along with people who go in for loud noises—

remember the guy we called Monk, out in Hawaii? I suppose the boy you referred to is Lester Leonard.''

Mac nodded. "Yes. I could see the shape of your plan when his hobby was described to me; I just telescoped your timetable a bit, and brought in Wickerman to make certain young Leonard's materials would actually do the job and that they were positioned to best advantage.''

I was a little ashamed of my outburst. Nobody likes to have an operation taken over by someone else, even by the top man; but his explanation was reasonable. I hadn't expected things to break quite so fast.

I said, "I was planning to ask for an expert to give the boy a hand; I'm glad Wicky's here to help him.'' Halfhearted apologies are a waste of time, so I went on: "Okay, you were right in speeding things up, sir. I thought I had more time. So we're going to finish the job by using Lester's whiz-bangs to demolish them and their café headquarters?''

"That is correct. Considering the number of restaurants they have bombed, it seems like poetic justice, don't you think?'' Mac's smile was thin and fleeting. He went on: "Afterwards, we will vanish, and Mr. Leonard and Mrs. Helm will surrender to the authorities and confess to striking this vengeful blow at the terrorists who killed the lady of the young man's dreams and the young woman's husband. I very much doubt that, considering the local outrage over the Howard Johnson bombing, they have much to fear in the way of legal action, particularly in view of the discreet pressures we will exert in their favor. And the menacing Legion of Liberty will become an international joke, its fearsome Council of Thirteen smashed by a couple of angry youngsters. Other victims of similar fanatics may be encouraged to take similar retaliatory action. It is really an excellent idea, Eric, and a very satisfactory conclusion of your mission. I congratulate you.''

Anytime he hands out a lot of praise, it means he's got a very dirty job coming up for you.

I said, "Let's hold the congratulations until we see the results of the bang, sir. And even if it's successful, there's still Bultman."

"I'm sure you'll be able to deal with him properly."

"When do the fireworks take place?"

"The execute is set at eight o'clock local time; Wickerman is certain his group can place the charges and get clear by that time. That's an hour ahead of New York time, if you haven't adjusted your watch."

"It's set." I studied him for a moment. "What about Dolores and Modesto?" When he didn't speak at once, I said, "I think we can assume that they're both inside 424; and that Angela was steering me to the building across the street just so her friends could shoot at me conveniently from their headquarters' windows."

Mac nodded. "We have seen nothing of Modesto, but I think your assumption is a good one. It is very fortunate for us."

"Fortunate?"

He went on calmly, "Yes, we are fortunate in having two people captive inside the place. Otherwise the gang members might have scattered in spite of their arrogant overconfidence. But everyone knows the American obsession with hostages. Why, great military expeditions have been mounted, shining political careers have been wrecked, whole U.S. administrations have foundered, all on account of a few unimportant citizens who happened to be in the wrong place at the wrong time. With two hostages at whom they can point their guns, our terrorists feel completely safe. They know no tenderhearted Americans can possibly bring themselves to attack the building under those circumstances, certainly not without days of meaningless negotiations."

His voice was dry. It's one of the subjects on which

316

he's slightly irrational, in his ruthless way. His solution of the airliner-hijacking problem would be to send up fighters to blow any hijacked plane out of the sky. He claims that, while it would be a little hard on the passengers involved, it would soon convince potential hijackers that there's no future for them in messing with the airways; and that would save more lives in the long run. The trouble is, he could be right.

I spoke without expression: "Are we going to make an attempt to get them out before the place goes up?"

He gave me his thin smile once more. He said, "That is a stupid question, Eric. You know that, with or without orders, or even against them, you would make the attempt, sentimental as you are, about people as well as dogs. But as it happens, that is why I had Mrs. Helm bring you here. You are the diversion of which we spoke; you will distract the opposition while Trask's team plants the charges. The silenced pistol I see in your belt is inadequate for this purpose. We want a loud and convincing disturbance. Use the weapons on the table. They are the ones favored by the CLL so the authorities will learn nothing from the distinctive cartridge cases, or the firearms themselves, if you have to leave them. Willard has volunteered to cover you as far as necessary." Mac paused for a moment, and continued: "How far you penetrate, and who you bring out, is up to you. The charges fire at eight no matter who is inside the building."

I said, "Including me." It was not a question.

He nodded. "Including you. Here is a sketch indicating what we've been able to learn about the premises. Is there anything else you need to know?"

"Nothing, sir," I said.

He'd made it pretty clear. He always does.

CHAPTER 33

WILLARD was lean and moderately tall, although an inch or two short of my height. He was also a respectable number of years short of my age. He was wearing jeans and a black turtleneck, with a dark blue baseball cap covering most of his blond hair; a good night-fighting costume. He carried one of the Skorpians and had his half of the spare clips tucked away somewhere. There were probably other weapons concealed about his person as well.

I was tempted to ask him to lend me his knife, assuming that he had one; but that would be kind of like asking to borrow somebody's toothbrush. Guns you can pass around; knives are personal. Besides, I always carry a tricky little belt-buckle blade that would serve in a pinch, but I still missed the Gerber I'd lent to Dana, now lost in enemy hands. I reminded myself that I had another silent weapon at my disposal, in addition to the .22: I had the junior-grade crowbar Dana had bought me, as good as a sap for anyone who had no strong prejudice against skull fractures. There wasn't much chance of my forgetting it. Tucked inside my pants, with the curved end hooked over my belt, it kept digging into me.

I whispered, "There's Number 427, front view." We'd sneaked up on Pacheco Street by way of a narrow alley that had brought us out across the street and a block and a half away. "Second block, second doorway. No welcoming light, you'll note. They may be expecting me at the rear, but I doubt it. Their girl Angelita told me that it was all clear back there and unlocked; I should just walk right in and make myself at home. She made it sound so good I doubt very much she expected to be believed. I think she wanted me to figure that she was lying, and hit the door she seemed to be steering me away from.''

"So I go for the front," Willard said softly.

"Don't stick your neck out," I whispered. "Just make them think you're going for it. Or, to be exact, that I'm going for it. Actually, I think you can safely assume that they're on this side of the street in one of the second-floor windows above the closed-up restaurant. They wouldn't have a clear view from the ground floor, somebody could park a car and block them; and how are you going to shoot from those big restaurant windows? The third floor would give them too much of a down-angle for easy target practice. So call it floor two, and I'm guessing that they have a lot of firepower zeroed in on the front of 427, ready to blast me the moment I try to get inside. That's the kind of trap they set for us once before, in West Palm Beach; and people do tend to repeat their best tricks.''

He nodded. "Suppose I find me a sheltered spot and just hose the living shit out of that doorway with this toy firearm? Hell, I have sixty rounds to play with. They'll figure it's you softening the place up for a banzai charge across the street and inside. Even after I quit firing, they'll hold their breaths for a while waiting for you to make your death-defying dash.''

I said, "Sounds good. It should give our three-man explosives squad a chance to do its stuff at the rear, and me a chance to crack the side door that shows on the sketch and slip inside to try for the hostages. But you'd better take a couple more magazines for that .32 squirter; I probably won't be doing so much shooting inside. One spare will do me. Here.''

He took the clips I handed him. "When I'm through,

I'll try to work my way around to that side of the building and cover your getaway.''

"If you can do it easily," I said. "But remember, if everything works, there'll be a girl coming out, kind of tall, dark hair. Red pants and sweater if they haven't put something else on her. Dana Delgado, code Dolores. And a short stocky dark guy I've never seen, clothes unknown. Could be a bit battered. Paul Encinias, code Modesto. And no matter who comes out or doesn't, including me, be sure you're well clear by eight. The Leonard boy's boom-booms could be more vigorous than he thinks; and that's no steel-and-concrete bunker. It could come down like a house of cards."

"You're the one who'd better worry about getting clear; you'll be inside."

I grinned in the dark. "Just one thing before we start the clock ticking. Any hole you pick, make sure it's solid. In West Palm they had a hell of a big gun, I figured fifty caliber. It was a single-shot, slow and clumsy, it took them five seconds or more to recover from the recoil and slap in a fresh round; but it sure made a sieve of an armored Mercedes, so watch yourself. I don't know that they've smuggled it into Puerto Rico, but they'd know how, and when you make up a special cannon like that, you yearn to use it."

"I'll keep it in mind. See you in church." But as I was turning away, Willard said, "Matt, have you fired one of these baby MGs before?"

I paused and looked back. "It's the first time I've seen one in the flesh."

"Use the folding stock," he said. "Shoot from the shoulder. The little motherfucker ejects straight up. If you try to do a Rambo, holding it down at the hip, you'll get a faceful of hot brass."

"Thanks."

It gave me a pleasant feeling as I moved away. A lot of

320

junior characters won't venture to give advice and risk being slapped down by senior characters who're too proud to take it. The fact that Willard had taken a chance on pointing out to me a characteristic of an unfamiliar weapon that might have caused me embarrassment showed that he was a pretty nice guy and that, having worked with me before, he'd decided I was. Okay, but it was time to forget about nice. I was going to have to get into the lousy building somehow; and I wasn't entering it to be nice.

I made my way cautiously through the narrow streets and lanes and alleys that were becoming reasonably familiar to me. The area still had that tense, silent, waiting feeling. There were lights at many windows, but I saw no silhouetted heads; anyone curious enough to look out had the sense to first darken the room behind him. I wondered how many of these people wanted a free Puerto Rico. Well, their political affiliation was their business as long as they kept it their business and didn't blow up members of my family; after that it became my business. I'd never been close to my son, and I hadn't wept for him yet; but there was a strange dark hole inside me where he'd been, like an open grave. I couldn't begin to fill it until I'd dealt with his murderers.

Dana Delgado was also in my mind, of course. I was trying not to think of her, or speculate on the degree of fear and discomfort she was enduring as a captive of a bunch of political maniacs. . . .

There was a guard at the side door of the restaurant building. He was standing under a small hanging sign that presumably read ERNESTO'S although I couldn't read it in the dark. Or maybe the place had had a special boozing room and the sign read LOUNGE, or BAR, or CERVEZA. The narrow alley was cluttered with beat-up garbage cans and loose trash. I took cover behind one of the cans and waited with the little rapid-fire .32 slung from my shoulder and the silenced .22 in my hand—I didn't want to make a lot of noise going in, although I expected to make plenty coming out. If I came out. I checked my watch: four minutes to go. Three. Two. One . . .

Even though it was well around the corner from where I hid, Willard's Skorpian seemed to make a shocking racket when it opened up. You'd have thought it was a real grown-up machine gun instead of a glorified pocket pistol. The dim figure I was watching stirred and stepped out into the middle of the alley to look in the direction of the uproar. Something gleamed in one hand, but I couldn't make out the nature of the weapon. The man was nicely silhouetted against the lighted street beyond. Using my battered trash can as a rest, I aimed the Ruger at his head, having a hard time making out the sights. I pressed the trigger carefully. The noise of the machine pistol in the street, firing neat little three-shot bursts, covered the small sound made by the silenced .22; I only knew when it went off by the slight jump of the recoil. The man fell.

I ran forward. He lay facedown with his hands clasped to the back of his head, rolling back and forth in agony. I reminded myself that Matthew was dead, and that I had no connection whatever with the Salvation Army. The white neck made a good target. After finishing him off, I looked around for his weapon—it's poor technique to leave live men or loaded firearms behind you—but I couldn't spot it in the dark and I couldn't waste time on a search.

I hurried to the door the dead man had been guarding. It was unlocked. Inside, I found myself in a small vestibule. A swinging-type door straight ahead was labeled BAR in faded letters. I could hear loud alcoholic voices beyond. Apparently, even though the place was out of business, they were employing it for its designed purpose, and to hell with the lousy imperialist pigs. If they'd heard the shooting at all, in there, they'd apparently decided it was just their friends upstairs taking care of the dumb government agent for whom such an elaborate trap had been set; let's have another to celebrate.

A stairway led up to the right. I could still hear Willard, outside, ripping off his tidy little bursts, *brrrp, brrrp, brrrp,* but in here the sound seemed to come from a considerable distance. I started up the stairs; then I turned quickly, as the bar voices became suddenly louder. The door had opened and a woman stood there: a large, bleached lady in baggy jeans with a big, soiled khaki shirt hanging loose outside them. There was an automatic pistol in her hand, one of the fifteen-shot jobs, a 9mm Beretta or imitation. Chivalry is dead, but it can still kill you; it took me a moment to decide that it had to be done.

If she hadn't been drunk, she'd have had me as I hesitated. If her piece had been cocked, she'd have had me. As it was, she had to wait for the automatic to stop waving around erratically; and then she had to struggle with the stiff double-action pull that cocks the action for the first shot. Subsequent shots come more easily, as the recoil does the hard work; but she never got that far. She never even got off the first one, not quite. I put three .22s into her face, not trusting the little bullets to do an instant job on the bulky body. She fell on top of her pistol, her straw-colored hair straggling, dark at the roots.

I waited a second or two to see if anyone would come after her. Nobody did. Somebody'd told a joke in there that had them all laughing. As I ran up the stairs I reminded myself that there were five rounds gone out of the ten-round Ruger magazine. I clapped in the spare to play safe. No problem distinguishing it by feel, slim and straight, from the one spare Skorpian clip I carried, fat and curved. Outside, Willard had also switched magazines and now was working on his second. I was glad I'd given him a couple of extras; at the rate he was putting out the lead, he was going to need them. The upstairs hall was

323

empty, with a splintery wooden floor that had once been painted brown, distempered green walls, and a single, hanging, twenty-five-watt bulb for illumination.

There were doors on both sides of the corridor, all closed except the second on the right, the street side. I started that way cautiously. There was still one floor above me, and I could hear voices up there; but apparently everybody in the place had been warned that there was going to be some shooting, don't panic, don't start milling around asking dumb questions and interfering with the executioners. Nevertheless, I hated to leave the stairs. At any moment somebody could come down them, or up them, and discover what a lovely target I made, trapped in the narrow hallway with no place to go.

I forced myself to move towards the open doorway on the right; then I stopped because there was a closed door to my left that seemed oddly familiar. It was a small door, perhaps a closet door, with the customary knob, old-fashioned porcelain; but it was also equipped, higher up, with a hasp and eye, and a padlock. I'd had a door like that described to me, although I'd been told it was located in another building. Maybe my tricky girl informant had had this one in mind, and had simply moved it over to where she needed it for fictional purposes. It was a coincidence I couldn't pass up.

I knocked softly. "Modesto," I said. "Friend here; don't get violent when I open."

There might have been a sound from inside, but Willard chose that moment to let off one of his well-controlled triple blasts, so I couldn't be sure. I put away the .22 and hauled out the crowbar, feeling very clever and foresighted to have brought it. Then I saw that the padlock hadn't been snapped, and why should it be? Even unlocked, it kept anyone inside from getting out; and this way they didn't have to produce a key every time they wanted to get in. I took a fresh grip on the little crowbar, now holding it by the straight cold-chisel end meant for prying—the hooked end is designed for pulling nails—just in case something hostile should jump out at me. I lifted out the padlock left-handed and opened the door.

It was a closet, all right. It was quite empty except for a man on hands and knees just inside the door. He was naked to the waist, bloody and dirty; and the face he lifted to me was so badly beaten that even if I'd known him before I wouldn't have recognized him now. But he was trying to get to his feet. I helped him, and steadied him.

"Modesto?" I said.

He had to make two tries before the right sounds came out of his battered mouth, but then his speech, although slurred, was quite intelligible and even a little formal.

"Yes, I am Paul Encinias, called Modesto. What remains of him."

"Can you walk?"

"If it is away from here, I can do it, if I must crawl like a snake." Then he shook his head quickly. "No. Dana."

"Where?"

"The devil-girl took her. Angelita. The little angel. What a name for such a monster!" He shook his head minutely. "They call her *El Martillo* now. That is the wrong gender, but a much more appropriate name."

So the girl had been elected to the Hammer spot left vacant by the death of Dominic Morelos. Mac would be interested, but I had other concerns.

"What about Dana? Is she all right?"

"Yes. All right. More or less all right. But we must find her, save her. . . ."

I sensed a movement behind me and spun to face the rush of a large man with a long knife, the narrow, tapering, Arkansas-toothpick kind of dagger that, unlike a Bowie, isn't worth a damn for chopping but is great for stabbing, which was exactly the employment he'd intended for it. I swung the crowbar at him backhanded. He leaped back and laughed, tossing the knife from hand to hand as he dodged and feinted, daring me to expose myself by making another effort to bash in his skull. The playful type. The cocky type, too sure of himself to alert the house to the intruder within the gates. He was going to nail my hide to the wall all by himself before calling in his friends to see his bloody trophy.

I made another tentative swing and, when he danced away, hurled the bar at him, using the smooth, knife-thrower's release. The hooked steel made a full one-eighty in the air and, chisel-end first, buried itself in his chest. He dropped his knife and reeled against the wall and sat down heavily, staring down at himself, seeming very puzzled by the metal sticking out of his dirty shirt like a curved umbrella handle.

"I'll find Dana," I said to Modesto. "Get down the hall and down the stairs and out. Here." I gave him the Ruger. "Shoot anything but a young fellow in jeans, a black jersey, and a baseball cap, named Willard. The piece is silenced so you won't bother anybody. You have eleven shots, ten in the clip and one in the chamber. Okay, on your way before we have more company."

He started off, but paused to look down at the pistol in his hand. "Silenced, you say?" Then he raised the weapon and put a careful bullet through the head of the seated man with the crowbar in his chest. He looked my way apologetically. "Just a promise I made when he was beating me. I told him I would kill him. I like to keep my word."

Well, we were all paying off old grudges here. He'd had a hard day and he had a little vengeance coming; but it gave me a new slant on chunky middle-aged men who sell ladies' dresses. I waited to make sure he was making it down the hall all right, even if a bit unsteadily. Outside, Willard had stopped shooting at last. I turned and approached the open door across the hall, cautiously. I heard a girl's voice speaking.

"Not to be so impatient, *amigos*. Stay with the gun. Wait. I said he would come to the front, did I not? With his *ametralladora*, he has thoroughly prepared the doorway to which I directed him. Nothing over there could have lived through that hail of bullets. Now, thinking it safe, he will cross the street and enter the building. Wait!"

It was my cue and I stepped inside, saying, "He is here."

I had a freeze-frame image of the room. Two windows. At the right-hand one a large weapon on a heavy tripod mount. A sleek, military-surplus gunbarrel attached to a crude bolt-action mechanism that looked as if it had been fabricated in somebody's basement and probably had. A small off-the-shelf telescopic sight on a rather flimsy-looking bracket sticking out to the left where the gun pointer crouched behind it holding something that looked like a camera cable release, presumably the firing device. The loader was on the right, beyond the gun; and the ammo he had ready was, as I'd guessed, standard .50 machine-gun stuff. I remembered how I'd threatened Angelita, promising that I'd get her no matter what kind of bullets her friends put into me first. The usual Helm hot air. After one of those massive, half-inch-thick slugs had knocked me flat, the way I'd seen it happen in West Palm, I'd have been in no shape to get anybody.

Angelita, or *El Martillo*—or *La Martilla*, if there is such a thing in Spanish as a female hammer—was standing at the window to my left holding a Skorpian just like mine, ready to back up the heavy fifty-caliber bullets with a shower of miniature thirty-twos. She'd shed her borrowed too-big jacket; but she was still wearing her pretty, blood-smeared blouse and her tight, tattered jeans. Dana knelt beside her, between us. Clearly she'd been placed there so she could have the pleasure of looking out the window and

327

watching me walk into the trap and die. Her hair was untidy and her clothes were dusty, but she wasn't sagging in the manner of somebody badly hurt. Her legs were free, but her wrists were taped behind her. Sudden hope came into her eyes when she saw me.

The girl with the gun made her decision instantly: Seeing me, she stuck her weapon into Dana one-handed before I could shoot, and reached down with the other hand to haul her up to form a shield. Angelita's mouth was moving as she faced me. Undoubtedly, she was telling me to drop my gun or she'd shoot Dana, the standard movie script; but she had nothing to say that I had to hear. We never play that game; and what they always forget is that you can't shoot two people with the same gun at the same time, at least not with a pipsqueak .32 that has hardly any penetration about at all.

There wasn't time to hold a long, stylized conversation about who was going to shoot whom if I didn't do what. We all take our chances, and the place was definitely going to blow within ten minutes or less. Dana might survive a few bullet holes; but unless I got her out of here, wounded or unwounded, she wasn't going to survive the explosion if our boy Lester knew his stuff. And neither she nor I was going anywhere unless I did a small job of local extermination first. . . . I'd already swung right as these thoughts were going through my mind, and the little Skorpian was already chattering away at the rate of seven or eight hundred rounds per minute, I couldn't recall the exact figure.

I took the loader first since he was farther away and might be able to find some cover behind his big weapon if I gave him time; then I turned the machine pistol on the man at the telescopic sight. It was an amazing little gun, really. With that feeble cartridge, it had hardly any recoil and no tendency for the muzzle to climb in rapid fire, unlike the more powerful 9mms or, God help us, the bucking, thrashing .45 Thompsons. You just pointed it where you wanted the bullets to go, and they went there and kept right on going there.

I didn't have as good trigger-control as Willard. I used six on one man and four on the other, wasteful; but they got the job done. The empties squirted straight up as I'd been warned, and bounced and tinkled around the room. I was aware that shots had been fired to my left. The bullets hadn't come my way and the reports had been oddly muffled, so it seemed likely that Dana was hurt, maybe dying, but there was no time for guilt or grief. I didn't even take time to look that way. I just dove and rolled, hearing Angelita's Skorpian start chattering again, the sound now unmuffled by a human body.

Bullets tugged at my shoulder and leg as I took my evasive action, no tidy bursts here. The little angel just clamped down on her trigger and sprayed her weapon like a hose. I think she put some into her friends as she tried to track me across the room, but her swing was strangely erratic. Coming up facing her, I saw the reason: She had the weapon braced against her hip, Lady Rambo, and she had her eyes squinched almost shut against the rain of smoking little empties that bombarded her. I put the sights on her and gave her one short burst, and another to make sure. I was getting so I could send them off in neat little threes like Willard. It was about time.

There was shooting elsewhere in the building now. I rose and walked forward. The girl was down, of course, but she wasn't quite dead. Her brown eyes were staring up at me, hating me, but she died before I could set my weapon to single fire and complete the *Martillo* part of my mission—it occurred to me that this was the second of their *Martillos* I'd terminated. I hoped they had no more. She'd been a tough, bright little girl; and it was too bad. It's always too bad.

I moved to Dana, who lay in a tight little ball, hugging

329

herself; but when I turned her over gently she relaxed a bit, looking up at me. Although some women might have blamed me for letting her get shot like that, there was no hatred in her eyes. At least not for me.

She licked her lips. "Did you . . . get her?"

I nodded. "I got her."

"She masterminded the Howard Johnson bombing, Matt, just like the others. She boasted about it. Well, if she's dead, that takes care of it, doesn't it? As much as it can ever be taken care of."

I clapped the spare magazine into the Skorpian. "Come on, let's get you out of here before this place goes bang."

"Matt, don't ever hate me," she whispered. "I'm sorry. I've been so sorry ever since I met you. . . ."

I didn't know what she was talking about, and there was no time to find out, nor was there time to make a medical diagnosis or put a Band-Aid where she hurt. I didn't even bother to determine if she could walk. I just hoisted her to my unwounded shoulder, hearing her choke back a cry of pain.

"Matt. Matt, have you got her?" It was Modesto's voice down the hall, slurred from the mouth damage. "You can come out, the corridor is clear."

"Coming."

With Dana over my left shoulder and the machine pistol in my right hand, I marched out into the hall—well, staggered out into the hall. I don't do enough of the muscle stuff to pack a solid lady around easily. There was another dead man out there, in addition to the one I'd skewered with the crowbar and Modesto had shot with the .22; the newcomer also seemed to have a .22 hole in his upturned face. As I stepped out of the room, there was a tremendous crash of sound behind me. For a moment, I thought Lester Leonard's charges were beginning to go off; then I realized that the gun pointer at the big rifle, still clinging

330

to his cable release, must have squeezed it hard enough, dying, to fire his artillery piece blindly out the window.

"This way," Modesto called. He was on the stair landing, holding the Ruger in both hands. As I approached, he fired up the stairs. With my ears ringing from gunfire, I heard no sound from the silenced pistol, but I saw it jump. Modesto glanced at me. "Go on down. Your friend is holding them off down there. Better let me have that weapon; I think this one is running on empty."

He wasn't exactly following the instructions I'd given him, but I was in no position to complain. I tried to remember whether or not I'd told him about the explosives being planted, but things seemed to be getting a little hazy. I passed him the Skorpian and got a better grip on my burden.

I said, "You've got a fresh clip, but don't hang around up here. Some charges have been set and we don't have much time."

"I'll be right behind you."

Heading down the stairs, with my knees buckling from the weight I was carrying, I saw Willard at the bottom; as I watched he put one of his trademarked little bursts into the bar door. Behind me, Modesto fired up the stairs; he had pretty good trigger control, too. You never know whom you're going to meet these days who's fought in somebody's war. Maybe I should retire and sell ladies' lingerie. I resented the fact that everybody was getting to shoot but me. All I got to do was carry a girl who was bleeding all over me—or was I bleeding all over me?—I couldn't tell. It seemed to take me forever to make it down that endless stairway, one precipitous step at a time. . . .

Then somebody took Dana from me and told me we'd better hurry. Sometime later there was a large explosion not too far away. It seemed to go on forever. Somebody called to somebody to look out; the whole rear wall of the building was collapsing. I thought with regret of the big fifty; I like oddball guns and it would have been fun to shoot a few rounds through the crazy thing. I thought of the girl called La Margarita and Angelita and a few other things. I thought of the little Gerber knife. Well, that at least could be replaced.

There was fire now, the light flickering on the wall by which I lay, don't ask me where. I saw the battered face of Modesto above me.

I licked my lips. "Dana?" I whispered.

He shook his head. "I'm sorry. They couldn't stop the hemorrhage."

Somebody in a white coat took inventory and told me I'd be all right although I had three bullets in me. It bothered me that I'd only counted two.

CHAPTER 34

HERMAN Heinrich Bultman's invasion force hit Gobernador two weeks later. Certain highly placed optimists with whom Mac was in contact had expressed the opinion that the demolition of the Caribbean Legion's San Juan headquarters and its guiding Council would undoubtedly cause the Kraut to postpone or even abort his plans. Mac had consulted me as the resident Bultman expert, and I'd told him they'd better stop dreaming. Bultman was neither a patriot nor a fanatic. He was just an old professional hit man using his skill and training and experience to teach a bunch of trigger-happy uniformed jerks, and the officials behind them, and the nation behind *them*, the inadvisability of shooting a friend, even a canine friend, of Herman Heinrich Bultman.

Sentiment was certainly a factor, but essentially it was the arrogant final statement of an aging and ailing assassin, I said, a reminder to the world that even in retirement the Kraut was not to be messed with. What had happened in San Juan wouldn't affect him; he'd felt no love or loyalty towards the CLL. To him, it had been just one source of manpower and intelligence; he had others. Of course the people upstairs had experts of their own, and to hell with the opinion of a guy who merely happened to know the guy in question. So it came as a dreadful surprise to them when the sun rose one morning, down there in the Caribbean, to show the Kraut's boys all ashore on one of Isla del Norte's more deserted and sheltered beaches, moving inland in a determined fashion. Apparently the government forces, relying on U.S. intelligence reports, had been caught with their pants at half mast.

When the U.S. Navy helicopter flew me past the battle zone in the middle of the morning, at a considerable altitude and a discreet distance off shore, I could see, through the 7×50 glasses they'd lent me, the tiny conflict going on over there on the shore beyond the grounded boats, a couple of which were burning. Except for the tropical surroundings—the blue water, the white sand, the green jungle—it looked like a D-Day movie seen on a small TV set at the far end of the room with the sound turned off.

"They seem to've gotten off the beach, but they're taking a pounding," I said to the helicopter pilot. "Did I see a couple of jets?"

"Yeah, those little countries always buy the flashy goddamn jets when they'd be a damn sight better off with some workhorse helicopter gunships. What the hell can you do with a jet except go fast and make a lot of noise and impress the girls?" He glanced at me. "We'd better get on down the coast before one of those government zoom-zooms makes a pass at us. We've got clearance, but the rocket jockeys do get trigger-happy. What are we looking for, anyway?''

"A rusty old LCT. I didn't see it over there.''

The pilot glanced towards the distant beach. "Nothing that big over there. They picked a calm night and came across from Montego in a lot of little stuff, it's only eighteen miles. I'll bet, calm or no calm, most of the boys were seasick as hell, but they seem to be doing okay now. Just the same, I'll be glad I'm not them when the government gets its ass in gear.''

"I seem to remember that somebody once said the same thing about the Maginot line.''

The pilot studied the sunny distant scene for a moment longer, and shrugged. "Well, however it goes, as my old pappy used to say, it's a good day for dying.''

We clattered on down the coastline. I watched the pretty shore go by below, and thought of another good day for dying—at least a lot of people had managed to use it for that purpose. The following morning, Modesto had come to see me in the hospital. They'd cleaned him up and patched him up and turned him loose; apparently he'd suffered no major fractures or ruptures from his beating, but he still had some dental work to look forward to. We didn't really have much to say to each other; we certainly didn't compare notes about a lady we'd lost. I asked him some questions and he answered them.

Finally he said, "She spoke to me just before . . . She told me to make certain you did not blame yourself. She knew it had to be done that way.''

"Thanks.''

"Vaya con Dios, amigo.''

I watched him go out of the room, a stocky little man with a business to run; and where he'd learned to handle pistols and automatic weapons was his business. A little later, Sandra stuck her head in the door cautiously, determined that I was awake, and enlarged the opening so that her companion could enter as well. Lester Leonard was wearing slacks and a gaudy sports shirt; the same thick spectacles were sliding down his nose. My daughter-in-law was wearing a summery dress; the first time I'd seen her in a dress since she'd met me in the airport in Miami Beach. They asked the usual silly sickbed questions and I gave them the usual brave sickbed answers.

Then I said, "I thought you kids would be in jail."

"I feel like a fraud," Sandy said. "Lester was the real hero, all I did was sit and listen to the shooting, and all the reporters want to make an antiterrorist Joan of Arc of me, so brave with my poor wounded arm, although really, ducky, do you think it's *right* to take the law into your own hands like that?" She grimaced. "We're being exported."

"Deported," said the boy.

She shook her head. "They're washing their hands of us and sending us home to the U.S.; that's still the same country, isn't it? It's got to be a different country to count as deportation, doesn't it? We're just being exported out of Puerto Rico." She glanced at me. "Oh, I called Elizabeth and told her about . . . everything. She sends you her regards."

So my former wife, the mother of my son, knew that the vengeance she'd asked for had been achieved. I wondered if, having had time to cool off, she'd still wanted it. I looked at the two young people by the bed. Both of them seemed to have put the grim retribution business behind them overnight. It was finished and they weren't going to brood about the dead, loved or hated, any longer. A callous attitude, perhaps, but a youthful and healthy one. I found myself wondering if they were merely getting along well because they were nice kids thrown together by exciting circumstances, or if they were becoming seriously interested in each other. Well, he was pretty far out on the screwball side, but a smart girl could do a lot with him,

335

and when she was through she might have a genius on her hands. I was sure Matthew wouldn't have wanted his young widow to mourn eternally. Then, as I had the thought, Sandra turned a little, and I saw that she did have a black mourning band on her arm.

"What's that for?" I asked.

She hesitated, and her expression grew serious. "Actually, a policeman gave it to me since I didn't have time to buy a black dress and he thought I should have something to show . . . That's one reason they're turning us loose, Matt. It gave them the excuse they were looking for; they could be bighearted and release us so we could attend Daddy's funeral." She shook her head quickly. "No, not the Caribbean Legion. It was that drug-chasing man who made me do a striptease, remember; the one whose agents got blown up in our Old Saybrook house? I won't pretend to be totally shattered, you know we never got along; but he was still my daddy and it's a shock. You always wish, well, that you'd tried a bit harder to . . ." Her voice trailed off. Then she grimaced. "I bet Lia looks great in black."

"Bob Tallman," I said.

"Yes, that was his name. The Dobermans killed him. Ugh."

Lester said, "Sandy, we'd better get going if we're going to catch that plane; and they won't like it if we don't. What's the phrase, *persona non grata*? Or *personae non gratae*, plural? Good-bye, sir. I hope you get well soon."

Sandra also told me to get well soon. I told them to have a good trip. Maybe I should have congratulated the boy on how well his home-brewed explosives had performed; but I wasn't sure he was really aware of the deaths for which he was responsible. It had been an interesting technical problem and he'd solved it. The passion that had driven him to it would seem strange and a little embarrassing now. It was better to let him go his own strange way without rubbing his nose in reality.

Mac came after lunch, in the same or another gray summer-weight suit. He told me I was doing very well and would probably be released in a few days. When I take the bad one that awaits everyone in the business, and am on my way out, I'll probably wait around out of habit until he can tell me officially that I'm dying.

"You seem to've pried the kids loose in record time, sir," I said.

"Under the circumstances, they were not eager to prosecute knowing it would inevitably become a news circus."

I said, "I hear Tallman really blew his stack."

"Yes. Of course Mr. Alexander Varek was well overdue. There is no grief in law enforcement circles, except for the fact that the act was committed by an officer of sorts. They're calling it temporary insanity."

"I gather it happened on the estate and the dogs killed him; but how did he get in? Security was pretty tight when I was there."

Mac shrugged. "Mr. Tallman was, after all, a professional, Eric; and he did a professional job of penetration. If somebody hadn't turned the Dobermans loose ahead of schedule that evening . . . Actually, the dogs didn't kill him, although that was the first report we heard. They simply rounded him up and disarmed him; one of the guards shot him." Mac stopped and smiled thinly and went on: "As a dog lover, you will like this. Mr. Tallman could easily have shot both animals as they were coming at him, but he didn't fire. He said before he died that they were good dogs just doing their jobs and he'd got the beast he was after, so why should he kill them?" Mac shook his head. "Anyway, you don't have to worry about him coming after you, as he'd threatened to do." He pulled the chair he'd taken closer to the hospital bed. "Now, is there anything you'd care to take up with me before I re-

337

turn to Washington? As I recall, you were asking about a code that didn't exist. Would you care to elaborate?"

I said, "I was just talking with Paul Encinias. Modesto. He told me he'd received a message from Washington a few weeks back. It had come through the computer by way of Dana—Dolores. It concerned some negotiations the Legion of Liberty had been conducting, or trying to conduct, with Sonny Varek. It appears that the CLL crew got a lot of its finances from the drug trade. And far from being the wild-eyed political fanatics blowing up people at random we were supposed to think them, they usually combined their politics with business. In other words, if you screwed the Legion on a drug deal, or refused to play ball, or whatever, you might just kind of accidentally find yourself in the middle of a loud patriotic protest incident. Boom."

Mac said, "I am quite aware of this. Modesto sent several reports on the subject. It was a detail you didn't need to know to perform your mission."

"Good old need-to-know," I said. "Anyway, that colorful old drug dealer up in Newport, Pirate Williams, had been shortchanging the Legion on the stuff he'd been getting from them, so he wound up victim of a terrorist atrocity, as an object lesson to others who might get greedy."

"That reminds me," Mac said. "A certain Mr. Benison of a certain drug agency called to let you know that a certain big fish in that neighborhood is taking the bait; he thanks you for not muddying the water."

"Well, I had no reason to interfere in his case, so I don't deserve much thanks. I'm all for interdepartmental cooperation when it doesn't hurt." I paused and went on: "So the Newport explosion was actually a punitive action in the line of business. Modesto didn't know the commercial reason behind the bombing here in San Juan that killed Dana's husband and kid; maybe there wasn't any. The Executive Board that managed the action end of things didn't

338

always consult the whole Council. Maybe when things got dull they'd set off a firecracker just for fun, so folks wouldn't forget the Legion was still around. But the West Palm Beach job was a business proposition just like Newport."

"To influence Mr. Varek?"

"To punish him for refusing to deal with them. Varek was a respectable citizen now, he told them, retired from the import business; he didn't want to deal with the CLL, he didn't want to deal with anybody. *No*, repeat *no*. There was some disagreement in the Council about what should be done about him. Normally they'd have slapped his wrist hard as a matter of course, but some members felt that Sonny Varek with his syndicate connections was too big to touch and they should just forget the whole thing. Modesto said that the message he received from Washington, signed Elsie, instructed him to throw his weight on the side of punitive action, suggesting the Varek daughter as a suitable target." I cleared my throat. "As we know, Modesto was successful in swinging the vote that way. Angelita, with her bomb squad, went for Sandra and missed by just a little. But she got my son."

Mac spoke without expression: "This order ostensibly originated in Washington? It was transmitted by computer?"

"Correct."

"Signed Elsie. Could Modesto identify Elsie?"

I said, "Yes. The routine communications Modesto received from Washington were signed Dolores. Dana. Special action instructions were attributed to Elsie. It was a private joke between Dana and Encinias. Somehow one of them had learned the full name of the man at the top of this outfit. Arthur McGillivray Borden. Borden's milk. Elsie the cow. So they picked that name to identify orders coming directly from you."

Somebody ran a cart down the hall outside. It had a

squeaky wheel. Watching Mac, I reflected that any hospital's medical equipment really ought to include an oil-can.

Mac spoke quietly: "Are you convinced of my guilt, Eric?"

I said, "It was pretty foolproof. There was no logical reason for the CLL to hit Matthew, so it wasn't possible to sic them on to him directly. But they preferred restaurants for their dirty work; and if Sandra went out to eat, who'd most likely be with her? If the bomb got both of them as they dined and wined, fine, I'd be mad enough to come back to work for you. If it just got Matthew, as it did, ditto. And if it only got Sandy, it seemed likely that her young husband would feel strongly enough to look up his secret-agent pop and persuade him to hunt down the miscreants. Actually, Matthew was a nonviolent type and probably wouldn't have reacted like that, but this wasn't known to the person setting it up, and the problem never arose."

Mac smiled thinly. "When can I expect to be shot, Eric?"

I studied him thoughtfully. "We've worked together a long time," I said. "I know you'd sacrifice my son, or me, or your son, or yourself, if the fate of this country really depended on it. But not just for a lousy antenna field on a lousy Caribbean island. Not just to track down one crummy bunch of terrorists when the world is full of them. Not just because we had an argument about a dog." I drew a long breath, and grinned at him. "Anyway, the last thing Dana said to me was that she was sorry."

He studied me for a moment, and spoke thoughtfully: "Mrs. Delgado? Dolores? Yes, of course, she had the opportunity; the message came through her."

"Actually from her, although Modesto didn't know that," I said. "She must have been pretty crazy with grief and anger in her quiet way. She wanted to strike back at

340

the people who'd killed her child. She'd been directed to us by a reporter, Spud Meiklejohn, who seems to have an inflated notion of my capabilities. He apparently gave me a big buildup. So she got the idea that invincible Super-agent Helm was the only man for her vengeance mission; but suddenly she found out that I'd had a fight with you and quit the agency. A stupid fight about a dog, when her baby was dead! At the time she didn't know me at all, of course. I was just a walking gun, a grim instrument of vengeance that had let her down. So, as she monitored her computer information on the CLL, she saw a way to bring me back to do what she wanted done. Why shouldn't I learn, as she had, what it was like to lose a child? She instructed Modesto, in your name, what action to take in the Council of Thirteen. When we met in your office afterwards, she behaved as if she hated me. She had to, after what she'd done to me. Of course the one she really hated was herself.''

"And that code business?''

"Just something she threw out in desperation, to side-track me, when she sensed I was getting close to the truth. I think she'd have told me everything very soon, but she never got the chance.''

And she'd cried the night we'd made love because she'd known that, after the unforgivable thing she'd done, we could never have more than this together. But I didn't tell that to Mac. . . .

The helicopter pilot's voice dispelled the memories that plagued me. "Smoke up ahead. Looks like a beached vessel of some kind, burning.''

It was a curving half-moon of a beach at the head of a sheltered cove. The ancient landing craft had run right up on the sand after first dropping the big stern anchor that was supposed to haul her back into deep water after her cargo had been put ashore; but the old vessel's life had finally come to an end and she would never float again.

341

The government jets had found her, smashed her, and set her on fire. It must have happened several hours ago, say about dawn, since there were no longer any visible flames, just the thick, black, greasy smoke.

I noted that the bow ramp was down. Maybe Bultman's skipper had had time to unload a cargo of tanks before the air strike, although this seemed a long way from the landing site. . . . Then, as we passed over, low, I could see that there had been no tanks. The blasted cargo hold was full of twisted, blackened wire that looked like tortured chainlink fencing, although that didn't make very good sense.

"Can you set me down?" I asked.

"I was afraid you'd say that. Sure, that beach is like a billiard table. But don't be long; those government flyboys seem to have got hold of some of those there high explosives I've read about, and I don't want any." He was silent for a moment; then he glanced back at the wreck and said, "Poor old girl. Well, she died with her boots on. I wonder if she remembered Normandy when they hit her."

Well, some people are sentimental about dogs and some about ships. Then we were settling in and climbing down to the sand. I still hurt enough in various places to make it a chore.

"Maybe you'd better stay and watch your bird," I said to the pilot. "You're supposed to be here in a strictly noncombatant status. If there's trouble, light out fast. If I'm dead, nobody wants the body; if I'm alive I can take to the brush. Just get that whirly with its U.S. markings to hell out of here."

"Check." But he walked a few steps towards the beached ship with me. "Hell, those are cages!" he said suddenly. "All smashed up now, but they started out as animal cages. The old bucket was a fucking Noah's ark; and there's a dog now. . . . Here, boy!"

Hunting-dog men go by the unwritten law: *Never touch,*

or give orders to, somebody else's dog. The ones who've had nonworking canine pets, however, seem to have a compulsion to run up to any strange mutt and make friends with it. I grabbed the pilot by the arm.

"Easy, that looks like a very disturbed pooch, *amigo.* You'd better get back to your chopper while I take a look around."

He went reluctantly. He still wanted to pat the pretty doggie. I had no such desire. A big, shaggy beast of the husky persuasion, the animal would have looked great in front of a sled on an Alaskan snowfield; in this tropical climate he made about as much sense as an igloo. He was drooling a little as he stood there, and I heard the low, rumbling growl that said clearly: *Buzz off, Buster, this is my territory.* But the smoke-blackened tangle of wire behind him had definitely been cages of some kind before the bombs hit and scrambled them. A lot of cages holding a lot of animals. Like the man said, a fucking Noah's ark, where we'd expected a shipful of secret weapons. There were no visible bodies except for the live one guarding the ship's bow door.

I said, "Relax, friend, nobody's going to trespass on your property."

I limped on, surveying the lush green vegetation that bordered the smooth sand of the beach. Something moved in the bushes off to my right. I saw the dog first, a small curly-haired terrier-type with a stub of a tail that was working very hard as he—excuse me, she—tried to play with something or somebody hidden in the brush. The little bitch heard me approaching and came running to dance happily in front of me on two legs. I was tempted to give this one a pat and an ear-scratch, but it seemed better not to get too friendly until I knew what the hell was going on. Getting no affection from me, the little dog ran back to its former friend. Not knowing what hid there, man or beast, I made the approach with care, gun in hand.

"I have been expecting you, Herr Helm," a voice said. "It is all right. I have no weapon."

I recognized the voice, of course. I said, "You'll excuse me if my normal paranoia prevents me from taking your word for it, Herr Bultman."

But when I reached a spot from which I could see him lying there, he had nothing in his hands. He made a strange black figure in some kind of protective clothing; after a moment I realized that he was dressed in heavy motorcycle leathers, complete with gauntlets and boots. There was also a helmet. He had the plastic face-plate pushed up. He'd apparently been caught by one of the blasts that had wrecked the LCT, and the leather was badly ripped along his right leg, side, and arm. There was blood on the sand under him. As I watched, he scratched the ears of the little terrier left-handed, lying there, and offered her the leather of his gauntlet to tug at, delighting her. However, after a moment she decided to favor me with her attention again.

"No, no," Bultman said, as I reached down to let her sniff my hand. "It is too bad, she is a nice little dog, but she has had the injection. Do not touch her. Will you help me off with this helmet, please?" When I had it off, keeping an eye on his hands in case of tricks, he said, "Protection. I did not know what stage of the disease they would have developed when the time came to release them; and I preferred not to be chewed, although considering my last medical report it would have made hardly any difference. I had very little time left anyway."

It showed in his gaunt, lined face. Of course the wounds made a difference, too. I said, "You didn't bring that bucket here alone."

"Bucket? Oh, the ship. The crew went inland, that was the arrangement. They wanted nothing to do with my cargo of sick dogs. I had to unload them myself. I heard the planes coming as I was finishing, but there were still a few left in their cages and I couldn't leave them trapped."

He laughed again, a short bark. "We all have our little weaknesses, do we not, my friend?"

I stood looking down at him. So he'd had a secret weapon after all. "You brought a load of dogs to Gobernador?"

"What did you think I brought, a load of tanks to help those patriotic fools dying twenty miles from here?" He saw the answer on my face, and shook his head at my stupidity. He said, "The people of Gobernador would not accept my healthy dog, their officials shot her to death, so I have brought them my sick dogs instead. The poor animals will not last long, the incubation period is ten days and they go fast after that; but I have been assured that they will last long enough to infect the entire island."

"Rabies?"

"Of course, rabies. It is endemic in many countries. We lived with it in Germany. You live with it in the United States. Let them learn to live with it here, since they cannot administer their quarantine decently."

"And your whole invasion plan was simply a diversion. . . ."

He shrugged, and winced at the pain. "It is a good plan. They have a chance, those gullible heroes, but most likely they will commit suicide by fighting over who is to lead them now, and be pushed into the sea. But they will kill many Gobernador soldiers before they go, and keep the government forces too busy to worry about a few infected dogs. By the time action is taken, my slavering pets will be well dispersed. . . ." He winced as a pain went through him hard. When it eased, his face was even grayer than before. He licked his lips and said, "I need a favor, Herr Helm."

"Do I owe you one?"

"It is the favor we all owe each other, in this business. I would prefer not to be finished off by the government troops, or my dogs. It is what you came here to do, is it not? I ask you to do it now. . . ."

When I returned to the helicopter, the pilot looked at me oddly; and he didn't speak on the way back to base although he'd bent my ear the whole way down. There were several other flying machines between me and Washington, but they all made it, unlike the invasion force. It held out for three days but, contained by the government ground forces and hammered by the jets, it surrendered on the fourth day after the landing.

CHAPTER 35

In Texas, the big yellow Labrador pup was very glad to see me. He was even happier, the morning after my arrival, to be taken hunting. It was a good day for waterfowl, gloomy and windy, but with no real rain to make things too uncomfortable. Bert Hapgood took us out to the same blind. The ducks flew well, I shot well, and Happy did a beautiful job of retrieving; but as usual he couldn't understand why we had to quit so soon, with plenty of birds still buzzing the decoys.

I was sitting on the embankment cleaning my ducks when I heard the four-wheel-drive pickup approaching. It stopped behind me.

"I'll be through in a minute," I said without looking around.

"Don't hurry," said a woman's voice.

I turned quickly. Mrs. Rosalia Varek was wearing snug, tailored jeans and a matching jacket. The jeans were tucked into little boots with high heels. Her hair was uncovered and she wore it loose to her shoulders today, black and glossy, the way I'd seen it one night in Palm Beach, with her husband's approval.

"No, no," she said. "You're a good doggie, but I don't need my face washed."

"Happy, down!" I went over and pulled him off her. "I said, *down*! What are you doing here, Lia?"

"I'm a widow now," she said.

"I know," I said.

"I have no intention of marrying again," she said. "I have the security I wanted."

I said, "Is that what you came here to tell me?"

"Last time he sent me to you," she said quietly. "This time I'm my own woman, and I'm here of my own volition. But if you can't figure out why, I obviously came for nothing."

I figured it out.

ABOUT THE AUTHOR

Donald Hamilton has been writing Matt Helm novels for over twenty-five years. An expert yachtsman, he has also written nonfiction books and articles on sailing. He and his wife live in Santa Fe, New Mexico.